A GARLAND *at* BITTERBARK CREEK

TAMMY MANNERSLY

A Garland at Bitterbark Creek
Copyright © 2024 Tammy Mannersly
All rights reserved.

ISBN: (ebook) 978-1-964636-19-1
(print) 978-1-964636-20-7

Inkspell Publishing
207 Moonglow Circle #101
Murrells Inlet, SC 29576

Edited By Nevada Lewis
Cover Art By Emily's by Design

DEDICATION

I would like to dedicate this book to a few important people. To the Santoro family in my real life – Mel, Dan, Aunty Jan and Uncle Steve. You have always been my second family.

To my wonderful publisher, Melissa Keir and Inkspell Publishing. Your encouragement and belief in my writing has meant the world to me.

And to my incredible parents, Ian and Rita, and our little fur-cloud, Bonamie. Without your love and support, I wouldn't be the person I am today.

TAMMY MANNERSLY

PROLOGUE

20 Years Ago

Her petite form sank slowly, lifelessly, into the murky water of the Garlands' dam. The sudden stillness made everything almost peaceful again. There was no more splashing, no more screaming, and the children restraining Jack held their breath as they watched. The chirping of birds returned, and in the distance he could hear the soft beat of music wafting across the hillside from his parents' annual picnic.

Jack's heartbeat shook his whole body, thumping loudly, deafeningly, in his ears. His stomach throbbed from his sister's painful punch and the nausea bubbling within. Bruises circled his scrawny arms from where his captors' small, nimble fingers had locked on, yanking him so viciously away from the edge. But their hold had loosened considerably as they watched someone they'd once called *friend* slip closer to the very bottom of the large dam.

Wasn't it just the other day they were rolling down the grassy hills together with the farm dogs? They had been laughing so hard. Breathless. Not a care in the world. But the car accident had changed that, and his mother's opinion of the Wendall family even more still. It was their fault his father had been injured. They were not to be trusted.

That's what Jack's mother had said. Yet Jack's heart hurt more now than it had in his anger.

He hated that he'd shared his sister's rage. Hated that in his blind obedience he'd made a decision he would forever regret. He knew it hadn't been the girl's fault, hadn't been her family's. Her loss had been greater. But Jack loved his father—an adoration his sister shared—and his family had desperately needed someone to blame. It wasn't right, but it was all he could do not to lose himself. The accident had been terrifying. But *his* father had eventually made it home. It was this little girl turned listless sea creature whose father would never return.

An eternity passed as all five children peered over the edge of the jetty into the depths below, watching the jet-black swirl of hair sink lower.

"Help." It was a quiet squeak of a sound, but it drew all attention to the youngest of the group.

His sister's cold, violently blue eyes shot to Ella.

The little girl flinched and released Jack. "Help," Ella said a little louder.

Jack's final two captors tightened their hold for an instant before releasing him. They both spun to face the traitor as she backed away, her wide eyes flicking between them, like a lamb hunted by wolves.

"Help." Ella's high-pitched voice sounded strangled as she began to cry. "Help!" she screamed, stumbling, her tiny feet tripping over themselves. Then she turned and ran along the jetty towards the shore. "Help! Mummy, help!"

His sister nodded for the other two children to follow and then threw the whip-like stick she'd been clutching into the dam. She watched it bob above the sinking child. Then her glacial gaze shifted to Jack. "If you are truly my brother, you'll leave *her* and come with us."

Jack held her stare. She sounded so much like their mother. Full of hatred. Was this the loving family he had betrayed his truest friend to protect? His love for that little girl disappearing into the depths had always been greater than anything he'd ever felt for his sister.

How dare he let himself believe otherwise.

His sister hurried after the others. Jack didn't wait to see if she'd turn to check if he was following. He just dove into the water and swam towards the whirl of ebony that marked the presence of that drowned mermaid, the sweet friend he'd known as *Sophie*.

CHAPTER 1

Wide grassy pastures and lush thickets of bushland whizzed past Sophie Wendall's window. The natural beauty, still crisp and golden and a little dry from the winter drought, took on a dreamlike quality as Sophie viewed it from the shelter of her mother's car. It was a familiar landscape, one that called to her in sleep. Vivid memories haunted her, reminding her of a life that had once seemed perfect. Before destiny had intervened.

Dawn had broken over an hour ago, gleaming above the hills behind them, and intense rays of full daylight had burst over the road. Coming alive with the glow of morning, the parrots, kookaburras and lorikeets sang a greeting to the light, excitedly heralding the birth of another blessed day. Even her mother hummed pleasantly to the lively country tune playing on the local radio station as it drifted from the small speakers to fill the atmosphere of the car. It was only Sophie who felt the foreboding, who developed a general malaise the closer their journey got to its end.

"Not long now, darling." Angelica nodded to the navigation device stuck to the windshield. The little red marker indicating their destination had appeared at the top of the screen.

Bitterbark Creek, her aunt and uncle's farmstay, was positioned on five hundred acres of heavily treed land. It sat on the outskirts of Moorhenvale, a traditional country town just northeast of Warwick, and had once been the place Sophie had called home.

Although their brief return was in celebration of her cousin Patrick's upcoming wedding, Sophie feared this immersion into a past life she wished to keep buried. During the twenty years she'd spent living in West End—the eclectic, trendy heart of Brisbane—she had never once considered making the trip back to the place that had stolen her memories and cursed her with heartache.

Her stomach churned as the image of a boy flashed to the forefront of her mind. Jackson Garland. The grin he'd given her when he'd been caught sneaking strands of hay into her braids. His endearing laughter when she'd slapped his hands away. Though she tried to deny it, his name was still seared into her soul. It had made his betrayal hurt even more.

"I'm trying to remember, Sophia." Her mum's voice sounded distant, thoughtful. "When was the last time you saw your uncle Nicholas?"

"You mean besides on Skype?" She picked anxiously at her fingernails.

"In person. I can't seem to place it."

Sophie gulped back a swirl of nausea. They had seen Aunt Robin, Pat and Laura many times over the years. Her cousin Laura had even stayed with Sophie in Brisbane for a month while she completed the technical exams for her photography degree. As for her Uncle Nick, it wasn't a surprise that her mother couldn't remember their last time together. It's said a person blocks painful memories to protect themselves.

"The hospital." Sophie distracted herself with the charming scenery outside her window. "He stayed with me until you arrived."

He had held her hand in the ambulance, while one

6

paramedic maintained her vitals and the other drove speedily to Warwick Hospital. At the time, they'd told him he was a hero, that she was lucky he'd known how to resuscitate her. But he hadn't been listening to them. He'd just kept telling her, over and over again, that it was going to be all right.

Angelica swallowed loudly. "Sorry, darling. I didn't realise."

The subject was still painful for them both. No one wanted to reminisce about the time their ten-year-old daughter attempted suicide.

Although Sophie's memories of the actual event were lost, she knew for certain that suicide hadn't been the case. It had taken years of therapy and arguing to finally convince her mother to discount the rumours that spread through the town. No matter what the Garland family and their ilk had suggested, the sudden loss of Sophie's father hadn't broken her young brain. Yet the stigma still haunted them.

Only a few things remained certain. Sophie had nearly drowned in the Garland dam that day. Several children had seen her jump in and not resurface. But *why* she'd gone into the water alone in the first place was locked in some cave of distant memory. Although she longed to know the truth, she feared the betrayals it might hold.

Now she was hurtling right into the mouth of trouble, and the thought of what her mind may unleash was more terrifying than the reception she expected from the townsfolk.

Beyond Sophie's window, a herd of Friesian cattle huddled in a paddock, their black and white spots juxtaposed against the dry, honeydew-coloured grass. It was so serene that for an instant she warmed with fondness for the familiar wilderness. She and Jack had chased each other through similar fields, picking dandelions and playing tag. Always smiling and laughing. Never wanting to be apart.

A vision of Jack's sullen face as Sophie and her mother left that last day filled her mind's eye. She knew he didn't want her to leave, but he and his family had given hers no other choice. He had picked their side. He'd kept his distance from her. He hadn't denied their lies. His choices had broken something between them, a deep connection they had built with trust and love. She could see he longed to have it back, but by that point it was much too late.

Sophie shook away the memory of Jack's haunted expression and tried to focus on the present. Perhaps she could enjoy this break in the country for what it was and reconnect with her beloved extended family. Her infamy must have transferred to a new victim after two decades. Why would the tiny town dwell on such prehistoric drama anyway?

She pinched the bridge of her nose. Who was she kidding? Small towns thrived on sordid history and gossip. The community probably knew she would be in town for Pat's wedding, and the Garlands wouldn't hesitate to fill them in on all the juicy details. Sophie squeezed her eyes shut. It would be a real test of character to remain polite amid the prying, but she wasn't about to give anyone the pleasure of seeing her squirm.

Sophie felt the car slow and heard the click of the indicator.

"Looks like we have a welcoming party."

Sophie's mother steered their navy sedan through the grand entrance of the Bitterbark Creek farmstay. Bronze horse heads crowned each parallel brick pillar. As the car's tires crunched on the dusty gravel driveway, excited yips rose over the noise to greet them. Boris and Banjo, two young kelpie-heeler crosses, were the second incarnation of the farm dogs she'd known as a child. They raced alongside the vehicle, jumping, trying to sneak a peek through the tinted windows.

Her mother laughed. "You would think they'd never had visitors before."

A smile tugged at Sophie's lips, the first since starting their trip. She glanced up at the long, sprawling ranch-style homestead, made of cream-coloured timber and sporting a corrugated iron roof the same shade as the frosty green grassland. "They're not the only ones," she said, catching sight of her family waiting at the top of the short wooden staircase leading to the wraparound veranda.

She waved as her mother parked the car and saw her Uncle Nick—a giant, burly man—hasten down the steps towards the vehicle. His dark brown eyes were friendly, so like her own and her mother's, and his toothy grin sparkled within the grey of his neatly trimmed beard. Like her mother, he'd let his jet-black hair ashen naturally, but their Italian genes shone through in their straight, regal noses, their raven-haired children and the Mediterranean tan of both families.

He had the door open before Sophie finished removing her seatbelt. Pulling her from the car, he scooped her up into his muscular arms, leaving her boot-clad feet dangling in the chilly morning air. She gasped for breath as his tight embrace caused the bones in her spine to crack loudly.

"Sophia." His gravelly voice sounded choked. "It's been too long, Chooky. Twenty years too long."

Sophie felt winded at his use of the special nickname and struggled to keep her eyes from welling up. Geez, she had missed him dearly. She cuddled him tighter before he lowered her to the ground.

"It's so good to see you again, Chook." He left one hand securely on her shoulder as his eyes moistened. "We're so happy you could make it for the wedding."

"It's good to see you too, Uncle Nick." Sophie clasped his hand in hers before turning to embrace the short shapely woman who had appeared beside them. Her pixie face and blond, almost silver hair gave her a doll-like appearance. "Aunt Robin."

"Sophie sweetheart, you're so beautiful." Robin regarded Sophie's white blouse and dusky bohemian skirt. "Too cosmopolitan for our little town, and look, you've dyed your hair."

Sophie tunnelled her fingers through her long golden mane. "It was time for a change, I guess."

"It's been like that for over a year now, ever since things ended with Mason," Angelica piped up. She was at the back of the car, greeting Pat, Laura and the two farm dogs.

"Thanks for the overshare, Mum." Sophie patted Boris and then Banjo before approaching her cousins.

"I didn't much like that boy." Uncle Nick sniffed. "Too focused on the social medias from what Laura told us."

"Dad," Laura scolded. "Throw me under the bus as the town gossip why don't you?"

Uncle Nick ignored his daughter's protest and greeted his sister with a hug. "Angie, you're so thin. Look at these twiglet arms. Doesn't that husband of yours feed you? Where is he anyway?"

As Sophie pulled Laura in for a hug, she heard her mother laugh.

"Stuart had a last-minute invite to speak at an architecture conference in Adelaide, but he sends his apologies. I did call earlier in the week to let you know."

"Remember, Nicky?" Robin asked. "That phone call on Monday? I told you Sophie's stepfather was called away and wouldn't be coming." There was a second of silence as Uncle Nick gave her a blank look, then she laughed. "Sorry, Angie, the past couple of weeks have been a blur."

"I take it you missed me then?" Sophie coughed, freeing herself from Laura's painfully tight embrace.

"You're all Laura's been talking about for the last year." There was a teasing glint in Pat's deep brown eyes. "You, and her time in the city."

"I'm surprised she hasn't moved out there yet." Sophie winked at Laura.

Laura's cropped black hair, delicate features and petite, tomboyish physique made her seem younger than her twenty-eight years. "Give me time. I'm still saving."

Pat stretched his arms wide. "Come here," he told Sophie, pulling her against his rangy body for a brief squeeze. "We've all missed you, Soph. It's good to have you home."

Home. The word bit into Sophie's heart like a knife.

"Thanks, Pat." She sighed shakily. "So, when do I get to meet the bride-to-be?"

"Be careful what you wish for," he warned. "Marilyn's at her mum's today, but tonight is the hens'."

"It's going to be wild." Laura slipped her arm through Sophie's, yanking her closer. "We've even got a stripper."

They faced the older members of the family, catching the tail end of their conversation.

"You're at my house now Angie, and that means you're always going to be well-fed." Nick wrapped his arm affectionately around his sister's shoulders. "We knew you'd be hungry after the long drive, so Robbie and I organised brunch. Come on, come inside, and once we've all eaten, we'll get you settled."

Laura dragged Sophie towards the stairs. "Oh, Soph, there's so much to catch you up on. I need to tell you everything before the girls meet tonight." Her eyes were bright with excitement. "April-Rose is going to lose her mind when she sees you. She's invited to the wedding. Pretty much everyone in town is coming."

An icicle of fear stabbed through Sophie's chest. *April-Rose Garland? Jackson's sister?* Before Sophie and her mother had left town, she'd seen the young girl blossom into a manipulative, bigoted bully just like her mother, Sheridan. From what Laura had told Sophie, April-Rose hadn't changed much in twenty years.

As though sensing her cousin's discomfort, Laura hugged Sophie closer. "Don't worry, Soph. April-Rose better be on her best behaviour if she wants to keep her invite. You'll see. It'll be fine."

Sophie frowned. If her gut had been telling her anything all morning, it was that the next few days promised to be some of the most difficult of her adult life. She hoped she had the strength to survive them.

TAMMY MANNERSLY

CHAPTER 2

Besides the guest rooms in the main house, Bitterbark Creek had six small self-contained wooden cabins dotted over the property. They perched in peaceful isolation, some on cleared countryside, others nestled between bush or hugging the weaving creek edge. With the wedding looming, all were now occupied with invitees.

As Angelica spun the steering wheel, following Pat's ute along the crest of another hill, Laura—who had joined them for the ride—tugged on the sleeve of Sophie's blouse and pointed out the window. "That's for the reception tomorrow. Think it's big enough?"

Stretched out on the flat lawn was a huge white outdoor marquee with clear French windows on the side panelling. Chunky timber furniture was arranged outside—high bar tables, picnic settings, a couple of garden benches—with a few hay bales for good measure.

"How many guests are invited?"

Her mother's voice drew Sophie's concentration back to the dirt road in front of them. The car passed another cabin and then veered down the hillside. Towering eucalyptus trees, she-oaks and shorter bitterbarks shaded the picturesque valley below. As the tires rolled over rockier ground, Sophie bounced in her seat.

"Almost a hundred." Laura leaned forward and held onto the back of Sophie's headrest. "Pat and Marilyn wanted to keep it small, but Mum and Dad invited everyone they could think of."

"Well, it's not every day your child gets married." Angelica slid a hand from the steering wheel to touch her daughter's knee.

Sophie raised her eyebrow sharply. "I love you, Mum, but if you get any ideas like that come my wedding, I'll elope."

Laura snorted at that, and Sophie smiled. With the car back on level ground, they travelled beside Gap Creek, its dark waters slow-moving and pristine.

"The wedding will be held down here, by the creek," Laura said. "It's where Pat and Marilyn used to get away from Mum and Dad when they first started dating."

"How lovely." Angelica admired the spot. "Before the cabins were built and Sophie came along, her father and I would ride the horses along that track and spend the night out here under the stars. It's probably where Sophie was conceived."

"Mum," Sophie chided, but her mother ignored her.

"It's a perfect place for a wedding, Laura. Maybe you'll be having yours here one day too?"

"Yeah right, Aunty Angie," Laura scoffed. "Normally you have to date before you get married, and to date you have to meet someone you actually like who is interested in you too. Where in town can I find a nice, normal queer girl who understands that I want more in life than what this little old-school community can offer?"

"You really need to move to the city, Laur," Sophie advised.

"I know."

Pat parked his black utility in front of a quaint khaki-green cabin, and Sophie's mother followed suit.

"Here it is," Laura chirped as she opened the car door.

"I hope you don't mind being out this far. Mum and Dad tried to keep the elderly guests at the house or in the closer cabins."

"It suits us just fine," Angelica said.

The crisp country air hit them as they exited the vehicle, but the warm rays of midmorning sunshine offered a slight reprieve.

Pat strode around the ute's tray and headed to the trunk of Angelica's car. "Let's get you inside and settled."

Sophie and Laura met him at the rear of the vehicle, just as a sharp whirring noise shrieked through the serenity of the wilderness around them.

Sophie flinched. "What's that?"

Laura nodded to the last cabin on the property, almost half a kilometre away. It perched on a slope to their right, closer to the winding creek bed. Below the front stairs was a tall dark-haired man, shirtless and bent over a long piece of timber clamped to a pair of sawhorses. He appeared to be wielding a circular saw over the wood.

"It's just Jack," Laura explained.

Jack? Sophie went cold. She had expected to see him, knew it was likely unavoidable. But so soon? And *here*, on her family's land?

"The maintenance was getting too much for Dad and Pat to do alone," Laura continued, "especially with Pat working in Warwick during the week. So they hired a handyman. He rents that cabin permanently now."

"Jack?" Angelica squinted in the man's direction. "Jackson Garland?"

The sound of his name made her breathless. Sophie stared at the sturdy-looking man in the distance. Was he really the same boy who used to hide blue-tongue lizards in her gumboots, who told her that he liked to be *it* when playing tag just so he could catch her? She caught a glimpse of his familiar profile, and her heart fluttered. How in heaven's name had her crush lingered throughout all the pain? Hadn't his betrayal been enough to extinguish that final flame?

"Yeah." Pat perked up at the subject, jerking Sophie's attention back to the conversation at hand. "We took him on when he returned to town after spending a few years in Melbourne. He's been with us for over a year now. Helped us renovate the cabins and put up new fencing. He's a very talented carpenter—he built the outdoor furniture for the reception."

"We saw those pieces as we drove down," Angelica said. "They were stunning. I bet they set you back a bit."

"Not at all." Pat shook his head as his sister snorted.

"No way. Dad let Jack use some of the trees at the far end of the property, the ones we harvest and replant for firewood," Laura told them. "He cracked the furniture out in his spare time. Wouldn't accept a cent for them. Said they were his wedding gift to Pat."

"Oh my, what a sweetheart." Angelica's hand went to her heart. "He always was a polite little boy."

"I wouldn't say that," Laura scoffed, "but he's like one of the family. He's always lending a hand to Mum and Dad."

Like one of the family. Sophie couldn't breathe. Her mother and the rest of them knew about Sophie and Jack's falling out. But the extent of the betrayal and heartache was more than Sophie had ever wanted to share. Then they had left town, and she'd hidden it all away. Twenty years may have passed, but the pain of losing him, of him pushing her away, hadn't faded.

"Here, I'll call him over. I'm sure he'd love to say hi and get to know his temporary neighbours." Without waiting for an answer, Pat started towards the far cabin. "Oi, Jack."

"No—" Sophie stretched out a hand, but Pat was already out of earshot. She cursed.

"What's wrong, darling?" Her mother looked concerned.

Her cousin's face twitched with mischief. She had been hinting at a reunion between Jack and Sophie for months, much to Sophie's annoyance. "What? I'm sure I told you he's been staying with us."

Sophie dug her neatly manicured fingers into the soft fabric of her skirt. "No, you didn't."

"Are you sure?"

Sophie could still hear Pat calling out Jack's name, and then, abruptly, the sharp whirring of the electric saw ceased. The silence quickened the rhythm of her heart, but she refused to look over at the two men.

Please no, she prayed silently. She could face Jack another time. Once she was ready. But would she ever be ready for that confrontation?

Angelica touched her daughter's shoulder. "Is everything all right?"

Laura stifled a laugh, and Sophie brushed her mother's hand away. It wasn't their fault they didn't know. Some secrets were too painful to share. She just couldn't tell them that Jack had said he was glad *her* father had died and not his. She knew he probably regretted it as soon as the words left his lips, but how could they have moved forward from that? How would they have healed a wound that deep? And then he'd pulled away. To protect her heart, Sophie had done the same. Destiny had forced them in different directions, but now they were right back where they had started. The hurtful memories seemed so much more real and painful when she was looking at him.

"I'm fine." Sophie winced. "But don't expect me to make conversation."

"Don't be antisocial." Laura hugged Sophie's narrow waist. "I know he'd love to catch up. He's always asking about you."

Sophie pushed out of her cousin's embrace. She knew Laura meant well, but Jack's opinion of her hadn't meant anything for a very long time. "Well, he can just keep on asking. I'm not walking down memory lane with that jerk anytime soon." She thrust a hand towards her mother. "Please just give me my bags."

Frowning, Angelica opened the trunk with a click of a

button and handed her daughter a hefty duffle bag and a wheeled suitcase. As Sophie lifted the silver handle free from the luggage case and turned on her heel, she collided with a damp, rigid wall of masculine muscles. Recoiling in horror, she stumbled backwards until the heels of her boots hit the side of her suitcase. As she wobbled, a solid arm slid around her waist, keeping her upright.

"Whoa, there. I've had women fall for me before, but not usually this quickly."

The smooth male voice dragged Sophie's attention to a familiar gaze. Jack's cool blue eyes, like the winter sky at dawn, held her captive. The memory of a gentle, secret kiss beneath the shelter of a weeping willow played across her mind, until the beat of his pulse shook her to her senses.

"Hey there, Soph."

Embarrassed that she'd allowed herself to linger in his embrace, Sophie swiftly withdrew. His hand stayed on her hip, emanating an unsettling but strangely pleasurable tingling, so she smacked it away. "I can stand by myself, Jackson."

"Just trying to help, Soph." His stubborn square jaw tightened around the words.

He had changed a great deal from the lanky eleven-year-old Sophie remembered. He stood much taller than her now, easily clearing six feet. While still lean, the bulk of his muscles was intimidating. With that body squeezed into those tight denim jeans, he looked like an off-duty superhero. Yet his flawless face was all charm and polish— like some movie star from the sixties. Only that shock of wavy jet-black hair and those fierce eyes remained the same. It had been that intense, affectionate stare that had mesmerised her back then as well, long enough for him to risk their first and only kiss. She'd wished it had lasted longer.

Sophie bit back her desire to argue with him. She just wanted to escape to the cabin, but he was still studying her. She was about to scold him for gawking when someone behind her giggled.

"This is going to be an interesting weekend." Laura winked.

Stepping around her niece, Angelica acknowledged the half-naked hunk. "Well, Jackson Garland, haven't you grown into a handsome young man?"

Jack raked his fingers through his hair. "Not so young anymore, Mrs. Wendall. I hit thirty-one earlier this year."

"It's Faulkner now, dear. I remarried. But call me Angelica."

"Sorry. Angelica. You look exactly as I remember— elegant and sophisticated, with the beauty of a Gustav Klimt painting. I see your daughter has been blessed just the same." He shot a look of blue fire in Sophie's direction.

She flushed under the weight of his gaze and then pondered his choice of artistic comparison. She hadn't known Jack to be interested in the arts.

"Oh my goodness." Angelica shielded her smile. "You're a sweet-talker, just like your father. Klimt is one of Sophie's favourite artists, don't you know?"

Yes, how did he know? Sophie caught Laura dodging her gaze and thought she'd found her mole.

"There's nothing sweet about Jack," Laura quipped. "Don't let the perfect smile fool you. It's like I've got two cheeky, bull-headed brothers around here now."

Pat grinned and slung an arm around Jack's shoulders. "Lucky me. I've always wanted a brother."

Laura poked out her tongue as Angelica laughed.

Sophie gestured to her mother. "I'm going to take my things inside." As she dragged her suitcase towards the stairs leading to the cabin's small veranda, she felt warm fingers lock around hers.

"Let me give you a hand." Jack was at her side again, pulling at the luggage handle.

"No, thank you. I can do it myself." Sophie yanked the suitcase closer in an attempt to discourage him, but he only followed the movement.

Warmth radiated from his body as he loomed over her, forcing her to raise her chin and meet his eyes. His closeness was so disconcerting. She remembered that kiss again. She wondered what it would be like to kiss him now. Her eyes lingered on his soft pink lips.

"I'm just trying to be neighbourly." Jack's smooth voice was nearly a purr.

Sophie yanked her gaze free of his distractingly perfect features and cut a glance back to the others. "Then maybe you should be helping someone who needs it." Her family stood by the trunk of the car, where several heavy bags still waited.

When she turned back to Jack, Sophie noticed his gaze drift over her body before his beguiling eyes met hers again.

"Don't worry, there's plenty of me to go around," he told her.

His smug grin irritated her. "Get a clue, Jack. I don't want your help."

Pain flickered in his expression. "It's been twenty years, Soph. Talk to me for five minutes."

"You stopped talking to me first," she growled, knowing how childish it sounded.

"Sophie," her mother chided.

Ignoring them both, Sophie jerked the suitcase forward again but couldn't dislodge Jack's hold. She tried pulling her fingers from beneath his hand, but his grip only tightened.

"I'm not denying it happened, Soph," he told her. "But we can't change the past, and I think we should move on. I know I'm different from the naive boy I was back then. Perhaps you could find it in your heart to try?"

"*Perhaps* you could start with an apology?" The words left her lips before she'd thought them through. She knew she'd likely cry if he tried to apologise.

"Will that even make a difference?" he grumbled. "You're clearly not ready to let go of the pain and move forward."

"Don't psychoanalyse me, Jack."

"I just want us to be friends before you leave town again, Sophie. Is that such an unreasonable request?"

She sneered at that. Then his hand was gone, leaving hers alone on the silver handle. When she realised she was free, she bolted for the cabin. She didn't want anyone to notice the tears welling in her eyes.

"I'll be seeing you around, neighbour," Jack called after her, that familiar affection already filling his voice.

Not if I can help it, Sophie thought.

CHAPTER 3

Jack watched Sophie hurry towards the cabin's front door, Laura rushing after her with the key. He felt his heart flip-flop with a burst of hope and anxiety. That couldn't be the same girl he'd made dandelion crowns for—definitely not the cheerful little girl whose hand he used to hold when crossing the creek, simply as an excuse to touch her. When had she become such a . . . *woman*?

He had seen recent pictures of her. The Santoro family had obliged whenever he'd asked about their beloved niece and cousin. Yet none of those photos had done justice to Sophie's true beauty. She had become willowy like her mother, with just enough fullness in all the right places. Her glistening black hair, which had fascinated him as a child, was now a striking golden blond. Even her dark brown, nearly ebony eyes had transformed with age. They were fierce and mysterious but hadn't lost that familiar warmth and softness he remembered.

Sophie disappeared into the darkness of the cabin, and Jack turned away. "I should probably go."

"Oh, no, Jackson." Angelica's kind words held an apologetic lilt. "Please don't mind Sophie."

"It's fine, mate." Pat slapped Jack's bare shoulder.

"You've already proved to us you're more Santoro than Garland now. You'll win her over in no time. Stay. I'm sure Aunty Angie would love to find out what you've been up to."

The tightness in Jack's chest eased at his dear friend's reassurance. He acknowledged Sophie's mother with a smile, noting the familial elegance and beauty that was so radiant in her daughter. "Another time, Angelica. I should get back to work. Nick's new rocking chair won't build itself." Jack pointed his index finger assertively at Pat. "And I'll see you tonight, buddy. Bachelor party. I hope you're ready."

Pat kicked at the ground. "Yeah, I'm not sure ready is the right word."

With a laugh, Jack patted the younger man on the back. He nodded at Sophie's mother. "Nice to see you again, Angelica. I hope we can find some time to catch up properly." His attention flicked to the yawning doorway of the cabin, where Laura had materialised. He wished Sophie were with her. "All of us, while you're both in town."

"Of course, Jack." She followed his gaze. "Maybe we could organise something after the wedding?"

"I'd like that." *I really would,* he thought, raising a hand in farewell. "You know where to find me."

Casting a final glance at the bridegroom-to-be, Jack headed back up the slope towards the cosy wooden shack that had become his home. A long-lost memory of daring a little dark-haired girl to jump from the barn loft into the hay pile below came back to him as he walked. She wouldn't do it alone, so they had jumped together. Back then they did almost everything together.

Halfway home, the mobile phone tucked in the back pocket of his jeans began to vibrate, interrupting his musings. Whipping it free, he checked the screen. *Hellbeast,* it read. He'd updated the name a few months back when his sister had renounced him. He'd really hoped she'd meant it that time. He considered the phone for a long moment before finally answering the call.

"What do you want, April-Rose?"

"Really, Jackson? You haven't heard from me in months, and that's how you greet me? I don't know why I even bothered to call."

"Well, that's the crux of it, isn't it? You did call, so you obviously want something. You better be quick, because I'm busy."

April-Rose huffed in annoyance. "Don't be like that, Jackson," she whined. "We're family and we always will be. You know that I just get . . . upset sometimes. It's your fault really. You irritate me on purpose."

Classic April-Rose. The narcissistic manipulator. She'd inherited the trait from their mother. Luckily it wasn't genetic. Jack rubbed the back of his hand over his eyes. "I'm hanging up now."

"No." It was a sharp demand. "Jack, please."

"Spit it out, April-Rose. I don't have time for your games."

She was silent for a moment, and he was sure she was choosing her next words very carefully.

"I heard the Wendalls are coming to town for tomorrow's wedding."

Jack paused and glanced back down the slope. Sophie had come out of hiding. She handed Pat the last bag from the car while her mother and Laura climbed the cabin stairs. As Pat walked back to the cabin, Sophie closed the vehicle's trunk and then glanced straight up, her eyes locking with Jack's for an instant before she hurried after her family.

Jack wished the sight of him didn't send her running.

"You mean Sophie," he growled into the receiver, "and you've known about that since May."

"Yes." It was a hiss. "When I tried to ask for your help the first time."

"It wasn't my *help* you asked for, April-Rose. You wanted me to stalk her." Jack felt his chest tighten. Turning away from the Wendall's cabin, he took the last few strides to his outdoor workspace.

"Stalk is a strong word, Jackson. I asked you to watch her. Just keep an eye on her. Make sure she doesn't get too comfortable. We don't want her getting any ideas about staying here, do we?"

Jack didn't agree. It had felt good to see Sophie again, to talk to her. God, he'd missed her. He snuck another glance down the hill. No one lingered outside the cabin now. Everything was still, peaceful. He sighed deeply, rubbing a hand over his chest where a dull ache had begun to gnaw at his heart.

"There is no *we*, little sister. Sophie can do as she pleases. I don't care."

"Don't you?" There was a smug scepticism in her tone. "I just thought you might, considering she has the power to ruin the nice little home you've made for yourself with your perfect new family."

Closing his eyes, Jack pinched the bridge of his nose. The thump of a headache pounded at his temples. He knew the Santoros weren't aware of every awful detail, but they knew enough, and they had accepted him. He was afraid to jeopardise that.

"How much longer do you think she's going to keep the truth to herself, Jackson? Twenty years is a long time to hold on to such a secret, and once she finds out that you've nestled yourself into her family, into her old life, she'll do anything to punish you. You'll see."

"You're wrong, April-Rose." He clenched his free hand into a fist. "Sophie isn't like that. We don't even know if she remembers what happened."

That was a lie. Laura had hinted to him that Sophie's memory of the incident was hazy. He'd hoped that meant there were some things she would never remember, but it was what she *did* remember that worried him.

"Don't be stupid, Jackson. If you want to keep this cushy life you've created to escape the Garland name, then you will listen to me and do as I ask."

"Is that a threat, April-Rose?"

"Of course not. I'm just trying to do what's best for you, that's all. If you agree to keep an eye on the little troublemaker and ensure her stay isn't too comfortable, then you'll guarantee your secret is safe. That's what you want, isn't it?"

What he really wanted was for the truth to be out. He longed to be free of the guilt that had eaten at him for years. There hadn't ever been a right time to tell the Santoros what he'd done. That he had been partly responsible for Sophie nearly dying all those years ago. He could never do enough good deeds—could never help the Santoros enough, love them enough—to make up for his sins.

"Jack?" His sister's self-satisfied tone cut deeply.

As he stared at the cabin at the bottom of the grassy slope, he thought he glimpsed a flash of ivory on the veranda by the door. Like a flicker of cloth, the shimmer of Sophie's white blouse. Perhaps he'd imagined it.

"Jackson?" The word was sharper this time.

He cherished the pristine scenery that had become his home, the eucalypts swaying slightly in the wind, the native flowers decorating the edge of the babbling creek and the bright blue sky that opened up to the heavens above him. Only the truth would set him free, but would it cost him everything else?

"Jackson," April-Rose snarled. "If I haven't made myself clear enough, I can break it down for you." There was a brief pause. "If you don't—"

"It's crystal," Jack snapped. "I'll keep an eye on Sophie, make sure she doesn't tattle on either of us. Right?" He sighed, his heart heavy. "Now, if you get the urge to call me again, fight it."

As Jack lowered the phone from his ear, his sister's screeching reply merged with the musical squawks of the birds in the beautiful bushland around him.

CHAPTER 4

The syrupy water of Gap Creek trickled along the grassy riverbank and around the ancient grey boulders that guarded its edge. Native flora were spectators along the shore, some standing tall, reaching for the sky, while others arched over, dipping their leaves or petals into the cool liquid below. The honeyed smell of wattle overpowered the spicy scent of the earth and the freshness of the water. Every now and then the tranquillity was disrupted by the excited squawk of a vibrant parrot or the chortle of a magpie.

Sophie sat on a weathered log by the bank, legs crossed, a sketch pad resting atop her knee. A cluster of indigo star-shaped flowers sprouting from a thicket of long emerald blades had caught her artist's eye, and she had set about capturing the vision in pencil. To her left, the sun's golden rays slanted through the trunks of the eucalypts and ironbarks, warning her that dusk was approaching.

She estimated there was still an hour or two before she and her mother were due at the ranch house for the hens' party. While Angelica had already opted out of the wilder events planned for that evening—choosing to join the group for dinner and then retire early—Laura had informed Sophie she wouldn't be given the same option. Apparently, being the soon-to-be-cousin-in-law of the bride-to-be came with obligations. She just hoped none of them included entertaining April-Rose.

As she tilted the pencil to shade a segment of her artwork, she heard the crunch and snap of a twig on the dry leaves behind her. Knowing it was probably her mother come to check on her, Sophie took her time, carefully etching the final scratch of graphite.

"Laura told me you're an artist."

She jumped and scraped a long, solid line across the page. *Crap.*

"Sorry, I didn't mean to frighten you." This time she recognised Jack's silver tongue.

"What are you doing here, Jack?" Sophie shot a scowl over her shoulder but saw only dark denim jeans with a sizeable bulge beneath them. Her mood grew fierier as she followed the black T-shirt–clad bulk of muscular chest upwards. Jack's smile greeted her at the top. "Do you make it a habit to sneak up on people?"

There was a shimmer of amusement in his eyes. "No, but now I'm enjoying it, so maybe I'll have to start." Stepping over the end of the log, he sat down beside her, blocking her easy escape. "I see you still like to draw. Laura told me you were a graphic designer for some fancy fashion company in the city."

"Sounds like my cousin has told you lots of things." Sophie had deduced as much after catching Laura's guilty expression earlier that day. She shifted away from him, but Jack just moved closer. His nearness was something she used to yearn for as a child. Now it was just infuriating.

"Thanks, I needed the room." He reached towards her. "Show me what you're working on." Pinching the sketchpad from her lap, Jack examined the pencilled drawing. "It's beautiful."

Sophie snatched it back. "It's ruined." She flipped the cardboard cover back in place. "Thanks to you."

It wasn't exactly true. The image was salvageable. It was

her peaceful afternoon that had been spoiled.

"Hardly. It's nothing an eraser can't fix."

"Like *you* know art."

"No. I know sketching. Before I find the timber and get out the tools, I always put my project ideas on paper, to see the full image and work out the dimensions."

She fought the urge to roll her eyes. It shouldn't have been a surprise that Jack shared her favourite pastime. They always had a lot in common.

"Good for you." Sophie patted his knee patronizingly and regretted it as soon as she saw him acknowledge the touch. She stood. "I don't have time for this. I have to get back and get ready for tonight."

As she tried to step around him, Jack stretched out a long jean-clad leg, blocking her exit. He grinned. It was the same look he'd worn as a boy while chasing her around the house, threatening to tickle her if he didn't get his way.

"What's the rush? The party isn't set to start for over another hour. Why don't you sit back down and talk with me for a little while."

Sophie crossed her arms. "You can't keep pretending as though nothing happened between us, Jack."

The memory of their kiss resurfaced. It was the day before the accident. Everything had been so perfect. Then she saw Jack's young face, the hatred etched there when he'd told her he was glad it had been her father who had died. She winced and shook her head.

"We can't just go back to the way things were," she told him.

"Why, Soph? Haven't we been hurting and hurting each other for far too long? Isn't it time to put the past behind us?"

How could she when she still didn't fully remember what that past entailed?

Sophie sighed and eyed the bodily barricade before her. She could step over him. Her escape could be that simple, but she didn't trust him to behave if she got too close.

"Come on, Sophie. I'm not asking you to act as though everything is fine. Just talk to me. See where we can go from there."

"It's the talking that's the problem. You're not the same little boy I used to tell all my secrets to."

"Well, I'm not some stranger."

"Close enough."

Jack studied her. "No, I don't believe it." He grinned again. "I know you missed me. You wouldn't still be standing here fighting with me if you hadn't."

"Excuse me?" Sophie scoffed. "Did you hit your head too hard falling from your ivory tower? I knew narcissism ran in your family, but I didn't realise stupidity followed."

He sighed with satisfaction. "I missed you, too, Soph. Why don't we hug it out?" He reached for her, and she stumbled backwards in surprise.

"There's such a thing as consent, you lunatic."

It was only after she'd regained her composure that Sophie realised Jack hadn't been serious—and that he'd started laughing.

"Shut up," she grumbled, feeling a little silly. She bit her lip to stop herself from sharing his good humour. When they were kids, she'd often made Jack laugh so hard he'd caught hiccups. His genuine laughter still warmed her heart.

"I've really missed this, Soph."

She wouldn't dare tell him she felt the same. He was making it harder for her to keep hating him. But she wasn't ready to let her pain go.

Sophie eyed his outstretched leg again. Jack had stopped laughing and now watched her like a confident predator observing its prey.

"Are you willing to risk it?" He nodded towards the route blocked by his outspread limb. "Bet I'm quicker."

She didn't doubt it. She'd seen the coiled strength in his muscles.

Sophie put her hands on her hips. "I don't have time for your games, Jack. Are you going to let me pass?"

With a smirk, he shook his head. "It's either this, or you sit and talk to me for five minutes."

Neither option was preferable, but she would rather take a chance at escape than risk opening her heart to him again. "You're a real jerk, you know that?" She didn't give him a chance to respond. She flung herself forward, madly dashing for freedom.

He caught her easily, his warm hands locking around her waist pulling her onto his lap with a thud.

"Damn it, Jack." She slapped her sketchpad against his thigh. "We're not children anymore."

"I can feel that," he told her, cuddling her closer. She wriggled, trying in vain to dislodge his firm grip as his breath tickled the fine hairs on the back of her neck.

Sophie froze as every nerve in her body came to life. It felt good to be in Jack's arms. He smelled enticingly familiar. Butterflies fluttered within her as that childhood crush burned ever brighter.

He held her there for the briefest of moments, until their breathing synced, and then slid her back onto the log. Sophie held his stare as he gently released her.

With a sigh, Jack rested his hands on his knees. "That didn't quite go as planned," he mumbled.

His deep voice snapped Sophie back to reality, and she squirmed further away. She raked fingers through her hair, lifting it off her heated cheeks. "You won," she panted. "Wasn't that the plan?"

He frowned, clearly distracted by his own thoughts. "I'd been hoping to convince you to give me a chance, to give our friendship another try, but I'm not off to a good start."

"Yeah. Not really," Sophie agreed. She would never admit it to him, but friendship hadn't been her first thought when she'd landed on his lap. Not even the second. She'd become consumed by something more carnal. Terribly inappropriate thoughts about someone she was supposed to hate.

Jack caught her gaze again, and she could see his

33

disappointment. It tugged at her heart.

He brushed his hand across his forehead. "Maybe this whole thing was a bad idea." Again, he shook his head, then shot to his feet with a dismissive wave. "I'm sorry if I upset you, Soph. Don't worry. I'll try to leave you alone while you're in town." Jack headed back towards the path and the cabin beyond.

He didn't really mean that, did he? Regret swirled uneasily in Sophie's stomach. She felt ill, her chest heavy. She might not have been ready for the friendship he was after, not yet prepared to forgive him, but that didn't mean they couldn't talk—about some things. Like the weather or the wedding?

A blend of remorse and confusion drove her to call out to him around the painful lump in her throat. "Jack."

His stride never slowed.

Sophie swallowed deeply and tried again, more certain of her decision. The lump in her throat eased. "Jackson."

He froze but didn't face her.

"I'm"—she ground out the syllable slowly, finding it difficult to release the words—"sorry."

He was a distance away now, partially hidden by the short shrubbery and a couple of low-hanging branches, but she could see him slant his head slightly to the side.

"You're sorry?" he hollered at her. "Does that mean you'll give me a second chance?"

"I didn't say that. But I'll talk to you, Jack. Not like we used to, but we'll talk."

"Good. Then be my date to the wedding tomorrow."

"What?"

"As my date, we'll have plenty of time to talk, won't we?"

Sophie gritted her teeth, irritation flushing her cheeks pink. Had she just been played? Had this been Jack's plan all along? He'd obviously learned a trick or two from his manipulative sister.

"Sophie?" His voice was all velvety charm as he called for her to answer.

She should say no, but she didn't want to. Jack was right. She had missed him. "Fine," she growled. It might have been a mistake, yet Sophie felt lighter just knowing she would definitely see him again. He had been her other half all through their childhood, the yang to her yin. Now that she was close to him again, the thought of him keeping his distance was as distressing to her as that yawning hole in her memory.

Jack glanced over his shoulder, and his captivating blue eyes held hers. "That's all I wanted to hear," he purred.

CHAPTER 5

A cacophony of shrill feminine voices, ear-splitting stabs of laughter and the lively thump of pop music rose into the sparkling night sky above the rooftop of the Stout House Bar and Grill. Women, in all blooms of life and fashions— some in formal attire, others in torn jeans and Akubra hats—mingled on the vibrant green imitation lawn and among the trendy white-painted wood furniture. Waitstaff paraded after-dinner nibbles, decadent bite-sized desserts and flutes of pink and gold champagne on sparkling trays, even though the private bar had a never-ending line of guests. As the alcohol intake soared so did the volume of voices, causing Sophie to long for the comfort of bed and the quiet of sleep.

"I know you've been avoiding it," Laura nearly yelled, leaning closer to Sophie's ear, "but you'll have to acknowledge April-Rose at some point tonight. She keeps looking over here."

She nodded to a group of young women in the centre of the room, where a statuesque redhead was looking down her perfectly straight nose at them. Her raptorial gaze assessed them as an undoubtedly feigned smile tweaked her red lips. Sophie eyed the woman's glittering emerald cocktail dress and immediately thought of an infamous wicked green witch.

"If she wants to talk to me, she can initiate it. I'm not about to pander to her." Sophie turned her back on the prying eyes of her nemesis and looked for her mother.

Angelica was conversing with a sun-kissed brunette sporting a silver crown and red sash, and an audacious woman in a snug cheetah-print mini-dress—Marilyn, the bride-to-be, and her Aunt Susan. Angelica let out a sudden burst of laughter at something Marilyn uttered, and her dark eyes danced as they met Sophie's. She acknowledged her with a quick wave from across the room.

"Not everyone treats April-Rose like the princess she pretends to be," Laura quipped. "Marilyn might run in the same circles now that her father's made it big in the property industry, but her parents are as down-to-earth as they come. They treat everyone like family. Just look at Faith over there."

Sophie followed Laura's subtle nod to Marilyn's mother, who sat at a nearby table with a group of middle-aged women. As she watched, the cuddly, high-spirited woman slapped the table and snorted with the same unusual but infectious laugh as her daughter.

Laura giggled. "You think she's the kind of person to fawn over April-Rose or Sheridan Garland?"

"No, of course not. I don't doubt that the Harts are lovely. It just irks me to see people worship April-Rose as though she's heaven-sent." Sophie waved a hand at the crowd before them. "Speaking of Sherry, where is the Queen of Moorhenvale this evening?"

"Probably tending to some important business. You know those spa days—they can really take a lot out of you."

"Actually"—the word was a saccharine drawl of venom dripping from the sharpest of smiles—"my mother had a prior commitment with an old friend. But she'll still be attending the wedding tomorrow with the rest of our family."

Laura backed up a step, but Sophie held her ground. She stared into the stormy blue of April-Rose's eyes and calmly took a sip of champagne.

April-Rose was the first to blink. She chuckled, seemingly amused by Sophie's silence. "Sophie, *honey*. It's been too long, hasn't it?"

"I'm pretty sure forever wouldn't be long enough, April-Rose." How was it possible Jack was related to this viper? For all his faults, all his betrayals, he could never come close to the devilishness of this woman.

April-Rose's laugh was laced with poison. "For a moment I wondered if you recognised me." She licked her apple-red lips and stepped closer. "Which is funny really, considering you've managed to refamiliarise yourself with my brother in less than a day." Her eyes flicked to Laura. "Has your cousin told you that she's to be Jackson's date to the wedding tomorrow?"

Sophie felt her cheeks warm. She'd had every intention of telling her cousin what had transpired between her and Jack that afternoon, but she hadn't yet found the right moment.

"So, Jack told you?" Sophie held her chin high. She shouldn't have been surprised.

April-Rose's cloying grin got even bigger. "Oh, honey. My brother didn't tell me. Marilyn did. Pat sent her a message a couple of hours ago. Apparently it's big news."

Sophie gritted her teeth.

Laura touched her elbow. "I can't believe Pat found out some town gossip before me," she said.

"Sorry, Laur. You know I would've told you, right?"

"Of course, Soph. You always tell me everything."

"Aren't you both adorable?" April-Rose didn't make the slightest effort to conceal her ridicule. "How lucky you are to have each other. Family is so important. That's why I'm looking forward to spending time with you and Jackson at the reception tomorrow evening, Sophie. We'll all be seated at *our* family's table."

Our family's table. The words rang in Sophie's ears. She was to sit with the Garlands? *Oh god, no.* Sophie's stomach dropped, and she felt like vomiting.

"No," Laura choked out. "That's not right. I'm sure you'll find that Sophie is sitting with my parents. It's already been arranged."

"Don't worry, Laura." April-Rose dismissed her with a flick of her wrist. "I've sorted everything. I mentioned to Marilyn how nice it would be if Sophie was seated with the Garlands, and she was happy to oblige with the last-minute change. There was an empty seat for Jackson's plus-one anyway."

Bile rose higher in Sophie's throat. She was an adult now. She couldn't be bullied into doing April-Rose's bidding. Could she?

"Unfortunately, you're mistaken, April-Rose. I'll be sitting with my mother, my aunt and uncle during the wedding and the reception. Jack's invitation does no more than ensure him a dance or two."

It might not have been exactly what she'd agreed to, but they could still talk while dancing. Maybe she'd been naive to think Jack would be seated with the Santoros, but he hadn't warned her otherwise. Perhaps he'd wanted her company *because* he'd already known of this unhappy fate?

"Oh dear." April-Rose's immaculately manicured fingers spread over her heart. "Sophie, had I known that's how you felt, I never would have suggested it. But Marilyn has agreed to let her father's business partner—a close friend of my mother's—attend, and he's to take your place at that table. How unfortunate."

A blaze of anger lashed through Sophie's limbs. She wanted to slap that grin off April-Rose's perfectly made-up face. As if she sensed Sophie's desire, Laura tightened her grip on Sophie's elbow. That reassurance eased the tension building in Sophie's chest and she sighed slowly. The wedding wasn't until tomorrow afternoon. She could talk to Pat and Marilyn and have things changed back. Maybe she could have this new arrival moved to the Garlands' table instead?

"It will be all right," Laura whispered.

"Never lose that positivity, Laura." April-Rose sniffed. "Even if it does reveal how naive you are."

Sophie saw red. How dare this she-demon speak to her cousin like that? She stepped forward ready to retaliate but halted at the sight of another familiar person.

"Sophie." The ultra-slim woman with a long, oval face and ombre—chocolate to blond—hair greeted her tartly as she handed April-Rose a fresh flute of pink champagne.

"You remember my best friend, Tiffany McDowall, don't you, Sophie?" April-Rose clinked her glass with Tiffany's. "She works with the family now as Garland Grain's chief marketing officer. She'll also be sitting with us tomorrow."

"Of course she will." Sophie didn't bother to hide her sarcasm.

Reconnecting with one childhood bully was bad enough, but two? How many more surprises were in store for her?

Knowing she'd won this battle, April-Rose winked at Sophie. "You ladies have a good night now." She grinned smugly as she headed back into her adoring crowd.

CHAPTER 6

At the foot of Bitterbark Creek's homestead, Jack shifted his grip on Pat's waist, hauling his severely inebriated friend higher in his arms. Boris and Banjo excitedly circled their feet, all bright eyes and lolling tongues. Jack offered the driver of the retreating vehicle a wave as it headed back along the driveway towards the road. When the crunch of the tires tapered, the pulsating whoop of a tawny frogmouth began in the sheltering gum trees nearby.

Banjo yipped, jerking his furry head towards the noise.

"Quiet, boy." Jack rubbed the dog's scruff affectionately. "Go on back to bed, both of you." He pointed up the stairs, then looked down at the pair of motley-coloured canines. "Go to bed. I've got to help your brother do the same."

The dogs padded over to the steps. Boris ran ahead obediently, but Banjo risked a couple of backsteps as though testing the command. Jack followed close behind them, supporting Pat's weight as the younger man struggled to find his feet.

"It's okay. I can do it." It was a merry slur of words. Pat rested his head on Jack's shoulder. "I can do—"

He slipped, but Jack caught him, holding tightly until he regained his balance. Pat threw his head back and let out a hoot of delight.

Jack quickly shushed him. "Come on, buddy, let's get you to bed. Left foot, right foot. We're nearly there."

"You're too good to me, Jack," Pat garbled. "You're like family to me. Like my brother." Pat tightened his grip on Jack's shoulder. "You know I wanted you in the wedding party. I mean, Laura was always going to be my best person, no contest, but you—I wanted you up there with me. You know that." Pat flopped his head to the side as he tried to look at Jack. "But you turned me down."

"I know." Jack halted at the top of the steps, steadying his friend. "I know, mate. I'm sorry."

Boris and Banjo looked longingly at them from where they'd retreated to their elevated trampoline beds. When Banjo inched a paw to the floor, Jack held up a hand in warning.

"No." Pat slowly shook his head, rolling his eyes, and then changed direction with a nod. "No, I get it. I know you're just trying to protect us, that you're trying to keep your family out of our business. You're a good friend."

Jack tried but couldn't muster a smile. He was certain Pat wouldn't think so highly of him had he known the full truth. Yes, he'd rejected the opportunity to be in the wedding party in order to protect the Santoros. But it wasn't just to ensure the Garlands didn't gore their toxic tusks into the wedding, embedding themselves until they'd conquered every inch of it. Jack hadn't wanted Pat to regret his inclusion in such a major milestone of his life. He feared the shame, the horror, the anger Pat would feel upon discovering the reality. Pat was right. Jack loved him like a brother, but that wasn't enough to change his past choices. Forgiveness was hard even for the best of people like the Santoro family. Jack refused to muddy their future memories of this special event if the truth came out and they couldn't find it in their hearts to forgive him.

"You're a great friend as well, Pat," Jack consoled. "I'm lucky to know you." He avoided his friend's gaze and looked towards the front door. "Now, you've got to help me, otherwise we'll never get you inside." As he pushed Pat forward, the younger man pulled back.

"I just have to know, Jack. I have to know." Pat dropped his head to his chest and raised a hand as though to steady himself.

"You okay, buddy?"

Pat nodded, long and slow. "Totally okay." When he opened his eyes, his brows furrowed. "Sophie . . . what are you doing with her? I don't think you've told me everything."

Jack felt cold and clammy. Had Sophie or Laura said something to Pat? Jack was already guilt-ridden over his agreement with April-Rose. Getting Sophie to come as his date to the wedding had filled him with such mixed feelings. She had felt so right in his arms by the creek. So soft and warm, smelling of jasmine and vanilla. He'd told Pat he'd asked her if they could try repairing their friendship. April-Rose thought Jack was helping to keep an enemy close. But Jack just wanted to spend more time with this enticing new version of his Sophie. He yearned for her to forgive him.

"What do you mean, Pat? I told you I wanted to build back that friendship we had as kids. That's all." Jack hated lying.

"Uh-uh, I think there's more to it than that."

"You're drunk." Focusing on the front entrance, he ushered Pat forward, but his friend fought him, digging his heels into the wooden floorboards.

"I am," Pat chortled, "but I'm not blind. You like her. You missed her. You always ask about her. Laura told me."

Jack's stomach twitched uncomfortably. Had he really been that obvious? "Like I said—you're drunk." He yanked open the screen door.

Pat sniggered. "That's not a no."

"It's not a yes," Jack snapped, fumbling the key into the lock. "Just shut up and let me get you to bed."

Pat guffawed wildly as Jack finally got the door open.

Quickly, he covered the younger man's mouth. "Shut it," he growled. "You want to wake up the whole household?"

Pat stifled his laughter, but merriment still flickered in his eyes.

"You going to behave?"

Pat nodded, swaying a little with the movement.

"Okay, then." Tentatively, Jack removed his hand and shepherded his friend over the threshold.

"You know," Pat whispered as Jack closed the door behind them, "I wouldn't be doing my job as her cousin, as family, if I didn't tell you not to hurt her."

"I'm not going to hurt her, mate," Jack assured him. His gut said otherwise. Perhaps it would be better if he encouraged her to leave town after all? The pain of losing her all over again would be nothing to the pain she and her family would suffer if the truth ever came to light.

"Good." Pat closed his eyes, his grin wide and content. "Then I won't have to hurt you either and that's that then."

Sighing, Jack readjusted his grip on Pat's waist, supporting more of his friend's weight. He was pleased Pat could sleep tonight with a clear conscience. He hadn't been able to do the same for twenty long years. All these lies were slowly killing him. God, how he wished he could reverse the ignorant decision he'd made as a child. He adored the Santoro family and the freedom and acceptance they offered him.

And Sophie? Jack pondered as they headed down the hall. Did he still love her, the girl he'd crushed on before knowing what a crush even was? She'd held his heart once, and when she'd left, he thought it would remain broken forever. Now she was back, he could truly feel again. But would he hurt her? Was she better off forgetting him? Those were the important questions. Right now, he didn't have the answers.

CHAPTER 7

The gentle flow of Gap Creek over rock and riverbed created a harmonious melody with the chirping of crickets and the croaking of cheerful frogs. Jack followed the rocky path along the winding water's edge, using moonlight and the torch he'd taken from the main house to light his way. He dodged another newly formed web, not wanting to disturb the dancing spider as it weaved a delicate pattern, and noticed a glint in the darkness, coming from the direction of Angelica and Sophie's cabin. Breaking away from the trail and crossing the gravel road, he headed towards it, peering through the shadows of the night's darkest hours. There was a dim light inside the cabin, as though a single lamp was fighting the gloom, but that wasn't what he'd seen. As he drew closer, he saw something glittering atop the steps.

"Wrong cabin," a feminine voice hissed.

Jack raised the torch, illuminating the veranda until he snared Sophie in its glow.

"Hey!" She raised an arm to cover her eyes and lowered the glossy white porcelain mug in her other hand.

Nipping his lip to keep from smiling, Jack tilted the torch away but kept her illuminated. His heart skipped a beat at the sight of her. Was it wrong of him to hope she felt the same? "Did you have a good evening?" he asked with interest.

Through the murky gleam of torchlight, she smouldered with annoyance. "Is now really the best time for a chat?"

He took a seat beside her, aiming the flashlight at the lime-green grass below. "It was that bad, huh?" He thought he caught her smirking.

"Well, I blame you for most of it." Her eyes roamed the darkness in front of them as she sipped her sweet-scented tea.

"And I wasn't even there."

"When a butterfly flaps its wings. . ." she whispered.

He had missed their banter. "Are you suggesting I created chaos with one tiny little act?"

She shot him a look, daring him to dispute it.

He chuckled softly. "I only wanted to give Pat a heads-up about our plan to go to the wedding together."

"Our plan?" Sophie spat her surprise.

"Yeah, you agreed." Had she changed her mind? He swallowed his nerves. "I thought it best he knew beforehand. I'd rather not spring any surprises on him during his special day."

"Right? So it had nothing to do with securing a change in seating arrangements either, hey?"

"I'm sorry. What?" Jack fought the smirk that tempted him. "Why would I care about where you plan to sit?"

"You're really going to pretend that you knew nothing about April-Rose moving me to your family's table?"

What had the Hellbeast done now? He shook his head. "I guess it makes sense that we sit together." *Keep your enemies closer.* It was one of his sister's favourite clichés.

"Couldn't you have just joined me at mine?"

Jack shrugged. His sister was used to getting her way.

"I should have known you had a bigger part to play in all of this, Jack. What did you and April-Rose do, concoct this devilish little plan in your secret lair somewhere?"

A loud burst of laughter escaped him, and he reminded himself that Sophie's mother was asleep inside. "I'm sorry, Soph. I'm not nearly the villain you want to think I am." He had made some terrible choices long ago. But like the Garland name, they had never defined him. He'd fought every day since to be a better man. "I swear, I never even mentioned the idea to my sister."

"So, what?" The dim glow of torchlight by their feet lit Sophie's face with the slightest hint of colour. "April-Rose just knew your intentions? Do you two share some kind of evil ESP?"

He chuckled. She had always been deliciously witty. "No. I'm not evil, just eager." He leaned closer, bumping the edge of his shoulder lightly against hers. "Eager to get to know you again, Sophie. Twenty years of silence will do that to a guy."

"You still talk as though we've got something to get back to. But things will never be as they were."

"Is that so?" A wayward strand of Sophie's honey-blond hair caught his attention, and he smoothed it behind her ear without thinking. Their eyes met and she didn't flinch away. The touch prickled his fingertips, and he ached to do it again. "Sorry." He dropped his hand to his lap and stared out into the darkness.

Sophie cleared her throat. "Yes, that's so." The hard edge in her voice had softened. "You really hurt me, Jack."

"I know." Pain gripped his heart at the sadness in her voice. He would only hurt her more if she stayed. But god, he wanted her to.

"You never called, never tried to reach me." She sighed. "I'm not sure I would have answered if you had."

"I wanted to." But how could he have apologised for everything he and his family had put her through?

"But you didn't."

"No. I didn't." He tightened his grip on the torch until his knuckles became white. Frustration had him wanting to yell or run, but he didn't want to leave her. He was at war with himself, with his family, not with Sophie. "If things had been different, Soph. If my family had been different. I like to think I would have tried harder."

"That's our answer then, isn't it?" She glanced back into the darkness and took another casual sip of her tea. "You can't choose your family, Jack. You can't change blood. We'll never get back what we lost. It just wasn't supposed to last. Our friendship, the innocence we had back then. None of it."

Then why did a spark between them still flicker? Why did he suddenly feel more alive, his heart fuller? If there was no hope, then how could still feel this way about her? The fear of losing her all over again threatened to suffocate him. He took a steadying breath. "I'm not ready to believe that."

"It doesn't matter what you believe." Sophie shrugged. "You can't fight fate, Jack." She stared at him then, those beautiful, mysterious eyes looking straight into his soul. "And if you don't believe in fate, then just try fighting April-Rose."

"My sister doesn't control me," Jack argued. Even as he said it, he knew it wasn't true. Look at how she'd convinced him to agree to keep an eye on Sophie despite his protests.

"Then tell her to return the seating arrangements at the wedding to their original plan," Sophie challenged. She pursed her lips, waiting for his answer.

Jack knew he'd been beaten. "I can't." His sister would sooner hang up on him than listen to his plea.

With another sigh, Sophie launched herself to her feet. "Exactly." She frowned. "Why bother trying to repair our friendship when April-Rose will do her darnedest to destroy it again?"

When Jack opened his mouth to disagree, she dismissed him with a wave. "Don't worry, Jack. I'll be gone in a couple of days and your comfortable life with the Santoros will return to normal."

"But—Soph?" What if he told her he didn't want her to go? Would she still leave? Fear chilled his fingertips and formed a lump in his throat.

Exhaustion lined her face. She shook her head. "Just go home, Jack." She motioned to the cabin in the distance. "Go home and get some sleep. After the wedding, it will be as though I were never here."

With that, she turned her back on him and stepped out of the torchlight.

CHAPTER 8

Sophie and Angelica's cabin was compact. The kitchenette shared space with the living room, the linoleum and timber floorboards drawing a line between the two. It contained just enough practical furniture to be comfortable. Modern appliances sprawled over the kitchen benchtop while a nutmeg-brown couch squatted directly opposite against wood-slated walls. A tiny dining table and four chairs huddled in the centre.

A handsome elderly woman with slender limbs and fine silvery hair twirled atop her head waited with perfect posture at the table as Sophie and her mother prepared black tea and golden biscuits. Her shrewd dark eyes met Sophie's, and she grunted her disapproval—a garble of guttural Italian—before swishing her fingers over her heart in the sign of a cross.

"What kind of man invites a woman to attend her own family's wedding on his arm, only to separate her from them?"

"Obviously an evil one, Nonna." Sophie tried not to laugh as she ignored her mother's scowl. She grabbed the tin of shortbread and sugar cookies from the counter. Placing them on the circular table, she took a seat beside

53

Isola Santoro.

"He's a good boy, Mama," Angelica chided. "Always has been from what I can remember."

"The Garland boy?" Nonna Isola snorted. "Bad blood is bad blood, my Angelica. I might live hills and fields away in Warwick, but the people at Sage Oak talk. They say all the Garlands are trouble, worse now with their patriarch dead and buried. Alcoholism, they say. The wife and that harridan daughter of his lead the business, and people are scared to work for them, scared to leave. They act as though they've got the only grain farm in the Southern Downs."

"Well, Mama, it is the biggest." Angelica placed a cup of tea before her mother and took a seat.

"Money can't replace a conscience, darling," Nonna told her. "Nor kindness or respect. People abandon that all on their own."

Sophie bit into a biscuit to hide her smirk. "I doubt April-Rose was born with a conscience."

"Sophia." Angelica shook her head, her cup of tea poised before her lips. "Don't encourage your grandmother. Prejudice is not something I want *our* family renowned for."

Nonna fixed her brown eyes on Sophie. "So, this boy, Sophia. Are you aware of his intentions? Do you expect them to be honourable?"

"Unlikely." Sophie remembered the way Jack looked at her last night. He had looked the same just before he kissed her years ago. She had hoped he'd take that risk again. "But there's no need to worry." Sophie patted her grandmother's hand. "I'm grown now. He and his family can't hurt me like they used to."

Nonna furrowed her wrinkled brow and directed her concern at Angelica. "Why do you let her do this, Angie? She is your daughter. Tell her to refuse this boy. Such an inconsiderate last-minute request. I don't want to see my Sophia hurt."

"I cannot." Angelica gestured to her daughter. "Like she said, she is all grown up now. She makes her own decisions."

"She doesn't know what is best for her," Nonna argued. "You must look after her."

Sophie bit back her urge to argue. She couldn't win an argument against Nonna.

"I always look after her, Mama. If I thought I could change her mind I would, but this boy is nice. He's not as bad as Sophie says. He'll take care of her at the wedding. He's a sweet boy. He and Sophie used to be friends."

"Friends? What sort of friend asks this of another?" Nonna Isola raised her hands heavenward and called out for the virgin Madonna.

My thoughts exactly, Sophie agreed silently. If only her Nonna's prayers could save her from another altercation with April-Rose. Her *friend* Jack definitely wouldn't.

Sophie heard a distant rumble. Was that the sound of a spluttering engine?

"What is that?" Angelica tilted her head, listening.

"Sounds like the four-wheeler." Sophie stood, heading for the screen door.

"Mama." Angelica caught her mother's attention. "Is Nicky coming back for you? I thought we were walking down to the wedding together since it's so close to our cabin?"

Nonna shook her head. "No, no. Nicky said he would see me there, that you and Sophia would take me."

Blinking in the glare of the midmorning sunlight, Sophie scoured the hill that led back to the homestead. As her eyes adjusted to the cheerful brightness, a chunky scarlet and ebony farm utility vehicle appeared on the crest of the hill before rumbling down the rocky dirt road, stirring up a whirlwind of dust as it sped along. Sophie couldn't make out who was driving, but from the slightness of their figure she suspected they were female.

"Who is it, Sophie?" Angelica asked. "Can you see? I hope everything's all right."

"I think it's. . ." Sophie squinted as the four-wheeler approached the cabin. "Yes, it's Laura"—she frowned as her cousin came into view—"and she's in her pyjamas."

Again, Nonna Isola hailed the virtuous Madonna.

When Laura decelerated and parked the vehicle alongside the cabin, Sophie slipped outside onto the veranda. "What's happened, Laur? Is everything okay?"

Laura switched off the grumbling engine and freed herself from the vehicle's caged cab. "It will be, Soph." She dashed up the stairs. "I think I've found a solution to our problem."

"Our problem?" Which problem? Sophie had many on her radar.

She assessed her cousin's attire. Although Laura was wearing a matching sleep-set adorned with palm trees and tropical fruit, her make-up was perfect, and her pixie haircut was neatly styled as though she'd just escaped the wedding beautician.

Laura grinned. "I talked to Pat. Since April-Rose ruined everything with the seating arrangements, he agreed to give you another option. He and Marilyn organised a few extra settings at the kids' table in case parents needed to handle any child-related dramas. He's happy for you to sit there instead or move if things become too difficult at the Garlands' table. He said there's room enough for you and Jack both." She paused to catch her breath. "I know it's not much, being the kids' table and all, but I thought it would give you an out when April-Rose and her mother become unbearable."

"Oh, that's wonderful." Sophie dragged her cousin into a quick hug. "I was just complaining to Nonna about it. You'll have to thank Pat for me when you get back."

"I knew you'd be pleased." Laura beamed. "After last night, seeing how April-Rose was with you, I couldn't stand to see her win. This way, you have the upper hand."

"You're the greatest, Laur, but what did you do? Escape the wedding prep to come down here?" She motioned to her cousin's face. "Why didn't you just send me a text?"

"All the phones are on lockdown until the actual

wedding. Marilyn doesn't want anything leaking out on social media before the event. Pat would've given me permission, but Marilyn's brother, Dale, is the other groomsman and Pat didn't want to put Dale in an awkward position. You know, to tell or not to tell Marilyn."

"So Pat let you take the four-wheeler?"

"He gave me fifteen minutes. He's timing me."

Sophie giggled. "You're lucky Marilyn and the girls are getting ready in Warwick or else you'd be sprung."

"Tell me about it. I love Marilyn, but she's been nudging bridezilla mode for the last couple of days with all the wedding stress."

"Are you certain she'll be okay with all of this? It's very last-minute, and she's already had to change plans once because of April-Rose."

"Sure. Pat will sort it all out with her later. It will be fine. I swear."

"Okay, good." Relief had Sophie sighing. "Thanks again, Laur."

"No worries, cuz." Laura patted her arm.

There was a scuffling of footsteps behind them as someone exited the cabin.

"What are you two talking about?" Nonna's eyes glinted with suspicion.

"Nothing, Nonna," Laura purred innocently, waving in her grandmother's direction. "I just dropped in to tell Sophie something, but now I've got to get back." She began inching down the stairs.

"Laura Carina Santoro, you will come back here and tell me why you are parading around in your undergarments in public."

Nonna's outrage only drew a wider grin from Laura, and from Angelica, who had slipped outside behind the elderly woman.

"They're not undergarments, Nonna," Laura defended. "They're my pyjamas and I've got to get back to the house. Pat's got the stopwatch running."

"Stopwatch? What is this?" Nonna exclaimed. "Are we having a wedding or a sporting race? Oh, Madonna"—she raised her hands heavenward—"why did you punish me with such unruly grandchildren? Have I not been good all my life? Have I not been faithful to our Lord?"

Sophie stifled a laugh as Angelica came to Nonna's aid, cuddling the older woman's shoulders and steering her inside. Laura climbed back onto the four-wheeler.

"It will be fine, Laur," Sophie called out. "I'll smooth things over with Nonna and explain why you stopped by."

Laura saluted her and started the engine. "See you at the wedding." She spun the four-wheeler around, giving Sophie a wave of farewell as she bumped along the stony road and into the distance.

It was only as the vehicle disappeared over the hill that Sophie realised the side pocket of her black palazzo pants was vibrating. Snatching her mobile phone free, she saw the screen glowing radiantly with a new message. With a tap of her thumb, she opened it. Her heart did that annoying little somersault she used to experience years ago whenever she saw *him*.

Sophie. It's Jack. What time are you heading down to the wedding? We could walk together. You have my number now, so call me. Anytime.

She considered calling him for a moment. Adrenaline buzzed through her at the thought of talking to him again. She had to kick this renewed desire for him. Like she'd said last night, she'd be gone in a couple of days. There was no need to fight for something that had no future. They had separate lives now. They were better off apart.

She switched the screen off. How had Jack gotten her phone number? Avoiding him was difficult enough when he lived just a stroll away. Now he could call her, or—heaven forbid—she could drunk-dial him once she returned home to Brisbane.

She slapped a hand to her forehead. She couldn't trust herself. She would have to block him or lose his number.

Could she be that rude? Probably not while they were supposed to be attending this wedding together, but after . . . maybe?

She glanced in the direction of his cabin hoping to catch a glimpse of him. There was no doubt he'd be drop-dead gorgeous in a formal suit. Maybe she should call him? She could help match his tie to her dress.

Oh my gosh. What was she doing? She couldn't let her heart run away with her head like this. This Jack wasn't the cheeky little boy she remembered. That boy was lost to her after that horrible car crash claimed her sweet, loving dad. This man was the same person who had shunned her afterward and ripped out her heart. She had to remember that.

Sophie breathed deeply and, with a silent prayer reminiscent of her grandmother's, she went back inside.

CHAPTER 9

The wedding's magical decor had transformed the lush jade-hued lawn beside the cola-coloured creek. White-painted wooden chairs with azure satin sashes stood in symmetrical lines, flanking each side of a lengthy gold aisle runner. At one end sat an ornamental sign welcoming guests while an elegant arch adorned with delicate ivory blossoms framed the other. The hum of conversation gushing from the guests concealed the swish-swash of the water but couldn't drown out the chirping of native birds.

As Jack waited—shifting from foot to foot—for his date to arrive, the glow of the receding sun warmed his back through his midnight-blue suit jacket and white dress shirt. He'd sent Sophie three text messages now yet received no reply. He wasn't game to send another. He wanted to call, needed to know she was still coming, but he fought the impulse, forcing it back with clenched fists and gritted teeth. It wasn't as though she had left town again without a goodbye. That was just his fear talking. She would show up. She had to. Eventually. Sophie wouldn't miss her cousin's wedding.

His heart leapt when he heard a feminine voice cut through the din.

"There he is. Jackson!"

April-Rose approached him, wearing a slash of red lipstick and an ostentatious amethyst gown. Jack's stomach sank and irritation prickled across his skin.

"You almost looked happy to see me." She greeted him with a tight embrace and a peck on his cheek. "Were you expecting someone else?"

She knew exactly who he'd been expecting. Jack pushed her away and scrubbed the back of his hand over his cheek. "I would have been pleased to see *anyone* else."

"Children." The glamorous woman behind April-Rose, with a cascade of champagne-blond hair and beautiful features frozen in time from surgery, admonished them. "Manners, please. We are not alone." Sheridan Garland pulled Jack close, popping a kiss on each cheek before linking her arm through his. "And how is my dear boy?" she purred, batting her lashes as she stroked perfectly manicured fingers down his jacket's sleeve.

Jack had spoken too soon. He would have been pleased to see literally anyone other than his own family. Gentler than he had been with his sister, he pulled free of his mother and gestured towards her showy silver ensemble. It was startlingly more *bride-like* than *guest-of-the-bride*. "That is an exquisite outfit, Mother, but I feel obliged to ask, whose wedding do you expect to attend? Pat and Marilyn's . . . or your own?"

"Jackson," she hissed in displeasure. "I realise we have not been on the best terms of late. However, I expect you to treat me with the necessary respect when we are in public. After all, I am still your mother. We are still family, no matter how much you seem to wish otherwise."

He didn't need reminding. Sophie had done a fine job of that last night. He couldn't change the blood running through his veins, but if he could, he would do it in a heartbeat.

"Why don't you both find a seat in the peanut gallery before all the best vantage points are taken?" he snapped.

Sheridan gasped as though she'd been struck. "Is that the Santoros' insolence rubbing off on you, son? Or do you just wish to wound me?"

"Save the charade for someone else, Mother. You're guaranteed my company for the evening, so try to use that time wisely." Jack nodded at the rows of seating. "Take a seat and I'll join you once my date arrives."

Sheridan stared him down. When he didn't flinch, she inclined her head in surrender. "You might try to deny it," she whispered, "but you are *my* son, and we, my beautiful boy, are more alike than you would let yourself believe." She patted his chest and then sauntered over to the rows of seating.

Jack stared after her. He felt sick. He knew she was wrong. She had to be. He had made mistakes and lived with them every day. But his childhood transgressions were nothing compared to his mother's sins. She was the reason he was riddled with guilt in the first place. If it weren't for her poisoning their minds, none of them would have gone down to the Garland dam that day and Sophie wouldn't have spent twenty years with hazy memories of the moment she nearly died. If it weren't for his mother, for his mistake, Sophie wouldn't have left town and Jack never would have lost her.

"I don't understand why you align yourself against us, Jackson." April-Rose fixed her devilish gaze on his. "We have always been in this *together*."

Together? His sister was deluded. Jack bared his teeth. Before he could respond, a shimmer of gold caught his eye. He stopped breathing and his heart skipped a beat.

"Lost for words, brother?" April-Rose prodded, unaware of his distraction. "Maybe it's time you reconsider your position."

"Reconsider yours," he told her, pushing her aside.

She cursed, but her voice was distant, muffled. His attention had been stolen by the most ravishing woman he'd ever laid eyes on.

Sophie Wendall strode confidently towards him in sexy strappy stilettos. She looked like she had just stepped off a runway from some prestigious fashion event or glided down from heaven. She wore a snug blue-grey gown detailed with intricate lace. Her hair was curled neatly atop her head and golden earrings glittered against her delicate neck. Her large dark brown eyes and those plump rose-coloured lips absolutely enthralled him. He barely registered her mother and the older woman with the same familial prettiness beside her.

"Do you need a tissue?" April-Rose jabbed her brother in the side with her elbow. "I'm sure you'd rather not drool all over your nice suit."

Jack coughed, trying to catch his breath. His pulse was wild. He couldn't speak, couldn't look away. Sophie had him spellbound.

Sophie's kissable mouth slid into a hard line upon seeing his unwanted companion. "Jackson. April-Rose." She greeted them both with mechanical politeness. "You remember my mother, Angelica. And this is my nonna, my grandmother, Isola Santoro." She stepped aside, ushering the elderly woman forward.

"So, this is the boy?" Isola asked, scrutinising Jack through squinted eyes.

Jack forced himself free of Sophie's piercing gaze. "I guess I must be, Mrs. Santoro. Though I'd be obliged to know what Sophie's told you in case I need to defend myself."

"Please, I am *Nonna* and have been for many years now." Isola clasped Jack's outstretched hand. "There is no need to be so formal." She looked up at him with a mischievous grin.

Jack remembered seeing such a grin on Sophie's own face when they were children, back when they were allowed to ride the ponies, just before they raced. Sophie always won. It made him like this *Nonna* all the more.

"And there will be no need for defence just yet, Jackson,

dear," Nonna continued. "You stand accused only of securing my granddaughter's company for this wedding." She leaned in, pulling him down closer. "I must say, I was initially disappointed when Sophia told me she could no longer sit at the family's table, that she would be seated with the Garlands of all people. But now that I see you"—she reached up and patted his jaw—"now that I see this handsome face, I better understand her decision to accept your offer."

"Mama," Angelica warned. "Let him be."

Was that a compliment? Jack crinkled his nose. "Th-thank you?" Though he liked her, the woman unsettled him as much as her granddaughter did. Their confidence was admirable but intimidating. He felt seen and accountable in ways completely missed by everyone else. It was one of the many reasons he had loved Sophie. She took the time to listen to him, to know him, and he'd done the same. How could he have ever abandoned her?

Jack noticed Sophie staring at him, her spellbinding gaze revealing nothing. He gently pulled his hand free from her grandmother's grasp. "It's a pleasure to meet you ... *Nonna.*" The nickname was strange on his tongue.

Before he could offer to escort them to their seats, April-Rose lunged forward and offered the elderly woman her manicured hand.

"Nonna," she said with feigned warmth. "How brave of you to travel such a distance at your age just to attend your grandson's wedding." She widened her crocodile smile at the old woman's frown. "I hope your stay here is not tainted with too many bad memories." She looked pointedly at Sophie. "After all, it must be very difficult to return to the town where your granddaughter sought to take her own life all those years ago." April-Rose sighed dramatically and laid a hand over her chest. "Perhaps she would have saved you some pain had her endeavour been successful. It's not as though she's amounted to much anyway."

Jack felt like he'd been punched in the gut. He wasn't a

violent man, but he wanted to slap some sense into his sister right then and there. How could someone so heartless be of his flesh and blood?

"How dare you—" Nonna huffed like a blustery steam train, but shock had stolen her words.

Jack saw Sophie clutch her mother's hand when Angelica wobbled. "I'm so sorry," he told them. How could he fix this?

Sophie just glared at April-Rose. Jack saw no point in retorting. His sister's attention had already moved on.

"Deidre, sweetie!" April-Rose waved at someone and strolled over to her next victim.

Nonna's cheeks were aflame as she watched April-Rose exit. "Horrid woman," she growled. Facing Jack, she aimed her nose skyward. "Your sister is much like your mother."

"Yes. I apologise profusely." He gulped like a fish, feeling helpless.

"That is not your duty," Nonna said. "Apologising for your family's sins will not erase them. Just know, I am watching you. We are wary of you—this Garland in our midst."

Jack choked a little and looked worriedly from Nonna to Angelica before his gaze settled on Sophie. The glint of fire in her expression, the hard line of her full lips, held more menace than her grandmother's words. He hoped she was saving that for his sister and not for him.

"Come, Mama." Angelica took her mother's arm. "Let's find our seats." She nodded courteously as they passed, heading for the crowd.

To Jack's surprise, Sophie stepped forward and slipped her arm through his. He flinched at her touch as though he'd been stung. He hadn't expected her to initiate such contact, especially after what his sister had just put them through. It meant all the more to him and he held on to her tightly.

"Shall we get this over with?" she asked him.

"Are you sure you're okay?" He tried to catch her gaze

again, but she wouldn't look at him.

Sophie shook her head. "Your sister just wished me dead in front of my own mother and grandmother, Jack." Her voice tightened with coiled rage. "So, no. I'm not okay, but right now my cousin's wedding is more important. Let's get through this and then I'll worry about the fact that April-Rose just declared war."

"Right." Jack mentally kicked himself for asking such a stupid question. Sophie didn't wait for him to ask another. She dragged him into the mass of people and over to the rows of chairs lining the aisle.

CHAPTER 10

From her seat beside Jack, Sophie watched Pat take his place in front of the floral arch. Her cousin looked so handsome and grown up in his tuxedo. Where was the skinny little boy who used to help her practice her times tables? Pat winked at her before waving to someone else seated on the groom's side.

"He's grown into quite the gentleman." Jack nodded proudly at his friend.

"He should be a good influence on you then."

"Does that mean you think I'm a bad influence?" he ventured warily.

She was ready to snap back, but when she saw the teasing glint in his eye, she softened. "I never would have fed my mother's terrible apple pie to the goats if you hadn't dared me to, or leapt from the barn loft after Uncle Nick refreshed the hay pile. That was all because of you."

He laughed wholeheartedly. "From what I remember, we did those things *together*. So, you're just as much a terrible influence as me."

She gasped, feigning offence. "Not even close."

His sincere laughter had her chuckling along with him. For a second, she pretended all the bad blood between them never happened. It made her yearn for the future they could have had. At that thought, her good humour gave way to incredible sadness.

The rumble of the white stretch Hummer arriving drew their attention and gave Sophie a chance to hide her welling tears. The electric suspense surrounding the bride's entrance jittered through the crowd as they heard the wedding party exit the vehicle on the opposite side.

At a nod from the celebrant, the pianist struck the keys on his portable keyboard, leading the elfish singer beside him into the haunting melody of "Kissing You" by Des'ree. Clothes rustled as onlookers swivelled to get a better glimpse down the aisle.

Sophie glanced over Jack's shoulder, her gaze landing on the two small flower girls. Tightly clasping hands, eyes wide in awe, they meandered forward. They dropped a yellow rose petal here, a white one there, careful not to stumble over the long tulle of their sunny princess-style dresses. A small blond boy in an adorable azure suit trailed after them. He carried a carved wooden box with a singular determination as he marched towards the celebrant.

Laura was next, arm-in-arm with Marilyn's sister Addison. She wore a feminine blue pantsuit that complemented her fellow groomsman. The sunflower shade of the bridesmaids' gowns matched the flower girls. Laura met Sophie's gaze and smirked before leading Addison to their respective places on either side of the celebrant. Marilyn's brother Dale and her best friend Camille followed along behind them. Camille's petite frame was tiny beside her towering escort, but her firm grip on his muscular arm kept them in step. Camille proudly waved to their audience as Dale flushed with embarrassment at all the attention.

"I think I've found your competition for the bouquet." Jack's warm breath tickled the fine hairs on Sophie's neck as he leaned closer.

Her heart raced at the sensation, but she kept her eyes

on Dale and Camille. "Wrong again."

"Not interested in walking down the aisle yourself?" He sounded surprised. "I thought things had been pretty serious with you and Mason?"

She spun back to him. How did he know about her ex? Realisation quickly dawned on her. "Laura told you."

"We talk. Like I said, I've missed you, Soph."

She caught a sadness in his eyes that mirrored her own feelings. Unable to hold his stare, she glanced back over his shoulder again, the tip of her nose just missing his. "That's not an excuse to stick your nose in my personal business."

"Why did you break up with him?" It was only a whisper.

Sophie risked a glance his way. Prickles of excitement flashed through her at his nearness. Yet she didn't want to tell him the truth. "What's that got to do with anything?"

Jack shrugged half-heartedly. "I didn't believe what Laura told me."

The breeze shifted and Sophie caught the sharpness of his cologne, the citrus of his shampoo. It was an addictive scent. She licked her lips. "Mason and I just had different priorities," she explained firmly.

"That's what Laura said." He sounded unconvinced.

And he wasn't you, Sophie thought, hoping that wasn't written all over her face.

As the stirring song reached a crescendo, she found her gaze tangled in his, trying to decipher his thoughts. It wasn't until Jack raised his hand and swiped a coarse fingertip lightly across her cheek that the spell broke.

"Eyelash," he said huskily.

Sophie blinked several times and pulled away. What was she doing? This was still the same boy who broke her heart. She couldn't just allow herself to be lured back under his spell. He wasn't to be trusted. None of the Garlands were.

She quickly turned her attention to the magnificent bride, who had already begun her procession towards her husband-to-be. Marilyn floated down the aisle, arm linked through her father's, an arrangement of yellow and white roses in hand. She looked like an angel in a pearly, off-the-shoulder bridal gown adorned with silver embroidery. A delicate gold tiara secured a complex knot of chestnut curls atop her head, while the rest of her hair cascaded down her back.

Pat gazed adoringly at his fiancée as she took her place beside him. The euphoria in Marilyn's smile, in the sparkle of her green eyes, tugged at Sophie's heart, causing her vision to blur once again. She felt a tear escape down her cheek and touched her fingertips to her lips, trying to keep her composure.

A sob from the front row drew Sophie's attention from the happy couple. She watched her Uncle Nick pass his wife a wad of tissues and then hug her close. The tenderness between them was just one of the many things Sophie loved about them.

"If there was ever a couple to aspire to. . ." Jack murmured.

Had he shifted even closer to her? Sophie kept her gaze fixed on the bride and groom. "Are you trying to give me relationship advice, Jack?" She could feel the warmth radiating from his body. If she breathed too deeply, she would touch him.

"Not at all, Soph." He feigned innocence. "Just letting you know what I think." When she cut him a glance, he gave her his best nonchalant expression. "In case you weren't aware."

"And what would you like me to do with that information?"

He leaned in, a breath closer, the tips of their noses touching. "Keep it in mind the next time you consider dating a loser like Mason."

Stunned at his nerve, she opened her mouth to argue, but a snappy shushing beside them silenced her.

Although she and Jack weren't the only ones having a muted conversation, April-Rose aimed a scorching glare solely at Sophie. In an aggressively swift motion, she lifted her index finger and pressed it to her lips.

"Ladies and gentlemen," the celebrant began. All attention returned to the bride and groom beneath the arbour, their grins ablaze with elation and devotion. "We are gathered here today to join two hearts as one."

CHAPTER 11

The rear door of a nearby four-wheel drive burst open and shrill feminine chatter spilled out. Sophie shifted to the side, ushering Jack to follow her as a carload of elderly women exited and headed for the wedding reception area. The enormous marquee and chunky timber outdoor settings were already brimming with guests. Those who required assistance had been chauffeured, while others— like her and Jack—had opted for the short hilly walk up the gravel road.

Merry music—a mix of pop, rock, and country— bolstered the already joyous atmosphere. Inside and outside, people mingled and nibbled on appetisers, while the married couple and their cohorts posed for photographs elsewhere.

As Sophie strode past Marilyn's vivacious Aunt Susan lounging on a bench with a pair of equally flamboyant women, she felt Jack slip his hand around hers. A prickle of pleasurable energy jolted up her arm. Yet she didn't pull away.

"I should probably tell you to keep your hands to yourself," Sophie said sternly. But she really didn't want to.

"I thought you might want the support." Concern softened his tone. When she didn't immediately answer, he looked down at her, searching her face. "I can let you go if you'd like. Just say the word."

Sophie stared at him. She remembered how he used to hold her hand to help her cross the creek. He had said it was to keep her safe, but even back then Sophie knew that wasn't his only reason. She shook her head. She was already his date, what further gossip would a little hand-holding create? "It's fine," she lied.

He stopped walking to look at her, analysing her expression. "I know this evening will be tough. Especially at my family's table and all. Just know that I'm here for you, Soph. If you need anything."

His earnestness winded her. Where was this conviction after the accident when she was all alone, when she needed him most? He was also partly responsible for the *tough* evening she was about to endure. Sophie studied his hand wrapped securely around her own. She might have enjoyed the feel of Jack's coarse fingers, his warm palm, but was it all just for show?

He drew closer, his face above hers. She admired how his familiar features had changed with age. If not the little boy she'd loved or the friend who'd broken her heart, who was this man Jack had become—and could she trust him?

"Ugh, Sophie. This is a public place. If you'd just unhand my brother until you're behind closed doors, it would be much appreciated." April-Rose nearly stuck her nose between them to force them apart.

Jack moved away but wouldn't release her even when she eased her grip. Sophie wondered if he needed the support—their solid link to each other—just as much as she did.

"Really?" April-Rose shared a look of exasperation with the perfectly preened, auburn-haired man behind her. "If *I* had moved to the city, I never would have let the cosmopolitan lifestyle change me into such a floozy."

Sophie blinked. "Excuse me?"

"You're excused." April-Rose blanked her with a

dismissive slice of her hand before slipping her arm through Jack's. "You must sit with us, Jackson. We're over there." She waved at Tiffany, who was seated at a wooden picnic table beside the marquee.

Jack's lips thinned. "Sophie and I were in the middle of a conversation before you interrupted, April-Rose." He wrenched his arm away from her.

"Nothing important, I expect." His sister threw a frosty glance at Sophie. "Come," she ordered Jack. "I want to dissect the wedding, and Tiffany specifically asked for your opinion."

"Tiffany is spoiled for opinions with you and Bradley over there." Jack motioned to the bulky man who stood like a sentry at his sister's back. "She doesn't need mine, and I strongly doubt she even asked for it."

"Are you suggesting I lied to you, Jackson?"

"Yes."

Sophie laughed unabashedly, earning herself a sneer from the flame-headed harpy and a smirk from Jack.

"How ridiculous." April-Rose aimed her nose skyward. "I'm your sister. You shouldn't doubt my honesty, but go ask Tiffany yourself if you require proof. She's rather smitten with you, warts and all. I can't think why."

Jack groaned. "Look, I may have promised to be on my best behaviour today, but don't push me. I know what you're trying to do, April-Rose. Sophie and I will join you when we're good and ready. Until then, go belittle Pat and Marilyn's wedding by yourselves."

"Whatever you say, Jackson," April-Rose huffed. "Though I think you'd benefit from working on your notion of *best behaviour*." She spun on her spindly stiletto heel and stormed away, dragging Bradley along.

Sophie watched them retreat. The man had looked so familiar. "Was that Bradley Harding?"

"Yeah." Jack nodded. "He works at the farm now— chief financial officer. Though I doubt he's much more than a glorified accountant. He got the title when he and April-

Rose got engaged."

Of course he did, Sophie thought. "So was getting to marry April-Rose part of the promotion or did he get engaged to her just to climb the corporate ladder?"

Jack laughed. "Either way, Bradley was hustled. Nothing could be worth a lifetime married to my sister."

"Not even for all your family's millions?"

"Not for the wealth of the whole world."

Sophie felt him squeeze her hand, strengthening their connection. "It's good to know money isn't your only mistress. Even though it's been controlling your family for generations."

"If you give us time to talk, you'll learn many more interesting facts about me." There was a ghost of a smile on his face. "I think you'll find I'm a lot less like my family than you remember."

"I doubt that. It will take much more than one nice night out to make me forget the past."

Jack bunched his eyebrows in frustration. "That was years ago, Soph. Isn't it time we moved on? We're different people now. We're not those hurt little kids who lost their fathers in a terrible accident."

When Sophie gasped, Jack winced as though realising his mistake. She stepped forward and stabbed her finger into his chest, hard. "*You* didn't lose your father that day."

Jack sighed. "I'm sorry. That came out wrong. I didn't mean to upset you." He scratched his fingers through his hair nervously. "My father may not have died in that car, but that accident still killed him. Survivor's guilt consumed him. He could never forgive himself. Only alcohol could ease his pain, until it eventually eased him into death." Jack took a steadying breath. "You're not the only one whose life was upended by that tragedy."

"You think I don't know that?" Sophie hissed. The pain was suffocating. Old heartache clawed to the surface. "Do you think I was blind to my mum's grief? To how my extended family suffered? Yet I didn't turn on the people I loved. I didn't abandon my friends, Jack. Can you say the same?"

Sophie could see the sheer weight of guilt rounding his shoulders. To see him in agony hurt her almost as much as his actions had all those years ago. She looked away, her cheeks hot, vision blurring. Her gaze fell on the table where Tiffany, Bradley, and April-Rose were sitting. Through welling tears, she saw a sudden apparition of their younger selves—the friends who had once filled her days with joy before her father's accident had altered their lives forever. The mirage drew her attention to who was missing. They were one little girl short. Where was Ella?

"Soph." Jack wrapped his strong arms around her, crushing her to him. "Don't cry. It always hurts to see you cry."

"Good." Her voice was raspy as she freed a hand to wipe away her tears before they could spoil her make-up.

She felt Jack's throat rumble in amusement from where his head rested atop hers, felt him stroke his hand over her back, tickling bare skin. The pleasant sharpness of his cologne relaxed her, and she sank further into his arms. Her heart flip-flopped uncertainly. Hating him had been so much easier when she was miles away, back in the city.

"All right. Enough." She reluctantly pushed out of the hug. "I'm fine. Let's not make a scene."

"Probably a bit late for that." Jack gestured in the direction of his sister and her companions, who were gawking in their direction like meerkats. April-Rose's nasty expression made Sophie clutch Jack's hand tighter. "Ignore them. Let's put this behind us and try to have a good time. After all, one of our favourite people tied the knot today and I plan on celebrating that."

Sophie remembered the glorious sight of Pat and Marilyn kissing beneath the floral arbour and agreed wholeheartedly. "I can't think of anything better."

"Good." He beamed. "Then, shall we?" He gestured to the huge marquee, which was thumping with the jolly beat of another country rock song.

Sophie didn't need to utter her agreement. She let him lead her towards the entrance, taking her first step towards their reconciliation.

CHAPTER 12

As the conversation at the Garlands' table jumped to April-Rose and Bradley's honeymoon plans, Jack found distraction in admiring the setting around them. Marilyn's family had spared no expense in creating the wedding of their daughter's dreams. The rooftop of the marquee was edged with radiant lights, creating a romantic atmosphere in the coming gloom of the evening. Tiny glowing bulbs twirled around table centrepieces like fireflies while blue and gold trimmings maintained the colour theme of the ceremony. There was an extravagant wedding cake on show in the corner and a space reserved for the live band.

Busy hired help removed dirtied dinner plates and ensured champagne flutes were always full for toasting. They weaved between tables and giddy guests, their duties becoming more difficult as alcohol continued to flow freely from the open bar. Some guests who hadn't paced their intake now found themselves with lubricated lips and loosened tongues. Jack's ears pricked as someone at his own table posed a particularly intrusive question.

"Come on, Sophie. Tell us. We used to be friends, you know?"

After demolishing her fourth glass of white wine and

toast-loads of champagne, Tiffany had moved on from polite conversation. Even when sober, there wasn't much she loved more than confrontation and gossip.

Jack had caught only the tail end of Tiffany's query but knew no good could come of it. "You don't have to answer that, Soph." He covered her hand with his own, once again offering support.

Sophie licked her lips, clearly considering her words. "We haven't been *friends* for a long time, Tiffany, so I don't see how it's any of your business."

April-Rose shot Jack a look as though indignant on his behalf. "Surely my brother has a right to know?"

"I couldn't care less," he growled. That wasn't exactly true. He didn't care about the number, only that Sophie's heart may have once belonged to another. The thought made him feel hollow inside.

"I can't see how my past love life has anything to do with Jack," Sophie disputed. "Let alone how it is of interest to any of you."

Jack clenched his jaw. Was it wrong to have hoped she'd feel differently? He had known she hadn't been pining for him for all these years. Yet he'd seen a glimmer of *something* in her return. Unease swirled in the pit of his stomach until Sophie squeezed his hand reassuringly. He looked at her, but her glare was locked on his sister.

"Can't you?" April-Rose let the words slither off her tongue. "You're dating now. I thought discussing past relationships would've been one of your first big conversations."

"Who says we're dating?"

Jack felt Sophie's grip on his hand weaken with her words and his heart lurched with the fear that she'd let go.

"The whole town." April-Rose's grin was so wide it nearly split her face.

"One date—to a wedding of all places—does not constitute a relationship."

Tiffany flopped back in her chair with a snicker. "I think

she protests too much."

Bradley nodded. "I think a wedding is an important event and one's agreement to attend with a particular partner denotes a certain interest in said partner and therefore a desire to continue that relationship." He flicked a look at his fiancée, and then at her mother, who was seated beside Jack. Sheridan acknowledged Bradley's comment with a bow of her head.

The charade was getting ridiculous. Jack didn't need to know the answer to Tiffany's question to be certain that his opinion and fondness for Sophie would never change.

"Are you a relationship expert now, Bradley?" Sophie scoffed.

"Well, Sophie, honey," April-Rose interrupted, "he—unlike you—is engaged, so he clearly has a better grasp of the whole *relationship* concept."

"Oh, enough." Jack slammed his hand on the table, rattling the silverware and glasses. Although the noise was nothing in the surrounding din, those around him jumped. "If Sophie doesn't wish to share her past with me, relationships or otherwise, that's our business, not yours. So, you can quit this hunting party and leave her alone."

"Ha!" April-Rose cackled triumphantly. "*Our* business! Well, that proves it, doesn't it? You're together. Sophie, sweetheart, we may be well on our way to becoming sisters-in-law."

Sophie gagged at April-Rose's declaration, and he couldn't blame her. He'd spent nearly half his life running from the Garland name.

"One big happy family," Bradley concurred, taking April-Rose's hand in his and placing a chaste kiss on her knuckles. Sheridan regarded the public display of affection with disapproval before looking away.

"There you go," Tiffany squawked triumphantly. "You're all nearly family, and sharing is what family does best. So, how many sexual partners would you say you've had in your lifetime?" She shared a wicked sneer with April-

Rose, then propped her elbows on the table and leaned closer to Sophie. "Six? No, ten?"

Bradley dabbed a cloth napkin to his mouth, attempting to hide his amusement.

"Leave it, Tiffany." Jack hit his sister's friend with an icy scowl, daring her to push him.

"What's wrong, Jackson?" April-Rose pouted. "It shouldn't be a difficult question. I thought you'd want to know how many lovers had ventured there before you." She touched a finger to her chin, feigning thought. "Oh, that's right, I forgot. Your standards have dropped dramatically since moving into the Santoros' tiny hut. Perhaps you prefer your women with STDs and a shed-full of baggage?"

"Watch yourself, April-Rose. My best behaviour has its limits." Jack's whole body was stiff with aggravation. This little truce he and April-Rose had agreed to in order to keep his miserable secrets safe was getting more and more difficult to keep. Jack had already started fantasising about what might happen if Sophie stayed. If April-Rose pushed him a step too far, he'd hang the consequences, no matter how harsh they might be. He had only agreed to his sister's plan so he and Sophie could walk down memory lane unscathed. But if April-Rose continued to put that in jeopardy, all bets were off.

His sister swirled her index finger in his direction. "Oh, is this your best behaviour?"

Jack's blood boiled. He was about to say something he'd likely regret when Sophie squeezed his hand again, drawing his gaze to hers. The firm, comforting look in her dark eyes told him it wasn't worth it. She stroked her thumb across his knuckles and the gentle sensation calmed him. Inhaling deeply, he drew in the sweet scent of her. Jasmine and vanilla. It hypnotised him.

"Now you're ignoring me? Real mature, Jackson."

Bradley huffed. "That's just rude, brother."

Jack reluctantly looked away from Sophie to glower at his sister's fiancé. "You're not my brother."

"Not yet." Tiffany sniggered.

"Ugh." Sheridan winced and touched her neatly manicured fingers to her forehead. "This conversation is giving me a headache."

Jack turned to his mother, hating that his first instinct was still to be concerned for her wellbeing. Would he ever outgrow her brainwashing?

She used this moment of compassion, of weakness, to seize his wrist. "There is no need to discuss this further, my darling boy." She fluttered her long mascara-covered eyelashes. "I will not have my son dating a woman who is likely still a suicide risk, no matter the extent of her sexual exploits."

"Right." Sophie sighed. "That's done it for me." She released Jack's other hand, leaving it cold and stood up. "Sorry, Jack, but I've had my fill of the Garland family for one sitting. The rest of you can rot." She saluted them. "Have a good evening."

The viscous sarcasm of Sophie's final words hung heavily in the air around them as she bounded off into the crowd of elegantly dressed guests. Jack felt an arctic vice grip his heart at the loss of her. He lunged out of his chair, determined to follow her—only at the last minute remembering his wrist had been shackled. His mother wrenched him back into his seat.

"And where do you think you're going?" Sheridan was all motherly reproach.

"Sophie's such a drama queen," Tiffany criticised. "She's got no self-respect, no class. She can't even behave properly in a social setting."

"It runs in the family." April-Rose tossed her hair over her shoulder. "But what can you expect? She's the offspring of a whore and a murderer." She caught Jack's gaze and stared him down. "What, brother? Have you got something to say?"

"You disgust me." He ground out each word through gritted teeth. "You're all repulsive." He glared around the table—at the pompously ignorant, the zealously mean, the twisted and vengeful—before aiming the ferocity of his hatred and self-loathing at the woman who bore him. "And you're the worst of them," he told his mother. "You did this. You *created* them and you *love* that."

Jack shook his head, trying to rid himself of the abyss roiling inside of him. He glowered at his mother, forcing her to see the twisted creature she'd constructed in him.

"I'm not like you." He jerked his arm free of her. "I never was, never will be. Come to terms with that, Mother, because it will never change."

Jack sprang to his feet, desperate to get away, to free himself from this vile family. After so much time away from them, basking in the peace of the Santoros' as part of their devoted clan, he felt tainted just being near these people. He felt that side of himself, the one conceived of all his mother's bitterness, her rage—the part of him she'd moulded for her own vindictive means—lingering just below the surface. A shadow on the edge of sunlight. But it wasn't real. He wasn't that person. It was only a facade. It could and would dissipate.

As Jack ran after Sophie, he reminded himself of who he was now. Who he *wanted* to be, regardless of what unforgivable sins lay in his past.

He was Jackson Garland. A country boy, a talented carpenter, a proud new member of the Santoro family. And Sophie Wendall's friend—even if she wasn't ready to acknowledge it. And he was a good man.

Wasn't he?

CHAPTER 13

Colouring books, pencils and crayons were strewn across the children's table. After taking a seat among her new companions, Sophie gladly accepted a plate of wedding cake from a passing waitress. She carved a fork into her dessert, watching the children tuck into their own chunks of the frosting-covered sponge. They stared back at her and giggled through icing-mottled mouths when Jack slid into a cushioned chair beside her.

"Why didn't you take me with you?" He leaned forward, trying to catch her eye.

Sophie savoured a mouthful of cake, running her tongue over her lips to remove the smooth sugary glaze. "I guess I didn't realise we were joined at the hip."

She thought of his hand in hers, how he had taken it before the reception, how he'd reached for it again at the Garlands' table. They may not have been stitched at the hipbone, but she'd relied on the reassurance and guidance of his warm hand in hers just the same.

"Sophie." That single word held a multitude of emotions.

She slipped another forkful of wedding cake into her mouth and refused to look at him.

Jack sighed. "Fine. Are you going to share or what?" He nodded at what was left on her plate.

"It's mine. Go get your own."

Jack sulked.

"No." Sophie hurriedly devoured another bite.

"Sharing is good for the soul, Soph." He inched closer.

"You're a brat, did you know that?"

He nodded slyly. "A sweet-toothed one." He opened his mouth a little and glanced between her and the cake. He was too darn cute to ignore.

Exasperated but won over, she sawed off a piece. Her fork hit the platter with a clink. She waved the utensil impatiently in Jack's direction. "Well, open up. Wider. Unless you'd like to lick icing off your nose."

He smirked but did as instructed.

Sophie watched his mouth as she fed him. She saw how he curled his tongue, felt him tug at the fork as his jaws closed. She found herself mesmerised by the intimacy of it all. Her eyes met his, and a hush fell upon them. It was only the two of them, unguarded, in the moment.

"Yum." Jack purred the word. "Can I have another?"

Sophie swallowed, returning to her senses. She felt jittery, her stomach uneasy. She hadn't felt such strong desire in a long time. What she felt for Jack was so much more than just a crush now. It was serious, heartfelt, and it scared her.

Laying the silverware on the edge of the plate, Sophie pushed the rest of the cake in front of him. "You can finish it."

Jack frowned, creases lining his handsome brow.

A faint tittering drew their attention to the other end of the table. A young boy—maybe five or six—with unkempt black hair and cute chubby cheeks grinned at them. "You forgot the *choo-choo*," he said. "My mum always makes the choo-choo train sounds when she feeds me."

The other children jumped into the conversation, their chatter drifting from eating habits to favourite pastimes. An hour and a few visits from happy parents later, Sophie and Jack were invited to assist in the task of colouring.

The petite ginger-haired girl beside Sophie handed her a purple pencil and then set to work on the book in front of them, scribbling a green pencil over all the sections marked with a three.

"I think Kirstie over there"—Jack pointed his yellow pencil at the little girl—"is a colour-by-numbers pro. Aren't you, Kirstie?"

Kirstie didn't answer, but her proud, partially toothless grin said it all.

Sophie shared a smile with Jack. "I suppose it would be polite of me to thank you," she said.

"Thank me? For what?" Jack looked genuinely astonished.

"For joining me after I escaped your horrid family, for keeping me company even though it meant keeping the kids occupied."

"Don't be silly." He chuckled. "I was happy to. Besides, it's what friends do."

Friends? Sophie's throat tightened. "So, was that your plan all along then?" Suspicion edged her voice. "Are you just doing all this to win me over?"

His grin faded. Sophie couldn't help her wariness. She was so afraid of getting hurt again. How could she trust that this time would be any different, that he wouldn't let her down?

Jack raised a hand as if to stop her spiralling thoughts. "Not at all, Soph." He shook his head. "Look, you might think I chose you over them, but I chose myself. I made the decision that *I* wanted to. Sure, your exit gave me an opening and I wanted to support you, but I made that decision purely for myself, to make *me* happy. I've spent so many years free of their clutches, first in Melbourne, now with the Santoros. I forgot how heartless they could be. It wasn't until I was trapped there with all of them that I realised how much their cruelty has festered over the years.

They feed off each other's nastiness. I don't want any part of that. I don't want anything to do with them. You have to believe me."

Sophie's heart pounded, but when Jack reached for her, she didn't pull away. She let him settle his hand over hers, let him link their fingers. This physical connection between them was becoming a habit and she didn't mind in the least. His touch grounded her, a feeling of familiarity, of home among the chaos around her.

"Please believe me, Soph. I'd rather be here with you, colouring with these cute kids, than anywhere else."

Sophie gnawed at her lower lip. Heaven knew she wanted to believe him, and she did—sort of. She just couldn't shake that last sliver of suspicion. Was it something about that day down at the Garland dam? Maybe it was better if she didn't remember. But whatever the source, her heart and head agreed she needed to be careful of entangling herself with Jackson Garland.

"Does that mean you're friends now?" Kirstie asked.

Kirstie's older brother, an auburn-haired boy named Phillip, jumped in. "No. They're more than friends, Kirst," he explained confidently. "See, they're holding hands."

He nodded at Sophie and Jack. Kirstie followed his gaze and watched Jack squeeze Sophie's hand.

"Yes, but Philly"—Kirstie spun back to her brother—"you hold my hand when we cross the road and you're just my brother."

"That's different," Phillip dismissed, going back to his drawing pad.

"Exactly." Laura appeared behind Sophie, startling them all. "I only hold my brother's hand when I absolutely have to."

"*Exactly,*" Phillip concurred.

"Or else I'll get cooties." Laura laughed.

Aware that Jack's hand was still in hers, Sophie blushed and quickly yanked her fingers free, feeling a little breathless. "Laura." She beamed. "I didn't expect you'd have time to break away from your best woman duties."

"Nice change of subject there, cuz." Laura winked. "I had to get away from the wedding party table. Dale's a lovely lad and we're mates, but he's been clinging to me something dreadful since we sat down. I'm guessing it has to do with Camille. They're not dating, you know, but the way Camille waltzed down the aisle with him got them pegged as the next to be wed. I think it's freaking the poor man out."

Jack gestured to the empty chair beside him. "You can shelter here with us until they realise you're missing."

"Just what I was thinking." Laura slumped heavily into the seat. "It's been a long night already."

"I thought you'd be enjoying yourself, Laur," Sophie teased. "You're usually telling me how dull Moorhenvale can be, and this is anything but dull."

"Says the woman doing a colour-by-numbers."

Sophie stifled a smirk. "You know what I mean. Why aren't you out there meeting new people, flirting?"

"You know why. This town is more hetero than a hotdog. If you can point me in the direction of all the single ladies, then I'll jump to it."

"Hello, there's one right here." Sophie raised her arm, gesturing to herself. She noticed Jack look her way as she did so.

"Me too." Little Kirstie followed suit, a huge smile on her face as she lifted her small arm skyward.

"Well, that's just wrong." Laura waved her own hand at the two of them as Jack chuckled beside her. "Down. Put your hands down. You." She pointed to Kirstie. "You're just a teensy bit too young, don't you reckon? Might be best if you finish university before jumping into the singles scene."

Kirstie giggled heartily and went back to her colouring.

"And you." Laura turned on her cousin. "Don't be a bad influence on the youth or I'll have to find you a new table to squat at." She feigned outrage. "And who do you think you're kidding?"

"Pardon?" Sophie cleared her throat and avoided Jack's

eyes.

"Don't *'Pardon?'* me, Sophia Evangelina Wendall. I saw you holding hands with that man." Laura stuck a thumb in Jack's direction.

Jack bit his lip to hide his smirk, but he didn't deny the allegation.

"Okay, *Nonna*," Sophie mocked. "You might have seen what you think you saw, but that doesn't mean anything."

She flicked a risky glance at Jack. There was something hidden in his mesmerising blue eyes that piqued her curiosity. Did he still feel this spark of chemistry between them, too?

"Oh, doesn't it?" Laura crossed her arms.

"We're just. . ." *Friends.* Sophie struggled to get the word out. The word felt like too much after all they had been through, and yet not enough to express the intensity of feelings she had for him. She was terrified to admit anything either way, but it was the first step to moving forward. "Jack and I are friends, Laur. Okay?"

When Laura shot an expression of disbelief at Jack, he nodded his agreement and looked just a little too satisfied.

"Sure thing, you guys." Laura was unconvinced. "Just remember that denial isn't just a crocodile-filled river in Africa."

"You're hilarious," Sophie scoffed. All this contemplation of friendship reminded her of something. Where was Ella? She hadn't seen the youngest of her old friends all evening. Why hadn't she been seated with the Garlands like the others? "So, since we're on the topic of *friends.* Do you know if Ella was invited to the wedding?"

Laura shrugged as though she couldn't place the name.

"Do you mean Ella Larsen?" Jack croaked.

Sophie noted his sudden seriousness. She instantly felt uneasy about broaching the subject. "Yeah, that's her."

"Oh, I remember her. She used to be part of April-Rose's clique." Laura grimaced and then shook her head. "No. She wasn't invited to the wedding. I hardly know what she's doing these days. I think someone told me she works in Warwick at a video store."

"A record store, actually," Jack corrected.

Sophie studied his face, taking in his wrinkled brow and tight lips. He didn't seem himself and it worried her. He blinked, as though shaking away clouded thoughts, and offered her a small smile.

"If you remember, Ella and I used to be friends as well," he explained.

"I remember." She tried to return his smile, but distrust wrapped coldly around her heart. What was he hiding?

Hesitant to probe any further, Sophie was relieved when Laura switched the conversation to their opinions of her best woman speech. As Kristie chimed in to say it was perfect and Phillip complained it had been too long, Sophie couldn't stop thinking about the look on Jack's face. He'd been scared. But of what? Of Ella? And if so, why? It had Sophie stumped. Yet if she were to fully trust him again, it felt as though this was something she needed to know. She just hoped Jack would tell her himself.

CHAPTER 14

A polished wooden dancefloor laid across the grassy field, where wedding guests stomped and jived to the DJ's mashup of trendy pop music. The darkest hours of night were rolling towards those small hours of the morning, the time when the herd separated and the elderly and families with young ones retired to their beds. The young adults, however—and those well into their thirties and forties—powered on, celebrating as though the night were still as young as they were or wished to be.

Jack's gaze lingered on the dancefloor, on Sophie sashaying her hips to the infectious melody. It was hard to take his eyes off her. He still couldn't believe she'd agreed to give him another chance. *Friends*, she'd called them. He hoped he could live up to the title this time.

After taking a final moment to appreciate Sophie's delectable behind, Jack sidled towards the bar. He'd thought to head for Dale, who—like the bridesmaids—had been left to fend for himself now that the bride and groom had withdrawn to their fancy suite at the Brumby and Bridle, the most prestigious hotel in Warwick. Dale caught his eye and waved a hand in greeting, but Jack found his mission suddenly disrupted.

April-Rose materialised from the dance floor and blocked his path. In the rhythmic flitter of strobe lights, his sister looked demonic. Her face glowed against the flashes of yellow, red and blue, her eyes sparkling and fangs glistening.

"I'm not in the mood for more of your games tonight, April-Rose," Jack grumbled.

"Of course, you aren't, brother. You're too busy playing your own."

Ignoring her, Jack glanced back over at Sophie. She was too occupied with Laura and the blaring beat of the song to notice his predicament.

"Did you think you could speak to your family in that hideous manner and just get away with it?" April-Rose forced him to acknowledge her.

"I meant what I said. *Every* word."

His sister's jaw fell, and her eyes lit with fury. "You can't speak to us in such a way, in public of all places, and expect us—Mother in particular—to just forgive you."

"I don't want forgiveness. I don't want anything from you, from any of you—*Mother in particular*," he spat, mirroring her scathing tone.

"Oh, you will. You'll come running back to us once you see that those Santoros can't offer you what you truly need. You think they love you? You think they care? Well, what would they really think, how would they really feel, if they knew the truth about what you did to their favoured little niece?"

The retort stabbed at his heart. That fear had only increased as he'd grown closer to Sophie again. On the dancefloor, Sophie and Laura were laughing, writhing to the tempo of the next song, oblivious to his secret. It was the proverbial piano waiting to smash against their heads and shatter their opinion of him to splinters. There was nothing Jack could do. He couldn't keep the secret forever. One way or another it would come out. He didn't think he would ever be ready for that day.

April-Rose clutched his shoulder, feigning support. "They're not like us, Jackson." Her voice was sweeter, compassionate—pure trickery. "They won't understand. But I do. *Mother and I* do. You were only looking out for your family, that's all. We would never judge you for that."

"No?" He jerked free. "Then, I suppose we're blameless, you and I? Our actions were completely justified?"

"Our actions were brought about by pain," his sister insisted, her eyes wide. "A pain she and her family inflicted upon us. That validates everything we did, everything we had to do. You know that I'm right."

"Stop it." He clenched and unclenched his fists. "Stop talking bullshit. You can't manipulate me like you used to, like you do to everyone else."

She opened her mouth, rebuttal ready, but he slashed a hand through the air, cutting her off.

"No," he roared. "Just shut up." He aimed his index finger at her face. "While I'd love to tell you to piss the hell off right now, there is, unfortunately, a problem you and I need to discuss."

April-Rose pressed her mouth shut into a hard line and glared, waiting.

Jack stepped closer and kept his voice low, barely audible above the pounding racket around them. He hated to do this, but he had no other choice. His sister needed to know what had happened. "Sophie has been asking about Ella."

His sister pulled away and stared up at him accusingly. "What did you tell her?"

"Nothing, but Laura mentioned that she works in Warwick now."

"Do you think she wants to meet with her?"

Jack shrugged and then nodded reluctantly. "Maybe."

"She can't! Ella could ruin us all." April-Rose stalked away a few steps, tapping her lips with her index finger, and then paced back. "Well, you have to do something. Convince Sophie that Ella's not worth her time."

"Really?" Jack crossed his arms. As if it were that easy.

"How do you suggest I do that?"

"Tell her she's crazy. Tell her she's a lying junkie. I don't care. Tell her something to change her mind. It isn't just your cosy life on the chopping block, Jackson. If Ella talks, we're all done for."

"You're not telling me anything new, April-Rose." Jack took a little pleasure in the fact that he could see his own fear reflected in his sister's eyes. They all had a lot to lose if the truth came out.

April-Rose leaned into him, grinding a sharp fingernail into his chest. "Well, then do as I say, brother. Sophie's only in town for a few more days. Do you think you can manage to keep an eye on her for that long? Or is that too difficult for you?"

He gulped at the thought of Sophie leaving, sadness tightening his chest making it difficult to breathe. He wished for her to stay. He'd fantasised about the possibility. Maybe his secret didn't have to come out. Or maybe they would all forgive him if it did. But there were too many maybes, too many ifs. He was sure of only one thing—his secret would be safe when Sophie left town.

"Remember," April-Rose snarled. "I could always get Bradley to handle this problem. I'm sure he'd love the opportunity to lure her attention in his direction."

Fear punched Jack's stomach. Surely Sophie would see through his sister's scheme? Bradley may have been handsome, but he was an utter bore—and he was engaged. Sophie had morals. She would never fall for it. "Don't you ever get tired of using your supposed loved ones as pawns? I thought Bradley might be safe now the two of you are engaged, but it seems as though his debt will never be paid."

"Don't be so self-righteous, brother. Virtue doesn't suit you." April-Rose flicked her long fiery locks over her shoulder. "Besides, he and Tiffany, they love it. Any excuse to gain a little control, a little power—by *any* means. They are ambitious and I'm very glad I can help them." She flicked a glance at Sophie, who was now well aware of their attention. "Perhaps I *should* ask Bradley to step in," she mused. "He's always been fond of a challenge. I'd be willing to bet he could suck her in and spit her out before her visit's up."

Instinctively, Jack stepped in front of his sister, shielding Sophie from April-Rose's line of sight. "Don't you dare let Bradley anywhere near her." He ground out each word with quiet rage. If April-Rose wanted to go to war with him as well, this would be how it started. "I can handle the problem with Ella. As you said, Sophie won't be in town long. She'll be gone before you know it and so will all our problems. Let's leave it at that."

"You better be right." She quirked an eyebrow at him. "Otherwise, I'm sending in someone I *know* can handle it."

Jack was doing everything in his power not to grab his sister by the hair and drag her out of the marquee. "If you've got nothing to add besides more threats," he seethed, "I believe we're done here."

"Jack?" Sophie's voice was like a cry from heaven, a brilliant white light of peace cutting through April-Rose's putrid gloom.

He tensed, worrying that she'd overheard, but the trepidation swirling in his gut still settled in her presence. She was close enough now that he could protect her. Jack caught his breath, ignoring his sister's sinister grin, and faced the woman who had, only hours before, granted him her friendship again.

"Sophie." He smiled down at her, and April-Rose silently retreated.

Sophie observed his sister's exit curiously. "Is everything okay?" Concern tugged at her beautiful dark eyes. "I thought you might need to be rescued."

Jack grinned at her intuition, though he was still roiling inside. "You weren't wrong. When does one not need saving from my sister?"

CHAPTER 15

The cool night air of the small hours, still shrouded in the gloom of moonlight, bit aggressively at the bare skin of Sophie's hands and ankles as she allowed Jack to escort her to her cabin. Like the remaining revellers who refused to acknowledge the reception's conclusion, the raucous amphibians and nocturnal insects sheltering along Gap Creek and in the woodlands beyond chattered on uninterrupted. The hubbub ebbed and flowed, shrill then baritone, complementing the tea-coloured currents rushing over rocks and around the riverbank.

Sophie felt another chill whip across her neck. Shivering, she hugged Jack's midnight-blue jacket tighter around her body.

"Here." Jack tugged the collar up to create a protective shield, brushing the side of her throat with his fingers.

The simple touch felt so intimate. It shot tingles across her skin. Sophie licked her lips as he smiled sweetly and looked away, back to the path ahead. "Thanks," she whispered.

Distant, discordant singing flared out from the illuminated marquee atop the grassy slope behind them, drawing their attention back to the dying celebration.

"Sounds like someone has got a hold of the band's microphone." Jack winced. "Let's hope Dale had enough sense to retire when we did." His vision clouded for an instant before his smile returned. "Nope, doesn't sound like him."

"I didn't realise you and Dale were such good friends," Sophie remarked, walking ahead. Jack lengthened his stride and fell into step beside her once again.

"I've gotten to know him better over these past few months. He and Pat are quite close, have been since they were teenagers apparently. They used to play footy together. He's a good guy—kind-hearted, easy-going, just a giant softie. I guess you could say he's a refreshing change to the alliances I was encouraged to cultivate growing up as a Garland."

Sophie pursed her lips in consideration. "I hadn't thought about it like that." Jack had sometimes turned down invitations to play at Bitterbark Creek. She'd known Sheridan had barely tolerated her and Jack's friendship. It made sense she would have been trying to force a connection with a more acceptable friendship group. Jack once told her that his mother's friends were stuck up, and that their children were even worse.

"You sound surprised." Jack tried to catch her eye, but Sophie kept her gaze on the rocky track at their feet.

"Just sorry you had to go through that," she told him. She had blamed Jack for so long and was still broken-hearted that he'd abandoned her when she'd needed him most. Yet being back here had reminded Sophie of who the true villains were. "I'm glad you've found a friend in Dale. I like him too."

"He's a good egg." Jack grinned. "I'm pretty sure that's why Camille is so smitten."

"Laura told me Dale has tried to let Camille down gently several times, but she's still pining for him." Sophie glanced over at Jack and noticed he was already watching her closely. The glint of moonbeams sparkled in his eyes.

"I can't blame her." He shrugged. "She knows what she wants and how she feels about him. I think she's incredibly brave to put her heart on the line like that."

"But at the risk of their friendship?" Sophie immediately thought of their own situation. Just being alone with Jack stirred such desire within her. She'd already agreed to give their friendship another go, but what if she wanted something more? Was it worth the risk to try, especially when she was still so fearful of getting hurt again?

Jack opened his mouth to answer and then seemed to think better of it. He shook his head as though tossing those thoughts away. "I think it comes down to whether someone would regret not speaking their true feelings and if they could live a lifetime with that."

"Could you?" Sophie asked nervously. Would he approve of her taking that risk with their friendship? Would she ever be brave enough, trust him enough?

Jack gazed out into the darkness, considering. He took a shaky breath. Sophie wondered if he was just cold or if her question had made him nervous. Or was it something else?

"I'd probably never forgive myself if I didn't try." He hugged himself, squeezed his hands into fists and headed towards the cabin she temporarily called home.

Sophie followed, feeling more divided than ever.

Another burst of loud vocals startled the early morning ambience. She and Jack stopped to observe the party animals who lingered inside the marquee. The wedding singer announced a final song and encouraged the crowd to join in. The result was a choir of slurred lyrics sung off-key.

"Sounds like they're getting desperate to call it a night." Sophie giggled weakly.

Jack nodded but didn't look at her. Had she created this sudden awkward atmosphere between them? She'd been stupid to bring up the subject of friendship becoming romance. It was just all the alcohol, the long evening, her tiredness. She'd ended up really enjoying her night with Jack. It wasn't smart to hope for more. But . . . if she really was his *date*, the night could end on something more than just goodbye.

When she sighed and hugged his suit jacket even tighter around her middle, Jack finally turned towards her. "And how about you, Soph?" He gave her a sheepish smile. "Are you ready for the night to be over?"

It was like he'd read her mind. She couldn't decide how to answer. Anxious butterflies took flight in her stomach as her pulse sped up. She slid her gaze from those intense blue eyes of his down to his lips. The thought of kissing him merged with the memory of their first kiss so long ago. She felt dizzy with desire. What was wrong with her? It had to be the alcohol, right?

"I don't know." She shook her head, clearing her thoughts. She had to pull herself together.

When she turned away, Jack wrapped his hand around hers and spun her back into his arms. He held her close and danced with her, making her laugh.

"What are you doing, Jack?" Sophie was breathless but content in his arms. Maybe this closeness was the *more* she'd needed?

"Dancing." There was a proud, joyous lilt to his voice as he led them, swaying, into a waltz.

"And why are we dancing?" She let him guide her around. This way, that way. The feel of his hand at her waist sent delicious tingles of electricity throughout her body.

"There's music playing," he said matter-of-factly.

"Right?" Though her stomach still fluttered with nerves, Sophie couldn't hide her elation. She was having fun, like the old times, with *her* Jack—the sweet, sensitive larrikin she remembered.

Jack released her into a twirl and then pulled her back. She giggled as she stumbled against him, clutching his chest for support. She was in no way sober enough to move gracefully.

"I also happen to think," he told her, his lips at her ear, "that with this being a date and all, you owe me at least one proper dance."

Sophie felt her heart somersault. "You do, do you? What do you call what we were doing on the dancefloor earlier?"

"No," he touched his cheek to hers. "That's totally different. There were five of us dancing together, if you include Dale and Camille, and none of it was especially worthy of a *romantic* date."

She couldn't believe her ears. Was he just messing with her? "What's this about romance?" Maybe Jack had noticed her looking smitten and decided to tease? For a second, fear gripped her chest. It wouldn't be funny. Sophie would be mortified.

Jack twirled her again. "All dates need a bit of romance, Soph. The trick is knowing just how much."

"You sound as though you're well-versed in these things, Jack," she scoffed. "You must go on many dates."

He leaned back so he could look at her. Curiosity flickered across his face, and then he hugged her close again, his face nestling near her neck.

"No." He breathed the word across the sensitive skin of her throat. "I haven't dated in a long time."

Her body responded to the sensation of his lips so close to her skin with a burst of desire, her nerve endings sparking like fireworks. She could barely muster an answer. "Now, that's hard to believe."

"Is it really?" Jack spun her out again. Once, twice, three times. Disorientating her until he'd compelled another laugh from her lips. "I'm not sure how it works for you, Soph," he said as he reeled her back in, "but I have to be interested in someone before I go out on a date with them."

"You sound like Laura." Sophie laughed. She felt euphoric. She was still a little drunk from the wedding reception, quite befuddled from all the twirling and absolutely intoxicated by *him*. "Okay. So, you're telling me no one has captured your interest recently?"

Again, he pulled back to look at her. "Define recently."

His tone was so suggestive. Sophie swallowed nervously.

She still couldn't tell if he was only kidding, so she shied away from his question. "Your meddling mother or sister must have tried to set you up with someone?"

Jack cuddled her closer and pressed his lips to her earlobe. "Nope."

"Now I know you're lying." She smiled. "April-Rose is obviously desperate to make a match between you and Tiffany. Think of everything she said at the reception. You must have been coerced into at least one date together?"

Jack leaned away to look at her, their noses almost touching. "Do you really think I'd go on a date with Tiffany?" He gave her an exaggerated look of shock. "You don't know me at all, do you?" He feigned disappointment and had her laughing all over again.

"Fine. I believe you." She giggled. "You're just waiting for the right woman to come along." She had meant to tease, but her words struck a chord in both of them and their dancing slowed.

"What if I've known who the right woman was all along? I was just waiting for her to come back to me."

Sophie nibbled her lower lip. *Was he being serious?* She felt quivery, apprehensive, and very aware of just how close Jack was standing. She didn't know if her heart could take it if he was only playing with her. With a shallow breath, Sophie swallowed her fear, her desire.

Groaning, Jack pushed her into another twirl before wrenching her back with obvious frustration. She collided with him, grasping at him as though reaching for life itself. Their dancing ceased as he hugged her waist and pressed the hard line of his body firmly to hers. She gasped at the firmness of his arousal and felt her pulse throb between her legs.

So, he hadn't been teasing. Whether it was the alcohol boosting her confidence or the perfect size of him pressing against her, Sophie was ready and willing to risk their friendship for the chance at a second kiss.

Staring into her eyes, Jack cupped her cheek and

caressed her neck with his fingertips. He leaned closer, brushing his lips over hers, his fevered breathing quickening her own. Sophie didn't make a move to stop him.

"It's you I've been waiting for, Sophie," he whispered as though fighting against himself. "It's always been you." Then his mouth covered hers, devouring her with a hunger to match her own.

Sophie melted against him, her lips dancing with his, content in his embrace. Jack's kiss was everything and more than she remembered. The awkwardness and innocence of their youth had become something sensual and tender. Her whole body lit up with sensation at his touch. She couldn't get enough.

They explored each other like that—lips, tongues, hands groping the other ever closer—until Sophie finally noticed the stillness around them. Only the peaceful sounds of the pre-dawn filled the cool spring air. She reluctantly broke the kiss to look back at the marquee atop the hill.

"The music has stopped." Her whispered words broke the spell surrounding them.

Jack followed her gaze. "Everyone's finally heading home."

She sighed and rested her forehead against his. "I think it's time we call it a night too," she told him hesitantly. "I can find my way back to the cabin from here."

She didn't want to leave him, didn't want to stop kissing him. But she was afraid of things moving too quickly and wondered just how much they'd both been influenced by their intoxication.

"I thought you might say that." He returned her deep sigh, but snuck in a final quick kiss, making her laugh again. "Goodnight then, neighbour." He smiled. "I'm sure I'll see you around tomorrow."

"Today," she corrected him. With tremendous effort, Sophie released herself from his embrace, their hands the last link to separate. She forced herself in the direction of the cabin until her resolve strengthened and each shaky step became firmer.

"Today," Jack called out after her as though not wanting her to forget. "I'll see you around later today."

Sophie felt like a giddy teenager as she threw him a grin over her shoulder. Her *date* had ended so much better than she expected and in no way similar to what she'd wished at the start of it. How was she going to keep any of this from Laura?

CHAPTER 16

Rainbow lorikeets squawked excitedly as they gobbled nectar from the blossoms in the tall flowering trees that shielded the cabin's view of Gap Creek. Half-drunk, they performed elaborate acrobatics, hanging upside-down in their efforts to find the most delicious buds. Then they zoomed off—the race cars of the bird world—zipping through the bright blue afternoon sky in a polychromatic flash.

When another feathered troupe flitted to Sophie's right, screeching juicy gossip to each other as they passed, she changed positions—sliding out of warrior one and into downward-facing dog. Pressing her palms to the spongy blue plastic of her yoga mat, she aimed her black spandex–covered rear skyward. From the cabin's small veranda behind her, an elderly female voice piped up.

"I still don't understand why you need to perform such an activity in your underwear, Sophia."

Through her parted thighs and the wooden slats lining the veranda, Sophie could just make out the look of disapproval on her grandmother's face. The older woman gestured to her own daughter beside her on the long, timber bench seat.

"Angelica, why do you allow your child to parade around like this? Surely, this is something for the indoors?"

"It's yoga, Mama," Angelica explained. "Don't they have yoga classes at Sage Oak?"

"Of course." Nonna pointed her nose to the heavens. "Though they never involve sticking one's behind out in such a way, nor are we obligated to partake dressed only in stockings and a brassiere."

"Leggings and a crop top, Nonna," Sophie corrected sweetly.

"Tomayto, tomahto. Either way, your very personal virtues are on display to the whole wide world."

Sophie giggled. "What *whole wide world*, Nonna? No one is even around today. Everyone's still recovering from last night. You and Mum are the only two getting a good view of my *personal virtues*."

There was a masculine cough to her left. "Not quite."

In the middle of lowering into plank pose, Sophie unbalanced and stumbled forward in a running step before righting herself. She dusted her hands on her pants and spun to face the intruder. "Jack? What are you doing here?" She blushed hotly at the sight of him, her thoughts immediately jumping to the feel of his lips on hers and the line of his body pressed against her.

"Actually. . ." He searched the ground, then the veranda, before meeting her eyes. "I came by to see *you*."

"You could have just messaged me." Sophie shot a look at her family, noting their sudden interest. They couldn't have known what had happened last night. Still, she felt as though she'd been caught in the act.

"If I'd messaged, I would have missed out on this impressive display." He gestured approvingly between her outfit and the yoga mat.

Sophie gave him an awkward smile and looked away. She couldn't believe he'd seen her head down and tail in the air like that. Talk about mortification.

"I told you, Sophia," Nonna said. "This is the type of

attention you encourage by prancing around in skimpy undergarments."

"No." Jack raised his hands, palms out apologetically as he glanced between the two women. "No, that's not what I meant at all." He laughed uneasily. "Sorry. I was referring to the exercise. I'd assumed most of us would be taking it easy today. Maybe having a lazy Sunday and resting after the festivities of last night, that's all."

Sophie watched him fumble his words, finding his sudden nervousness endearing. Her thoughts drifted back to their embrace the night before. She desperately wanted to do it again. But was it a good idea when she was going back to the city in a few days? She still didn't know if she could trust him.

Both her mother and grandmother moved to a better vantage point against the veranda's railing to watch what was unfolding between Sophie and Jack.

"Look." Jack lowered his voice and took a wary step towards her. "I had a good time last night, Soph. With you." He tunnelled his fingers through his jet-black hair. "If I'm being completely honest, I wanted to know if you were free for dinner tomorrow night. Maybe we could go out?" The hopeful lilt in his voice was contradicted by the anxiety crinkling his brow.

Sophie wasn't used to seeing Jack so nervous. He had always been the confident one, the one to lead her astray with his mischief. She couldn't say with certainty that he wasn't trying to do so now. Yet he seemed truly fearful of her rejection. Her heartbeat quickened, and then she remembered that she'd already set her mind to another task that afternoon.

She hadn't been able to shake Ella from her mind. It might have been a mistake to visit her old friend, but she was curious to know what had happened to her. She hoped there might be something of their friendship left to salvage, just as she had with Jack. Ella had always been a sweet, generous girl, if a little quiet and easily led. Sophie wanted to tell Jack her intentions but thought better of it, recalling his odd reaction at the reception when she'd brought up Ella.

Sophie shook her head. "Sorry, Jack. I'm busy."

"Doing what, darling?" Her mother called out. "We don't leave until Wednesday."

Sophie scowled at her. "I didn't say no. Just not tomorrow." When her mother tilted her head sceptically, Sophie whispered to Jack, "I'd planned to go into Warwick tomorrow. I don't know what time I'll be back."

He quirked an eyebrow. "To do something in particular?"

Sophie frowned. She didn't really want to lie to him. How could this new friendship stand if it was built with lies? "Just some shopping." It was half true. She had planned to visit Ella at the record store.

"Maybe I could meet you there after?" He shrugged. "Or go with you if you want company?"

"No, it's okay. I'm fine by myself. I don't know how long I'll be." *Still the truth*, Sophie thought.

Jack nodded. "Sure." He regarded the curious women observing them from the safety of the veranda and then hazarded another step in Sophie's direction, leaving them only arm's-length apart.

The fine, sensitive hairs across Sophie's skin flared at his closeness. "What if you came by my cabin afterward? We could have a nice, no-pressure dinner—just relax, talk, spend some more time together?" The hope in his blue eyes prompted butterflies to dart around in Sophie's stomach. She really wanted to say yes. God, she wanted to kiss him again. She nibbled at her lower lip, completely torn. "What do you think?"

His gaze dropped to her mouth. Was he also thinking about their kiss last night?

"She says yes." Her mother's voice cut through the tension. "Sophie would love to have dinner with you tomorrow night, Jackson."

"Mum," Sophie snapped, at the same time her grandmother said, "Angelica!"

"Mama, he's a good boy and he likes her. What's wrong with them having a little friendly dinner?"

"It isn't proper." Nonna jabbed her finger into the air. "Dinner at his house? Anything could happen. Why would you put your daughter in that sort of situation, especially with the Garland boy of all people?"

Sophie laughed. "Yeah, Mum. Can't you see this one's trouble?" Sophie slanted a look at Jack. His grin made her giddy. He clearly wasn't nervous anymore, not now he'd got his way.

"I know you're teasing, darling, but you two used to be good friends," Angelica justified. "It would be beautiful to see that again."

"I feel much the same way, Angelica."

Sophie's mother mooned over Jack's affectionate tone as she nodded her approval.

"Very well," Nonna surrendered. "If this is to go ahead, Jackson Garland, then you must have our Sophie back by ten o'clock."

"No, Mama. Eleven."

"Hello?" Sophie huffed, and waved at them. "I'm pretty sure that's my decision." She shared a look of hopeless irritation with Jack.

He chuckled. "Families, huh?"

For a second, Sophie had forgotten just who she was talking to. No family was more controlling than the Garlands.

Resigned to her fate and quite pleased at the possibility of more kissing, Sophie sighed. "Okay. I'll meet you for dinner afterwards. I'm not sure what time that will be, but I can call when I'm on my way."

"Perfect." He beamed. "I'll see you then."

CHAPTER 17

Divided by rose bushes and other blooms, the quaint town centre of Warwick was a juxtaposition of time and culture. It incorporated greenery among the urban sprawl, the plain against the cosmopolitan. Early twentieth-century shopfronts were home to fast food giants, trendy clothing stores and livestock suppliers. Old-fashioned pubs sat proudly on most corners. Grand historic churches circled around town like points on a compass. It seemed customary for those in the country to respect few things more than their religion, their land and their beloved community.

Seated in the shelter of her mother's navy sedan, Sophie watched as a professionally dressed group slipped out of the café adjoining the narrow Warwick Music store. All had a takeaway coffee in hand. As they strolled past the car, their jolly conversation was a welcome distraction to Sophie. She couldn't stop wondering if she'd made the right choice.

"Soph? Where are you?" Laura's voice emanated from the tiny speakers on Sophie's phone.

"Warwick."

"Why?" It sounded as though Laura couldn't think of anything worse.

"I wanted to see Ella." Sophie tried to peek inside

Warwick Music's decorated facade. The spray-painted design made for a better wall than the window it was.

"Again, I ask, why?"

"Because, I ..." Sophie trailed off, glimpsing a figure near the glass, but the dark shape was obscured by the shop's stylised name. "I don't really know."

It had seemed like such a good idea the other day. Things had been going so well with Jack, she thought perhaps she could also rekindle her friendship with Ella, especially now that the other woman had freed herself from April-Rose's clique.

Was that really why she was here? Sophie didn't want to dig deeper for the answer.

"Well, that's a fabulous motive." Laura's sarcasm dripped through the phone. "But I think I know the real reason."

Sophie rubbed her forehead. "I don't think I want to hear it, Laur."

Her cousin ignored her. "You want to know what happened to you, don't you? You want to find out the truth of what happened *that* day. You can't ask April-Rose and her posse. You're too afraid to ask Jack. So you're seeking out the stray?"

A lightning bolt of realisation struck Sophie. Was that true? Yes, she had hoped her memory would return, wished the trip back might spark something. Yet she'd been unsuccessful so far. But the thought of uncovering what lay hidden in her mind truly scared her.

"I don't know, Laur." Sophie touched her temple to the coolness of the car window. "Maybe? I thought I could go on as I am, that I was better off not bringing that trauma to the surface. But being back here, spending time with Jack, seeing April-Rose ... I keep feeling like the memories are just out of reach, as though I need just one more thing to pull back the curtain."

"I think you should have asked me to come along."

Sophie knew her cousin would have dropped everything

to go to her aid. She tapped the steering wheel in an anxious rhythm. "Maybe this isn't such a great idea after all?"

"I'm not saying that. You might finally get the answers you're after."

"Yes, but what if don't like those answers?" Once Sophie got those memories back, they'd be there to stay. Could she live with whatever she discovered?

Laura was silent for a moment. Sophie could hear the faint bop of music through the phone.

"Are you at home?" Sophie asked.

"I'm at my desk organising some wildlife shots for an international photography contest," Laura rattled off automatically, and then snapped, "but don't try to change the subject."

"I don't know what to do, Laur. Give me some guidance." Sophie gripped the wheel with white-knuckled intensity. Her gut was knotted tightly with nerves, and she was feeling flushed, hotter than she should have been with the car's dashboard fans whirring fresh air towards her.

It had seemed such an easy task moments before. Go into the store and say hello to Ella. Make friends again. Piece of cake. Now that Sophie was questioning her motives, so much more seemed to hang on her actions.

"I think," Laura began cautiously, "that you called me for a reason."

"Yes, for moral support." Sophie checked the storefront again and then the car's digital clock. It was nearly two o'clock Monday afternoon, which meant she'd been hiding in the car for a little over an hour.

"Ah, but why would you need my moral support?" Laura queried as though she'd already found her answer. "Unless, of course, you planned to ask more than just how Ella has been doing these past twenty years?"

Her cousin had a point.

"Crap." Sophie couldn't keep fooling herself. She was here trying to solve her own mystery. What was she thinking? She'd be home in a couple of days, why ruin everything now?

Because I need to know what happened. The thought was Sophie's own, yet it seemed to come from someone else. She struggled to acknowledge it. The truth wouldn't define her, but it would help her move forward.

"I want to know." Sophie sighed wearily. "I need to know what happened to me."

"I've known this about you for a long time now, cuz, but the first step is always acknowledgement."

Sophie ignored the teasing lilt in her cousin's voice. She was finally onto something. She could see a little clearer. She didn't want to forget this.

"I think I noticed something about Jack the other night," she explained. "Do you remember? We were all at the kids' table. Did you see how he reacted when I asked about Ella? He looked scared. Not much scares Jack."

"I don't know about scared. I guess he didn't seem himself when you brought her up. It could just be the difficult history between them, between all of you."

Sophie shook her head even though Laura couldn't see it. "I think I hoped finding Ella would help me figure out what Jack's been hiding. I want to trust him, but something feels off with him. What if it's got something to do with my lost memories?" She sighed, feeling the swirl of mixed emotions weighing heavy on her chest. "You're probably right, Laur. I'm afraid to ask Jack about that day. He might not tell me the truth, but maybe Ella will."

"Well, whatever you find, cuz, I'll always support you. You're not alone, okay?"

Sophie's vision clouded with tears at her cousin's sweetness, but she scrubbed them away. "Thanks, Laur. I love you." Clearing her throat, she tried to shake off the suffocatingly serious atmosphere that had crept in. "Now, why aren't you here with me again?"

"Because my stupid cousin forgot to invite me."

Sophie chuckled. "How terribly slack of her."

"I know, right?" Laura groaned. "She's lucky I love her

too."

Sophie imagined Laura's cheeky but affectionate grin, and it warmed her heart. Now that she was feeling brave enough to acknowledge her motives, she admitted that she was scared to face this situation without her cousin. She just hadn't wanted to drag the younger woman deeper into her drama.

"Now, Soph," Laura lectured, "you do know you actually have to leave the car and talk to Ella to get your answers?"

"Yes. I know." Sophie laughed again. "Thanks for the pep talk."

"No probs. I expect a full debrief when I see you next."

"It will likely be tomorrow." Sophie's smile faltered. "Apparently, I have plans tonight."

"Plans?" Laura's voice raised an octave. "What plans?"

"With a certain *friend* of yours," Sophie hinted. "We're supposed to be having dinner together—at his cabin." Sophie worried about how that would go if she got the answers she wanted from Ella.

There was a squeal of delight from her cousin's end of the line that quickly rose to a shriek.

Sophie waited patiently. "You quite finished now?"

"What happened to not trusting him?"

"I still don't. Not completely." Maybe if Ella could offer her some answers, she could put her mind at ease?

"Jack's a good bloke, Soph. I'm sure whatever you discover about the past, you'll get through it together." Laura paused and her tone became playful. "Even Dale thought you made a cute couple."

"Oh my gosh." Was everyone trying to play matchmaker? "I hope you corrected that assumption, Laur. Jack and I are not a couple."

"Not yet."

Sophie ignored her cousin's teasing and noticed a woman approach the glass-panelled door of the shop. She was curvy, with heavy make-up, cropped burgundy hair and a dense fringe. Stepping outside, she lifted a tattooed arm to pin an A4 poster on the corkboard display beside the entry. When she stretched upwards, the shorts of her ebony overalls threatened to reveal the curve of her behind but stopped at the very tops of her thighs. Chunky black boots adorned her feet and piercings glittered on her ears.

Sophie barely recognised Ella. This woman hardly resembled the jubilant little girl whose friendship was often torn between Sophie and April-Rose. Although Ella had always been in awe of April-Rose's popularity, she'd had too kind a heart to fit within the brainwashed clique. She was so unlike Bradley and Tiffany, who wouldn't do anything without April-Rose's say-so. Their parents—all friends of the Garlands or associated with Garland Grain—had encouraged the six of them to play together. When April-Rose pulled the others away, Ella would often sneak off with Jack and Sophie. April-Rose had regularly rebuked her for it. Perhaps it was Ella's fondness for seeking friendship outside the clique that eventually got her kicked out of it.

"Laur?" Sophie asked, still a little lost in her thoughts. "When was the last time you saw Ella?"

"I dunno. I've probably seen her around, but I don't think I've spoken to her for a few years. Not since she and April-Rose went their separate ways."

"So, you don't know what she looks like now? If she's changed?"

"Why?" Laura yelped eagerly. "Can you see her?"

Sophie frowned. "I won't know for sure until I go inside."

"Then go inside," Laura ordered. "What are you waiting for? Stop procrastinating and just go do it. You can tell me all about it later." Laura caught herself and amended, "Sorry, I mean tomorrow. Now, go."

"Fine." With a chest-heaving sigh, Sophie said farewell and ended the call.

As she dragged in a breath of fresh air and a burst of much-needed courage along with it, Sophie opened the car door. She slunk inside the Warwick Music store and was greeted with the grumble and clang of old-school rock and a dusty, organised mess. Records, CDs and DVDs were stacked on shelves and racks beneath the buzzing glow of tired fluorescents, while guitars and other instruments straddled supports against the far wall. Besides the feisty-looking woman Sophie had seen, there were only three other people inside the store. A grey-bearded man in a leather jacket stood at the back assessing a bass guitar, and a teenage couple in dishevelled school uniforms rummaged through CDs, debating the significance of an indie band's new single.

"Be with you in a moment," a husky voice drawled from behind the cluttered counter. The woman Sophie hoped was Ella lifted a small crate of cassettes onto the glass top.

"Tapes?" Sophie queried. "Do people even buy those anymore?"

The woman shrugged. "We tend to sell a lot online." She gestured to the box. "These are second-hand—vintage—but in good nick."

"Vintage?" Sophie pointed at a case with a photo of the Backstreet Boys posed against a white-panelled wall. "Even this one?"

"You'd be surprised at what people want to collect." The woman smirked. "Interested? They're two dollars a pop or six for ten."

Sophie waved a hand. "No, thanks."

"What can I help you with then?" She pushed the crate to the side.

"Well, I was wondering. . ." Sophie's stomach churned. This was her last chance to back out, to keep things as they were. The weight of her lost memories would surely ease over time.

No, she was clutching at straws. Twenty years had passed and the ache of not knowing had only worsened. *I can do this.* She swallowed deeply. "Are you Ella—Ella Larsen—by any chance?"

The woman parted her lips in cheerful surprise, poised to reply. But as she studied Sophie, her expression became cold. Sophie's heart sank.

"You're her, aren't you?" she accused. "You're Sophie Wendall? I heard you were coming back to town." She shook her head. "Geez, I barely recognised you."

"I could say the same." Sophie offered a smile, but it wasn't returned.

"It's been a long time."

Sophie nodded. "Twenty years."

Ella crossed her arms. "What do you want?"

"I thought maybe we could talk."

"About what? The good old days?"

"That's part of it. Yes." Sophie nervously surveyed her surroundings, checking for eavesdroppers. "I need someone to be honest with me about that day at the Garland dam."

"*Honest?*" Ella mocked. "The truth tends to hurt, you know?"

"That's what I'm expecting." Sophie felt her heartbeat thumping high in her throat, its echo filling her ears.

Ella assessed her silently, as though trying to deduce Sophie's true intentions. After a moment, she exhaled, exhausted. "I'd heard your memory was vague." She glanced warily around the shop and then rested her hips against the serving counter. "Wondered if it might have been a ploy. I know I'd choose to forget if I could."

A chill of fear washed over Sophie. "Please tell me why." Her throat felt raw.

Remorse softened Ella's hazel eyes. "If you're sure?" At Sophie's insistent nod, Ella continued, "I finish work at five. We can meet up then to talk."

Relief loosened the rope of tension constricting Sophie's chest, and she nodded. "Thank you."

Ella smiled weakly, like she'd immediately regretted her offer.

The store's front door clicked open and drew their

attention. Although it took Sophie a second to register the identity of the tall raven-haired customer, Ella's reaction was instantaneous.

"What's going on?" It was a fearful whisper. "What is *he* doing here?"

Dumbfounded, Sophie glanced from Ella to Jack and back again. "I don't know, Ella. I mean—" She frowned at Jack.

"Hi," he greeted her, his genial grin wilting as he watched Ella slowly retreat from the counter.

"Hi?" Sophie was utterly confused. "What are you doing here, Jack?"

He shrugged. "Lucky coincidence really. I thought I'd hunt for some new records for tonight."

Ella shook her head aggressively. "No. Get out," she ordered, jabbing her index finger at the front door. "You're not welcome here. Both of you. I don't know what game you're playing, and I don't want any part of it. I don't want anything to do with you, April-Rose or your horrible family. Go make someone else's life miserable."

"Ella?" Sophie gasped, reaching out to console her old friend. She couldn't understand how things had escalated so quickly.

Ella slapped her fingers away. "Just get out. I'm not kidding, Sophie. Leave me the hell alone."

The shock of rejection, of losing the opportunity to finally get some answers, hit Sophie hard and she felt tears well in her eyes. She had been so close. So very close. What could she do now? She wasn't ready to let it go.

"Best to do as she says," directed a gravelly voice behind them. The middle-aged man with the silver beard who'd been appraising bass guitars approached them, his expression one of concern rather than menace.

"I'm so sorry, Ella." Sophie wiped her eyes before looking over at the man. "We didn't mean to upset her."

He bowed his head as though he understood. "I'll look after her," he reassured them.

Feeling lost and grief-stricken, Sophie cast a final glance at her old friend. Ella's fierce disguise was cracked, overtaken by ruddy cheeks and glistening tears. Sophie hated that she'd hurt her so and wished she could understand what they'd done. But for now, she would leave the poor young woman in peace. Sophie took Jack's hand and led him outside into the stark, cleansing sunlight.

CHAPTER 18

Jack gripped his shaking hands in his lap. He hoped Sophie hadn't noticed. Ella's verbal assault still rang in his ears, the deafening drone even worse in the silence of the car. He'd joined Sophie in her mother's navy sedan, offering to stay with her until she calmed. She was still wiping at her eyes, her cheeks flushed, lips swollen. Part of him was furious with Ella for upsetting Sophie, and yet he completely understood the young woman's reaction. She had every right to hate the Garlands, to hate him and his family. The Garlands and the Wendalls weren't the only ones affected by what happened that day at the dam. The repercussions continued to inflict pain on several families.

Jack felt sick. He couldn't shake Ella's terrified expression from his mind's eye. Seeing Sophie so distraught had him even more worried. He hadn't wanted her to get hurt. Hadn't wanted Ella to suffer either. There seemed no way for the truth to come out without injuring those he cared for. He wished they could all move on, forget about the past and focus on their future. But what he'd done, what his family had done, had left a giant scar within all of them, one that only honesty and forgiveness could fade.

Oh, why wasn't he braver? Why couldn't he just own up

to his mistakes and tackle the consequences? Why had he formed such a stupid alliance with his sister? Surely Sophie hating him and rushing to leave town was better than trusting April-Rose? But if the truth were out, the Santoros would hate him too. He couldn't lose them all, not his new-found family and the person he'd always held dearest to his heart. The agony of it all took his breath away.

Stop it! Jack yelled at his spiralling thoughts. He had to pull himself together. Sophie needed him.

"Are you okay?" he asked cautiously, knowing it was a silly question. Neither of them were okay.

She looked at him, still dazed. Worry creased her forehead.

"Soph?" he tried again, taking her hand in his, hoping the connection would steady them both. "That thing with Ella, please don't take it personally. She's been through a lot."

"What do you mean?" Her voice was hoarse from crying.

How did he answer that without revealing it all? Jack didn't want to lie, and he definitely didn't want to use April-Rose's suggested solution. Ella had never been a junkie. She was just a person in pain. Jack could relate.

"She's not the same girl you used to know," he explained. "When her mother passed away a couple of years back, she changed. She distanced herself from everyone. She became angry, nothing like the bubbly little girl we knew." Jack shifted in his seat, twisting his body to face her. "Grief does terrible things to people. Maybe she just wants to leave the past behind for good?" It was the closest thing to the truth he could offer her.

Sophie stared out the windscreen as though considering his words. Her hand was right there in his, yet she still felt so far away. What was she thinking? When she looked at him again, he wilted under the intensity of her gaze.

"Why are you here, Jack?"

He gulped a little at the accusation in her voice, but knew

it was justified. "I told you. It was a happy coincidence."

But it wasn't. Not exactly. He hadn't realised Sophie would be in the record store at that moment. He had intended to talk to Ella, to see if he could plead with her not to reveal anything if Sophie came by asking questions. Jack hadn't even been sure if Sophie would. He just had a feeling. He had fought with himself all morning about what to do, delayed seeking Ella out until that moment. Had it been self-sabotage? Had he waited so long to approach Ella in the hope that Sophie would have already found her and learned the truth? Ever since Sophie had returned, Jack had been in a constant state of equal parts fear and hope. If she discovered what really happened, it could destroy his life but also put him out of his misery.

Jack winced at the sharp stab of a tension headache.

Sophie studied him closely. "Just a coincidence?" she asked. "But you knew I was planning to come in to Warwick this afternoon."

"Yes, to do some shopping." He licked his lips. Why was his mouth suddenly so dry? "I hadn't realised that involved visiting the music store. It was nice to run into you though." He tried for a small smile, but she didn't reciprocate.

"Until it wasn't." She sighed. "Poor Ella. I wish I knew how we upset her. She seemed okay with me initially. But then you arrived. . ." Her voice trailed off and her attention turned to the shopfront, perhaps hoping for another glimpse of Ella.

"She and April-Rose had a tough friend break-up," Jack offered. Still not a lie. Just not the whole truth. "I'm probably guilty by association. Seeing you and me together, maybe it reopened old wounds?"

"Maybe." Sophie nodded and was silent for a second. "She didn't sound keen to reacquaint herself with your family ever again."

Jack felt his stomach drop. He knew Sophie wasn't necessarily insinuating anything, but it still hurt to be connected in such a way. "They're only my family in name," he reminded her.

Sophie squeezed his hand in hers. "So, you were really out here buying a record for tonight?"

"Or two." It wasn't a lie. He'd had every intention of doing so. The internet could be spotty out by the cabins, and he had always been too old-school for CDs. He didn't really need a new record, but it had been the perfect excuse to visit the store.

Sophie shot a curious gaze his way. "Why did you decide to visit Warwick Music?"

Hadn't he already answered that question? The confusion must have shown on his face because Sophie's features softened, and she tried again. "I mean that shop in particular. You told me that Ella worked at a record store in Warwick. This is the only one I could track down. You said you *used* to be friends, but from what I gathered you hadn't seen each other in years. If you knew how much bad blood was between her and your family, why even risk it? Was the shop you usually visit closed or something?"

Suddenly the reason behind all her questioning clicked into place. She didn't believe his excuse for a minute.

"Actually, I usually buy online," he told her. "Warwick Music was a last resort." He shrugged. "I guess I just wanted to organise something special for tonight." He wasn't lying, even if it was only half the truth. He had desperately wanted to make a good impression on her.

His gaze drifted to Sophie's lips. He couldn't stop thinking about their kiss after the wedding reception. He wanted to do it again, wanted to kiss more of her, wanted to keep her close. Yet to keep her in town would be to bring about his own undoing. Jack's tension headache panged painfully at his temples.

"You don't have to do anything to make tonight special for me, Jack." She caressed the back of his hand with her thumb. "It's nice just to spend some more time with you." Sophie sounded genuinely pleased, and Jack's heart swelled.

"What are your plans right now?" He could hardly look

at her when he asked. What if she turned him down? "Are you still shopping, or would you also like to spend the afternoon with me?"

"Well. . ." Sophie's grin widened and then faltered as she looked back at the Warwick Music shopfront.

When her vision glazed over in thought, Jack wondered if she was considering reaching out to Ella again. How could he stop it? He wasn't with Sophie twenty-four seven. He couldn't stop fate. If it was supposed to happen it would, and there was nothing he could do about it.

Something triggered Sophie to glance back in Jack's direction. She smiled warmly. "Sorry. Ignore me. Must be still processing." She shook her head as if trying to expel unpleasant thoughts. "I'd love to spend the afternoon and evening with you, Jack."

Had he heard her correctly? The moment was so surreal. "You would?" He probably shouldn't have let on that he was so surprised. *Play it cool, Jack. Play it cool*, he told himself.

She beamed at him. "Of course. It would be great for us to catch up and chat properly."

Jack's grin faltered at the word *chat*. What exactly did Sophie want to chat about? The weather? His time in Melbourne? The past? He was pretty sure he could guess it in one. With Ella no longer an option, was Sophie hoping that he would provide her with some answers? He was in no way ready to tell her. He'd have to be on his guard with her, and on his best behaviour. Sex and secrets never mixed well. He hoped to rekindle their relationship, not send it up in flames.

CHAPTER 19

Stony, coffee-brown soil crunched underfoot as Jack led Sophie along the narrow track, trekking deeper into the heavily forested landscape beyond Bitterbark Creek's cabins. A light breeze, blissfully cool in the otherwise temperate afternoon, swayed the trees and rustled leaves as though in jubilant applause. Monochromatic magpies added their own warbles from the bushy branches above as they gazed down curiously at the visitors to their territory.

Jack had suggested the short hike upon returning from Warwick. He knew of Sophie's fondness for the outdoors and loved that the simple pleasures in life still brought her so much joy. The fresh air and exercise would do them good after their dramatic encounter with Ella too. Perhaps it would also keep Jack's head clear enough to avoid any of Sophie's probing questions. He desperately didn't want to lie, but if she put him on the spot. . .

Beside him, Sophie inhaled deeply as though relishing the scent of pine and eucalyptus. "Thank you. I don't do this often enough."

"What? Walk?" He smirked at her.

"No." She swatted playfully at his shoulder. "Spend time outside, enjoying the trees, the wildlife. I rarely get a chance in the city. I might wander around the botanical gardens or drive to the coast, but nothing quite as magnificent as this."

"Yeah," Jack agreed. The farmstay's property was his own piece of heaven. He admired the towering tree trunks, how they stretched for the bright blue sky. The birdsong in chorus with the babbling creek had become the peaceful soundtrack to his new life. "I never want to take it for granted. After having it on my doorstep for so long, I'm not sure I could live without it."

"I'm glad you understand how lucky you are, Jack," Sophie said earnestly. "The Santoros did a very kind thing inviting you to live here with them. Bitterbark Creek means a lot to my family. The place is full of memories. To come home and find a Garland living here with them—it was a shock, to say the least."

He grimaced. It felt like he'd been punched in the stomach. Would he ever be free of his family's reputation?

"Sorry. I didn't phrase that well. It's your mother and sister I worry about." Sophie gnawed at her lower lip. "What if your being here puts my aunt and uncle in harm's way?"

"I wouldn't let that happen." Jack looked away, his shoulders slumping with the weight of her question. Could he really make that promise? He may have been a Garland in name, but he had a smidgen of the power they held in this town. If they wanted to hurt the Santoros, there wouldn't be much he could do. He had always prayed his mother and sister had more important people to destroy.

Sophie slipped her arm through his, offering him a sweet, supportive smile. "They've really taken to you, and I don't just mean Pat and Laura. I saw how Aunt Robin and Uncle Nick were with you at the wedding."

"They call me the adopted son." He laughed softly. Nothing had ever meant so much to him. He hadn't known what it truly meant to be *family* until he had lived among Sophie's.

"Please don't do anything to hurt them," she whispered.

What? Jack stopped walking and stared at her. It was like

she could see right through him. He couldn't stop thinking about what the Santoros would say if they knew the extent of his sins—if they spoke to him again at all. What if they could never forgive him for his part in what happened? He couldn't bear the thought of hurting them like that.

"Sorry," Sophie said. "I would never forgive myself if I didn't say it."

"No. You're just protecting them. I get it." He gulped back his own pain. "You do know how much I care about them though, don't you, Soph? They took me in when I needed it most. They shared their home with me, their love." Jack's chest tightened. Sophie had to understand that his deep affection for her family was genuine. "Bitterbark Creek has become my *home*. The Santoros are the family I *chose*, and I wouldn't be happy, wouldn't be the man I am now, without them." When his fingers trembled, Jack curled them into fists to hide it.

"I really want to believe you, Jack." Sophie held his gaze, and he could see the sincerity in her eyes.

"But you still don't fully trust me." He knew he was venturing into dangerous territory.

"Again, I really want to." With a sigh, she pulled free of him to tug her black cardigan tighter around her shoulders. "You're just not making it particularly easy for me."

She continued along the track and Jack hurried after her. "What do you mean, Soph?" As if he didn't already know.

She cursed under her breath and threw up her hands, fighting some internal war. "I wasn't planning on saying anything, but this whole thing with Ella has got me so confused."

"How so?" Geez, could he be any more obvious? No wonder Sophie doubted him.

"Jack." The stern look in her eyes ordered him to drop the pretence. When he didn't, she huffed in frustration. "I saw the look on your face at the reception when I mentioned Ella. Something wasn't right. Then in Warwick today—what was that? Was it really a coincidence you were there? And why was Ella so upset?"

"I told you—," he tried.

"Yes, and I'm telling *you* that I don't believe you."

Jack swallowed, fighting the lump in his throat. "What do you want me to say, Soph?"

"I want you to tell me the truth, Jack."

He couldn't meet her eyes. Instead, he stared through the dense bushland, drawing on the serenity of the natural world to calm him. He couldn't answer her without revealing everything. It was all tied together. If they talked about Ella, they'd have to talk about the mistake that almost got Sophie killed.

Jack felt Sophie rest a hand on his shoulder and the connection immediately eased the tension twisted in his chest. "I'm sorry, Soph. I want to tell you, but. . ." He couldn't think of an explanation that wouldn't incriminate him further.

"From the look on your face, I'm guessing this is a Garland family issue."

"You're not wrong." At least he could admit to that much.

"Well then. Maybe you're not ready to trust me either, Jack?"

He looked at her, utterly shocked. Besides the Santoro family, she was the *only* person he trusted. Yet as he stared into her beautiful dark eyes, he wondered. Maybe she was right. Jack didn't trust Sophie to forgive him upon learning the truth. He couldn't see how she could. He didn't trust her not to abandon him, not to break his heart. He might have been keeping secrets to protect his new life, but he was also protecting his heart from being ravaged by loss all over again.

"I do want to tell you, Soph." He really meant it.

She offered a tentative smile. "Just admitting that there's something you're not ready to tell me is reassuring. You're a good guy, Jack. I can see now that you always have been, but I think you doubt it yourself sometimes. You're a

Garland, but you aren't *them*. What they've done doesn't reflect on you."

"Doesn't it?" Irritation flared within him. He wasn't angry with Sophie, but she'd hit such a sensitive nerve. "I've only been free of them for a few years. My time in Melbourne and with the Santoros may have shielded me from a lot, but I can't erase history. What we've done—I can never undo it, Sophie. I may never be free of the guilt."

Guilt. His constant companion for years, ever since the fatal car accident that took Sophie's father. He was sick of feeling this way. He couldn't survive another thirty years in this agony. Something had to change—and something had. Sophie had returned.

Jack's cheeks were hot as he wiped at his watery eyes. To his surprise, Sophie took his hand and secured it in hers. The solid connection ignited the adoration he'd always had for her.

"You don't have to deal with this all on your own, Jack. I'm here. We can talk even when I go back to the city. But if you're not ready to talk to me, then talk to Pat or Laura. Even Uncle Nick or Aunt Robin." She pulled his hand to her heart and held it there as she stared into his eyes, willing him to really hear her. "We all care about you, Jack. You are not alone."

Jack couldn't help himself. He leaned forward and pressed a gentle kiss to her lips. A blush crept over her cheeks when he pulled back to look at her.

Sophie inhaled sharply. "Jack—" she attempted, but he wrapped his arms around her and kissed her again.

It was a velvet caress, lips moulding, dancing in perfect harmony as he drank in the sweet taste of her. The emotions that ruptured within him only confirmed the notion that *this*—right here in his arms—was where Jack longed for Sophie to stay.

CHAPTER 20

The electric kettle on the kitchen countertop clicked off automatically as the water inside boiled. The sound drew Jack's attention away from Sophie, who sat outside his cabin beside the rustic fire pit, captivated by the glowing flames. Reluctantly, he dragged himself from where he'd been loitering by the front door and collected two porcelain mugs. It took his eyes a moment to adjust from the darkness outside to the warm gold of the indoor lighting. At the small sink—shiny and tidy after an earlier dinner—Jack prepared the tea as the distant crackle of the fire called to him. It was only when he took a heated cup in each hand that he noticed another noise drifting through the otherwise quiet cabin.

The electronic serenade of his mobile phone grew louder with each repetition. Leaving the beverages on the dining table, Jack hurried into the bedroom. Snatching the device from where he'd left it charging on the bedside table, he frowned as the screen illuminated the words: *Unknown Caller.* He wandered back into the living area before deciding to take the risk and answer the call.

"Hello?"

"Jackson?" His mother's inquiry was sharp, impatient. "What are you doing? Why didn't you answer my call immediately?"

"Because I have a life, Mother. I also didn't recognise the caller. When did you start withholding your number?"

"I've borrowed a friend's phone. Mine . . . it ran out of battery."

There was a muffled voice on Sheridan's end of the line. Something masculine, disapproving, and somewhat familiar. Jack couldn't distinguish the words.

Did his mother have a new beau? His father's passing had been exceptionally difficult for her. She'd taken a keen interest in Bradley before April-Rose set her sights on him. But it had been innocent flirtation. His mother always cared too much about reputation to take the risk of dating someone twenty years her junior. Jack hadn't seen her show any interest in men since then. Maybe she had met someone new? Perhaps a positive influence to help distract her from her devilish pastimes? It was something Jack could hope for anyway.

"Do you have company?" he teased. "Or are you out? If you were at the house, you could have just used the landline."

"My social life is none of your business, Jackson."

Her agitation made him grin. "It's so unlike you to be out this late, Mother. Even with friends."

"I did not call to be interrogated," she blustered.

"Well, why did you call at all, Mother?"

"Your sister asked me to check on you, to see that all is as it should be, that there is no growing threat from Sophie or that Larsen girl."

"Really?" Jack scoffed. "April-Rose has you playing errand girl now? Why didn't she just call me herself?" He strolled to the front door to check on Sophie. She was still perched comfortably before the blazing fire pit, a woollen blanket cuddled around her.

"She's with Tiffany, completing the last of the arrangements for her engagement party. She only has another fortnight before the event."

"So you waited until eleven in the evening just to ask me if I'd done as ordered?"

"I would have called earlier, but I had plans."

"Well, I'm busy too," he growled, his indignation matching his mother's.

Silence reigned for a brief moment and then Sheridan's voice softened. "You know your sister. She always gets her way."

"It runs in the family."

"Don't be like that, Jackson. I know we've had our differences—"

"Problems," he corrected.

"And," she went on loudly, "your behaviour at Patrick and Marilyn's wedding reception was in many respects unforgivable, but I *do* forgive you, my beautiful boy. I always forgive you. I know your sister's teasing was just too much for you that night. I know you didn't mean all those horrid things you said."

"Hmm." He pretended to ponder her words. "I'm pretty sure I did."

"You're talking to me, Jackson—your mother. There's no need to continue this charade."

"What charade, Mother? The one you're performing right now?"

"Jackson?" There was hurt in her voice now, but was it even real? She lied so often that Jack struggled to know the difference.

"Save it for another fight, Mother. Like you, I have company, and I'd rather get back to entertaining than prolonging this conversation."

There was a gasp of vexation through the phone line. "Jackson—"

But Jack didn't want to hear it, didn't want to drag things out any longer. Shaking his head, he disconnected the call.

Little did his mother and sister realise that the threat no longer resided with Sophie or Ella. It lived within their own blood, within him. He was so tired of keeping secrets. Jack wanted to look in the mirror and not hate the person staring back at him. He would face it all. Soon.

Leaving the phone behind, Jack grasped a mug in each hand and hurried out the front door. When the phone called out to him again, he ignored it and descended the few stairs to where Sophie waited for him.

"Should you get that?" she asked as he handed her a cup.

"No." He gave her a reassuring smile and settled on the timber bench beside her. "I'd rather talk to you."

There was a coyness to her grin as she glanced away, back into the fire. "So, who was on the first call?"

"My mother," he groaned.

"Wow, she really does expect you to be available at all times to address her every whim."

"You have no idea." Jack sighed.

Sophie's attention drifted back to him. "Here." She offered him half the blanket.

When he accepted it, wrapping it around his shoulders, she shuffled closer until she was snug against him. The sensation of her body, so close and inviting, had him swallowing back a sudden urge to claim more than was offered.

"You're so warm," she murmured, her focus back on the flames. Then—beneath the protection of the woollen barrier—she slipped her hand into his. "Even hotter than the fire."

Jack stared at her. She was stunning. He took in her elegant profile, the contented expression there, and how her flame-tickled golden locks framed her beauty like the sun's rays. Everything seemed so perfect, so right. Was it time? Should he tell her the truth?

"Soph?" he started, still enthralled by their closeness.

She made a short, distracted murmur in response.

"You know how special you are to me, how much I care about you? I never want to hurt you."

"I know, Jack." She yawned. "We've been over all of this already." She sipped at her tea and then rested her head on his shoulder.

"Even as kids," he continued, "you meant the world to me. I wanted to be with you all the time."

She snuggled against him. "I remember feeling the same way about you too."

He exhaled lengthily, desperate to drag up the courage to say what was needed. He could do this. "But when my father almost died, something changed inside me."

At the mention of his late father, Sophie stiffened. Jack didn't want to overwhelm her, but he had to keep going. If he stopped, he might never be brave enough to start again.

"I was too young to process the grief, to mourn properly," he explained. "I let it control me, let my mother's hatred and my sister's anger manipulate me. Had I been older, wiser, I hope things would have been different. As it was, I allowed them to turn me against you, against your whole family, and I think that killed me just a little inside."

Sophie squeezed his hand lightly as though reassuring him she was still there, still listening. That brief sensation gave Jack so much hope. If Sophie could understand his side, maybe she would eventually find it in her heart to forgive him.

"Almost losing you was the turning point for me. It was the moment I realised who I wanted to be—and who I didn't. I just wish I could have figured it out earlier."

Was he saying any of this right? It sounded muddled to his own ears. Jack lowered his mug to the bench beside him and then scrubbed at his forehead. His heart was thudding against his ribs, like someone attempting to kick down a door. He felt nauseated, dread swirling in his gut. The thought of what he might lose, of his whole world falling apart, terrified him. But he had to press on. He was so close.

"I've played it over and over in my mind. I've spent so many years wishing I could go back, that I could change things. Maybe then you wouldn't have left town. You wouldn't have left *me*. Maybe then we would have grown up together and learned how to get through it all—how to survive what happened to our families—*together*?" His heart clenched at the thought of what could have been, and he forced his misty gaze back to the fire. "Maybe then I wouldn't have been alone, fighting every day against the rot that slowly destroyed my family."

Jack heard the clunk of Sophie's cup on the timber bench. She freed her hand from his and enfolded him in her arms. He nuzzled into the crook of her neck and drank in her sweet scent. Her embrace was exactly the reassurance he needed. He was doing the right thing.

"I'm so sorry," Sophie whispered, her breath tickling the sensitive skin of Jack's neck. "I've spent so many years trying to hate you. After my father died, you changed so much, you pushed me away, and it broke my heart. I never really knew what you were going through." Sophie raked her fingers through his hair affectionately. Jack hugged her closer, clinging to her compassion. He could stay like this forever, in her arms. But he had a duty to do. He had to tell her his secret.

Then all of this will end. The thought wailed through Jack's mind, clawing at his heart. He had only just got Sophie back. Was he willing to risk losing her again just to be honest? But it wasn't only that—Jack also hoped that telling Sophie his secret would help clear her murky memories.

His thoughts were at war. Fear fighting against his wish to heal. Which direction should he choose?

"Jack." Sophie's sweet voice was soft and choked with emotion. "You can help me understand what you were going through and why you acted as you did. I know that will make us stronger. Maybe we can face the future together?"

Jack cuddled her closer, and in the span of one sharp breath, he decided. *Yes.* It was time to take that terrifying step. Sophie deserved to know the whole truth. Jack needed them to move past this. It was the only way to give their new relationship a decent chance. But as he opened his mouth to begin, Sophie pulled back to look at him.

"Now that we're sharing secrets," she posed timidly, unaware that he was yet to fully disclose his own. "That day . . . at the Garland dam. What really happened, Jack? I don't . . . remember."

Her words froze him solid. She really didn't remember any of it? Laura had insinuated that Sophie's memory was hazy, and during their time together it had quickly become obvious his betrayal wasn't something she remembered. But to not remember *anything*. . .

Jack hesitated. He'd just been presented with the perfect opportunity. He could tell her the truth from his own perspective, unhindered by the need to help her piece together foggy memories. What was he waiting for? He licked his lips, trying to find the words. But as he searched, his whole confession, the sorry sonnet that had rolled around and around in his thoughts for years, abandoned him.

He frowned at Sophie, feeling helpless as she stared at him with those gorgeous dark eyes. Could he stand to see the agony of betrayal fill them? He desperately wanted to soothe her anxiety. Yet the truth he had to offer would do the complete opposite. He saw only one way forward. The coward's way.

Jack swallowed deeply. He cupped a hand to Sophie's cheek, regretting his decision even as he made it. He knew it would haunt him for the rest of his life.

"Soph." Solemnly, he shook his head. "Neither do I."

Dread consumed him. What had he done?

CHAPTER 21

Warm rays of sunlight pierced through cotton-wool clouds in the wide cyan sky, sparkling like glitter as they struck dewy tree leaves and damp flower buds. Tiny green pink-cheeked musk parrots flittered from branch to branch in the flora overhead, squawking their approval, while the hooves of two horses clip-clopped against the stony earth of the winding dirt track below.

Sophie locked her legs tightly around the belly of the gentle chestnut mare she was riding. "How did you get me to agree to this again?" Sophie called out to Laura, her knuckles white as she gripped the reins. It had been much too long since she'd been atop a horse. Riding the ponies had been one of her favourite pastimes. Now she was used to her feet flat on the ground.

Laura and her jet-black steed, Wonder, were leading the way up the hilly trail. She giggled. "This was your idea, cuz. You're the one who asked to go horse-riding."

"Yeah, in the safety of the riding ring." Sophie had hoped starting small would help build her confidence. "It was your idea for us to trek up to the Bitterbark Creek lookout."

"What's the difference?"

"Flat ground," Sophie groaned.

Again, her cousin laughed. "Just keep your knickers on, we're almost there. Then we can dismount, have a rest and admire the view."

"That's assuming I can unlatch myself from this thing."

"She is not a *thing*. She's Butterscotch."

"I was talking about the saddle."

Laura emitted another hoot of laughter as Sophie attempted to loosen her fingers from their death grip on the leather straps.

"Besides," Laura continued once she had her breath back, "I wanted you all to myself. If we'd stayed back at the farm, Mum and Dad would have been all over you. I thought you'd prefer privacy when you tell me all the juicy details."

Sophie freed one clammy hand for an instant, wiping it over the fabric of her ebony jeans. "What juicy details?"

"You know," Laura drawled. She glanced over her shoulder when her words were met with silence. "Aw, come on, Sophie. You have to tell me what happened last night. Was there *love* in the air?" She wiggled her shoulders for emphasis.

Sophie quickly hid a smile.

"I'll take that as a yes!"

"I never said that Laur." The feeling might be there, but it was too early to announce anything. Besides, she was supposed to be heading back to the city soon. She didn't know about Jack, but she wasn't ready for a long-distance relationship. Maybe they were better off not getting lost in something deeper than friendship.

"It's written all over your face, Soph. You can't deny it." Her cousin's triumphant grin was so irritating.

"Fine." Sophie cleared her throat. "It's not *not* a yes."

"What does that even mean?"

"It means I like him—you know I've always liked him, even when I hated him—but a relationship beyond this weekend might not be viable."

"*Viable?*" Laura mocked. Wonder chose that moment to release a tremendous snort. "Did you hear that, cuz? Even my horse thinks you're full of crap." Laura cackled until she noticed Sophie's glare of disapproval. "Hey, don't blame me. It was the horse." She patted Wonder's neck. "So, did you spend the night?"

"Laura," Sophie chided. Heaven knew Sophie wanted to, but something about how the conversation changed as the night went on had pricked her doubts. She wanted to trust Jack, to let him in, but she wasn't sure he trusted *her*. She felt in her gut that something was still off. It made her just a little hesitant to share his bed.

"What?" Her cousin shrugged. "These are the juicy details I was talking about."

"Should we really be discussing this right now?" Sophie glanced at the wilderness around them. They were alone, but she was still uncomfortable disclosing such information.

"Is that a yes I hear?" Laura asked devilishly.

"No," Sophie harrumphed. "No, I didn't stay the night."

"Well, that explains it." Laura clicked her fingers. "Now I know why you're so grumpy this morning."

"I am not grumpy."

"My apologies. What's the clinical term these days— sexually frustrated?"

"Do you want me to turn my horse around?"

Laura scoffed at the threat. "I doubt you could get Butterscotch to stop, let alone figure out how to point her towards home."

Sophie smiled despite herself. She reassessed her white-knuckled grip on the reins. With her rusty riding skills, she'd struggle to even attempt such an incredible feat as a horsey U-turn.

"Fine," Sophie conceded. "These are all the juicy facts I'm willing to offer up. No, I didn't stay the night. I wanted to and Jack did ask me, but I needed time to process."

"Process what?" Laura shot a quizzical look over her shoulder. "The whole concept of the birds and the bees?"

"No, Miss Smarty-Pants. Geez, you're in right form this morning, aren't you?"

Laura grinned. "I slept well. Thanks for noticing. So, what is this mysterious thing you had to process then?"

Sophie swallowed uneasily. Jack's admission had brought them closer, and she found comfort in the knowledge that she may not be alone in her strange amnesia. But it had also frightened her. Was he really telling the whole truth? He'd sounded so sincere when telling her about his life back then, how alone he'd felt after the car accident and then after losing her. But when he told her about his own memory loss, it was as though he didn't want to say too much, didn't want to think on it for too long.

Unless it was because the emptiness of that day was so painful? Sophie understood the agony of desperately wanting to remember something, no matter how small, only to keep hitting a wall. She didn't want to believe Jack was lying, but he was still hiding something from her. Did it have something to do with Ella? As she let those scary thoughts swirl in her mind, Sophie clenched her fists even tighter around the leather reins.

"Soph?" her cousin urged cautiously.

"Jack told me. . ." Sophie gulped in air to calm herself. "He said he can't remember anything either—about that day at the Garland dam. He agreed that it must have been so terrible that we blacked out the memory."

"Really?" Laura seemed surprised. "No," she disputed with a shake of her head. "No, Soph. That can't be true. I'm sure he remembers more. He's never actually told me what happened, but he never mentioned any kind of memory loss."

"I don't know, Laur." Sophie really hoped Laura was wrong. "Maybe it was just too painful to talk about. That's how I've felt."

"Why wouldn't he have just asked his sister?"

"You know what April-Rose is like. Who's to say she wouldn't have kept the truth from him, forbid the others from telling him until it would serve her best?"

"Okay. Good point," Laura agreed. "But for twenty whole years? And what about Ella? I doubt April-Rose has any control over her now."

The barrage of possibilities made Sophie feel queasy again. "That's the other thing I wanted to tell you, Laur."

The gravelly mountain track had levelled out in front of them, and Laura halted Wonder so she could meet her cousin's gaze. "Oh no. I don't like the sound of that." As Sophie and Butterscotch neared, Laura reached for the reins. When Sophie handed them over, Laura eased the horses alongside.

"Yeah, it's not good news." Deflated, Sophie sighed. She had wondered how much to tell her cousin. She'd worried about casting Jack in a bad light with the Santoro family. She didn't want Jack's obvious secret-keeping to affect the life he had with them. But after last night, after what felt like yet another lie, Sophie needed someone she could trust to help her work through everything. After Jack had abandoned her and broken her heart all those years ago, the one person who was always there for her was Laura.

She watched her cousin dismount and then attempted a shaky descent of her own. Finally on flat ground, Sophie wobbled unsteadily for a few steps before encouraging Butterscotch to follow Laura and Wonder over to the fenced edge of the Bitterbark Creek lookout.

"Unfortunately, I didn't get anything from Ella." Sophie felt the weight of her disappointment in each word. She had pinned so much hope on discovering more from Ella. Perhaps she gave up too soon?

Laura wrinkled her brow. "Do you think April-Rose is somehow forcing the old clique to keep secrets?"

It wasn't a farfetched accusation, but it still didn't explain Ella's meltdown. "Not exactly." Sophie kicked at the loose stones with the toe of her ebony boot. "Ella wasn't exactly friendly when she recognised me, but she had seemed willing to talk—until Jack walked in."

"What? Jack was there? At the music store?" Laura's mouth was so wide she was in danger of catching flies.

Sophie nodded. It sounded more suspicious every time she said it out loud.

"I thought you were meeting up with him at his cabin later on? What was he doing in Warwick?"

"Buying a record apparently."

It was a weak excuse, but it wasn't that unbelievable. Jack had sounded so sincere. But that didn't mean she had the full story. Had he hoped to speak to Ella before Sophie? But why? Sophie thought of the fear that crossed his handsome face when she'd asked about Ella at the wedding. What was Jack afraid of? Was it Ella? Or what she might say?

"I smell a rat," Laura declared. "It might not be Jack— he's a great guy. It's likely April-Rose. For all we know, she could be manipulating Jack just like she did when they were kids."

Sophie tapped a hand to her chest. "I swear he's afraid of something, Laur. Maybe it is April-Rose? Maybe she's holding something over him? I know he doesn't want to hurt me, any of us. But something is off. I hate to say it, but I really do think he's lying. I just don't understand why."

"Okay." Laura shut her eyes for a second. "Let me get this all sorted out in my head. Ella was willing to talk to you until, low and behold, Jack walks into Warwick Music . . . to buy a record."

"Yes."

Butterscotch chose that moment to nicker and shake her lovely chestnut mane, startling Sophie. She flinched and then patted the horse's neck in apology.

Laura tilted her head in Butterscotch's direction. "I'm no horse whisperer, but I think she's agreeing with us. There's something very odd going on."

"I'm thinking *odd* might be just the tip of the iceberg."

Jack. Ella. Her lost memories. There was definitely a deeper mystery there. Sophie just didn't know how all of it was connected yet. The only way to find out was to dig, but did she have the courage to drag those skeletons to the surface? Sophie wasn't sure.

Turning her attention to the lookout, she took in the incredible scenery before them. She admired the towering indigo mountain range in the distance, the dense green treetops below and all the sprawling honeydew fields of Bitterbark Creek in between. "I could never get tired of this view."

"It is spectacular. But it doesn't quite have the draw of the city, does it? The activity, the nightlife."

"The sirens, the random strangers yelling in the street at all hours of the day or night." Sophie chuckled when her cousin shot her a glare.

"Come on, it's not that bad," Laura groaned.

"Says the woman who's spent little more than a month in an actual city."

"No." Laura waggled a finger at Sophie. "Says the woman whose dream is to become a city-slicker." She smirked as she appraised the picturesque sight. "I'm pretty sure I was born for all that noise, the bright lights and the faster pace. You can have all of this." She waved a hand, engulfing the stunning landscape. "Just give me the commotion and culture of the city."

"You don't mean that, Laur. Would you really give up all of this?" Laura loved Bitterbark Creek. It was her home and always would be, but she had been in awe of the modern and cosmopolitan since childhood. A quiet little town in the country didn't provide all the action she yearned for.

"The city has so many opportunities, cuz. Opportunity to further my career, find my community and maybe even broaden my dating scene. I would always come back here to visit, but I foresee a very happy future in the city one day. I just have to take the leap."

"You'll get there, Laur." Sophie touched her cousin's shoulder reassuringly. "One day very soon."

Laura sighed contentedly and then shot a quizzical look at Sophie. "And what about you? I know how much you love it here. You always have. Could you see yourself moving back?"

"You want to swap places, do you?" Sophie laughed softly.

"It's not a bad idea." Laura winked. "How about it though? What do you see in *your* future?"

Sophie's heart leapt at the thought of living among all this beauty, all the time, and of being so close to Jack. But there was still so much she didn't know. She needed to know what Jack was hiding before she could make such a life-altering decision.

She took a calming breath and tried to think rationally. Could the little town of Moorhenvale offer her the life she longed for? Could Bitterbark Creek be her home once again? It had seemed so unlikely mere days ago. Yet this idyllic sanctuary of woodlands and mountains had ignited something within her that she'd only ever admitted to in dreams. This charming farmstay among the fields and forests had always secretly been her home. Her trauma couldn't take that from her. This was *where she should be*.

Question after question swarmed her. Was home truly where the heart was? And, if so, where would Jack Garland fit? As her friend? Her lover? Maybe something even more? Or would being with him, loving him, make her pay the ultimate price?

That fearful look on Jack's face flashed across her mind again. What was he afraid of? What was he hiding? And would Sophie be able to forgive whatever it was?

Turmoil roiled in her gut. She looked at Laura. "I do love it here, and you're right. I still love so much about Jack. But I'm terrified of making the wrong decision." Shaking her head, Sophie stared out at the wilderness she yearned to call home. "I think the only way I can move forward is by finally facing what happened to me."

CHAPTER 22

The farmstay's timber barn was filled with the pungent scent of dirt, hay and horse manure. Its cathedral ceiling rose high above the stalls, the lighting overhead bouncing off the caramel of the bare wood, warming the interior with a golden glow. At the far end of the building, Snow and Apricot—the remaining horses who were temporarily sharing a pen—could be heard clomping around and whinnying enthusiastically.

Taking a break from mucking out the empty stable, Jack leaned on the handle of his rake and crossed one boot over the other. He wiped the back of his hand over his damp forehead. "Thanks for helping us out today, Dale."

The slightly taller and bulkier man brushed a sweaty palm over the dirtied fabric of his white singlet. "Not a problem, mate. I don't have to be back at the office until next week, and this is the perfect excuse to get away from my ma for a couple of hours."

Jack grinned. "It's been that bad, huh?"

"You've no idea," Dale grunted. "You know how Addy and I took time off to be there for Ma in case she sulked while Marilyn and Pat were honeymooning in Bali?"

Jack nodded.

"Well, it's been nonstop sulking. What's she gonna be like when Addy and I fly the coop? It'll be a full-on meltdown that's what. If that happens, I'm moving interstate."

Jack laughed. "Then you'll really cause a meltdown."

"I know she does it out of love, and I love her too, but does that love have to be so smothering?"

"I'd take smothering over manipulating any day." Jack sighed.

"Sorry, mate." Dale inclined his head apologetically. "Forgot who I was talking to. You really drew the joker when it comes to families, didn't you?"

Jack shrugged and lifted his rake again, tossing soiled straw into the two wheelbarrows beside them. There was no point in brooding. Blood was blood. It was the people he chose to love and spend his time with who really mattered. "I prefer my adoptive family anyway."

"Yeah, the Santoros are awesome. Wish we could all have Marylin's luck in marrying into such a tight-knit clan."

Jack smiled. Marrying into the Santoro family? That would be the ultimate salvation, wouldn't it? And marrying Sophie? That could very well be a dream come true. It was a shame he lied to her when she'd desperately needed the truth.

Damn, he was such an idiot. By trying not to hurt her in the moment, Jack would only hurt her worse down the line. He clenched his jaw and used the exercise of shovelling straw to work through his frustration. How could he fix this? When she found out, would she hate him even more now that he'd straight out lied to her? Although . . . she was returning to the city soon. Maybe she would forget all about it, forget all about him once she returned to her normal life?

His heart sunk at the thought. Jack tried to swallow back the pain, but his throat burned. He scraped harder at the hay littering the cement floor causing the tines of the rake to grate audibly.

"So, Sophie?" Dale began warily. "What's happening

there?"

"Self-sabotage," Jack choked out. Geez, he hated himself for what he'd done to her, the lies he was still telling. He was ruining everything. He should have just told her the truth. But he still couldn't shake off the fear of what would happen when he did.

"What was that?" Dale propped his rake beneath his elbow. "If I'm being too nosey, mate, just tell me."

With a groan, Jack stopped working and scratched a hand through his tousled hair. "No, Dale. It's fine. Maybe talking will help."

Dale slapped a hand against Jack's arm. "I'm here for you, buddy. Get it off your chest."

Jack grimaced. Would his friend feel the same way if he knew just how horrible a person Jack really was? "I think I've done something unforgivable."

"Like what? You dating someone else?"

"No. Nothing like that." Jack rubbed his brow, feeling a tension headache building there. "I lied to Sophie about something important. Something *very* important to her."

"So? Fix it." Dale shrugged as though the solution was a simple one. "Tell her the truth."

"She may never speak to me again." Just saying those words had Jack's heart constricting. He couldn't bear to lose Sophie.

Dale cocked an eyebrow. "Do you think she'll talk to you again if she finds out the truth somewhere down the track? Or if she hears it from someone else?"

"No," Jack grumbled. How had his friend become so clever all of a sudden?

"Then do the right thing."

Jack groaned. His stomach was knotted with regret. "I'm worried it won't be that easy, Dale, and that. . ." He hesitated and stared down the corridor towards the open barn door and the bright sunlight beyond. "And . . ." Jack couldn't bring himself to say it—it hurt too much.

"And what?" Dale probed. "You think she won't be able

to handle it? That she won't understand?"

"No." Jack's voice wobbled.

"What then?"

"I think she'll leave." Each word cut painfully into his heart.

"I thought she was supposed to be leaving tomorrow anyway? Aren't her and her mum heading back to the city?"

"It's not just the leaving I'm worried about." Jack's shoulders slumped. "What if I tell her the truth and I never see her again? What if she never talks to me again? I just got her back, Dale. After twenty long years. I couldn't bear to lose her like that again." He groaned in frustration and rubbed his hand across his eyes, trying to relieve the tension building behind them. "I want her to stay, damn it. She's too important to me. I want her in my life. Now I've gone and ruined it all by lying."

It may have been wrong of him to hope for Sophie to stay, may have been a selfish wish, but he was the happiest he'd ever been now that Sophie was back. He didn't care if his mother and sister turned on him, or if encouraging Sophie to stay in Moorhenvale led her to discover all their secrets. He needed her to stay. He longed for them to grow closer, for this relationship blossoming between them to become something even more special. But then he'd wrecked it by telling her such a ridiculous lie. No doubt she knew he was full of crap.

Oh god. What if she had already left town without telling him? Jack clutched his chest as anguish sliced through. *Don't be silly*, he told himself, forcing himself to breathe. There was still the big family dinner planned for that evening.

"Wow." Dale blew out a breath as the horses in the far stall nickered excitedly. "You went to a dark place there, mate. You're really stuck on Sophie, aren't you? I'm so sorry. I didn't realise." He clasped Jack's shoulder reassuringly. "This is serious, then. It needs to be handled a little more delicately."

"You're telling me." But was there anything he could do?

Maybe he really was a true Garland, like his mother had said. Evil and heartless just like his sister.

"What's so serious?" Nick Santoro's booming voice erupted behind them, drawing their attention to the small internal office down the opposite corridor. Nick shut the office door and strode over to them.

"I'll let you field that question on your own, mate," Dale murmured.

Jack shot his cheeky friend a look. "Thanks a lot."

"So, what is it then? Something I should be worried about?" Nick stuck his thumbs through the belt loops of his jeans and looked over their hard work. "You boys are doing a great job. I really appreciate the help, especially while Pat's away and we've still got so many wedding guests around. Hopefully that will change tomorrow when most of them head home."

"That's actually what we were talking about," Dale piped up, flicking Jack a proud grin as though salvaging his role as the supportive friend. "The guests heading home." He poked an elbow into Jack's ribs. "It might be nice if some of them could stay, don't you think?"

Nick passed a look between Dale and Jack. "It's always nice to have family visit," he agreed, "but *visit* is the operative word. I'm not sure life would be quite the same with my mama running around the farm."

Jack chuckled at the thought of little Nonna Isola roaming around the fields in gumboots and a flannel shirt, utter chaos in her wake. The image eased some of the tension in his tight shoulders.

"But Sophie?" Dale prodded, and received an instant glare from Jack.

"Sophie?" Nick studied the two younger men. "Of course, I would love Sophie to stay. She is my other heart, my other daughter." His dark eyes sparkled. "Sophie." He chortled, gaiety illuminating his angular features. "Pardon me for not catching on immediately." Then he shifted and directed his next question to Jack. "You're hoping Sophie will stay?"

Jack shot another glower at Dale. Some friend he was.

Over the last year, Nick Santoro had become like a father figure to Jack. He was a strong and dependable man who'd offered Jack the support and encouragement his own father had never provided. Jack valued Nick's opinions and advice and didn't want to disappoint him. Until now, he hadn't considered what Nick may think of his growing relationship with Sophie. What if Nick disapproved? That was another chink in Jack's already weakening armour.

He bit his lower lip as he sought the right words. "Do you think it might be something she'd consider? Staying, I mean. Staying here?"

Nick's jolly countenance fractured for an instant as he ruminated over the question. Then he beamed. "Of course, Jack. Sophie loves it here—always has. It might take some convincing on our part, but her mum's been telling me how much good it's doing her." He nodded decisively. "We'll see what we can do to encourage her to stick around."

"You can ask her tonight, Jack," Dale advised smugly, as if he were a problem-solver extraordinaire. "At dinner. Didn't you tell me the family was getting together?"

"Good point." Nick nodded. "It's a perfect opportunity."

Jack sighed. "And what if she says no?" God, just the thought . . . He tightened his grip on the rake to distract himself from the pain.

Nick squeezed the younger man's shoulder supportively. "I wouldn't worry about it, Jack. Like I said, our Sophie loves it here. But if it happens, *we'll* think of something to turn her decision around." He shared a conspiratorial wink with Dale. "You should come too, Dale. For our Jack's moral support. Bring Camille. You know how Robbie loves to entertain."

Dale grimaced at Camille's name. "Do I have to?"

Nick tilted his head. "No, but it would be the nice thing to do. Especially while her best friend is out of the country.

If you like, you can tell her you were entrusted to invite her on my behalf."

Dale's glum expression caused a tickle of good humour to bubble up inside Jack. "Maybe this is a prime opportunity for both of us, buddy? I'll help you with your problem if you help me with mine?"

"Deal." Dale snatched Jack's hand and shook it forcibly. "I'm holding you to that, mate."

So it was decided. Nausea bubbled in Jack's stomach. Would Sophie agree to stay at Bitterbark Creek? He chewed his lower lip again. He couldn't think about the alternative. He had to show her how much she meant to him, how desperately he wanted her to stay.

The merry sound of laughter drew the attention of the younger men, snapping them free of their thoughts. They looked over at Nick to see a huge grin splitting his face.

"Between the guests and your shenanigans, it's going to be one interesting night."

Jack and Dale shot each other a look, but they didn't challenge Nick's prophecy. The night would either go very well or very, very badly.

CHAPTER 23

Stretched across the emerald lawn in front of Bitterbark Creek's homestead was a long timber refectory table. It was dressed with a patterned table runner, elegant place settings and a multitude of condiments and beverages. Sophie admired the colourful paper lanterns strung overhead and around the building's veranda. Their soft illumination complemented the moon in the star-speckled sky. Guests crowded around the table as the delicious scents and inviting lights drew them like curious insects to a flame. Their buzzing chatter, rising and falling jovially, diffused the stillness of the evening until the piercing tinkle of a silver bell carved all sound into silence.

Aunt Robin was poised at the top of the wooden stairs of the ranch-style house, tucking the bell into her apron. The family's two obedient farm dogs watched from their beds beside her as she lifted a huge platter of barbequed meats, presenting it to the masses below. She waited until she had everyone's attention and then grinned. "Tucker's ready."

Sophie's mother and a short grey-haired woman—Robin's sister Barbara—followed Robin to the dinner table. Each carried their own porcelain platters of cooked meat and meat alternatives.

On the outer edge of the small crowd, Sophie and Laura huddled close.

"Mum loves to make an entrance," her cousin whispered. "She should have been an entertainer. She treats that veranda like a stage."

"I seem to remember us doing something similar as kids." Sophie smirked.

Laura poked her thumb in Aunt Robin's direction. "That's probably where we got the idea."

"Hey." Jack's deep, smoky voice rumbled beside them. "Where are you two ladies sitting?"

"Yeah, can we sit with you?" Dale made a subtle gesture at Camille, who was still chatting with Uncle Nick. "She's a nice gal and she means well, but I'm already exhausted."

"What if we don't want to entertain *your* guest?" Laura protested.

"Aw, Laur." Dale sidled up to her and wrapped an arm around her shoulders before slipping it around her neck in a loose headlock. "You ain't got a choice, because that's what *friends* do for each other."

Laura wiggled as Dale lightly scrubbed the top of her head with his knuckles until she worked herself free. "Jerk," she snarled, and landed a punch on his shoulder, causing a small cry of pain to briefly interrupt his smug laughter. Grinning at her victory, Laura led Sophie to the far end of the table. "Fine, you can sit with us." The words were thrown over her shoulder. "Next time just remember the magic words."

"Pretty please?" Dale fluttered his eyelashes coquettishly.

"No," Jack amended. "Tim-Tams."

Laura winked at him and slumped into a chair. "Who knows their sister from another mister?"

Jack beamed at that and caught Sophie's eye. She smiled back at him. She could almost forget he was hiding something from her. She was always so much more content when he was around. He brought out the best in her.

Sophie thought of Jack's kisses, his touch, and longed to be wrapped in his arms. She had tried to be careful, but in truth, she'd already lost her heart to him again. He'd swept her off her feet the first day she'd seen him all shirtless and sweaty, and then every time after.

As Sophie took a seat beside her cousin, allowing the men to sit opposite, an excited squeak from Camille startled her.

"Ooh, lucky me." The young woman skipped over to them, her summery dress swaying. "I get to be head of the table." She grasped Dale's hand as she plopped down.

Laura choked back laughter when Dale gently snatched his hand away.

"Friends, Cami. You agreed," he told her.

She shrugged innocently. "There's nothing unfriendly about holding hands."

"It's not the unfriendly I'm worried about," he groaned. "It's the too friendly."

"You can never be *too* friendly." Camille giggled.

When Dale rolled his eyes, Sophie and Jack swapped amused glances.

Again, the shrill tinkling of the little dinner bell sliced through their conversation, drawing their attention along the refectory table to where the older guests were seated.

Uncle Nick gestured towards his elderly mother and offered the group an apologetic smile. "Nonna has kindly requested to say grace over our lovely meal. Would everyone please take a moment and join hands?"

Around the table, Sophie's friends, family and other guests linked fingers. Her eyes found Jack. For a fleeting instant, he hesitated, casting a look in her direction as though wishing to take her hand instead, before finally closing the circle.

"For some of you, this might be an old-fashioned tradition," Nonna began, throwing a knowing look at Sophie's end of the table. "However, when we find ourselves surrounded by such good people and delicious food, it is only right that we show our gratitude."

Sophie met Jack's tender smile with one of her own. She was very grateful to have him back in her life. She wasn't ready to go home, but at least this time they would stay in touch.

Unless she chose to stay? Sophie had been ruminating over the possibility for a while now. Staying in town would give her more time with Jack, and more time to uncover any secrets from her past. But she hadn't decided. She hadn't even broached the topic with her mother, let alone the rest of the family. Would they even support her, especially if they knew what she planned to do during her stay? She doubted her mother would be okay with her poking around in old trauma. Angelica preferred to live in the present and focus on the future. But Sophie needed to put the past to rest before she could properly move forward. She looked at the other end of the table, where the elders of her family were seated. Sophie didn't want to hurt any of them, but she truly felt that this was something she had to do.

When Nonna bowed her head in prayer, many guests followed suit. A few chose to just close their eyes or look on.

"Blessed are we in health, in love and in life," Nonna praised. "We thank Almighty God for this fruitful bounty and for everything thy goodness has bestowed. In his name, Christ, our Lord. Amen."

"*Amen.*" It was an almost unanimous chorus from the attendees.

"Namaste." Camille pressed her hands into prayer and bowed, garnering inquisitive looks from those seated nearby.

"Namaste?" Laura questioned. "Let me guess, you're trying out Hinduism?"

At the opposite end of the table, chatter resumed and the clink and scrape of cutlery on dishes commenced.

Camille frowned. "No. Yoga."

Laura caught Sophie's eye and winced.

"There's this fabulous new place in Warwick. They do hot yoga," Camille explained. "I heard somewhere that it's supposed to sweat the fat right out of you."

"I don't think that's how it works, Camille," Dale said, piling meat onto his plate.

"Sure, it does. I've already lost a kilo and I've only been doing it for two weeks. Oh, that reminds me." Camille jolted and pointed at Jack. "What's the goss with Bradley and Tiffany? Isn't he engaged to your sister?"

Jack picked at a bread roll. "As far as I'm aware. The engagement party is the Saturday after next."

"Well. . ." Camille purred eagerly, leaning forward as if to divulge a secret. "Last Wednesday—after my hot yoga class—I saw them eating dinner together at Ronaldo's, the Italian place over on Grafton Street. They looked pretty cosy."

Laura scooped out a ladle of green bean salad. "How *cosy*?"

"I only watched them for a moment, but I saw Tiffany whisper something to Bradley. By the way his eyes lit up, it didn't seem like they were talking about the weather."

"They were probably talking about the upcoming engagement party." Dale pointed a roast chicken leg at Jack. "Aren't they both helping April-Rose plan the thing?"

Jack nodded apathetically.

"There you go, Camille." Dale gestured his greasy hand at Jack in validation. "A man and woman can go out and do things together without it having to mean anything romantic or sexual. Look at what people say about us, and we're just *friends*." He emphasised the word.

"But this was more than just friends, Dale. They were having dinner together. Just the *two* of them," Camille said, as if that proved everything. When Dale didn't concede, she pleaded with Laura and Sophie for support. "You agree with me, right? It's weird for a guy and girl to have dinner alone together at a nice restaurant if they're just friends.

Something else is going on."

Laura shrugged. "From what I've heard around town about the two of them, it wouldn't surprise me to learn it wasn't an innocent dinner."

"See." Camille threw a defiant look at Dale.

"That doesn't prove anything, Camille," Dale argued around a mouthful of food.

"Whatever. You agree though, don't you, Sophie?"

Sophie chose her answer carefully. She knew Jack loathed his family connection, but she didn't want to say anything that might upset him. "I think it's likely none of our business, but who knows what they're up to? Maybe karma has finally come for April-Rose."

At that, Camille snorted with laughter. "*Karma*. Is that a yoga joke? Oh, I like you, Sophie. We need to keep you around."

Laura applauded. "You tell her, Cami. I think she ought to grace us country bumpkins with her presence for a while longer."

Sophie laughed. Had she been that obvious during their horse ride? She knew Laura loved having her around, but now, with a mystery to solve, she seemed more keen than ever.

"You know my man Jack will back that." Dale angled the neck of his beer at his friend. "He's been walking on cloud nine ever since Sophie arrived."

The group fell silent as their attention zeroed in on Jack. Sophie was sure he wanted her to stay too, but a part of her feared rejection. She glanced up at him nervously. When he met her gaze, the tenderness in his expression warmed her insides.

Camille eyed the two of them. "What's going on here then? Looks like Cupid's been working his magic," she teased.

"Don't go jinxing it, Cami," Dale chided. "I don't want Jack holding me accountable for what might have been."

"You're such a worrywart." The petite blonde snorted.

"Anyone with eyes can see that they're smitten with each other. I just want them to admit it." Camille moved her wine glass aside to lean further across the table. "So, what do you say, Sophie? Do you fancy young mister Garland here?"

Sophie saw Jack cringe at the use of his surname. It tugged something deep in her heart. She wished she could take his pain and embarrassment away. He really was a Garland only in name. Seeing him vulnerable like that had her feeling brave and she wanted to protect him. Sophie decided to follow her heart.

"Actually, Camille, I'm pretty sure Jack and I are dating."

Jack brightened. "We are?" His voice was hushed, so innocent that Sophie wanted to climb across the table and into his arms to reassure him.

"Dating?" Laura hooted. "Finally, she admits it."

Sophie laughed.

Dale pumped his fist into the air in celebration. "Yeah, baby." He swatted Jack on the back, making his friend blush.

Camille reached over and whacked Dale's shoulder. "See? I was right."

"Ow." He sulked. "Fine. Okay. Whatever. You were right."

She frowned pensively and then grinned. "That could mean I'm also right about Bradley and Tiffany?"

"Not a chance, Cami," Dale grumbled. "That's just girly superstition."

"*Girly superstition*." Laura snorted. "I didn't realise there was such a thing."

As Laura and Camille went into teasing attack mode against Dale, Sophie studied Jack. His grin was still so bright, but he looked as though he couldn't quite believe it, like her declaration was a dream come true. Her heart swelled and her fingers were itching to touch him. In that moment, all her fears disappeared. She knew the real Jack. He was still that handsome little boy who had read her stories when the summer storms rolled in, who had snuck her extra chocolate cake when she'd been sick, who had kissed her in secret down by the creek.

When the group erupted in laughter again, Sophie and Jack joined in, the sound of their shared happiness drifting up into the midnight-blue sky.

CHAPTER 24

The glowing moon caressed the ground with pale light as a lone cloud skirted its rim. Although bright, it was no match for the towering trees edging Gap Creek, where slippery amphibians and energetic insects serenaded the flowing waters. As Jack waved the lit torch over the dark, pebbly path, a flash of headlights and the crunch of gravel drew his attention back towards the main house. Gripping Sophie's hand tighter, he tugged her away from the road. She skipped quickly to his side, careful not to drop the rolled tartan blanket clutched under her other arm. Headlights blinded them as a silver station wagon approached, the double-toot of its horn spearing through the gentle noises of the night.

"Have a good one," Robin's brother-in-law hollered, waving through the open window as he and Barbara rolled on by.

Jack had barely returned the gesture before a second engine rumbled behind them. The Santoros' stocky red and black farm utility vehicle approached, front lamps dazzlingly bright. It paused beside them, motor spluttering as it idled.

"You two behave yourselves now," Nick bellowed over the clamour. "You've heard Angie's story about how Sophie was conceived by this creek."

Feminine laughter bubbled from the seat beside him. Moonlight sparkled off Angelica's grin. "Your uncle's a cheeky one, darling. Ignore him and enjoy your evening."

Nick beeped the horn in farewell and sped off, the vehicle bouncing over the rough terrain.

"Goodnight," Jack and Sophie called in unison.

"I thought you were the bad influence," Sophie told Jack." She giggled. "Clearly I underestimated my own family." She skipped forward, pulling him along.

Jack beamed at her and quickened his step. He'd been in seventh heaven ever since she'd said they were dating. It felt like he was dreaming. He knew Sophie still didn't fully trust him, that she had every reason not to, but it made him adore her even more knowing she was willing to take a chance on him.

There had been no perfect time to tell her the truth that evening. Then she'd kissed him, quickly and sweetly, and asked him to come with her to look at the stars. That kiss was all he could think about now, all he wanted to think about. He desperately wanted to do it again, to curl her into his arms. Now that they were all alone, in the dark, his restraint was waning.

"Where are you taking me, Soph?" Jack aimed the torchlight ahead, illuminating the path and the trees alongside the creek. "To the most secluded spot on the property?"

"Maybe." She flashed him a cheeky grin. "Would that be such a bad thing?"

"No." Jack chuckled and pulled her into his arms. "But I don't think I can wait." He snuck forward and kissed her. The delicious taste of her, the softness of her touch, made him ache for more. Yet when he deepened the kiss, she pulled away with a laugh.

"They say good things come to those who wait," she teased, and then hurried away, out of his reach.

Jack chased after her. His heart thudded against his ribs

in excitement. Amusement fizzed between them as they shared glance after glance, smirk after smirk, on the verge of laughter. Yet Sophie never quite let him catch her. Jack felt mischievous and secretive, but in only the best way, a feeling he hadn't felt in such a long time. The tension between them was electric and Jack couldn't wait for it to snap.

They reached the green clearing in front of Jack's cabin—a secluded spot over the rise—just as the buzz of sexual energy peaked and prickled in the air around them. Sophie managed to drape the patterned blanket over the spongy grass at their feet before Jack threw the torch to the ground and spun her into his arms.

She yelped in surprise when he pressed his lips to hers again, but swiftly returned his hungry kiss. Sophie's rapid heartbeat matched the pounding of his own as their mouths and tongues danced to a sensual rhythm. When he allowed his hands to wander, to grasp the firmness of her bottom and the sleek arch of her lower back, he felt Sophie do the same. The sensation of it all built an insatiable eagerness in him, a desperation to touch more of her, to feel her bare skin against his.

With a hand at her waist, Jack guided her down to the ground and felt her smile into the kiss as he stretched weightily overtop. As he pressed himself against her, the flimsy material of her slitted skirt shifted, and she opened her long legs to embrace him. When their bodies connected, she gasped into his mouth, but then pressed a hand to his chest, gently pushing him upwards to look into his eyes. Reluctantly, Jack rolled onto his side.

"Jack," she panted. Her expression became more serious as she stared up at him. Her kiss-swollen lips only added to her beauty in the glow of the moonlight. Unable to help himself, Jack stole another peck. He relished the way Sophie's lips readily greeted him before she pulled away again. "Jack." She laughed this time.

"Yes, Soph?" he asked innocently, even though the devil

in him ached to kiss her again.

"I never actually asked you if you were happy that I'm staying." She glanced away, furrowing her brow. "Dale said what he said, so I just assumed. . ."

As her voice trailed off, Jack chuckled slightly. "Soph, does it look like I'm unhappy?" He cocked an eyebrow when she looked at him again, and she laughed.

"No, but it's good to hear you say it."

He leaned close, letting his lips flutter over hers. "Well then, hear this. I want you to stay for as long as you want. Forever if you want to." He kissed her briefly. "Or, at least until your aunt and uncle kick you out." He winked.

"Nice," she scoffed, shaking her head.

"Hey." He shrugged nonchalantly. "When that time comes you can move in with me?" He'd let the words fall playfully, but they weren't a joke to him. He swallowed nervously as he waited for her response.

Sophie must have seen through his charade, because her gaze softened and she lifted her head to return his kisses with a peck of her own. "I couldn't think of anything more perfect," she whispered. Then she kissed him again and pulled him closer, until he was lying across her once more.

Jack allowed her to take the lead and lost himself in the kiss—the way Sophie swirled her tongue, the velvet caress of her lips, how she tunnelled her fingernails through his hair. He enjoyed feeling her desire, her longing for him. It reassured him that he wasn't the only one whose feelings were so intense, who felt that they were meant for so much more together. That they belonged together. Sophie wanted him too.

When she slid on top of him, legs astride, he was already painfully hard and aching for her. He stroked his fingers along her burgundy cotton blouse and over her patterned skirt before pushing the fabric higher and baring the silkiness of her thighs. Slipping his hands beneath the material, Jack filled his palms with the lush curves he found there.

Sophie moaned into his mouth. When she shifted her hips eagerly, pressing herself against him, it shot a pang of desperate yearning through the length of him. Jack groaned, feeling breathless, but hungry for more. He snuck his hands beneath the hem of her shirt and found her perfect breasts bound only by delicate lace. Brushing his thumbs over each sensitive nipple, Jack coaxed them to hardened peaks. He yearned to lick them, to taste them. Sophie gasped at the sensation and broke their kiss, seeking his hands and covering them with her own as she arched her back.

"We don't have to stay here," Jack told her, his voice hoarse. "We can go inside."

"No." Sophie shifted against him, making him groan. "If I move, I'll think." She kissed him, nipping at his lower lip. "And right now, I don't want to think. I want you."

Those three words rang triumphantly in Jack's ears, like the ding-ding-ding of the victory bell when besting a game at the local fair. It wasn't quite *I love you*, but it was a step in the right direction.

"I want you too, Soph," he admitted, hoping she could hear the adoration in each word.

Hugging her close, Jack rolled her beneath him until he was once again nestled between her thighs. He kissed her passionately, sucking the breath from her in carnal moans. Sophie pulled at his shirt, yanking it up over his head and tossing it aside before unfastening his jeans. Jack skimmed his fingers down her ribs, over her hips, then hooked the lace of her panties and tore the garment from her thighs.

He snatched a foil packet from his back pocket and slipped on some protection before he lost himself completely. Then Sophie was touching him, stroking him, caressing him with her fingers as she pushed his pants lower. He ached with hunger for her and almost growled when she opened to him and wrapped those incredible legs around him. As he found her centre, a dewy heaven, he drove inside and they gasped together, floating on the same cloud of ecstasy.

She was utter perfection, everything he had ever longed for, the one person who had always felt like home to him. A twin soul. And now she was his again. *His* Sophie.

Spellbound by the feel of her in his arms, the way she reacted to him and the intensity of their embrace—their pulsating rhythm building faster, harder—Jack surrendered to the pleasure and contentment of it all as the fireworks of ecstasy burst within him.

Sometime later, still cuddled peacefully in a tangle of limbs, Jack and Sophie admired the sky above them. With the torch out and the moon's once radiant shine declining, the dark sky had filled with an opulence of sparkling stars. A tawny frogmouth whooped from a nearby thicket of trees, harmonising with the whisper of cool wind and the whooshing flow of water over the riverbed.

When Sophie lovingly snuggled closer, euphoria—stronger than he'd ever felt before—overwhelmed Jack and he thought his heart might fly right out of his chest. He longed to spend all night, every night like this. To have Sophie cuddled in his arms amid the tranquil wilderness of his new home.

He was already in love with her, wasn't he? He had fallen head over heels the moment he saw her again. Nothing could have stopped it from happening. It felt meant to be.

As Jack reminisced about their initial meeting, he remembered the call from his sister that followed. Fear struck his heart. What would April-Rose and his mother think of this revelation? They'd never forgive him . . . but he'd found his perfect family, his perfect partner in life.

Would these perfect people still love him once they learn the truth? The thought came unbidden, and Jack stiffened. No matter how much he loved them all, no matter how much he'd tried to change, it might not be enough.

"What just happened? Your heart's dancing." Sophie tapped his bare chest lightly, mimicking the palpitations. "What are you thinking, Jack?"

He propped himself up. "Only good things, I promise." He wished it was true.

"Hmm. Pretty vague answer." She swirled a fingernail over the sensitive skin around his nipple, making him flinch. "What is it with you Garlands and secrets? Maybe I'll just have to coax it out of you?" She brushed her lips against his chest, covering that taut pink protrusion, now hard and erect.

At the twist of her tongue, Jack inhaled sharply, feeling the sensation much lower on his body. When she released him and shot him a challenging look, he laughed. "It's not a secret, Soph." He stroked the silk of her golden hair. "Not really."

"Well then?" she said, sensing his hesitation.

He kissed her forehead, partially in placation, but mostly out of adoration. "I was thinking that I didn't realise I would feel this way." *Not so soon*, he added silently.

"What way?" she inquired, oblivious to what he was thinking.

God, could he really say it out loud? Jack kissed the tip of her nose. "That I'm. . ." He cleared his throat. It was too early, wasn't it? What if he scared her away?

"That you're what, Jack?" Sophie propped herself up so that she could look at him more clearly.

To hell with it, he thought. *Better to say it now than regret remaining silent later.*

Jack cupped her cheek, caressing the velvet skin there with his thumb as he gazed into Sophie's beautiful eyes. "That I think I'm in love with you," he told her. He pressed his lips to hers and let the electricity of their connection make his case.

When he finally released her mouth, kissing her chin and cheeks for good measure, Jack could feel that the beat of Sophie's heart had quickened. He smiled and nuzzled her nose with his. "You don't have to say anything in return," he reassured her affectionately. "I just needed you to know."

She stared up at him, her expression unreadable, almost

mesmerised, and then finally smiled at him. "I love you too, Jack," she said, her voice hushed as though she were afraid to say the words aloud. "I think I always have."

Jack's heart warmed. He felt the same way.

CHAPTER 25

Although the blush of sunrise had blossomed along the horizon, like a bruise from a blow thrown in the battle of daybreak, the night was not yet ready to concede defeat. Sensing that the presence of morning was just over the mountains in the east, the kookaburras stirred and began to croon their ode to the coming sunlight. Hoping to arrive ahead of the light to avoid detection, Sophie flitted from her romantic tryst with Jack on bare tiptoes through the crisp grassy field, towards her quiet little cabin.

While Jack had offered to escort her home, Sophie hadn't been prepared to tackle any probing questions had they found themselves discovered. Their affection for each other was hardly a secret, but she hadn't told her mother about her decision to stay. Sophie hadn't considered how staying might affect her life back in Brisbane, and she wasn't ready to discuss how her temporary life would work here. Should she extend her leave or work remotely? How would she shop for groceries or return to her apartment in the city without her mother's car? She was sure a good sleep would help her solve those more practical issues, if only she could make it to her bed.

Sneaking a glance over her shoulder, Sophie spied Jack's

silhouette lingering on the rise, watching her, waiting for her to arrive safely at the cabin. Just the sight of him warmed her heart, eliciting another grin as every cell in her wearied but sated body demanded to head back. She had considered lingering in his arms and spending the morning together at his cabin, but she knew that would have aroused more suspicion.

It had been difficult to unlatch herself from his embrace long enough to put this short distance between them. Even now, she ached to be near him and could feel every nerve tingling like sputtering fireworks at the thought. As if in answer to her own feelings, Jack stepped forward. That small movement made her smile, pleased that he too felt the pull between them. Reluctantly, she gestured for him to stop. Returning to her mission and concerned the dawning sun might shine a different light on their magical evening, Sophie quickened her pace. Memories of their night together flooded her mind.

He'd said I love you, and she'd bravely returned his affection. Was it sensible? Probably not, but she had never really stopped loving him. Not even after the accident, when he withdrew from her and she was sure her love had turned to hate. At least now she knew why, knew that his family was to blame. Jack's mother may have tried to fill her children with hatred, but his love for her—their love for each other—had flickered on inside like a candle refusing to go out.

With a sigh, Sophie mounted the stairs to her cabin. Slipping the key into the lock, she opened the door and crossed the threshold into the blackness inside. Her bare foot slid on something papery, startling her. She snatched an ivory rectangle from the polished floorboards and shut the door behind her. It was a simple envelope. She switched on the small light above the kitchen sink and flipped the envelope over to reveal her name scrawled on the front. Intrigued, she opened it and read the scribbled handwriting on the lined page.

Sophie,
I want to talk. It's time you knew the truth. Meet me at 9 p.m. tomorrow. Our old hideout. Don't tell anyone and come alone.
E.

"E?" Sophie could think of only one person. "Ella?"

Strange, she thought. Ella was so adamant in her refusal to speak to her. What had made her change her mind?

Sophie gnawed at her lower lip as a cyclone of emotions swirled within her. She desperately wanted to know the truth but was also terrified. If Jack was involved . . . she wasn't ready to lose him after finally reconnecting. She loved him, but would she be able to forgive him?

She fought to catch her breath as her vision clouded with tears. A salty droplet landed on the letter, smearing the ink as it spread. Having the truth within her grasp should have made her happy. Sophie had hoped for answers for so long. She scrubbed at her eyes, tossing her tears on the floor with a violent shake of her hand. She'd been in limbo for twenty years, an empty black hole weighing down her heart. Of course her emotions were all over the place. Sleeping with Jack, confessing their love for one another, had only made her more vulnerable, pulled her in too many directions.

"Sophie?" The hoarse voice snapped her thoughts free of their spiral.

Her mother stood at the edge of the kitchen, her features only half-lit in the lamplight. She regarded Sophie blearily. "Oh, darling, what's wrong?" Angelica glided forward and stretched her arms wide, catching Sophie in a tight embrace.

It was too much. Sophie gave in to the outpouring of emotion. Violent sobs shook through her until her throat was painfully raw. Tears drenched her cheeks and soaked into her mother's hair and nightgown, but still Angelica held her close. When Sophie finally started to settle, she searched for an explanation as to why she was so distraught at this odd, dark hour. But as she pulled away, she felt Angelica touch the letter still clutched in her hand.

"What is this, sweetheart?"

Sophie locked her fingers around the paper. "It's something Jack gave me," she lied, her voice raspy. She knew her mother would disapprove. Angelica preferred to focus on their future. "He wants me to stay in town a while longer." She pressed a hand to her heart as she hiccuped another sob. "It's okay, Mum. These are happy tears, that's all."

Angelica crinkled her brow and smoothed her fingers over Sophie's cheek, brushing back loose waves of silky sunlight-coloured hair. The intensity of her mother's stare nearly brought on another onslaught of sobs, but Sophie fought them back.

"Really, Mum." Sophie tugged the letter free of her mother's grip. "Everything's fine." She forced a smile. "Happy tears, see?"

"Happy tears," her mother parroted with a nod, but the suspicious lilt in her voice betrayed her. "So, are you going to stay, darling? Or are you just happy Jackson asked you to?"

"Both, probably." Sophie tucked the letter safely back into the envelope. "You know how much I love Bitterbark Creek, but it also means a lot that Jack wants me here with him."

"You like him, don't you?" Angelica smirked. When Sophie didn't answer immediately, she continued, "What's not to like? He's a lovely boy."

"I know he is, Mum." Sophie fought the urge to roll her eyes at her mother's matchmaking. It was definitely too early to tell her that they'd shared the L-word. If Angelica knew that, she'd have them engaged and married in no time.

"Oh, Sophia," Angelica chided. "Admit you like him. You always have. There's no harm in that."

Sophie shook her head in amusement. Did everyone know? "I think it's time I go to bed, don't you?" She brushed a kiss on her mother's cheek. "Goodnight, Mum."

"Sophie?" her mother implored, but Sophie kept on walking.

She ignored her mother's repeated *Sophie? Soph? Sophia?* and headed for her bedroom and the rest and rejuvenation it offered. Heaven knew she needed the energy to face the coming evening with Ella.

It was that meeting that occupied Sophie's thoughts well into the following afternoon, even as she floated peacefully atop the liquid horizon of the swimming pool, swirling her fingers and toes to create a ripple of weak waves with glittery tips. The hot noon sun lounged overhead, its white-gold beams blinding when they hit the slick terracotta tiling or the shimmering water. By the far end, a couple of yellow wasps raced each other along the water's edge, bouncing on the cool fluid like rubber balls before flitting away, only to swerve around and go again.

At the click of the gate and the clink of glass against glass, Sophie righted herself and turned around. She had a split second to notice a fresh pitcher of virgin mojito mix on the table before Laura barrelled towards her.

"Bombs away!" her cousin yelled, launching herself skyward and pulling her knees to her chest. She hit the water with a *thwack*, creating a small tsunami of whitecaps that washed over the deck. Sophie clutched at the side, dragging herself to the shallows while she waited for the surge to die down. Boris and Banjo circled the pool, pressing close against the fence line and yipping their excitement and desire to be included.

Bursting back through the roiling surface, Laura shook her head, shooting spray in all directions like tiny damp bullets. "So, where were we?" She slicked back her short hair and blew the water from her nose. "That's right. You said Ella snuck onto our property in the middle of the night to leave you a little love letter."

Sophie perched on the pool's underwater step. "Not quite, Laur. It's supposed to be a secret, so indoor voice, please."

"But we're outdoors?"

Sophie scowled. She didn't want her mum or aunt and uncle or—God forbid—Jack to overhear. She already felt as though she was somehow betraying him by going through with meeting Ella. Should she be on his side, supporting him after Ella's furious reaction at the music store?

"Don't fret, cuz. I'm good at this cloak-and-dagger stuff. That's why I'll be coming with you tonight."

"Pardon?" That had not been part of Sophie's plan.

Laura swam closer. "I'm not letting you go alone again, Soph. Don't worry, I'll keep my fedora and trench coat away from the glow of any streetlights. She'll never know I'm there."

"There aren't any streetlights where we're meeting, Laur." Sophie huffed. "Besides, you just want to go to get a good look at her."

"Of course I do." Laura smacked at the water distractedly. "Where are you going where there aren't any streetlights? Where is this *old hideout* anyway?"

Sophie swirled her feet in the sun-streaked depths below her. "The woods behind Ella's mother's cabin."

"The woods?" Laura shrieked. "Now I'm definitely going with you."

"What, you weren't serious before?" Sophie teased.

"Don't be cute, Soph. We're talking about *the woods* here, the birthplace of many gory horror movies. Do you really think it's a good idea to go trekking through the wilderness in the dead of night?"

Sophie whirled her feet around faster, creating a surge of bubbles that spiralled upwards and ruptured when they reached the open air. "It's only nine—not *the dead of night*— and I'll be fine. We're meeting at the troll's cave. We camped out there a couple of times as kids. It's not far from the cabin. You can see the lights through the trees."

Mouth agape, Laura slapped the water again. "Now there's trolls? Sophie, maybe neither of us should be attending this potential massacre?"

"Laura," Sophie reproached, biting back a laugh.

"Laura what?" her cousin grumbled. "Laura, please come with me to the big, scary woods in the middle of the night, to find the cave where the trolls live?" She crossed her arms over her navy bikini. "Well, I'm just not sure anymore. It might take some begging on your part." Laura shot her a sulky expression.

"So what, it's fine to skulk around Bitterbark Creek at all hours of the night, but the thought of going into the forest turns you chicken?"

Laura shook her head with indignation. "Ella's mad. I'm sane. There's a difference."

"I think I'd need to see proof on both accounts to agree." Sophie laughed and then raised her arms for protection as Laura splashed water at her.

"For all your rudeness—I'm glad you decided to stay." Laura swam closer and sat next to Sophie on the underwater step. "Though I'd prefer if your decision had more to do with wanting to spend time with your beloved family rather than longing for more hanky-panky with Jack." Seeing Sophie's surprise, Laura bumped their damp shoulders together affectionately. "Speaking of hanky-panky, how was last night? Did you *look at the stars together*?" Laura made googly eyes at her.

With a playful shove, Sophie pushed Laura off the step and into the depths, making her cousin laugh and hop on tiptoe to regain her balance.

"That's answer enough for me." Laura beamed. "So, was it worth the wait? Are you all smitten with him now? Are you going to get married and have twenty kids?"

"Don't make me bash you with a pool noodle," Sophie threatened, gesturing to the pile of foam toys by the fence line.

Laura put her hand to her heart. "Is that any way to treat your favourite cousin?"

"Who told you you're my favourite?"

"You know what I'm getting from all this antagonism?" Laura warily waded closer. "That you're engaged and have a summer wedding planned."

Sophie stifled another giggle. "You won't stop until I tell you, will you?"

"Nope."

"You'll follow me around all day until you get what you want."

"Probably."

Sophie sighed. "Fine, you brat. I'll give you the overview."

"The *overview*?" Laura blew a raspberry through puckered lips. "Surely I—as your most favourite cousin in all the world—deserve a play-by-play?"

"Take it or leave it, Laur," Sophie ordered. "It's still early days, and I need to get the whole situation straight in my own mind before I go sharing my deepest feelings with anyone else."

"Oh. So, there are *deep* feelings, hey?"

Sophie laughed again. "You're insufferable."

"This is not news, cuz." Laura grinned proudly.

"Look, we had a really good time together last night. I like him, he likes me. We're seeing where that takes us."

"Did he say that?"

"Not quite that way, but yes."

"So, he told you that he *loves* you, he *adores* you, he wants to *marry* you?" Laura gushed as she swirled around in circles.

"Now you're just making things up," Sophie protested, although her cousin wasn't too far off track.

"No, but I can read between the lines, and I know Jack. He's been smitten with you since forever, Soph. I doubt much has changed in the past few days. If anything, being around you only made those feelings grow stronger." She bobbed down further in the water and waggled her head from side to side, feigning indifference. "I mean, you're kind of great. So I get it and all. Like, I love you too."

Sophie smirked. "You know, for a cheeky brat, you're

also a bit of a sweetheart."

"I know," Laura said smugly. She swam over to Sophie again and then tapped her damp fingertips on the tiled edge. "Not to put a damper on your love fest, but are you still worried about what you told me yesterday? About Jack's memory and whether there's anything hinky going on there?"

Sophie tightened her grip on the curved pool step. "A bit." She swallowed the nausea bubbling to life in her gut. Her instincts were warning her not to believe his story. Half of her was desperate for Ella to have the answers, while the other half wanted to go on in blissful ignorance. Was it better to know the truth, or live with a lie if it meant keeping this profound happiness? Sophie just didn't know.

She sighed. "If I had to bet on it, I would say he's lying about not remembering. I just can't understand why. What's he hiding?"

"Maybe Ella might know."

"Exactly." Sophie nodded. "I think Jack would be upset if he knew I planned to meet with her. I know it wasn't a coincidence that he happened to show up at Warwick Music on the same day I was in town. Something is going on there, and if I want to know the answers, I have to speak to Ella."

"So you don't think Jack would tell you the truth now, after everything, even if you asked him?"

Sophie adjusted the shoulder strap of her slinky black one-piece as she rolled the question around in her mind. "I honestly think he wants to, Laur. He gets this look sometimes. But something keeps stopping him."

"April-Rose?" Laura slicked back the loose strands of her fringe.

"Maybe? Or his mother?"

"Right then." Laura winced. "So, Ella and the troll's lair is our best bet?"

"The troll's cave," Sophie corrected. "I promise it's not nearly as bad as it sounds."

"It better not be. I don't think my life insurance covers

slaughtered by trolls."

Sophie splashed a wave of water at her cousin. "What about death by pool noodle?" She laughed as Laura ducked underwater to avoid the mini tsunami headed her way.

CHAPTER 26

Rustic buildings, some a little dilapidated, stood side-by-side along the short stretch of Moorhenvale's sleepy main road. With only a singular lane each way, it was a sneeze-and-miss-it sort of country town. Coming from a small community with modest annual wages, the storekeepers had learned to share their shop space. The tiny news agency was also the post office. The local pub included the general store. The hairdresser split a shop with the barber. Being off the highway in the middle of nowhere meant the town had limited tourists, just those dropping in for a driver reviver break before passing on through. So it was the petrol station with its bakery and café that often triumphed in trading.

Jack left his ute parked on the cracked cement in front of the complex and strode past the small gathering of day-trippers in the alfresco dining area. He entered the bakery through the sliding glass door, where the sugary scent of cakes and biscuits mingled with the spicy aroma of pastries and fresh bread. It hit his senses at the same time as the coolness of the air conditioning. Both were welcoming sensations at midday on a Wednesday. Though he didn't frequent the store, preferring to rustle up meals at home or join the Santoros at the homestead, today was a special occasion. Sophie was staying and Jack hoped to use something sweet to persuade her into having dinner with him again that evening.

"Jack," crooned a middle-aged woman behind the treat-laden display counter, her hairdo and clothing style reminiscent of the fifties. "What a lovely coincidence to see you here today." She adjusted her sparkly horn-rimmed glasses.

He offered her a warm smile. "Why do you say that, Val?"

She started to gesture towards the far corner of the small shop but was interrupted by a patronising drawl.

"Jackson. What a shame we hadn't known of your intention to visit Valorie's fabulous establishment today. We could have invited you to join us."

Jack saw April-Rose and her bore of a fiancé and felt exhausted already. He didn't have the patience for them today. He wanted to get back to Sophie. When he returned his attention to Val, her expression was sympathetic.

"Bradley and April-Rose are here tasting cakes for their upcoming nuptials." Val walked out from behind the counter. "I have more samples out the back if you'd like to give them a hand?" With her back to his sister, she tossed him a look of helpless apology before waltzing over to April-Rose and clearing the dirtied plates.

"I'm fine. Thanks." Glancing around, Jack noted the rest of the tables inside were all vacant, undoubtedly the collateral damage of his sister's presence.

"What a shame." His sister feigned dismay. "I'm certain your input would have been vital."

Val sniffed in irritation as she carried the dishes back to the kitchen.

Crossing his arms, Jack readied himself for a fight. "I'm surprised, April-Rose. I didn't think a smaller business like the Moorhenvale Bakery would be worth your attention. I seem to remember you referring to it as 'small-town and stale.'"

"I would never be so vulgar. Perhaps you're remembering your own words?" His sister swung one skinny leg over the other and relaxed into her chair. "Besides, Bradley and I like to support our local businesses, don't we, sweetie?" She looked at her fiancé, squeezing his hand. The tinny, electronic tune of a mobile phone cut into their fabricated moment of affection.

Bradley snatched a sleek phone from his pocket, checked the screen and then signalled to April-Rose that he would be a moment. Pressing the phone to his ear, he answered. "Yes, Sher—is everything okay?" He shot a look of concern at April-Rose.

"Is that my mother?" she asked him.

Bradley shook his head.

April-Rose eyed her fiancé a moment longer before tossing away her thoughts with a flick of her red hair.

"Since when?" Jack asked, not missing a beat. His question drew his sister's focus back to him. "The only local business you support is your own."

"You're quite mistaken, brother," April-Rose said earnestly. "Caring for your constituents is very important to a politician."

"A politician?" Jack looked between them in shock, wondering what fresh hell was about to rain down on him.

"Yes. Didn't you know?" April-Rose chuckled, obviously delighted to be delivering the news. "Bradley will be running for council office in the next election."

"Of course he is." Jack had to laugh. Surely no one would be stupid enough to vote the idiot in. Especially when it was clear that April-Rose would be the puppetmaster.

"It might be eighteen months away, but respect and admiration should be earned at every opportunity, Jackson."

"Is that right?"

She laughed again, then shook her head. "My apologies. I forgot that *respect* is a foreign concept to you. Do you need me to explain what it means?"

Anger flared hotly under Jack's skin, but he thought

better of firing a sharp response in retaliation. He was done. Drawing in a steadying breath, he cut a quick, flippant wave through the air. "I'll leave you to it then." As he turned to exit, his sister's shrill voice held him back.

"I'm worried about you, Jack." She imitated concern. "What will you do now that Sophie has left town? You two had become so close. I can't imagine losing such a *good friend* all over again."

Jack clenched his fists as her words struck home, digging his fingernails into his palms. April-Rose may have succeeded in rattling him, but he could still take pleasure in the fact that he knew things she didn't.

"Why April-Rose—don't you know?" Jack sauntered forward and clapped his hands together proudly. "Sophie intends on *staying* in town. Her new date of departure has not yet been decided. She is welcome to stay at Bitterbark Creek indefinitely, and I personally hope that she never leaves."

Nick and Robin had said something similar when Sophie had asked permission to stay. Even Angelica had enthusiastically supported her daughter's decision.

A buzz of satisfaction invigorated Jack when he saw his sister's saccharine smile droop. April-Rose threw a look at Bradley, who appeared to have heard the tail end of their conversation. They shared an almost calculating look before Bradley focused back on his phone call.

"Yes, yes," he confirmed with someone on the other end of the line. "But we might have a problem."

April-Rose watched her fiancé curiously and mouthed 'Tiffany?' in his direction. Bradley shrugged and then nodded enthusiastically. That brought the smile back to April-Rose's face.

"Reckless move, Jack," she scolded, shaking her head at him. She stood and stalked closer. "Did you think I'd just forget about your promise?"

He sneered at her. *What promise?* She'd threatened him, and he'd been too weak in the beginning to say no. Well, now he would either tell Sophie the truth himself or let the cards fall where they may. "Your games of blackmail and extortion leave no room for promises, April-Rose. You wanted to get your way at any cost. But it doesn't matter. I decided that doing the right thing was more important."

"The right thing?" She studied him. "You've told her then?"

Jack struggled to hold her predatory gaze. "Not exactly." But he would—and soon. He'd been hoping to tell her tonight at dinner.

"Then you've told the Santoros?"

Jack sighed. He needed to speak to Sophie first and find out how much she hated him before he braved that task.

"Not yet," he said defiantly, "but I plan to."

April-Rose just laughed at him. "If you ask me, Jackson, it sounds as though you *want* me to tell them." She crossed her arms like a teacher addressing a child. "Is that it? Are you too frightened to confess to your own misdeeds? Do you want to make it all my fault when you and I know we both played a part in what happened to your precious Sophie?"

"It was your idea, April-Rose," Jack spat.

"Yes, and without your help it never would have worked."

"I didn't know the extent of what you'd planned," Jack growled angrily. "You said you wanted to punish her, not *kill* her."

"You can't minimise your involvement by lumping blame on me, Jackson. You agreed to help and you did. End of story. So, now you either tell Sophie the truth and lose everything, or tell her to get the hell out of town like I told you to so we can all get on with our lives."

"I *will* tell her, April-Rose." Jack mirrored his sister's stance, crossing his arms over his chest to protect his heart from further verbal wounds. "You can't keep this a secret any longer. I will tell all of them. You can be sure of that."

"Fine. Don't come complaining to me when your world

falls apart." She paused. "Just do one thing, brother. If not for me, then for yourself. Make sure you tell Sophie soon. If you don't and somebody else gets in first, she might be less understanding."

Jack wondered if his sister was still trying to protect herself. Someone like Ella, someone who wasn't a Garland, would hardly spare his family's feelings when telling Sophie what happened. And offering his own perspective might make his actions appear less heartless. He certainly didn't want to make his sister any more promises, but April-Rose was right, regardless of her motives. If he wanted to stand a chance of keeping Sophie in his life, she needed to hear the truth from him.

Jack sighed deeply, but it failed to relieve the painful tension in his chest. "I'll make sure I'm the one to tell her," he agreed.

April-Rose glanced at Bradley—waiting for her at the table like a good spaniel, whispering earnestly into his mobile phone—and Jack felt compelled to ask a final, niggling question. "One last thing."

His sister glanced over her shoulder at him and arched an eyebrow inquisitively.

"Is Mother seeing someone? Romantically, I mean."

April-Rose's cold eyes snapped to Bradley. He straightened under her stare but didn't break from his conversation. She shrugged and swiped her hair over her shoulder. "We're not aware of any such connection. I think she may have shown some fondness towards one of our industry associates, but I don't believe there has been anything serious. Even if there was, Jackson, it's hardly any of your business."

"Of course." If his mother was seeing someone, it was in secret. "You both have a good afternoon," Jack said dismissively. Then he made for the security and serenity of the sanitising sunshine outside.

CHAPTER 27

The warm midafternoon sun drained energy from all of earth's creatures and encouraged sleepiness like a comforting lullaby. The birds that had been so boisterous and excitable earlier now nestled groggily in the highest of branches. Even the frisky breeze that had danced throughout the morning had finally hushed into nothing but an occasional tickle of tender leaves. It was only the insects that didn't retreat. Honeybees flitted in search of sweet nectar, while cheeky black flies swerved and dodged the swish of tails and the slap of hands.

"That's the last of it." Angelica shut the navy sedan's boot and tapped the top resolutely. "I'll drop your nonna off at Sage Oak and get her settled before heading back to the city."

"Text me when you get there?" Sophie spread her arms for a hug.

"Of course, darling." As Angelica embraced her, an elderly voice from the cool shade of the cabin's veranda interrupted them.

"I told your mother to start the journey earlier," Nonna complained. "I was ready to leave after breakfast, but she wanted to spend lunch gossiping with Robin and Nicky."

"Don't sulk, Mama," Angelica chastised. "You enjoyed yourself just as much as the rest of us. If we'd left early, you would have missed out on good company."

"And that lovely tea cake," Sophie added. At her mother's questioning glance, she grinned. "Laura swiped us some to eat by the pool."

Angelica returned Sophie's smile and headed up the stairs towards her mother. "Besides, the journey isn't a long one. It's only a couple of hours to Brisbane."

Nonna made a *pfft* noise and crossed her arms. "I don't like knowing my baby is driving such a distance at night."

"Sunset's not until after six tonight, Mama. We've got plenty of time." Angelica helped Nonna to her feet.

"I hope so." The older woman didn't sound convinced.

Angelica wrapped her arm around her mother's shoulders reassuringly, supporting her down the steps and steering her to the car.

"You take care of yourself." Sophie cuddled her grandmother gently.

"You also, Sophia—my beautiful girl. Your mother and I want you to be careful during your stay alone. Remember you've always got your aunt and uncle here for support if anything happens." She clutched Sophie's hands tightly.

"I know, Nonna." Sophie was immensely grateful that Uncle Nick and Aunt Robin had been so supportive. She'd worried they'd lose income with her monopolising the cabin and had offered to pay the going rate, but they wouldn't hear of it. Uncle Nick said it filled his heart with joy to have his second daughter back home. His sweet words had made Sophie teary.

"I mean it, dear," Nonna continued. "Don't go putting your trust in the wrong people. Make sure you know their true intentions before getting in too deep."

"She's very subtle, isn't she, darling?" Angelica teased. "We're glad you've rekindled your friendship with Jackson, but we know how difficult things may still be between you and . . . other members of his family. Perhaps it would be best to keep your distance from them for now?"

"What your mother means, my Sophia, is that the Garlands can't be trusted." Nonna linked her arm through Sophie's and led her towards the passenger-side door. "Personally, I wouldn't believe a word from any of them—even if they were locked to a lie detector—but we know you like Jackson and he seems like a good boy. Just remember—the poisoned pear doesn't fall far from the cursed tree, as they say, so protect that big heart of yours and be prepared for anything." She grabbed Sophie's face and pecked a kiss on each cheek.

"I'll be careful, Nonna." Sophie chuckled. "You have a safe trip home." She opened the front passenger side and helped her grandmother inside. Sophie wondered what helpful tips her grandmother would offer if she knew what she really had planned for her time in town, especially for that evening. Dispelling more of the Garlands' lies was probably at the top of Ella's list.

After shutting the car door, Sophie wiggled her fingers in a final wave and turned once again to her mother.

"Your nonna's speech might have lacked the tact I was aiming for," Angelica clarified, "but she hit the point directly on the head. Leave the Garlands alone, and hopefully they'll do the same. There's no need to reopen old wounds."

God, what would her mother think if she knew Sophie was going into the mouth of the troll's cave tonight to do just that?

Angelica cupped her daughter's cheek before dragging her close for another hug. "I love you, baby. Be safe and call me when you want to come home. I'll be happy to drive out here again and pick you up."

"Thanks, Mum. I should be okay though. Laura's already offered to drive me back. Uncle Nick said she could take the Pajero. I think she's looking forward to staying in the city for a night or two."

"Fine, if you're sure." Angelica squeezed Sophie tighter

and then stepped back. "Stay in touch, okay? Give me a call anytime. We'll catch up for dinner when you return."

"Sounds good."

Angelica hesitated for a moment, studying her daughter, before finally releasing her grip on Sophie's hands. She rounded the sedan's trunk and opened the driver's side door. "Bye, darling."

"Bye, Mum. Drive safely."

Angelica winked at her and slid behind the wheel. As the engine rumbled to life, Sophie backed away and watched the vehicle roll down the gravel drive. Once it had reached the property's rocky road, she waved enthusiastically until the car disappeared over the grassy rise.

Now all alone, she felt even more resolute in her mission. Her mother's worries about delving into the past had weighed on her while she was around. Sophie hated the thought of upsetting her mother, and she was still terrified of seeing Ella, of discovering what had really happened. Yet she needed to do this. She had to know the truth. It was the only way she could focus on the future and the only way she'd know if she could ever truly trust Jack again. And she desperately wanted to.

When the sound of the engine was no more than a distant rumble, Sophie hugged herself tightly and spun around to face the cosy cabin.

"Hi." The sound of Jack's deep voice jolted her. He looked broodingly handsome in his tight black shirt and dark denim jeans but offered her a gentle, endearing smile. "Sorry, I hadn't wanted to interrupt. You looked deep in thought." He nodded towards the dust cloud hovering above the road. "Are they heading home?"

"Yeah." Sophie glanced back over her shoulder. "It's probably for the best. I'm not sure Uncle Nick could survive much longer with Nonna around."

Jack laughed. "No, I've heard that same tune from him as well. I'm very glad *you* decided to stay though."

The raw emotion in Jack's tender words warmed

Sophie's soul. She went to him, slipping her arms around his neck and dragged him close.

"Are you okay?" He nuzzled her neck and rubbed a hand along her spine.

Sophie nodded against his shoulder. "I'm just glad to see you."

She was grateful to have him here, to have his support. It felt slightly less daunting to have someone else on her side—besides Laura—with whom to ride the emotional rollercoaster she was about to strap herself into. Even though she suspected he was lying about what he remembered, Sophie truly believed Jack had her best interest at heart. He would probably disapprove of her looking into the past, but surely he could understand why she needed closure.

Sophie breathed in the comforting scent of him, heated skin mingled with something natural and citrusy like the aroma of his favourite soap. As though relishing the feel of her so close, Jack hugged Sophie tighter. After a lengthy moment, she reluctantly pulled back.

"Just dropping in for a visit, are you?" She left her hands atop his shoulders, enjoying how grounded and secure she felt when touching him.

He grinned. "Actually, I came around to find out if you had dinner plans. I've got a pinot grigio chilling in the fridge and one of your aunt's famous blueberry tarts for dessert. Are you interested?"

Excitement bubbled inside of her until she realised that Jack's dinner plans coincided with her secret mission to meet with Ella.

"I'm so sorry, Jack," Sophie told him, disappointed. "I would absolutely love to. Aunt Robin's famous blueberry tart and your good company would usually guarantee my attendance in a heartbeat. But I've unfortunately already got plans this evening."

"Oh." His cheerful face fell, and Sophie saw her disappointment briefly reflected in his handsome features before he tried to shrug it off. "Of course. That's okay, maybe we can take a raincheck?"

"Definitely." Sophie stroked the side of his neck lovingly. "Maybe we could try for tomorrow night instead?"

"Sure." He gave her a small smile. "So, what are you up to tonight? Sorry, do you mind me asking?"

"Not at all." Sophie shook her head as her stomach knotted. What could she tell him that wouldn't make him worry? "I'm seeing Laura tonight." She really didn't want to lie.

"A girls' night then? Are you heading out for dinner or staying in?"

She nibbled at her lower lip. "We haven't decided."

He frowned and then raised an eyebrow sceptically. "I thought Laura would have bullied you into something already. She has her favourite haunts and prefers to go out if given the chance."

Sophie grinned at his obvious fondness for Laura. "I'm starting to think you know my cousin better than I do." She briefly touched her lips to his.

"What can I say? She's my little sister from another mister, just like she said." He returned her sweet peck to the lips. "Okay, fine. You have your fun night together and we'll plan something for tomorrow."

"Thank you," she gushed, relieved at how easy that had been.

"I guess I'll leave you to it then." He still sounded a little down. "There's always Nick's rocking chair to busy myself with in the meantime."

She kissed him again, and he slowly unwound himself from her. Just before he let go of her fingers, that last link of physical connection between them, he furrowed his brow and clasped her hand in his again.

"Sorry, Soph, I just have to ask. . ." He looked at her with concern and caressed the back of her hand with his thumb. "You're not thinking about doing anything silly, are you? It's just . . . I have this odd feeling, like you're keeping something from me."

Join the club, she thought. Maybe it was good for Jack to experience the sensation for himself.

"I think you might have to define silly," Sophie teased, hoping to calm his worries without giving too much away. "I am going out with *Laura* after all."

At that, Jack's lips twitched with humour. "Sorry," he shook his head again. "I guess I'm the one being silly. It's just—I've been thinking about Ella and was starting to worry you were going to try to speak to her again. I know you'd like to know what really happened to you that day at the dam, Soph, but Ella isn't the best source."

Surprised and a little miffed, Sophie clenched her jaw stubbornly. "How could you possibly know that, Jack? Unless there's something you're not telling me?"

He widened his eyes at the accusation and licked his lips. "I'm not saying I know anything for certain, Soph. I just don't want to see you get hurt."

"You don't know that I will."

He quirked a dark eyebrow. "If you go digging up demons, you will."

"You sure talk as if you know something, Jack. Tell me—is what you said the other night true?" Somehow asking him directly hit her harder than thinking about it or discussing it with Laura. It made it real. "Do you remember the day at the Garland dam or not?"

Jack opened his mouth to speak and then stopped. His expression darkened, and he shook his head. "I remember."

Jack's admission filled Sophie with a mixture of hurt and exhilaration. She grabbed both his hands and pulled him closer. "Then please tell me," she begged. She was so close to filling in the black hole of memory that had burdened her for so long. She was near tears.

"I was going to," Jack began. "I wanted to talk to you tonight."

"Then tell me now." When he wouldn't look at her, Sophie lifted his chin, forcing him to meet her eyes. The sadness and fear she saw there tugged at her heart. She wanted to protect him, but she needed answers. Why hadn't he told her? What was he so afraid of? "Jack, please."

"I can't," he said. His lower lip quivered. He looked like a broken man, consumed by fear. "I love you so much, Soph. I can't lose you again."

"I love you too," she whispered. It hurt her to think it, but if he couldn't tell her, how could she ever trust him? Even if they did love one another. She needed to know the truth, and if he wasn't going to help her, then she was done. "Sorry, Jack. I don't think I can do this."

"What?" He gulped, and his eyes reddened with nearing tears.

Sophie looked down at their entwined hands, then released his and took a step back.

At the rejection, Jack's face fell. "Please, Soph. I'll tell you. I will. I just need more time." He reached for her.

She backed away from him. "You've had time, Jack. I'm sorry, but I can't wait for you to get over whatever has got you so torn up. I've got a chance to learn the truth tonight. I'm not going to pass that up."

"You're going to see Ella?" Fear flashed in his eyes when she nodded. "Please don't do this, Soph," he begged.

"I don't think you understand just how much I need this, Jack. I *want* to move on—but I can't while this emptiness consumes me."

"I do understand. Honestly, I do, Soph." His face was flushed, his voice breathy with terror. "You have to believe me when I say that I hate myself for being so weak, for not being brave enough to face this and tell you the truth." He opened his mouth as though trying to force himself to say something, but nothing came out. "Damn it!" he yelled in frustration. "I love you, Sophie. I'm a miserable mess of a man who has done terrible things, who fears he'll end up just like his horrible family if he doesn't work hard every day to be a better person. I'm not the same boy who abandoned you after the accident or the same boy who was at the

Garland dam that day. I just need you to know that whatever Ella tells you about me, I'm a better man now. I'll never make the same mistake again."

Sophie didn't know what to say. She couldn't find the right words. So she cupped Jack's face with her hands and kissed him. She tried to send him all the love, all the support and understanding she could muster in that single kiss. Then she pushed free of him and hurried for the security of her little timber home.

His pleas and promises didn't change anything, but Sophie believed him. No matter what she learned from Ella, he would still be her Jack—the man she loved. But whether she could open her heart to him again after learning the truth was something she wouldn't know until all these secrets finally saw the light.

CHAPTER 28

The darkness was thick and impenetrable, even with the moon idling above the leafy treetops. On the dirt track below, Sophie and Laura shone their flashlights over rocks and pebbles, the rays of light jiggling and shimmying to the crunch of accompanying footsteps. Sophie had spent the rest of the afternoon trying not to think of what had happened between her and Jack. She didn't want to let him go, didn't want to lose him, just as he didn't want to lose her. Yet they couldn't move on until they were on equal footing, until she had her memories back. She hadn't been able to bring herself to tell Laura yet. Sophie had been drawing on her cousin's chirpy good humour to cheer her and remind her that she was finally achieving what she had always wanted. All thanks to Ella.

There was a screech from the canopy, a wind-slapping flap of wings, and Laura's torch beam shot skywards to search the foliage.

"Geez." Laura clutched her chest and slowly lowered her torch. "Give me a heart attack, why don't you?"

"I guess I should have warned you." Sophie winced. "These woods are notorious for flying foxes."

"Are they also notorious for serial killers?"

Sophie laughed and then stopped abruptly. It felt too loud for the dense silence of the forest around them. "No, they're usually pretty peaceful, and look—" She paused and pointed through the trees behind them. "You can still see the lights of the cabin. Not scary at all."

"Hah," Laura scoffed. "A lonely cabin, viewed through a prison of trees. It's like a scene right out of *I Know What You Did Twenty Years Ago.*"

Sophie linked her arm through Laura's and dragged her cousin forward. "We should count ourselves lucky Ella even bothered to keep the lights on," she teased. "Without their beacon, we could end up wandering the woods, lost for all eternity."

Laura elbowed her playfully in the side and Sophie giggled.

"You think you're so funny, cuz. You just wait until we meet that troll of yours. Aren't we heading to his cave?"

"What makes you think the troll is male?" Sophie left Laura and headed over to a rocky rise in the ground. She shone the torch across it, revealing a stony hill, and scanned the dark earth below. The beam of light revealed a soiled plastic body in a tattered tiny blue outfit with a shock of bushy crimson hair. Sophie gasped. "She's still here."

"She? That *thing*—sorry, that doll," Laura corrected, "is a *she?*"

"Yes." Sophie crouched and reached for the precious item, but then she hesitated and decided not to disturb the little toy. "Her name is Puggle. She's Ella's troll, and this"— Sophie pointed to the gloominess beyond—"has been her cave since before I can remember."

Laura flicked her flashlight into the blackness of the small hollow. When the light suddenly illuminated a human face, she jumped back and emitted a shrill squeak. "Oh my gosh," she panted. "You nearly killed me. Why didn't you say something?"

Ella pushed herself off the shallow inner wall she'd been leaning against. "You two losers were making enough noise on your own. I didn't see the point in adding my voice to the chorus." She flipped her cropped burgundy mane and uncrossed her arms to reveal a grey jumper slashed with a fierce scarlet slogan. The heavy make-up around her eyes gave her an almost vampiric presence in the dimness.

"What the eff is right, Ella," Laura said, gesturing to the writing across the other woman's outfit. "What were you thinking hiding in there? Were you hoping to scare the crap out of us? Or is this where you plan to hide our bodies?"

Ella twitched her red lips and tilted her head. "Firstly, Laura Santoro, there was never supposed to be an *us*. It was a single invitation. And secondly—don't tempt me." She took a menacing step forward and looked Laura up and down. "I know where you live." She grinned.

"Ladies." Sophie raised her hand, displaying it like a stop sign to the two women. "There will be no killing tonight." She glanced over at the shadowed face of her cousin. "Laura, behave yourself, and Ella. . ." She waited for the other woman to peel her gaze from the youngest Santoro. "Let's start over. I'm sorry for letting this one tag along, but I didn't want to face this alone. I hope you can understand and are still willing to have this conversation."

Ella's eyes were slits, gauging Sophie's sincerity. Then she shrugged. "Don't sweat it. We're good. I don't mind little Laura joining us."

"*Little Laura?*" Her cousin gawped. "I'm only two years younger than both of you."

Laura's outburst drew Ella's attention like a predator to prey. Sophie bumped Laura's shoulder to silence her.

"Besides"—Ella turned back to Sophie—"I should be the one apologising. I overreacted when I saw Jackson on Monday. The Garlands just seem to bring out the worst in me. I probably have post-traumatic stress disorder from all the years they made my life a living hell. I find it best to avoid them whenever I can."

"All of them? Even Jack?" Sophie felt her stomach swirl anxiously.

"Well, no," Ella reassured her. "Jack usually keeps to himself. But seeing the two of you together—I wasn't prepared for that, and it freaked me out. He's not the Garland he used to be, Sophie, but he's still no angel. He has his demons, same as the rest of us."

Sophie nodded and nervously tightened her clammy grip on the torch. She knew he wasn't innocent—otherwise he wouldn't be so terrified of telling her the truth. She hoped his sins were as she'd expected. Decisions made and actions taken by a good-natured little boy poisoned by his upbringing in the Garland household. Now she knew the extent of his mother and sister's control and manipulation. She had been so young when he'd pulled away. She hadn't been able to understand how torn he'd been. His desire to love and support his family had been used against him, and his obedience and loyalty used to trap him.

Of course, she had no confessions from his mother or sister to cast full blame their way, but she knew the heart of the man she loved. Years and years may have passed since their youthful days together, and their new relationship may be in its early days, but Sophie was one hundred percent certain of one thing. Whatever had happened in the past, whatever he had done, Jackson Garland was a truly good man at his core. Nothing Ella said tonight could change that opinion. But Sophie was certain there was plenty Ella could say that would *surprise* her.

Laura inched forward warily. "What do you mean when you say they made your life a living hell? Something beyond their general unpleasantness?"

Ella put her hands on her hips. "Well, I still blame them for my mother's death. So what do you think?"

Laura grimaced as though Ella's words had physically struck her.

"Your mother's death?" Sophie repeated. "What did they do, Ella?"

Ella sighed. "Just remember, Sophie, you asked for this." She paced for a moment and then leaned back against the rocky cave wall.

"For me, all the drama began after that day—the day you ended up in the dam. The Garlands fought hard to keep everything under wraps. Even though I was only ten at the time, Sheridan and April-Rose threatened to ruin my life if I ever revealed anything. They said no one would believe me and that if I told anyone, they would say it was my fault. It took a little while, but eventually my mum noticed something was wrong and managed to get it out of me. Then, like any good mother, she tried to protect me."

Ella briefly closed her eyes and rubbed the back of her hand over her forehead self-soothingly, distorting her bold slab of fringe. "When my mum confronted them, they immediately fired her from Garland Grain. She had been Barton Garland's secretary for nearly ten years. She had started shortly after I was born. After my father's aneurysm had left her to parent me on her own.

"Mum tried to find work. She had the experience and asked all around town, but the Garlands' influence was inescapable. People she thought were friends turned on her. The few family members we had in Warwick attempted to support us financially but didn't want to get involved. They knew what happened when you messed with the Garlands."

Laura shared a grimace of disgust with Sophie.

"It was around my twelfth birthday when my mum decided enough was enough." Ella was staring at the ground now, lost in her memories. "She threatened to tell the whole town about what really happened at the dam. Sheridan found out and asked that they meet to talk things through." Ella paused, and when she finally glanced up again, her eyes had become glassy and distant. It was as though she'd pushed herself to a place beyond feeling in order to protect herself from the pain.

"My mum went away that day," Ella told them. "She went to visit that she-demon Sheridan and didn't come back the same. She lost something of herself. Something changed in her. She lost the light, the drive that had been pushing her on, encouraging her to seek justice. About a year later she had her nervous breakdown, and five years after that I put her into care. She lasted ten more years as an empty shell before she passed away and I lost her completely. She was only fifty-five."

Ella clenched her fists and shook her head in frustration. "I know they did something to her," she snarled. "Sheridan threatened her. Whatever happened at Garland Manor that day broke my mother, and I'll never forgive them for that."

A cold chill slithered down Sophie's spine. The depth of Jack's fear was beginning to make more sense. Whatever happened must have been incredibly horrific or incriminating if his mother had been willing to destroy Francesca Larsen over it. Sheridan was protecting herself or her children from something, but what—

Oh, Sophie thought. *Of course*. It was *their* fault. Something clicked into place in her mind, like the spin of a dial on a safe. Unlocking a hazy memory, familiar yet distant. It all made sense now. Sophie's stomach roiled. She felt like vomiting.

"I'm so sorry, Ella," Sophie whispered. She wanted to help her old friend, but there was nothing she could say to take away Ella's pain.

"So, that's it?" Laura scoffed incredulously. "You just gave up? How can you let them get away with that?"

Sophie glared at her cousin, but Laura just ignored her.

"You misunderstand me." Ella shook her head. "I have every intention of getting revenge for what they did to me and my mother, but escaping Moorhenvale is my first priority. Once I'm safe and financially secure in Brisbane, then I'll drop the bomb that's hanging above their pretty Garland heads. They know they can't keep me silent forever."

"I'm glad to hear it." Laura nodded approvingly. She winked at the feisty woman. "And you want to get out of town? We might have more in common than I first thought, Ella. Maybe we should have a chat about our escape strategies one day?"

"Be careful what you wish for, *little Laura*." Ella smirked. "I'm likely to hold you to that."

Sophie looked from her cousin to her childhood friend, noticing the chemistry fizzing between them. Feeling a little like a third wheel, she cleared her throat. "Do you two need a moment alone," she ventured cautiously, "or should we move on?"

Laura threw a little look of shock in Sophie's direction and Ella chuckled.

"We should move on," Ella agreed. "I'd rather not be out here all night. So, you want to know what happened twenty years ago, this big secret the Garlands would do anything to protect?"

Sophie nodded.

"Okay, but— are you sure you're ready to hear it? I've heard around town that you and Jackson have got something going on. If you don't want that ruined, you can walk away now."

Laura took Sophie's hand in support. Deciding to take that step forward, knowing she couldn't come back from this, Sophie nodded sharply. "Yes, Ella. I'm ready. I need to know."

Ella gazed off into the darkness. "Right then. Where do I start? Tell me the last thing you remember."

"Okay. . ." Sophie blindly stared at the ground as she searched the recesses of her memory. "I remember that we were all at the Garlands' property that day. They were having their annual party to celebrate spring and the grain harvest. Mum had forced me to go along. It had only been a couple of months since the accident, since my dad had died, and I wasn't coping very well. My friends"—she motioned to Ella—"were pulling away from me and seemed to blame me and my family for what had happened. I felt so alone.

"I remember leaving my mother with the Santoros. They were watching Pat and Laur compete in the sack race."

Clouds descended over the memory. "Everyone loved the games and activities. The party used to be the highlight of the year, the event all of Moorhenvale couldn't wait to attend." Sophie shut her eyes for a second, trying to focus. "I'd left Mum and made my way into the crowd. I was looking for my friends—Jack, April-Rose, Bradley, Tiffany and you, Ella. I was searching the crowd and . . . I guess I must have found you all together somewhere."

A misty blankness shielded the rest of that day. Sophie shrugged, at a loss for how to properly describe the emptiness. "That's all I can remember. The next thing I recall is being in the back of the ambulance with Uncle Nick. He was holding my hand, talking to me, telling me everything was going to be all right."

Ella frowned. "You don't remember us finding you at the gazebo?"

Sophie shook her head slowly.

"You've got no memory of the *adventure* April-Rose promised you?"

Laura growled. "I knew it had to be that harpy's fault."

Ella clenched her jaw angrily, her distaste for her former friend clear. She forced words out through gritted teeth. "Well, April-Rose convinced you to go down to the Garland dam, to play a game away from the adults. She said we were going to cut you from our group after what had happened with your father and hers, but she promised to let you stay if you joined us on an adventure."

Ella stared hard at Sophie as though trying to pierce through her mind and trigger the memory. "You believed her, Sophie. You were so worried about us rejecting and abandoning you that you did exactly as she said. Then April-Rose led everyone down to the dam. The rest of us didn't know what was about to happen. We knew she was angry after your dad passed away. We didn't really know why. We just followed her like always. We were all too scared or stupid or desperate to be popular that we never questioned her." Ella hung her head and sighed. "I deeply regret that now."

"It's okay," Sophie whispered. "I remember what it was like back then. We were all at the mercy of April-Rose's whims. She'd proclaimed herself queen of our little circle and none of us challenged her until it was too late. I don't blame you for that, Ella."

"But we were horrible to you out there, Sophie. We bullied you mercilessly. All of us. I know we were egged on, but we all played our part. We were like animals—like hyenas hunting. I got caught up in her anger. It was like a sickness. It wasn't until things escalated that I came to my senses." Ella covered her face with quivering hands.

Sophie fought to speak past the painful lump burning the back of her throat. "We were just kids, Ella," she croaked. She wished Ella's words would bring it all back to her, so she could have all the pieces of herself again. But it just wasn't happening.

"I'm not sure that's a good enough excuse." With a sniff, Ella lowered her hands and stared into the darkness. "Sure, we were young, but what we did out there changed us. None of us were ever the same after that. Some of us, like April-Rose, became a million times worse."

Ella took a deep, steadying breath. Then another. Silence reigned until Laura lifted a cupped hand as though begging for her palm to be filled with the truth.

"So, what happened next? You got Sophie out onto the jetty and then what? You all knocked her unconscious and pushed her into the water?"

Ella swallowed. "Not exactly."

"Well, what then?" Laura urged.

When Ella cast a look of concern her way, Sophie gestured for her to continue. "Go on. I have to know."

Inhaling harshly through gritted teeth, Ella rubbed her arms a few times as though warming herself. "Okay." The word trembled over her lips. "It got bad when we were out there, Sophie. Really bad. Some of the things we said were so awful. Unforgivable. At first you argued with us, but then you were crying. You screamed at us to stop, but we didn't. April-Rose told you to get in the water, but you wouldn't."

Ella rubbed her forehead as she looked at her feet. "Everyone was yelling at you to get in. There was some pushing and shoving. You desperately tried to keep your balance and avoid the edge. That was when April-Rose pulled a stick from her pretty pink party dress. A thin, whip-like branch. A little longer than a school ruler. I didn't know she had it. She struck you with it over and over again, Sophie. She hit your hands, your fingers—whatever she could reach. I think the pain stopped you from fighting back. Then she told you to get in, that we wouldn't let you leave until you had swum all the way back to shore by yourself. It was a long way, but you could have made it. You were always a good swimmer, but I think the dark water and the thought of what might be beneath the surface scared you. April-Rose knew that."

Ella pushed free of the sturdy rock wall and began pacing in the shallow cave. Arms crossed tight, she breathed deeply, in and out—like a runner preparing for a race. "When you refused, she would hit you again. She whipped your arms, your legs, and managed to back you to the very edge. You were crying uncontrollably by that point, telling her to stop, begging us to help you. We just kept shouting for you to do it, to jump in and swim, or we wouldn't be your friends anymore."

Again, Sophie noticed Ella's lips quiver and her eyes darken. "Then your heel slipped. It went over the edge. You grabbed hold of the stick. It all happened so quickly. April-Rose tried to yank it free and kicked you in the shins. You let go. Maybe it was the pain? The fright? Then I saw you falling over the edge, your body slipping into the water. You reached out as you fell, for something or someone to help you—but no one did."

Clearly traumatised herself, Ella gaped at Sophie. "You went in so fast. I don't think any of us moved. I just remember your eyes, how wide and white they were.

Then—the noise." Ella cringed and lifted her shoulders to her ears to keep from shivering. "That horrible noise as your chin hit the wooden plank of the jetty. Your head went back at an odd angle—just jerked right backwards—and you disappeared. There was nothing but a splash of water on the jetty where your feet had been a moment before, and then there was nothing." Shock still gripped Ella even after twenty years. "You were right there in front of us, Sophie, and then . . . you just weren't."

As Ella went silent, the quiet of the dark night filled the cave once more, and Sophie could hear her own pulse thundering in her ears. Her friend's distress had lured all her own hurt and pain to the surface, even though Sophie still couldn't remember. She wished she could understand why. At least now she knew why Jack was too terrified to tell her himself. Who would ever want to admit they'd done something so horrible to someone they held dear, someone they loved? No wonder Jack thought he wasn't a good person. As for April-Rose—she'd been nasty even as a child, but Sophie never would have expected her to do something this malicious.

"Is that when you went to get help?" Laura asked. "My dad told me you came running up to the party, shouting for help."

Ella looked troubled and shook her head remorsefully. "Not quite, but soon after."

"I just can't understand it." Sophie hugged herself comfortingly. "Why would April-Rose do such a thing? We had been close before my father died. We'd grown up together. Maybe we weren't best friends, but we used to have a lot of fun. All of us did. That's something I remember well. What changed?"

Scowling, Ella steadied herself against the cave wall. "I don't really know, but I'm betting Sheridan does. She's always had an unhealthy amount of control over her children."

"Up until recently," Laura corrected.

"True." Ella nodded. "April-Rose now rules the roost at Garland Grain, and Jack is apparently running free at Bitterbark Creek, or that's what I hear."

"Yes, Jack's with us," Laura agreed. "Although I can't imagine him ever behaving as you described. But then look at you. You seem like a good egg now too."

"Uh, thanks." Ella frowned.

"While you two might have grown up and got your act together," Laura continued, "no one can say the same of April-Rose."

Ella shrugged. "Like I said before—she's a million times worse."

"You're not wrong."

"I still don't get it," Sophie said. She felt restless. She had hoped for answers, but now that she had them, there were only more questions. "So, April-Rose forced me out on the jetty? Why? Because she wanted to scare me?"

"Payback," Laura proposed. "For the car accident that injured her father. She's as vindictive as her mother."

"No. Sorry," Ella interrupted, raising her hands to halt their hypothesising. "It wasn't April-Rose who got you out on the jetty that day."

"What?" Laura looked quickly at Sophie before turning back to Ella. "But you told us that all five of you bullied her under April-Rose's direction."

"I said April-Rose was the one who guided us down to the dam and took the lead once we were on the jetty, but she wasn't the one who encouraged Sophie to walk the plank, so to speak."

"Well, who was it then?" Laura prodded. "Bradley? Tiffany? I'm sure they're both hiding homicidal tendencies."

Sophie's stomach dropped. Something familiar niggled at her again. She felt dizzy and shivery. The answer was right on the tip of her tongue.

"Was it you, Ella?" Sophie queried warily. She felt her heart leap fearfully into her throat. Was that what this feeling was? Knowing someone she cared for had betrayed her? She blinked back the hot tears that threatened to cascade down her cheeks.

Ella stared hard at Sophie, as though once again hoping the lost memory might seep through so she wouldn't have to say it out loud. "No, Sophie." Ella sighed. "It was *Jackson*."

CHAPTER 29

The lush grass of the green field beyond the Bitterbark Creek homestead was still moist from an early morning downpour. Unlike the sunny days earlier in the week, Thursday had dawned with a grumpy rumble of thunder and the crotchety crack of lightning. Although the sun had finally risen beyond half-mast, the gloom of low-hanging clouds fought to bury the day's light. The air was sticky with humidity—a harbinger of further rain—and only the cool, wispy breeze that toyed with the leaves of the ironbark and eucalyptus trees made it bearable.

At the threshold between the main house and meadow, Jack loaded a brightly coloured tennis ball into a red ball-launcher while Boris and Banjo crouched at his feet, poised and ready to run. He flicked his wrist, hauling the sphere skywards and into the distance. The motley farm dogs yipped joyfully as they raced the length of the lawn and back, competing for the filthy green orb, while spectating birds cheered them on with frenzied tweets.

When one of the canines returned the ball—covered in globs of dirt and drool—to Jack's feet for the umpteenth time that morning, he scooped it back into the launcher and raised it again. Distracted, as he had been all morning, Jack smoothed his free hand over the back pocket of his jeans, feeling for his phone. Had it vibrated again? Had he received another text? Had Sophie changed her mind? Questions had been circling his thoughts for the past hour, and he hadn't been able to stop himself from checking the screen obsessively.

Earlier, Sophie had messaged him to say she couldn't have dinner together that night, that she needed some space, some time to think. He understood that for what it was. Their old friend had told her the truth. Sophie likely knew everything about that day at the Garland dam, all the horrendous things Jack had done. Now she had to decide whether or not she could ever forgive him.

Jack's heart lurched in his chest at the thought of never seeing her again. She could decide to leave, to return home to the city without a word. He'd been keeping an eye on her cabin, checking now and then for a light on, a window open, just to reassure himself that she was still there. He couldn't bear to think of the heartache he'd feel if he woke up one day to discover her gone. Why hadn't he had the courage to tell her the truth himself? He'd really tried yesterday, but the words wouldn't come. Now look at what he'd done. Ruined everything just as expected, living up to the Garland name like a good little heir.

You are the most miserable coward to ever live, he told himself. *You had the chance to be honest with the woman you love and you blew it. Now, she'll never forgive you, not if she knows what's good for her. Loving you will only hurt her.*

Jack gasped back a sob and whacked a fist over his heart, the pain helping him keep it together, helping him stay strong. He couldn't give up. He loved Sophie dearly. He didn't want to be the Garland he feared he was. He wanted to be someone she could trust, someone she could imagine a future with. He was trying so hard to give her the space she needed. But it had been just a few hours, and he already felt as though his whole world was crumbling. How would he survive if she needed days, weeks?

He took a deep breath to calm himself, but it was shaky and broken, and he didn't feel better. At his feet, Boris and Banjo sat whimpering and wide-eyed. Their concentration darted between him and their ball as they eagerly awaited the moment it would be lobbed once more across the yard. Their sombre whines cleared Jack's troubled thoughts.

"Sorry boys," he apologised with a grimace. "Here you go." He retracted the skinny stick and tossed the tennis ball across the field. Both dogs fired off in the same instant, like fur-covered rockets.

Unable to stop the compulsive need to examine his mobile phone, Jack snatched the device from his back pocket and checked the screen.

It was clear. No messages. Nothing. Of course Sophie wouldn't change her mind. She'd asked for space. Jack had to respect that. He had to stop obsessing.

"Waiting for something?"

Laura's voice, so loud and close and unexpected, made Jack jump. Her usually jovial tone and expression had been replaced with something more solemn.

"You could probably use some good news right about now." She crossed her arms.

Before Jack could find the right words to respond, Boris and Banjo made their boisterous return. At the sight of a potential new ball hurler, they waggled their tails with renewed enthusiasm. Dishevelled from the wet grass and his brother's slobbery nips, Banjo laid his prized toy at Laura's feet and then inched back, waiting. Laura snatched up the ball, curled into a pitching stance and heaved it towards the horizon. The dogs discharged like shotgun rounds after a clay pigeon, locking on their target, their snouts pointed skyward.

Jack swallowed in an effort to soothe his parched throat. He couldn't meet her eyes, so he just stared out across the greenery, observing the motley mutts leap and brawl over the bouncing ball. "I assume you know everything then?"

If he could find relief in anything, it was that Laura was

likely with Sophie when she discovered the truth. If she couldn't have been with him, learned the truth from him, then at least she hadn't faced it all alone.

"Not everything." Laura propped her hands on her hips. "I've yet to hear it from you."

Something about her tone lifted his spirits just a little. "Does Sophie feel the same way?"

There was a pregnant pause. Joyous canine yips and the thunderous padding of paws joined the tweeting birds and the cheeps of their chicklets to fill the lengthy silence.

"Sophie told me that she asked you to tell her the truth yesterday, and you didn't. After hearing what Ella had to say, seeing how traumatised she was by it all—I get it, Jack. I understand why you didn't want to. But what made you think it was a good idea to keep this secret to yourself for so long? To not even tell me or Pat?" Frustration tinged Laura's words, and she sighed. "We are supposed to be family."

"We are," he agreed hoarsely, feeling tears well in his eyes once more. He twisted the red ball-launcher between his fingers, wringing out his nerves as he strangled the plastic contraption. "I couldn't lose you, Laur. Any of you. I didn't want your opinion of me to change. I didn't want you to hate me as much as I hate myself."

"Jack." She sounded so serious, so tired, nothing like the Laura he knew. "We could never hate you—and it was twenty years ago. You were just a kid. We all were. Sure, what you did to Sophie, what you all did, was horrible. Especially considering Sophie had just lost her father. But the worst of what happened was still an accident. None of you planned for her to nearly drown."

Laura's compassion and understanding lifted a little more of Jack's suffocating guilt, and he felt his lower lip quiver. How could she be so kind to him after everything he'd done?

After tossing the tennis ball again for the eager farm dogs, Jack scrubbed away his welling tears. "Thank you,

Laur," he gulped. He shook his head. "But I don't know what's true anymore. I'm not sure it was an accident." He stared down at her, feeling pain rip through him at the nightmarish memory. "After the car crash that took Jim Wendall's life, April-Rose convinced me that Sophie needed to be taught a lesson, that we needed retribution for almost losing our father too. She'd said a swim from the middle of the dam would force Sophie to earn back our friendship, and if she didn't make it, she didn't deserve us."

"And you believed her?" Laura asked warily, but her voice was free of judgement.

Jack hung his head, the pain in his chest almost crippling. "Not at first, but she eventually won me over with my mother's help."

He ground his teeth together as he recalled the two of them bombarding him until he finally conceded. He'd been a coward back then as well. They'd told him that if he cared about his family at all, their reputation, their honour, then he would do this for them. *What was one little swim compared to the love of your family?* his mother had asked. But she and his sister had known Sophie had always been afraid of that water. So had he.

Jack looked at the ground again as Banjo dropped the drool-covered ball at his feet. "I coaxed Sophie onto the jetty that day believing that ridiculous punishment would solve everything, but I don't know if that's really what my sister had in mind." He threw the ball again and then finally met Laura's gaze. "To this day, Laur, I still question whether or not Sophie was supposed to make it out of the water alive."

Wide-eyed, Laura sucked in a breath and released it very slowly. "That's some pretty heavy stuff, Jack."

He nodded sadly. "Which is why I kept it a secret."

She stepped closer to him and put a hand on his shoulder reassuringly. "But sharing burdens is what family is for," she told him. "You can trust us, Jack. You can tell us these difficult things. Especially me. Pat. Even Mum and Dad. We all know who you are, what makes that heart of yours tick. We would never turn our back on you for a mistake you made as a child. No matter how unforgivable you think it is. We've all made bad decisions—sure, not all so life-altering as yours—but it's how you move forward from them that really matters."

Laura rested her head against Jack's arm as they both looked out over the field. They watched the dogs having a pounce and play with each other before snatching up the ball again and heading back to their humans. When Boris dropped the ball at Laura's feet, she straightened and patted Jack on the shoulder.

"You're a good guy, Jack." She smiled softly. "Stop doubting it and believe it. I think you've hated yourself long enough. You don't need further punishment from the rest of us."

Jack swallowed back a wave of emotion as Laura picked up the tennis ball and threw it into the distance.

"Is that also Sophie's opinion?" Jack couldn't look at her as he asked the question. He feared he already knew the answer.

"Sophie needs some time," Laura explained as she dusted her hands together, trying to rid herself of the dirty, slobbery muck from the ball.

"Of course." The words scratched at Jack's throat.

Of course Sophie needed time to decide whether she could forgive him, if she could still love him. Her text message hadn't included much detail, but Jack had read between the lines. He felt his face flush as tears blurred his vision again. He was going to lose her.

Laura stopped wiping her hands and frowned when she saw Jack's face. She pressed a hand on either side of his shoulders, supportively. "*Some time* does not mean *forever*, Jack. Just give her a couple of days. Sophie loves you, she told me as much, but wounds like this don't heal overnight. Respect her wishes, give her space to process and you'll make it through this together. You're already through the toughest part."

At that, Jack's lips quivered again, and he dragged Laura into a tight hug. He fought the urge to sob, to let his emotions get the best of him. The relief, love and support his new *sister* brought him was overwhelming. He didn't know if what she said about Sophie was true, but her reassurance had bolstered his waning hope.

"Thank you, Laur." He cuddled her tighter and felt her do the same. "Really. Thank you."

"I love you too, Jack." She chuckled softly. "We all do."

Jack relaxed into the hug and sighed. He allowed a tear or two to swirl down his cheeks before he broke the embrace and wiped them away.

Feeling stronger and more sure of his place in the Santoro family and at Bitterbark Creek, Jack braved a suggestion. "I guess I should tell your mum and dad what's been going on?"

"Probably not a bad idea." Laura nodded. "But believe me when I say it won't change their opinion of you. We all love you, Jack. To us, you're a Santoro now, not a Garland."

They shared a small affectionate smile, and then the playful pups were back. With adoration and excitement in their eyes, they nudged the tennis ball towards Laura's feet. She seized the plastic ball-launcher from Jack's hand, collected the ball and tossed it away, sending the farm dogs running wildly after it.

CHAPTER 30

A blustery breeze chased flocks of cumulus clouds across the bright blue sky, clearing space for sunlight to sparkle over the fertile field below. Reaching a crescendo, the gusts thrashed through a wonky line of adolescent eucalypts, whipping them about like the inflated tube figures adorning a car dealership. As though mocking the frailty of their younger companions, the taller trees skirting the border of the Bitterbark Creek property rustled their leaves riotously.

The hot Friday morning had melted into a humid afternoon, and the promise of a storm from the west could be felt in the mugginess of the air and the crackle of the wind. As Jack swung the weathered axe, splitting timber into another load of firewood, the wild conditions cooled the sweat trickling down his bare back. Chopping wood had been therapeutic for him. He'd been struggling with patience. He desperately wanted to see Sophie, needed to talk to her, but was fighting the urge. No good would come of anything until she was ready. He had to wait, no matter how frustrating it was.

Jack had been surprised by how well things had gone yesterday with Laura. Where he'd expected shock and judgement, there had only been support and empathy. She blamed his family. She put it down to their controlling influence over him—the brainwashing, as she called it—but Jack knew a portion of the fault still lay with him alone. If he hadn't listened to his mother and sister, hadn't encouraged Sophie out onto that jetty, none of them would be suffering through this turmoil. He was as much at fault as the other Garlands.

Jack lumped the split firewood on the well-stacked pile to his right before lugging another chunk of log onto the chopping stump. He scrubbed at the perspiration beading his forehead and then snatched up the battered axe, preparing to attack his next timber victim and continue to brood.

After their chat, Laura had been eager to help him create a plan of action to tell Sophie and her aunt and uncle his side of the story. Laura had suggested that a family dinner next Thursday evening, almost a week away, would be their best bet. Jack had questioned whether Sophie would be ready to see or talk to him by then, especially since she'd requested space. Laura had said they'd just have to wait and see. If given the chance, Jack would open his heart to Sophie and tell her everything now. But his previous cowardice had cost him all control over the situation. Now it was a waiting game. Patience was supposed to be his friend, but it didn't feel like it.

Jack hadn't realised how much Sophie's silence would eat at him. Their connection had strengthened so quickly that being cut off from her made him feel lost. Having her near had tethered him to his truest self, to what mattered most in life. Without her, Jack worried that the Garland characteristics he feared would leach back into his soul.

As Jack lost himself to his thoughts, his palms grew clammy and his grip on the axe handle weakened. While a week of waiting gave him time to prepare his confession, it was also plenty of time for his anxiety to bury him. His whole body was heavy with it. His mind on a nonstop loop.

Lowering the axe to his side, Jack searched the treetops above, taking refuge in the beauty there as he once again rubbed sweat from his brow. After a few deep breaths, his spirits lifted, and his thoughts began to calm. He needed a brief distraction to pull him back from the edge.

The chirruping of his smartphone startled him. He lunged, snatching it up from the long knobbly log he'd tossed it on, and then answered the call before he registered that it was from an unknown number.

"Hello?"

"Jackson? Why do you sound out of breath?"

Any good mood he'd managed to cobble together dissipated abruptly at the sound of his sister's shrill, demanding voice. For a split second, he considered hanging up on her, but curiosity made him behave.

"Why are you using an unknown number, April-Rose?"

There was a growl through the speaker. "Not that it matters to you, brother, but my phone's been misplaced."

"You mean you lost it?" Jack bit back a laugh.

"Have you lost your hearing, Jackson? I said *misplaced*."

"Right. Well, I hope you find it soon. There's a lot of important information on that thing." Since coming into power at Garland Grain, his sister had enjoyed having all the company's money accessible right from her phone. She used to laud it over him, what she could do with a click of a finger. Jack knew she loved the control. She could micromanage every cent like a dragon counting treasure in her coffers. He hoped she'd finally updated her ridiculously simple passwords.

"You think I don't know that?" Her voice was tinny through the device. "Tiffany is going to use the find-my-device application to locate it once I hand back her phone. Look, can we return to the point of my call?"

"You wanted to know why I'm out of breath?" He offered quickly. "Well, you see April-Rose, there's this thing called work and—"

"Jackson!" She cut him off with a screech.

"Yes," he drawled, pleased by his ability to agitate her.

"Have you quite finished?"

"What do you want, April-Rose?"

"I was hoping you could offer me some reassurance," she said sweetly.

"I thought you were the top predator in these parts, little sister, and that you feared nothing."

"I know you love the sound of your own voice, brother, but maybe just this once you could be silent and let me finish."

Jack released an exaggerated gasp. "Pot calling kettle."

"Obviously, it's necessary for me to make my point quickly," she barked. "Did you or did you not tell Sophie about that day at the dam?"

Jack felt his impish smile wilt as he considered his answer. He didn't want to admit he'd been such a coward. He hadn't just been afraid of Sophie and her family hating him once the truth came out. He was terrified of what his own family might do to ensure the secret didn't spread. Jack didn't know exactly what happened to Ella's mother, but he had his suspicions. He didn't need to know. His mother and sister were capable of anything. They had proved that several times over.

"I had hoped to hear you'd completed the duty yourself," April-Rose said. "At least then I'd know our family was represented fairly."

"It depends on how you define fair. If I'm to tell Sophie the reality of what happened, it will be the absolute truth. I'm not smoothing out the jagged edges of our indiscretions with careful compliments and tidy wording."

"So you'd dig our grave alongside your own? Does family mean nothing to you, Jackson? I thought you'd at least protect us where your own social standing was at stake."

"Clearly you don't know me at all, little sister."

"Clearly." The word was a snarl. "Well, I'm calling because it appears someone has already beaten you to the dreaded task. And I don't believe what Sophie heard painted us in the bright light we're accustomed to."

"You don't say?" Jack couldn't care less. He was too preoccupied about whether Sophie would ever speak to him again. Would she ever forgive him?

"This is a serious situation, Jackson. I don't understand how you can be so flippant about it all. What would happen to us if the whole town found out? How could Garland Grain continue to do business here? Our reputations would be ruined."

Jack shook his head slowly. "I don't think your current reputation is anything to be proud of, April-Rose."

There was a tempestuous huff of air through the speaker. "Would it please you to see Mother and I destitute? To see us banished from town in humiliation, ostracised like criminals?"

"*Criminals* isn't exactly inaccurate. Don't be so dramatic. Whatever consequences come our way, we deserve them. They always say karma's a bitch."

There was a sharp squeak of disbelief. "You can suffer your consequences, Jackson. Take your karma with a smile, but I plan to get ahead of this."

"And how do you propose to do that? Escape Moorhenvale with your millions?"

"No. I intend to tackle this problem at the root. Sway Sophie's allegiances and all will be resolved."

Jack laughed. His sister couldn't be serious. "You can't bribe her with money, April-Rose. She's not like the others you've forced to retreat or made to disappear. She won't be manipulated."

"Really? Because from what I've seen, brother, you've been doing a fine job of it yourself. I've heard it's like you've got her under some kind of spell. Shame it probably wore off when you were too weak-willed to tell her our version of the truth."

"*Our version of the truth?* What—that she slipped and fell?"

"That's the way I remember it."

Jack clenched his fist and bit back the insults lingering on his tongue. He stalked away a few paces and then back again. "My intentions may not have been honourable in the beginning, but I have not been manipulating Sophie in the good old Garland way. I have been trying to get our friendship back."

"Is that all?" April-Rose coughed cynically. "I've been told you're after something much more intimate."

"Watch yourself, little sister. I don't have the patience to spare today."

She laughed at him and then sighed. "Don't fool yourself, Jackson. You're playing Sophie just as I intend to. It's just our goals that differ."

The swelling anger in his chest was suffocating. "Stay away from Sophie," he ordered. "She's the least of your worries. If your phone has gone missing, you need to put all your energy into finding it. I'd hate for someone to figure out the passwords to those banking apps you love so much." He let his irritation and condescension bleed into his words.

"Cut the haughty tone, Jackson. You might not like my methods or motives, but deep inside you know that what I do, I do for the benefit of us all—the entire Garland family."

"Don't make me laugh. You've never cared for another person in your whole life."

"That's not true," April-Rose said vehemently. "I *loved* our father."

"You and me both," Jack agreed grimly. "But even he wouldn't stoop this low to shield us."

"Think what you like, brother. You can't stop me. I plan on meeting with Sophie and convincing her one way or another that it's best she sees things from our perspective. Who knows—we could become friends again too. I might even invite her to my engagement party." There was a concerning thread of malice in her suggestion.

"The promise of friendship, money or any accolades of popularity will not tempt her to the dark side," Jack warned.

"Sophie can't be bought."

"I guess we'll see, won't we? Remember, Jackson, if those options don't work, I've got numerous other cards to throw down."

Jack grimaced at the thought of his sister's earlier threat. The beat of music and the thump of shoes on the dance floor at Pat and Marilyn's wedding came rushing back to him as April-Rose's words replayed in his mind.

I could always get Bradley to handle this problem. I'm sure he'd love to have the opportunity to lure her attentions in his direction.

Jack had heard rumours about his sister's perverse games, using Bradley, Tiffany and whoever else to snare peoples' affections and control them until April-Rose was ready to strike. He was certain Sophie would be too clever for that, but then again, savvy businessmen and women had been successfully caught in his sister's trap. Just the possibility unnerved him.

"Don't even go there, April-Rose. Sophie will see straight through you both."

"Can you be so sure?" she challenged. "I'm willing to try *anything* to ensure her silence."

As Jack opened his mouth to snarl back, his sister cut him off with a slice of her reptilian tongue.

"Good chat, brother," she said, her sickeningly sweet tone as false as her love for her fiancé. "I'll be sure to keep you updated on my . . . progress."

He roared her name into his smartphone—fear, fury and frustration all scraping his throat—and nearly missed the dull, decisive *beep, beep, beep* of the disconnect tone.

CHAPTER 31

A rainbow of buds and blossoms, mainly roses, peonies and tulips, grew in a perfect arrangement in the neat, enclosed garden of the Eden Tea House. The view—both from the well-maintained Queenslander's veranda and from the picture windows brightening the elegant individual rooms—provided unparalleled beauty and class. High tea was the establishment's specialty, and they were renowned for their delicate French patisseries, delicious bite-sized cakes and exquisite herbal tea concoctions.

Sophie hadn't considered a visit to Eden's to be a priority while in town. She and Laura preferred the quaintness of Moorhenvale's bakery-slash-petrol station over the poshness Eden's exuded and expected of its customers. She doubted she would have even driven past the place had she not received a phone call from April-Rose Garland of all people, inviting her to attend the Saturday morning high tea.

"Tell me again, why are we going through with this?" Laura asked.

Sophie followed her cousin's gaze to the assortment of women seated around them on the wraparound veranda. Some were grey-haired, others youthful, but all appeared cheerful as they dined on sweet tea and even sweeter treats.

"April-Rose wouldn't give me a choice," Sophie explained. "She said she'd come by Bitterbark Creek to collect me if I couldn't make my own way. I bargained to have you come along so I didn't have to face this on my own."

Sophie was glad of Laura's company but would have preferred to be doing anything other than meeting one of the two Garland women who had caused her and her family so much grief. Yet she'd believed April-Rose when she'd threatened to show up at the farmstay to haul Sophie into the car herself. She hadn't been so blunt, of course, but Sophie understood her. April-Rose always got her way, no matter how much Sophie fought her. Perhaps their forced meeting would be an opportunity for Sophie to teach April-Rose she couldn't always win out?

"So *you're* the person to blame for my being thrown into a flower bowl of prissy femmes?" Laura smoothed her hands over her black slacks as her knee began a fidgety bounce. "To think I trusted you not to lead me into the world of high heels and summer dresses."

"Behave, you." Sophie stifled a smile. "I'm pretty sure we can still be thrown out of a fancy place like this."

Laura cast a suspicious look at the other customers. "You think they have a white-gloved security force hidden in the back somewhere, just waiting to control the situation if some radical makes a scene?"

"I'm guessing you're the radical in this scenario?" Sophie raised an eyebrow when her cousin ignored her to continue her spiel.

"Imagine ten nonnas—aprons freshly pressed and scowls set—all coming to evict you from your cosy chair." Laura shivered dramatically. "Terrifying."

Sophie swatted playfully at her cousin's forearm. "Stop it."

Snorting in amusement, Laura glanced beyond Sophie to the veranda's entry and abruptly choked on her good humour. Her look of alarm had Sophie spinning around.

April-Rose sauntered over to them, her sleek silver frock shimmering as she bared her fangs. Behind her, Tiffany hurried to keep up, her high heels clicking quickly like the paws of an eager lapdog. Sophie had a flashback of the two of them as little girls, looking eerily similar. Tiffany had always longed for what April-Rose had—money, status, power—but she'd never quite managed it. April-Rose wasn't skilled at sharing the spotlight, so it was unlikely Tiffany ever would.

"Sophie. Laura," April-Rose purred when she reached the table. "It's so lovely you could meet with us today." She moved a chair between them and slid into it, severing their invisible link of support. "And what luck we have with the weather. Beautiful, isn't it? Perhaps we'll get to repeat this occasion in the near future."

Laura gagged automatically before remembering where they were. April-Rose's gaze lit with fire. In a viper-quick flash of fingers, she snatched Laura's hand off the clothed tabletop before the other woman could recoil.

"How absolutely thrilled we are to have your company, little Laura Santoro," April-Rose cooed patronizingly. "When Sophie suggested you join us this morning, Tiffany and I were overjoyed at the thought. Weren't we, Tiffany?"

Her accomplice rounded the table and flattened her flouncy blue dress as she took the remaining seat. "We were indeed, April-Rose."

Laura yanked her hand free. "Have I missed a town memo or something nominating my new descriptor as *little*?" She scowled at April-Rose. "You're the second person this week to call me that."

"Well, you are petite, lovely." Tiffany aimed her bleached smile at the youngest Santoro.

"Yes, Laura," April-Rose agreed. "Take it as a compliment."

"Was it meant in that way?" Sophie raised her eyebrow. Releasing a hearty laugh, April-Rose placed a hand on her breast while her obedient henchwoman added her own giggle to the cacophony. "Such great banter we have. Just like old times."

"Why don't you just get on with it, April-Rose?" Sophie sighed. "There's no need to draw this farce out any longer than necessary."

"What do you mean, Sophie? Tiffany and I wanted to show you some geniality, that's all."

"Of course you did."

Wide-eyed with faux innocence, April-Rose showed her empty palms. "You clearly don't believe me, so—please—tell us why you think I asked to meet with you today, and I'll advise you of your accuracy or lack thereof."

Sophie relaxed into her chair and crossed her arms. "No. If you're truly trying to be friendly, April-Rose, then there's no need for games. Be honest and tell me why you really arranged this meeting."

"Fine then. No games." April-Rose spread her lips in a secretive smile. "Since we've heard rumours you intend to stay at Bitterbark Creek a while longer. . ." She paused purposefully.

Sophie began to expect a particular direction of conversation. Was April-Rose about to throw some threats around, whip up a little blackmail to chase her out of town? Considering what she'd learned the Garland matriarch was capable of, it was entirely likely April-Rose had learned a few tricks. What was it her nonna had said? *The poisoned pear doesn't fall far from the cursed tree.*

April-Rose fluttered her lashes coyly. "Well, we—Bradley and I—thought you'd be honoured to receive an invitation to our engagement party next Saturday. That is if you're not planning to leave before then?"

Startled, Sophie blinked several times. Was this a new form of punishment? "You're inviting me to your engagement party?"

"Yes. Laura's coming, aren't you, little Laura?" She patted the young woman's arm, making Laura flinch. "All the Santoros are. You'll find most people in town have already RSVP'd. It seemed only fair to allow you the opportunity to attend as well."

"Allow me?" A sharp laugh escaped Sophie. She was primed to point out the absurdity of the offer when a trim waitress with green eyes and a ginger braid politely interrupted them to deliver a tiered tray of delicacies. Once another graceful waitress had placed two elegantly painted teapots on the neatly laid tabletop, between upturned teacups, dessert plates and cutlery, April-Rose snapped her fingers in the woman's direction.

"Sweetie, can you bring us a bottle of champagne? We're celebrating the renewal of an old friendship." She dismissed the server with a wave of her hand, but when the woman's meek mumble of a reply clearly wasn't satisfactory, April-Rose flicked a glare over her shoulder. "Is there a problem with my *simple* request?"

The waitress wrung her hands until her fingers were red. "I'm so sorry, Miss Garland, but Eden's isn't licensed to sell alcohol."

April-Rose's gaze became icy. "Oh, I see. You must still be in training." When the young woman moved to disagree, April-Rose cut her off with a snarl. "You *must* still be in training, otherwise I fail to see the reason for your *major* misunderstanding. As I'm sure your manager will tell you, when your establishment has the privilege to serve a member of the Garland family, small exceptions can be made to ensure mutual happiness and goodwill."

Sophie nearly snorted. She couldn't believe people still jumped whenever the Garlands clicked their fingers. Although, since she learned about Ella's mother's experience, it was becoming more obvious by the minute that the Garlands were a real threat. It made her question whether she was truly ready to go down this path. Was she prepared to take on the Garlands no matter the cost?

The waitress considered April-Rose's explanation, but before she could make a decision, she was once again interrupted.

"My apologies, Miss Garland." An older lady appeared, impeccable in her lilac dress and tasteful make-up. She touched her colleague's shoulder as though encouraging her to retreat, and addressed April-Rose. "Did I hear you request champagne?

"Yes," April-Rose huffed. "I understand that *won't* be a problem."

"Of course. Shall we charge it to the card we have on file?"

April-Rose flicked her wrist dismissively as though the matter were settled. With a nod, the woman hastily withdrew.

"This used to be such a fine establishment, but clearly their hiring standards aren't what they used to be." April-Rose flared her nostrils.

"The first thing they learn should be that the customer is always right," Tiffany agreed heartily.

Laura frowned. "But they're not licensed? They aren't obligated to provide a service they're not legally allowed to offer."

"Oh, pish-posh, little Laura. I'm a Garland and they know that. Some rules don't apply."

"You wouldn't know this, being a Santoro and all"— Tiffany eyed Laura with disapproval—"but wealth and status garner respect in all areas of life."

Laura aimed a look of astonishment at Sophie, seeking her assistance.

"Don't even bother, Laur," Sophie said. "It's obvious that money and assumed importance have warped their sense of reality."

"There's that cheeky banter I've missed." April-Rose bared her teeth at Sophie. "But, come, let's be civil now. Look at all the delicious treats we have here." She gestured towards the tiered tray of desserts. "I placed the order myself, choosing only the best for my dearest friends."

Laura scoffed but covered it with a cough when hit with

the redhead's steely gaze.

"Go on now, Sophie," April-Rose encouraged. "I can tell by your figure that you enjoy indulging in sugary sweets—and," she added quickly to cover her insult, "we have two types of herbal teas on offer while we await the champagne."

"Miss Garland?" The woman in the lilac dress cleared her throat as she approached.

April-Rose inclined her head in the woman's direction.

"My apologies for interrupting, but it appears we have a small problem with your bank card."

"Small problem?"

"Yes." The woman glanced around the table as though deciding whether or not to proceed in mixed company.

"Well?" April-Rose hissed. "The quicker you spit it out, the quicker we can sort it."

"Your card—it's been declined."

"Impossible. Try it again."

"We've tried it three times. Perhaps you have another?"

Sophie shared a look with Laura as April-Rose pursed her lips tightly and considered the offending suggestion.

What happened to the Garland millions that were just a card tap away? Perhaps the wealthy person's trifecta of money, status and power could buckle and fall like a house of cards if just one factor was removed. Maybe this small mishap would remind the youngest Garland that she wasn't quite as invincible as she thought.

April-Rose rummaged around in her handbag and snatched a small gold card free from her purse. She waved it in the air for the older woman to collect.

"Thank you." The woman bowed before backing away. "Your champagne will be out directly."

April-Rose's furious gaze scorched a hole in the lady's back as she watched her scurry inside.

"I'm not sure about you, Laur," Sophie queried as she pushed her chair back from the table and stood, "but I've suffered through about all I can handle for one morning. I think this is our cue to leave."

"What?" April-Rose gaped. "Before we've finished our conversation?"

"Before the champagne?" Tiffany blurted in unison.

"Before I do something I'll probably regret."

Laura concurred with a smirk as she shifted her own chair back and rose to her feet. With her hands on her hips, Sophie stared down at the meanest Garland. "There was never friendly conversation on the agenda, April-Rose. You know that I know the truth of what happened all those years ago. That's why you brought us together today."

Sophie had caught on to her *old friend's* tricks the moment she picked up the phone. She'd just been deciding how best to tackle it. Keep it cool and sly, and not let on that she knew, or face it head-on and risk the wrath of the Garlands? April-Rose's attitude with the waitress and the champagne debacle had been her final two straws. Sophie was ready to lay out her hand. If the Garlands wanted to challenge her, they could bring it on. She wouldn't go down without a fight, not until everyone in town knew exactly what Sheridan and April-Rose had done to her, to Ella's mother, to countless others.

April-Rose straightened in her chair, her posture tense as she spoke through gritted teeth. "And what truth could that be, pray tell?"

"I thought we'd agreed to no more games, April-Rose. Look, I'm not sure who told you. I'm guessing you've got informants all over the place. But from what I can tell, you're making a last-ditch attempt to smooth past grievances to protect yourself." Sophie shook her head and feigned sympathy. "No matter what you try, it's not going to work this time. You can't buy me or manipulate me into believing we could ever make up. You and Tiffany think money and status equal power? Well, I think the truth trumps both of those. I don't yet know what I plan to do with the information I've uncovered, but you can be sure that I won't stop digging until I know *everything*."

"Go Soph," Laura cheered proudly. She threw a snide look in Tiffany's direction. "That's my cousin right there."

Sophie smiled politely as Tiffany paled and April-Rose turned red with rage. "It's been swell, ladies, but Laura and I have better things to do and nicer people to see. Enjoy that champagne. I'm sure it tastes almost as good celebrating failure."

Not giving them the chance to argue, Sophie strode towards the exit with Laura skipping along in tow. As they passed a bewildered waitress carrying a bottle of champagne and four flute glasses on a silver tray, they heard April-Rose screech behind them.

"Well—I'm rescinding the invitation to my engagement party, Sophie. Don't think you're still invited after that outburst. That goes for you too, Laura Santoro."

Sophie wanted to laugh. As threats went, being uninvited to an engagement party was hardly life-altering. Did April-Rose have any other cards to play, or had she just learned that there were times she had to fold?

After abandoning April-Rose and Tiffany, Sophie and Laura spent the rest of the day in town, window-shopping at the trendy stores, lunching at the Stout House Bar and Grill and even snagging a sunlounge each on the rooftop bar after a few games of pool.

Now, the blue-tinged lavender of the late afternoon sky blanketed the antiquated town centre of Warwick with a moody atmosphere of cool hues. With Saturday evening looming, all tourist-friendly boutiques had shut while the assortment of restaurants dotted throughout had brightened and begun to buzz with hungry patrons. As the streetlamps blinked to life, vehicles filled the parking along Palmerin Street, their occupants gathering in cheerful crowds on the previously quiet sidewalks.

Laura checked the rearview mirror and then glanced over her shoulder before reversing the silver Mitsubishi Pajero onto the popular street.

"Are you sure you don't want to stay a little longer?" Laura asked Sophie as they headed north. "It looks like it's going to be a busy night."

"What?" Sophie chuckled. "You haven't had enough fun today?"

Laura winked mischievously.

Sophie was exhausted and ready to head back to Bitterbark Creek to collapse into bed, but her cousin was still buzzing.

"You've got unlimited energy, Laur." Sophie smiled affectionately at her cousin. "Maybe you really are suited to the craziness of city life?"

"That's what I've been telling you, cuz."

"It's a shame you've got to take this old lady home, otherwise you could have had a night out on the town."

Laura whooped. "A night out on the town," she parroted. "We're not back in Brissy, in Fortitude Valley, Soph. Out here, what we did this afternoon was *out on the town.*"

"So, you did have fun?" Sophie teased.

Laura tapped her hands rhythmically on the steering wheel. "Why don't you use those sassy chops to talk about something you've been avoiding all day?"

"And what's that?" Unperturbed, Sophie gazed out the passenger-side window at the slowly passing shopfronts.

"When are you going to talk to Jack?"

Oh gosh, Jack. Sophie had been avoiding him and the topic of talking to since they'd first heard the truth from Ella. She'd been upset, angry. And then disappointed that he hadn't trusted her enough to tell her the truth. She'd seen how traumatised Ella was over it all and knew he must feel the same way. But it didn't remove the sting of his deceit, of his silence. She didn't know when she'd be ready to talk to him and didn't know what to say. She wanted to forgive him. But she didn't know if she could trust him again.

"Laura." Sophie released her cousin's name in a lengthy whine.

"Sophie." Laura mimicked her cousin's sulky tone.

"Do we really have to talk about this now?"

"Well, you can't avoid him forever."

"I know, and I don't want to." Sophie pressed her head back into the headrest. She missed him already.

"What *do* you want then?"

"I . . . don't know." It was almost a whisper and very much a lie.

Sophie knew what her heart craved, but she wasn't sure if it *should*. Could she truly forgive Jack for not only his part in the past but for lying about it too? She didn't know. She was certain there was more to the story, and she wanted those answers.

"What I need is to talk to Sheridan," Sophie decided.

"Sherry?" Laura asked, surprised. "That's a bold move."

"It's like Ella said—Sheridan Garland has always had an unhealthy amount of control over her children. We know she played a part in turning Jack and April-Rose against me and my family. What I don't fully understand is why. What had we ever done to her? What had I ever done to the Garland family? *My* father was the one who died. Maybe once I get some answers from her, I'll finally know what to say to Jack."

"You do need to hear him out too, Soph." Laura's tone was unusually serious. "Now that he's ready to talk about it, it will be good for both of you to work through it."

Sophie shifted in her seat to stare at her cousin's profile. "I'm sorry, but when did you become the mature one?"

"I don't know," Laura joked. "I must be coming down with something." She spun the steering wheel and drove the Pajero right, onto Grafton Street.

With a half-hearted chuckle, Sophie returned her attention to the darkening road ahead of them. "I just need some time to work things out on my own first. I don't want to say anything I'll regret, Laur. I promise I will make time to talk to Jack."

Laura glanced over at her, a sparkle in her eyes. "Good

girl. I'm proud of you."

"Yeah, yeah. Hardy har har. Maybe you could use your own sassy chops to pick a new topic of conversation?" Sophie propped her elbow on the windowsill and rested her chin in her palm, letting her attention drift once more to the activities on the street outside. She heard Laura's light huff of laughter beside her and then a sudden sharp intake of breath as she, too, saw what Sophie did.

"Was that Bradley and Tiffany—"

"—having dinner at Ronaldo's?" Sophie finished.

"Together?"

"Yeah."

Sophie frowned and looked out the window again even though they had long passed the restaurant. Laura was stealing glances at her, silently seeking some sort of explanation.

"They're organising things for Bradley and April-Rose's wedding, right?" Sophie snatched an excuse from the ether. But geez, it hadn't looked innocent. It was just as Camille had described—*intimate*. "They were probably just talking about the preparations, maybe even the engagement party?"

Laura's pinched expression suggested she thought otherwise.

"Tiffany and April-Rose are best friends," Sophie tried again. "They always have been. I'm sure it was just an innocent friendly dinner, that's all."

"It looked pretty cosy to me."

Sophie couldn't argue. "Just like Camille said at dinner the other day."

"Yep." Laura steered left onto the Cunningham Highway. "I don't want to join the gossip queen in my assumptions, but something fishy is going on."

"Yeah. It definitely looked suspicious. Maybe April-Rose has more than me to worry about. That would explain her lacklustre threats this morning."

"I mean, I don't know about you," Laura pressed a hand to her heart, faking misery, "but I am seriously scarred from having my invitation to April-Rose and Bradley's engagement party revoked. I don't know how I'll cope."

Sophie laughed and playfully poked her cousin in the arm. "The only thing you're sad about is missing out on all the fancy food."

Laura tossed her head back, laughing. "You got me. Still, I think the tides may be turning, and our dear April-Rose might not be prepared for the tsunami that's about to hit her."

After everything Sophie had uncovered in the past twenty-four hours, she couldn't agree more heartily.

CHAPTER 32

The wide cerulean sky above Sophie's cabin was cloudless, an almost limitless expanse of perfect blue, with only the sparkle of the Sunday afternoon sunshine pricking a hole in the exquisite hue. While the chirruping crickets were enlivened by the springtime heat, lethargy was gnawing at Sophie. From her position on the timber floor of the cabin's veranda, laptop perched on her legging-covered thighs, she closed her eyes and embraced the sedating warmth.

She'd spent the morning and afternoon completing work for the office—preparing a prospective sales advertisement for the marketing team and fabricating a funky slogan for a new T-shirt design. She didn't have the same applications on her personal computer as those on her work device, and the internet connection was running a little slow, but her boss—half of the sister duo who'd created the rising fashion brand *Smooch & Blossom*—was appreciative of what she could complete while working remotely.

She had been reading an email to that effect when weariness had overwhelmed her once more. Lost to the darkness behind her eyelids, Sophie relaxed against the sun-seared slats of the veranda's balustrade, enjoying the heat on her shoulders and neck. She was on the verge of dozing off into a sublime micro-nap when the joyful screeching of a posse of drunken lorikeets startled her awake. Straightening, she shook her head and blinked several times before refocusing on her email account. In the brief period she'd succumbed to drowsiness, a new message had appeared.

The subject line read RE: *Appointment with S. Garland.*

Sophie hesitated, letting the cursor hover over the subject line for just a moment before clicking the email open. She hadn't expected a reply so soon, especially after the chilly reception she'd received over the phone that morning.

Last night, on their arrival home from Warwick, Laura had swiped what she'd believed to be Sheridan's personal number from her parents' address book and passed it on. Though it should have been obvious Sheridan would require those she classed as beneath her to make contact through an intermediary, Sophie was still surprised when she heard the unflappable voice of Sheridan's personal assistant. The woman had been quick to dismiss her, hanging up tersely instead of prolonging their dispute. So Sophie tried another course of action and contacted the Garland matriarch via her work email at Garland Grain. While there was a chance her PA checked that as well, Sophie believed a control freak like Sheridan would at the very least view all emails that came to her inbox.

Sophie scanned her reply.

Mrs. Garland will acquiesce to your request and will meet with you at 10 a.m. sharp this coming Tuesday at Garland Manor.

Sheridan's hasty agreement made Sophie wonder if she might have her own reasons for desiring the discussion. Was she hoping to intimidate Sophie into leaving town? Or had she joined April-Rose's bandwagon, praying better-late-than-never friendliness would win Sophie's silence?

Sophie read the single line of text again. She felt queasy.

Sheridan would have the answers she sought. Sophie was sure of it. Swallowing deeply, she rubbed her temples and felt her pulse quicken, stirring her formerly drowsy limbs. She had started this journey and would see it through. She didn't intend on quitting until she'd uncovered enough to trigger her lost memories to resurface.

There was a creak from the veranda's stairs. Sophie flinched in fright and almost hurled the laptop into the side of the cabin. She muttered a curse as she righted the device and then glanced up at the intruder.

"Jack?"

"Sneaking in some city work between farm chores, I see." Jack offered her a cautious smile as he ascended the final step.

Sophie hastened to her feet. She felt a little awkward considering she hadn't spoken to him since Wednesday afternoon, before her enlightening chat with Ella.

"Sorry." Jack reached forward, palms out, as though approaching an anxious animal. "I didn't mean to make you uncomfortable. I—" He stopped and glanced away. "I thought. . ." Shaking his head, he straightened and started again. "Maybe this wasn't such a great idea. Sorry, Soph. I just miss you."

She missed him, too. Part of her wanted to run to him, to be scooped up in his strong arms, while the rest feared the thought of diving back in too quickly. She couldn't afford to get hurt again. She didn't know how much more heartache she could take. Closing the laptop, Sophie clutched it in front of her like a barricade.

"It's okay, Jack. Like I said in my text message, I just needed some time to process everything."

"And I've ruined that by coming here, haven't I?" He squeezed his eyes shut and muttered a curse. "I'm such an idiot. Please forgive me. I can leave if you want me to, Soph."

Sophie opened her mouth, considering, and then she looked at him—*really* looked at him. Jack's eyes were red with sunken dark circles beneath them as though he hadn't been sleeping. He looked drained, his shoulders slumped, hair scraggly. There were new creases around his eyes and a deep pinch in his brow. He looked like a broken man, like the guilt he'd felt inside all these years had finally cracked the surface. It hurt her heart to see him that way, in so much distress. She couldn't send him away.

Sophie sighed. Maybe it was time they both stopped letting the past hold them back. It was too late to change anything now. If they could love and accept each other as they were, maybe they could finally move towards the future together.

"You don't need to say anything, Soph." Jack took her silence as dismissal and moved to go back down the steps.

"No, Jack. Wait." She hurried to his side. "Would you like to come in? We could talk for a bit?"

His expression brightened before wariness took over. "Are you sure?"

"Yes." There was nothing more she wanted in that instant than to see the man she loved happy again. Sophie released her white-knuckled grip on her laptop and took his hand in hers. She led him to the cabin door and over the threshold. Once they were inside, door shut behind them and her laptop safely on the table, Sophie faced him.

There was desperation in Jack's blue eyes, the flicker of an internal battle. He sucked in a breath and shook his head. "I'm sorry," he said as he dragged Sophie into his arms and placed a hungry kiss on her lips.

She stiffened for a moment, questioning whether this was a good idea, and then melted into the embrace. Jack kissed her like his life depended on it, like he feared he'd never get another chance to do so. Sophie struggled to keep up with him, to catch her breath as the kisses grew hotter, deeper. She needed air, but she didn't want him to stop.

After some time away from Jack to think things through, Sophie had felt their connection severing, a distance yawning wide between them. Yet now, back in Jack's arms, everything was as it should be. It was like their souls had entwined the moment their bodies had embraced. Reunited with her other half and finally whole again. She believed they could take on anything if they were together.

Sophie gasped when he pressed her closer, feeling the hard length of him against her belly. He broke the kiss to look at her, a question in his eyes. She nodded her agreement. She wanted him. She had never wanted another man as badly as she wanted Jack Garland. She looked over her shoulder at the back of the cabin.

"Bedroom?" she suggested.

He swooped down to catch her lips in his again and they stumbled towards the bedroom doorway. At the edge of the bed, Sophie unbuttoned his shirt as he kicked off his boots, both of them stealing kisses where they could. Jack peeled off her white singlet and tossed it to the floor. She unzipped his jeans. There was a mad desperation in the way they stripped off their remaining clothing and fell onto the bed, naked and wrapped in each other's arms.

Jack nipped her lower lip and then dropped his kisses lower, over her chin and down her throat. The hair on his chest pricked her nipples taut as he moved down her body. He kissed a hot trail over her breasts, caressing her there, taking her nipple between his teeth and circling his tongue around it before moving to the next. She arched up to meet him when he kissed below her navel, his hot breath tickling the most sensitive spot between her thighs. When his mouth covered the centre of her, kissing her there with such hunger, such desire. Sophie moaned and closed her eyes, lost to the pleasure of it all. Jack nipped at her heated flesh, licked her deeply, probing, suckling until she couldn't take it anymore.

Sophie grabbed his shoulders and hauled him back into her arms. She was throbbing with such a need for him that she couldn't wait any longer. She grabbed the foil packet Jack had thrown on the bed and reached between them to slip it in place before guiding him inside her. Jack groaned, pushing deeper into her hot, wet embrace. Sophie panted as he began a rhythm that quickly increased in intensity. She clutched at him, wanting more, holding on to him as the delicious sensation of him filling her, completing her, dulled all other senses. There was only Jack, only Sophie, and their love for one another. When Jack grunted and burst inside her, Sophie hit her own climax and moaned, the fireworks of ecstasy gripping her. As she held Jack in her arms, her body tremoring in delight, Sophie knew this was where she belonged. Jack and Bitterbark Creek were her home. No grave childhood mistakes or traumatic incidents could ever rip that from her.

An hour flew by before their tryst was interrupted by the chirp of a mobile phone. Uncle Nick had called for Jack's assistance with a fallen gum tree over the dirt road in the back pasture. They needed both the ute and the four-wheeler to shift it before nightfall so that it didn't affect the bus of school kids visiting tomorrow.

"I can call Nick back, tell him I'm busy," Jack suggested solemnly. "Maybe Dale can help him?" Jack reached out and took Sophie's hand in his, caressing her palm with his thumb.

Sophie nestled deeper into the swirl of sheets on the bed. "No, don't worry," she reassured him. "We'll have more time another day."

"We've barely talked about it, Soph." He sighed. "There's so much I want to tell you, that I want to apologise for."

"We have plenty of time," she told him.

"Do we?" He was fearful again. He'd told her he'd been terrified she'd leave after discovering the truth from Ella. He said he couldn't bear to lose her again.

She smiled softly. "I'm not going anywhere, Jack."

He released a ragged breath. "We could meet tonight?"

"I'm supposed to be meeting Laura."

"Again?" He said it with a little smirk. "At least I know

who the favourite is."

She gently tossed a pillow at him. "I think what we did—several times—this afternoon is proof *you're* the favourite." She laughed.

"I wish I could stay." He leaned back over to place another kiss on her lips.

"I wish you could too." She cupped his cheek and kissed him back.

Sophie meant it, but a part of her was happy to let Jack leave. They'd discussed a little of what had happened at the Garland dam twenty years ago and why Jack had behaved as he had. He wouldn't stop apologising until Sophie reminded him, with a hand over his heart, that she loved him, and that whatever his past sins may be, they did not define him. Jack wasn't done with his confession—and neither was Sophie—but Uncle Nick's call had brought their time to an end.

As he dressed, Sophie found herself relieved that she hadn't had the chance to tell Jack about her meeting with his mother. She knew he'd likely try to talk her out of it. She may have been ready to move forward with him, but that didn't mean she'd forgiven the rest of his family. She wanted answers, retribution for Ella's sake at least. And the only way to get the whole story was from the snake herself, the self-appointed Queen of Moorhenvale.

"Tomorrow then?" he asked hopefully.

"Maybe?" She nibbled her lower lip. "I've got a few things planned, a lot of work to catch up on, and I promised to help Aunty Robin and Uncle Nick around the place too."

He cocked an eyebrow at her suspiciously. "You're not still going to avoid me after this, are you?" He tried to make it a joke, but she could hear the unease in his voice.

"No," Sophie said. She just wanted some breathing room until after she'd talked with his mother.

Jack didn't look convinced. "If something's wrong, Soph, please tell me."

"Oh, sorry, Jack." She shook her head and pulled him

back down onto the bed until he was once again leaning over her. "Nothing's wrong. I promise." She kissed him and tried to show him how deeply she cared for him with each touch of her lips. She hadn't meant to worry him, but she didn't want to confide in him and risk him thwarting her plans.

"Okay, I believe you," he chuckled when she finally freed him. "Fine then, if you've got a busy couple of days ahead, come to the Santoro family dinner on Thursday night. Laura helped me with a plan for telling everyone about what happened that day at the dam. Maybe by then you'll feel comfortable enough to tell me what's got you so distracted?"

When she narrowed her eyes at his observation, he laughed again.

"I'm no genius, Soph. But I can tell there's something you're still not telling me. Hopefully the more we talk, the more we'll trust each other. I'm in no hurry. We've got our whole lives to work through whatever needs working through and to heal whatever needs healing. I'm just over the moon that you're giving me a chance to prove how much I care, how much I've always loved you."

Sophie's throat tightened at Jack's words and her gaze became misty. His support meant the world to her, and his resolve to not question her further proved how much he trusted her.

"I love you too," she whispered, pulling him in for one final tender kiss. She reluctantly released him and then playfully pushed him away. "Now go be a good adopted son. I'll see you on Thursday night if not before."

Jack smiled sweetly down at Sophie, lifting her hand to his mouth and kissing the back of it. The look in his eyes was one of complete adoration. "Thursday night," he vowed.

CHAPTER 33

Alongside the timber barn and the sprawling meadow often enjoyed by Bitterbark Creek's horses was a small pasture securing a menagerie of visitor-friendly creatures. While a few patches had been gnawed by sharp teeth and stomped by heavy hooves, the rich emerald-green lawn flourished tall and wild—especially beneath the rustic fence where it harboured a brave number of sun-yellow dandelions. From its perch on a wooden rail, a black and white butcherbird puffed its belly and began to chortle a cheerful morning song, encouraging one of the field's larger inhabitants to join the chorus with a long, monotone moo.

"You tell him, Lola." Uncle Nick grinned and unfastened a prickly bale of hay from the back of the four-wheeler.

The light tan Jersey cow bobbed her head—likely to shoo free a pesky fly—and appeared to approve of her owner's remark as she did so.

With a giggle, Sophie ceased patting Banjo's silky head through the timber slats and stood up, watching the dog collapse lazily beside his buddy Boris on the cool overgrown lawn outside the paddock. Unconcerned with the action around them, the pups looked on sleepily while Nick scooped up the hay bale and carried it across to the penned yard. Inside, Sophie and Aunt Robin caught the heavy load with gloved hands and then carted it across the ground to rest next to the water trough, where the remnants of a previous bale remained.

When Robin used a small knife to remove the twine encasing the sallow-hued feed, Brandy, the heftier of the two dairy cows, moseyed over to investigate. She pressed her moist muzzle into Sophie's covered palm, nuzzling there and garnering herself a pat on the flank before she lowered her nose to the straw.

"Patience, young lady," Robin told her, pushing at the sturdy bovine's cheek until the animal backed away a step, then two. "We'll have to do this fast," she told Sophie.

Crouching, they yanked clumps free, strewing piles of hay around and loosening the dense block of feed until it was easier for all the animals to access and devour.

"You've got company," Uncle Nick called from where he supervised on the sidelines.

Jumping to their feet, the women skipped to freedom as the farm animals closed in. The trio of Merino sheep, the Jersey cattle duo and the pair of Pygmy goats advanced excitedly on their breakfast. Even the plump bantam chickens came running from the other side of the small pasture, abandoning the food scraps and poultry pellets sprinkled around their own coop to inspect the new bulk of chow.

"They're an insatiable lot." Aunt Robin stopped to admire the scene now that she and Sophie were safe at Nick's side.

"Greedy buggers," her husband agreed, "but lovable just the same." He unclipped the lock to the metal gate, pushing it ajar to let his wife and niece exit.

"A lot like these two." Robin pointed to the farm dogs, who leapt up at the clinking sound of steel against steel. They brushed against her shins and twirled in front of her until she removed her gloves and bent to pat them. "Hello,

I'm back. Yes. You are both good boys for waiting. Very good boys."

The frisky canines lapped up the affection as Nick refastened the gate. "You can tell who their favourite is." He winked at Sophie.

Sophie's mind immediately jumped to the afternoon the day before, to her intimate encounter with Jack, when she'd reassured him that he was her favourite. The thought made her smile, made her miss him. She had noticed him outside working that morning and had waved before scurrying off to help her aunt and uncle with the morning chores. She yearned to spend more time with him but didn't trust herself not to blurt out her intention to meet with Sheridan. They would just have to wait until after that, until Thursday evening as they'd planned.

"I think you'll find no one's their favourite," Robin corrected her husband. "They make a fuss of anyone and everyone, especially if they've got food."

A likely story," Nick smirked. "Speaking of favourites. . ." He broached the change in topic warily. "Your aunt and I were thinking about having our favourite niece and our favourite adopted son over for a special dinner on Thursday." He glanced at his wife. "It's our final night together before the newlyweds return and regale us with stories of their adventures overseas, so we thought it would be nice for us all to have a chat."

"*You* thought it would be nice?" Sophie eyed her uncle suspiciously. His script reeked of her cousin's scheming. "Did Laura say something to you?"

Although she had caught up with Laura the night before to tell her that she'd contacted Sheridan Garland, Sophie hadn't braved the topic of her and Jack, their reunion or the fact that they had been intimate several times. Sophie wanted to tell her but knew Laura would delve into the nitty-gritty and ultimately ask how her future conversation with Sheridan might affect things. She didn't have the energy to face such a big question so soon. She loved Jack, and that was all that mattered right now. Since Laura wasn't aware that Sophie and Jack were back on good terms, her cousin had obviously sent in the B team to matchmake.

"Yes, Laura will be there," Aunt Robin offered vaguely. "She's promised to help me with the cooking."

"Clever, Aunt Robin." Sophie pointed a finger between her relatives. "But I'm on to you both. Come on, what did Laura say?"

"Nothing, Chook." Nick wrapped a burly arm around his wife's shoulders. "We're just looking forward to having the five of us together."

Sophie took off her gloves and crossed her arms. "So, none of this has anything to do with the fact that I told Jack I needed some space?" Sophie knew Laura was behind this sneaky suggestion. Why wouldn't they admit it? Jack had already invited her, and they had started working things out. Her aunt and uncle's intervention was hardly necessary.

Robin patted her husband's chest as though advising him to let her speak. She gave her niece a warm smile. "We don't know anything about your personal business, sweetheart. The dinner is just a nice opportunity for us all to talk to each other."

"There's no need to keep up the act, you two. I know Laura put you both up to this."

"What act?" Robin pulled her best poker face.

"It's not like you've both kept the quarrel a secret, Chook," Nick contested. "We all saw how happy you were together at the wedding and the family dinner afterward. Since then, you've been of mixed moods, distant, and Laura says Jack has been moping around his cabin."

"Aha!" Sophie exclaimed. "Laura does have a big mouth."

"I'm sorry to say that's not a state secret." Robin took hold of her niece's hands. "She was worried about you, and so are we. Even your mother agreed that you seemed more content here with Jack than you had been in a long time."

Uncle Nick placed his warm palm on Sophie's shoulder.

"We don't know what happened between you, but your aunt and I think you're good for each other. You always have been."

"I agree." Sophie nodded, startling them both.

"You do?" Robin blinked in surprise.

"But Laura said. . ." Nick glanced at his wife.

"Laura was trying to help, and I love her for that, but there's no need. Really." She squeezed her aunt's hands in hers to reassure her. "Jack and I made up yesterday." *Several times*, Sophie thought to herself. "We have a lot to unpack and work through, but we plan on doing that together."

"Well, I'm glad to hear it," Nick chuffed, wrapping an arm around her shoulders and pulling her in close for a side-hug. "You always were a matching pair. I'd hoped you would find a way to reconcile. I know you've been through a lot together over the years."

"So, Thursday night dinner then?" Robin frowned in confusion. "Is that still happening?"

Sophie nodded when her uncle released her from his embrace. "Yes. Jack asked me himself. I just haven't had a chance to tell Laura. There's been a lot going on recently."

"We've heard a little of it, sweetheart." Robin beamed. "From what Laura told us, Jack's isn't the only old friendship you're rekindling."

Sophie huffed. "Are there *any* secrets in your household?"

"Not with Laura around." Nick chuckled.

"Ella sounds as though she's grown up to be a lovely young lady," Aunt Robin commented.

Her uncle grinned. "She always was a good-humoured little girl, but Laura says she's become quite the wit."

"You don't say?" Sophie couldn't hide her amusement. Sounds like her cousin had a bit of a crush.

Aunt Robin's eyes widened as though she'd been hit with an idea, and she looked at her husband. "We should invite Ella to our Thursday dinner."

Before her uncle could answer in the affirmative, as his

broad smile suggested, Sophie interrupted. "Might be best if we hold off. I believe Jack and Laura have something particular planned."

"That's right." Robin clicked her fingers. "Laura said Jack had something important to discuss with all of us. Maybe next time?" She looked to her niece and husband for approval.

"Next time," Sophie agreed as Uncle Nick nodded. "So, is there anything Laura didn't tell you about what I've been up to recently?" Her cousin may have a big mouth, but Sophie hoped Laura still knew when to keep things to herself. Sophie's upcoming meeting with Sheridan Garland was definitely one of those things.

"How would we know that if she never told us?" Nick cocked an eyebrow.

"Good point. Well, just know that your cheeky daughter and her big mouth have a pinch coming their way for all their meddling."

Nick barked out a laugh. "I'm sure Laura knows what she's in for, Chooky. This isn't the first time she's been caught meddling, and it won't be the last."

"He's right, sweetheart." Robin slipped her arm through Sophie's. "Unlike some people, our baby knows whatever mischief she hatches, she also catches."

Sophie was pleased to hear it, but she was even more pleased that her loving family was supportive of her blossoming relationship with Jack. Uncle Nick was right. She and Jack had always had something special, even as children. She'd made the right choice in forgiving him, loving him, trusting him. Jack may have been a Garland, but he was a Garland at Bitterbark Creek now, and a perfect fit for her family. A perfect fit for Sophie.

CHAPTER 34

Garland Manor was an enormous, bespoke Queenslander-style mansion. Raised high to endure the state's intense summer heat, it dominated the immaculately maintained acreage that had belonged to the family for over a century. A newly renovated barn stood to the right of the property, and a lavishly landscaped garden wrapped around the left. Rose bushes of all colours bloomed across the estate. They sprouted from elegant pots on the grand external staircase and billowed over balcony planters on the gazebo-like wings at each end of the vast dwelling.

Everything about the place was so familiar to Sophie, though maybe grander than it had been twenty years ago. However, there remained one thing in particular she couldn't assess from her current perspective. The Garlands' dam. The broad body of murky water that still filled her with a mixture of terror and curiosity was just across the back pasture and down a slope. She felt unsettlingly drawn to it, an unearthly connection to the place that had forever claimed a part of her and caused her family such grief.

Shaking free of those dark thoughts, Sophie exited the Santoros' silver Pajero and immediately regretted turning down Laura's offer of company. Earlier that morning—

after rebuking her cousin for meddling—the two of them had left Bitterbark Creek under the guise of visiting the Moorhenvale Bakery. While Laura had agreed to help with Sophie's alibi, she'd also hoped to come along, but Sophie didn't want to risk jeopardising the meeting with Sheridan.

As she frowned up at the magnificent country home and headed for the front gate, her smartphone buzzed. She pulled it from her handbag and glanced down at the screen. The dazzling midmorning sunlight bounced off the shiny surface, but she could still read the message from Laura.

Are you there yet?

When Sophie went to type her reply, her phone vibrated again.

I think I should have come. Don't let that she-devil bully you. Make sure you get the answers you need.

Sophie quickly tapped the keypad but was interrupted by yet another message that shook the mobile phone.

I mean it, Soph. This may be your only chance to get Sherry's perspective.

As Sophie made her way through the gate to the front stairs, she deleted her unsent message and tried again, this time managing to deliver a response before her cousin dispatched another comment.

You're not helping, Laur. I'm feeling the pressure enough as it is.

She switched her phone to silent and gazed up at the stylish butterfly staircase that climbed up to a central landing before ascending to the elaborate veranda. As she mounted the first step, she felt her phone shudder once more. Looking quickly at the glossy screen, she was surprised to see Jack's name appear. He still had no idea of her plans to meet with his mother.

I'm so glad you agreed to come on Thursday. I miss you, Soph.

Those two simple sentences tugged at her heart. She missed him too. The magnetic pull between them felt stronger than ever. Sophie had to clench her teeth and squeeze her eyes shut against the coming tears. She didn't want to cry, didn't want to appear weak, but she was so stressed and afraid of what Sheridan would reveal. She was juggling so much—emotional turmoil, work, secrets—she didn't know how much longer she could last without crumbling.

Taking a deep breath, Sophie tried to clear her thoughts and calm her nerves.

"Miss Wendall?" a curt female voice inquired from above.

Sophie wiped her eyes and steadied herself. "Yes," she nodded, climbing the final few timber stairs. "I'm here to meet with Mrs. Garland."

"Of course." The plain-faced elderly woman—rigid in her navy housekeeper uniform—gestured for Sophie to follow her as she marched towards a hexangular wing. The dull thumping of their footsteps on the wooden flooring sounded ominous against the quiet morning, where only the cheeps of crickets, the hum of curious bees and the faint tweets of birdlife broke the peaceful silence. When the veranda opened into a gazebo-like space, the housekeeper motioned towards the lavish outdoor furniture setting. "Please take a seat. I will inform Mrs. Garland of your arrival."

Once the housekeeper disappeared through a connecting door, Sophie sat on the cushioned lounge, debating the perfect posture. After crossing her legs one way and then the other, readjusting the fall of her violet skirt each time, she began fiddling with the frilled pillows beside her. Each minute that passed heightened her nerves until the butterflies in her stomach were flapping so wildly she thought she might be sick. Then she heard the click of the door latch and froze, on the verge of flight or fight, waiting to see what kind of monster would appear.

From her impeccably applied make-up to her flawlessly arranged champagne-blond hair and designer outfit, everything about Sheridan Garland told the world how rich and incredibly important she thought she was. She wore her arrogance like a badge of honour, proclaiming with just one look that she was out of everyone's league in every way.

Sheridan locked her glacier-blue gaze on Sophie's and sauntered over to her. Fear chilled Sophie's limbs and an anvil of dread replaced the wave of nausea in her gut.

"I want it known," Sheridan began sternly as she positioned herself opposite Sophie, across the glass coffee table, "that had it not been for recent events of *your* making, I would not have agreed to a meeting such as this. Yet, seeing as you've put me in a particularly difficult situation, forcing us all on a course that I can only imagine will end in destruction, I see no point in hiding the truth any longer. In fact, if everything works out as it should, I doubt I'll still be around to deal with the consequences of your interference."

Sophie gulped deeply as she digested Sheridan's words. Clearly, the woman expected the fallout from Sophie's inquiry to be immense if she was also planning to leave town.

Sheridan crossed one slender leg over the other, mirroring Sophie's body language, and then twirled a hand in the air dismissively. "Though I suppose if I'm to have a fresh start elsewhere, I need a clean slate. So tell me. Which of my darkest secrets should I divulge first?" She stared intimidatingly at Sophie as though trying to prompt a response.

Sophie felt locked into some sort of awkward staring contest. Was Sheridan serious? Her dramatic, cryptic monologue sounded almost rehearsed. Though Sophie still jittered with adrenaline, her fear of the monster before her had weakened substantially. She relaxed into the overpriced chair with a laugh. "Gosh, Sheridan. I had expected a cold reception, but that was priceless. You complain that *I'm* destroying *your* life, as if you haven't done the same to countless others? And what, you're just going to leave town rather than face what you've done? I didn't realise you were such a coward." Sophie shook her head and laughed again. When did the woman she'd once considered to be the mother of all evil become an old dragon puffing only smoke?

Sheridan just blinked at her. "*We*, my dear Sophie. We plan on leaving this thankless place, and I resent being called a coward. While your prying into the past may have escalated the timing of my departure, I'm leaving because I'm not needed anymore, hardly wanted. My children barely acknowledge me unless they want something or are forced to be amicable. Why would I wish to stay? I have agreed to talk with you today to clear the air. I've begun to see that it's the only way to move on. Perhaps doing you the courtesy of revealing the truth will be my legacy, a redemption of sorts before I shake off this tattered shell and become anew."

Sophie frowned, considering the mysterious choice of words. *We plan on leaving.* But after the harsh criticism of her children, Sophie questioned if that would include April-Rose. "I'm surprised you feel any guilt over past events, Sheridan. I hardly believed you had a conscience."

"Don't be so naive, Sophie. I have felt the weight of these secrets just as you have felt the absence of their truth. I do not regret their creation, only the need to maintain their secrecy. Ensuring the silence of others over all these years has been the most exhausting punishment. I am very ready to be rid of it."

"I'm guessing April-Rose feels much the same if she's aware of you speaking with me today?" Sophie laid the verbal trap suspecting Sheridan's answer to be very much the opposite. April-Rose would not have been still trying to manipulate Sophie only days before if she planned to make her escape. Sheridan's partner had to be someone else. "With you both leaving town soon, what will happen to Garland Grain?"

Sheridan blinked with indifference. "My daughter is not aware of our meeting or of my plans to leave town. She would not be understanding or receptive to either action. Yet mother knows best, and what's best for me is to move on and start a new life with the only person who still holds a place in my heart. Garland Grain is no longer my concern, and from what I have heard, my dear daughter's choices have run it into the ground. She is old enough to weather the consequences without my assistance, and I will no longer allow her poor decisions to reflect negatively on my own life."

This was not the conversation Sophie had expected upon arriving at Garland Manor. Sheridan and April-Rose had always been inseparable, but somewhere along the line, something must have gone very wrong between them—whether April-Rose was aware of it or not. It left Sophie wondering again who Sheridan planned to leave town with.

"Now." Sheridan sniffed. "If you're quite done interrogating me, may we move forward?"

Sophie fought the urge to roll her eyes at the Garland matriarch. "By all means," she said sarcastically.

"Very well." Sheridan arched her perfectly trimmed eyebrow. "It won't come as a surprise to hear that I have never liked you, Sophie. My aversion to the Wendalls and Santoros runs deep, but I've seen how determined you are to unearth the truth, a tenacity that is familiar to me. You're a fighter, and you would do anything to protect this life you've created, your family and most of all, yourself. That is something I respect. I hope it will aid you in understanding my perspective and the motives that influenced my actions. I would like to believe you might have done the same things in my situation."

Sophie spluttered in surprise. Of all the outrageous assumptions Sheridan could make, this was likely the worst. "Don't waste your time trying to manipulate me into sympathising with you, Sheridan. I know you'd love for me to believe you had no other choice. But the fact is, I would never go to the lengths you have. I don't consider people to be expendable." Sophie thought of what Sheridan had done to Ella's mum. It was unspeakably heartless. Only a truly evil person would ever threaten the life of a child.

Sheridan narrowed her gaze in assessment. "You talk as

though you've already discovered the whole truth. Yet I believed you'd come here today to find more pieces of your puzzle. Perhaps I was wrong?"

"I know all the facts, Sheridan. Everything that happened back then. It's the *why* I need to make sense of it all. I hoped you could provide some insight."

"I shouldn't be surprised," Sheridan growled. She repositioned her hands in her lap. "So, how did you find him then? Did you track him down to that dilapidated nursing home in Stanthorpe? I knew that old degenerate wouldn't be able to stay silent about the crash forever."

"Crash?" What was Sheridan talking about? "I meant that I'd discovered the truth about what Jack and April-Rose did that day at the Garland dam, and then what you did to Ella and Francesca Larsen to keep them quiet."

"Oh, that." Sheridan flicked her hand to signify the triviality of those matters. "My children were such obedient little angels back then. And as for Francie Larsen, that was nothing but a bit of harmless intimidation. She just took it too far."

"*She took it too far?*" Sophie queried hotly. "I heard about what happened to Ella's mother after her meeting with you. She was only trying to protect her daughter."

"As was I." Sheridan jutted out her chin defensively. "All I did was show Francie a few pictures of Ella—at play, at school, at home—and then I explained how easily something could happen to her daughter. An accident or something worse. Especially if she told anyone about what she knew."

Sophie winced in disgust. "Was protecting April-Rose and Jack from the consequences of their actions really worth destroying the Larsens' lives? Or should I say the consequences of your actions? You're their mother. They listened to you."

Sheridan sighed tiredly and for a split second looked her true age beneath all her artificial features. "Life would be much simpler now if they were still the obedient children they once were. As I said, Sophie dear, I did what was necessary to protect my family, and I would do it again."

"And I suppose it was also your idea to spread the rumour of my attempted suicide throughout town?" Sophie crossed her arms tightly as anger consumed her.

Sheridan's small grin was sharp and unbothered. "For the majority of my life, protecting the Garlands and our family name was my priority. I'm so pleased you can understand that now."

Rage filled Sophie as she stared Sheridan down. "No one can ever understand why the devil does what she does."

"I'm not the devil, Sophie. I'm just a mother."

"The mother of evil, maybe?" Sophie spat. "April-Rose sure is a chip off the old block."

Sheridan tilted her head and then gave a noncommittal shrug. "I don't disagree, but whatever my daughter is, she has been my burden to bear. Though that, too, will soon come to an end."

Sophie was tired of Sheridan's cryptic musings. Her thoughts went to Jack. Every moment she spent in his mother's company had her sympathising with him all the more. She was so relieved he'd managed to escape the evil and cruelty of his family to live with her own. She only wished she'd realised the extent of what he was going through sooner.

"And where does Jack fit into all of this?" Sophie asked. "Both your children were behind the awful events of that day, but I know Jack would never have done such a terrible thing without your influence."

"Jackson has always been a sweet boy. Too soft-hearted for the games needed to maintain our power and social standing. It's one of the reasons why I named April-Rose my successor, though even that wasn't to be the success I envisioned." Sheridan frowned.

"So, you encouraged them to take me down to the dam that day?" Sophie prompted. "To what—drown me?"

Sheridan chuckled icily. "Nothing so blatant. You have

to understand, Sophie. I hated your family and loathed your mother. I still do. I wanted you all to suffer as I had, to endure the pain and loss that I dealt with every day. I hoped if something happened to you, it would be some small form of compensation that would make my life more bearable. I did nothing more than use what I had at my disposal to fulfil that desire."

"You *used* your children?"

"Yes, of course." Sheridan was unmoved, her expression as brazen as her tone. "They are mine. They would have done anything for me and their father."

Goosebumps shivered across Sophie's arms. She thought of a young Jack being manipulated and mistreated by his own mother, and it tore into her soul. "How could you make them do such a thing? What could you say to them, to Jack, to turn him against me so heartlessly?" she whispered. She was almost too afraid to ask.

Sheridan gazed down her nose at Sophie like a hawk locking eyes on its prey. "I did what any wronged woman would have done, Sophie dear. I shared my abhorrence with them, my absolute detestation for the entire Wendall clan. I terrified them with the possibilities of what might have happened had their father died instead of yours. I blamed your family for everything, for every one of our family's problems. I simply showed my children the truth. Jack took longer to convince, but his sister and I got him over the line, forced him to see our perspective, to choose between your family and our own. From that point it was easy. A simple suggestion of exiling you, punishing you, became a mission for them. And by that time, they had their own hatred and their own vengeful desires to drive them. All I had to do was wait for the perfect moment to make it happen."

Stunned and disgusted, Sophie covered her mouth. Repressed pain leapt to the surface and smothered her, squeezing her heart like wet clay. Poor Jack. Sophie wished she could hold him close. She longed to take away his guilt, his pain—just as she knew he wished to rid her of her own.

How could Sheridan have done such a terrible thing to her own children? They had loved her, trusted her, would have done anything for her. And she exploited them, poisoned them. Maybe she really was the mother of all evil everyone thought she was?

Something else Sheridan had said begged for attention. She leaned forward. "You said *crash* before." Sophie gulped out the words as dread roiled in her gut. "Did you mean the accident? The car accident where my father died? And who did you think I'd spoken to? Who lives out in Stanthorpe?"

As though considering her response, Sheridan took the time to smooth her beige skirt over her thighs before she broke the silence. "I spoke too hastily earlier, but I suppose the harm is already done. With things as they are, the rest will likely come out soon enough anyway. I've revealed to you the repercussions, why not also the cause?" She sighed. "Truth be told, your family and mine weren't always at odds, Sophie." She paused to let that sink in. "There was a time long ago when your mother and I were friends, before she married your father, and before I married Barry. We'd met through school at Warwick State High. We were in the same clique and would spend most weekends together, hunting boys at the local drive-in or the town pool. Chances were we would have continued very much the same way had we not met the famous *Barton Garland* that summer." Her gaze became distant, and she smiled almost nostalgically.

"Angie had just turned sixteen and, while boys had always been on my radar, she was only starting to show interest. Although we were from the same area and knew much about the Garlands, neither of us had ever met Barry before. That year, he'd returned to town after graduating from Brisbane Boys Grammar, where he'd spent most of his schooling, boarding there in the city. When we met him that day at the pool, it was as though lightning struck me. I knew I had to have him, but he became besotted with your mother. It went on that way, month after month, me chasing him, him chasing Angie. The friendship between your mother and I deteriorated until that loner Jim Wendall rode his motorbike into town. His arrival and Angie's corresponding infatuation solved all my problems, and I was able to make Barry *mine*." Sheridan offered Sophie a proud, shark-like grin. "And for a while things were good. But love like that doesn't fade so easily. Throughout your mother and father's marriage, throughout my own, even once the children were born, I knew that Barry had never stopped wanting her, loving her. He denied it, but I never believed him. I became convinced they were having an affair. I hated your mother for it, for taking his love, that deepest, truest love I could never have while she was still around. That was about the time Barry started drinking. We were always fighting. He'd stay out late—probably with your mother, other times with your father—being *friendly*." Sheridan's mouth puckered like the word was bitter on her tongue.

"He even gave Jim a job at Garland Grain, a position directly under him, so they could spend more time together." Her lips peeled into a snarl. "Manipulative bastard. He denied it, but I knew he was doing it, all of it, to get to Angelica." She paused as if to compose herself. "His drinking worsened. Sometimes your father would even drive him home. It was one of those nights, after we'd had another vicious row, that the accident occurred."

At the thought of her father, of the accident, Sophie felt the raw, cavernous ache of loss that had remained buried in the depths of her soul awaken, lurching agonizingly upwards into her chest.

"You know your father wasn't even supposed to be there that night," Sheridan continued, exasperation sharpening her tone. "Barry called him, drunk as a nectared-up lorikeet, whining about our fight, threatening to do something ridiculous like leave me and the children or end his miserable life, so Jim ran off to the rescue." She huffed in vexation. "I believed that there was still something worth saving in my marriage back then, and I blamed the Wendalls for destroying my family. I never would have said this then,

271

but . . . perhaps things would have been very different had Jim just stayed home. It would have saved us all the heartache."

Sophie sniffed. Her eyes welled and her throat burned, but she fought through her raging emotions. "You said you thought I'd spoken to someone in Stanthorpe, someone who knew about the accident. Who did you mean?"

Sheridan stared hard at Sophie. "An old acquaintance and a necessary thorn in my side. As Barry spiralled out of control, I required someone to assist me in keeping his string of misdemeanours quiet. At that time, Chief Ambrose was a well-respected leader in law enforcement and a revered member of our community. He was also a greedy sycophant who would do almost anything for money. No one ever questioned his orders or his actions. No one ever had any need to. So, that night, the night of the accident, the two of us did what was necessary to protect my family and the Garland name."

Sophie's heart lurched in her chest, stealing her breath away. "What does that mean?" she managed to whisper. She knew there had been more behind her father's death than what was in the final police report.

"Sophie." A flicker of something menacing shifted in Sheridan's eyes. "Surely you've worked it out by now."

Sophie's eyes widened as an impossible thought entered her mind. No. It couldn't be that. It just couldn't be. She felt as if she were about to crumple in on herself and fall into an abyss of tears and pain and sadness.

"That night twenty years ago," Sheridan continued coldly, "the night your father died—Jim Wendall *wasn't* driving the car. My husband, Barry Garland *was*."

CHAPTER 35

The distant cackle of a clan of kookaburras announced the setting of the sun and the approaching evening. Although moody mauves and fiery oranges still lit the sky outside, repeating their daily war against the shadows of dusk, the artificial light inside the timber cabin was warm, bright and revealing. In the cosy living space opposite the practical kitchenette, Sophie lounged on the couch. Her bare feet didn't quite reach the other half of the sectional sofa, which bent ninety degrees at the corner of the wood-panelled wall. She gripped her mobile phone in her lap, the screen illuminated with the word *Mum* and a photo of her mother's smiling face. Her thumb hovered cautiously above the green *call* symbol, and she bobbed her toes—right foot, left foot—in a reflexive countdown.

Since escaping Garland Manor that morning, Sophie had spent the daylight hours relaying her and Sheridan's conversation to Laura and then subsequently dissecting it, every word, over and over until the shock had finally worn off. Neither of them had expected so many secrets or that those secrets would be so scandalous. When exhaustion had finally forced them to part ways, Laura had advised Sophie of two things she believed absolutely necessary in order for her cousin to move on. Firstly, and more obviously, Sophie needed to tell Jack what she'd discovered and hear the rest of his account of that day at the dam. Then, Angelica deserved to hear the truth about the car accident that claimed her husband's life.

Sophie tapped her index finger against the smartphone's casing, watching as the screen once again fell dark. While she had yet to complete the first task on her list, she had been working up the courage to call her mother for almost an hour now. She was afraid to hear the pain fill her mother's lovely voice. She didn't know how Angelica would cope with the anguish. Even so, her mother had every right to know—no matter how much it would devastate her.

Inhaling deeply, Sophie sought to muster up some bravery with the fresh gulp of air. Then, on an exhale, she tapped the screen, setting it alight before touching her thumb to the green button. As she pressed the icy glass display to her cheek, she heard the ringing cease.

"Hi, darling."

Sophie felt her heart jolt at the enthusiasm and tenderness in her mother's voice. "Hi, Mum." She did her best to sound upbeat.

"How are you going? Still enjoying your time in Moorhenvale?"

"Yes." Sophie drew out the word in a lengthy hiss, considering whether to elaborate as she did so. After all, at what point in the conversation was it appropriate to reminisce about a loved one's passing?

"Are you sure, darling? You don't sound good."

Sophie shut her eyes tightly and pinched the bridge of her nose. It was impossible to feign cheerfulness when she felt like crying. "Well, it's just—I'm okay. For the most part, I've enjoyed myself, and I'm glad I stayed."

"That's good?" Her mother sounded none too convinced.

"Yes, it is." Sophie nibbled her lower lip. "I've been spending a lot of time with Laura."

"And with Jack?" There was a hopeful lilt to Angelica's voice. "I may have had an update from your aunt and uncle the other day."

"Yes, and Jack." Sophie's heart warmed at the thought of him, and she wished she had him here with her in this difficult moment. But they had a tough conversation ahead of them as well, and she couldn't drag him into this one when it was so closely tied to the other.

"I'm so pleased to hear it, darling. Uncle Nick said you two have become very close."

"We have." A sob caught in Sophie's throat as emotions swirled within her. She stared at the ceiling, taking a moment to gather her thoughts and steady her breath.

"What's wrong, Sophia? Did something happen? Something between you and Jack?"

Sophie squeezed her eyes shut again and focused on her breathing. She didn't want to cry. "Yes and no, but not like you think." She sighed in grief and exhaustion. It had been a terribly long day. "But that's not why I phoned, Mum."

"Well, for whatever reason you did," her mother soothed, "I'm glad you called me. You know I'm always happy to hear from my baby."

"I know, Mum." Sophie nervously smoothed her hand over the fabric of her black tights and then scraped her fingernails up her thigh. "Actually, I called because I need to talk to you about something important. Something serious."

"Oh?" Worry reverberated in that one syllable. "You're sure you're okay? You're not hurt?" Another thought must have dawned on her mother, because she gasped. "It's not about Uncle Nick or Aunt Robin? Our Laura? Oh god, or Pat and Marilyn?"

"No, Mum. Nothing like that. Everyone's fine. I'm fine." Sophie scolded herself for not getting to the point. "It's . . . I, um . . . I went to see Sheridan Garland today."

"Oh?" There was that word again, this time edged with alarm.

"I needed some information. I thought she could help put the past behind me."

"And did she?" Her mother couldn't hide her scepticism.

Grimacing, Sophie tilted her head from side to side. "In a way, but there are a couple of things we should talk about."

"Like what, darling?"

"Well, to begin with," Sophie blurted, "Sheridan admitted that she was the one who spread the rumour of my attempted suicide after the incident at the Garland dam. She said she did it to protect her family and their reputation, but she didn't care in the least about how it would affect ours."

A black hole of silence answered her.

Sophie waited for another instant and then asked, "Mum?"

She heard a sob, then a sniff, and Angelica cleared her throat. "Yes, darling?"

"You heard what I said?"

"I heard." Her mother was painfully sombre.

"And?" Sophie waved her hand in the air, gesturing for more, even though her mother was blind to the motion.

"And I think, in the future," her mother ventured, a protective edge strengthening her words, "you should keep your distance from that evil woman."

"Mum?" Sophie grasped for something further. "Is that all you can say? Because of Sheridan's lies, we were ostracised from the town. Everyone thought I had tried to kill myself. Even you believed that." Fury boiled within her, and she gasped, her breath ragged. "I spent *years* in therapy. After losing Dad, then barely surviving that day at the Garland dam, that rumour nearly destroyed my life all over again. Yours too. The Garland family did that to us."

"I know," Angelica interrupted, her hoarse voice cracking. "I know, Sophie. That was the darkest of times. I sometimes wonder how we made it through. That vile woman was determined to take everything from us." Her mother drew in a harsh breath that bordered on a sob and coughed to cover the sound. "Though I try not to let the past suffocate me with remorse and grief"—she sniffed, her voice wet with emotion—"my biggest regret of all was not trusting you, not believing you. But you were so young, darling . . . and I was so naive. I wish I'd never believed Sheridan's lies, but I was terrified. I couldn't lose you, not after losing your father. I only put you in therapy to help. Everyone told me it would." There was a muffled cry on the other end of the phone, followed once more by silence.

Sophie closed her eyes and felt the warmth of fresh tears welling beneath her lids. "It did, Mum. It's okay. I know you were only doing what you thought was right. I was just so lost, so alone, when no one believed me. After Sheridan's confession today, I just needed you to know what really happened. I never tried to hurt myself, I never tried to leave you. What happened out on the Garland dam that day wasn't my fault."

Although Sophie was still tense with conflicting emotions, in revealing just this one truth she had lifted the weight that had been hanging heavily on her soul for twenty years. After her discussion with Sheridan, Sophie had hoped she would remember something, but her mind remained painfully blocked. She had nearly every piece of the puzzle in place. She'd heard nearly all there was to hear, except Jack's full story. Sophie wondered if her memories would ever return or if they had been lost forever.

As slow tears trickled down her cheeks, Sophie calmed her breath and gentled her death grip on the phone. "Mum?" she probed gently.

There was another sob and a sniffle before her mother returned to the line. "Th-thank you for telling me, my baby." Angelica sounded like she was on the verge of weeping. "I am so sorry. I wish things had been different. I wish I had known the truth—that I'd known what Sheridan had done. I never would have . . . I never would—" Her words caught again, and she cried. "I never should have trusted that woman."

Sophie swallowed the sadness thickening her own throat. "I'm so sorry, Mum, but there's more. More Sheridan told me about what happened back then." She inhaled shakily. "More about Dad. I need to tell you, but I also need to know that you're okay to hear it. Otherwise, I can wait. We can talk another day or when I get home."

Sophie didn't want to wait, couldn't fathom carrying that burden of truth around for so long, but she didn't want to cripple her mother with sadness. It was Sophie who had jumped into the viper's nest to delve into their traumatic past, not her mother. So her mother shouldn't be forced to face the revelations until she was ready—if she ever believed she would be.

A hollow silence pierced through the phone line.

"Mum?" Sophie ventured again. "Are you okay?"

"Yes, baby." The words were breathy and laced with fear. "I heard. I'm okay. I'm ready." She sniffed a couple of times. "You can tell me."

Sophie wasn't convinced, but she knew there was never going to be a good time to break life-altering news. If her mother said she could handle it, then Sophie believed her. Angelica had always been a strong woman, just like Nonna, just like Sophie had always prayed she herself would become.

"Okay." Sophie sighed and dug her fingernails into the flesh of her thigh, using the fleeting pain to steady her thoughts. "Sheridan told me you used to be friends back in high school, before you met Dad and Barton Garland."

"Yes," her mother said thoughtfully. "That's right."

"Apparently Barry always had a soft spot for you, a bit of a crush?"

"Barely." She spluttered in surprise. "Mainly when we were still teenagers, before I met your father, but we were good friends for years."

"Really? Sheridan told me she believed you shared more than just a friendly relationship. She thought it was something much more intimate."

"What? Barry and me?" Her mother actually laughed. "I think we kissed once, maybe twice, during the summer we met—before I met your dad, and before Barry and Sheridan got together. That was all. Barry was a good friend to your father and me, and I remember that something about that used to make Sheridan uncomfortable."

"No. Not uncomfortable, Mum. She was furious. She was convinced that you were having an affair with her husband—or at the very least, that he was still in love with you and trying to seduce you away from Dad."

"What?" Angelica gasped. "Are you serious, Sophie?"

"She told me as much this morning. It was why she behaved as she did, why she lied about the incident at the dam—she's the reason it even happened. She hates us, Mum. That's why she turned her children against me all those years ago, and that's why she lied about the accident."

"The accident?" Panic deepened Angelica's voice. "The car accident that killed your father?"

Hearing her mother's distress sapped all of Sophie's courage and left her unable to find the right words. Like a goldfish, she opened and closed her mouth, scrambling to regain her nerve. How could she tell her mother what Sheridan had said? Sophie didn't want to break her mother's heart. But her mum needed to know.

"Sophie?" Her mother's voice wobbled with trepidation.

Sophie took another calming breath and slumped against the sofa. "Yes, Mum. I'm talking about the car accident. The day Dad died."

"What about it, Sophie? What did you mean Sheridan lied? Tell me. I need to know."

Sophie had been right. Her mother needed to know the truth. She deserved to know. It wouldn't make things right, but it would help them finally move forward together.

"Mum." Sophie bit her lower lip to stop its trembling. "Sheridan told me that Dad *wasn't* the one driving the car that night. That story was something she'd concocted with the chief of police at the time—a Chief Ambrose?" Sophie heard her mother's gasp of recognition. "Actually, it was Barry who was driving. He'd gotten in the car, started the engine before Dad could stop him. So Dad joined him, hoping to convince him to pull over. He had tried to get Barry home safely, but it was Dad who never made it home."

Sophie felt the ache of loss score her throat as it dragged a sharp sob out of her and caused fresh tears to form. How could she have blindly accepted the original story? Sophie felt as though she'd let her father down, let the kind, generous man she'd known be remembered with hatred and disappointment by everyone in town. All over a kind act that had turned deadly. But everyone had always revered the Garlands, and who would ever have questioned the chief of police?

Sophie scrubbed at her eyes and runny nose, leaving her face wet and ruddy with emotion. She was furious and frustrated but knew she'd had no power back then to change anything. Even her mother wouldn't have stood a chance against the all-great-and-powerful Garlands. Her kind, good-humoured dad had just been collateral damage in the Garlands' manipulative games for wealth, power and reputation.

"Dad was just trying to do the right thing." Sophie sobbed into the mobile phone. "He was trying to help Barry, as he always did when Barry and Sheridan fought, and he paid the ultimate price for it. He was being a good friend, and then Sheridan and that Chief Ambrose used his death to clear the Garland name of any wrongdoing." Sophie couldn't catch her breath. Her rage was suffocating. "Everyone in town accepted it without question. They were content to blame us, to ridicule us, rather than face the Garland family's wrath."

"Sophie?" Her mother spoke softly, her voice oddly calm.

"Everyone turned on us," Sophie cried. "Do you

remember? They weren't surprised, they said. Jim Wendall had always been a wild one. They'd praised heaven that Barry had survived. Oh Mum, and the rumours? We couldn't escape them." Weeping gently now, anger aching through every limb, Sophie covered her face as an uncontrollable tremor shook her shoulders.

"Sophie, darling?" Angelica tried again.

But Sophie was spiralling through twenty years of pain and anger, and it was too late to pull herself free. "How could they do that to us? We were like family to them, all of them. We knew everyone in town. And Sheridan—that *witch*. She deserves to go to jail for what she did, for her lies and all the pain she's inflicted. She doesn't even care, Mum. She feels no remorse—nothing. She destroyed our lives, and it doesn't bother her in the slightest. It never has. She let us believe Dad's death was his own doing, made you think what happened at the Garland dam was mine. But it was theirs—the Garlands—who were behind everything, and Sheridan is the worst of all."

"Sophie," her mother soothed, but Sophie could barely hear her over the sobs that were still racking her body. She missed her father, her life at Bitterbark Creek and the innocence of her sweet childhood relationship with Jack. Before everything had been taken from her and her family.

Cries of grief ripped free of her throat, coming from that deep dark place inside of her that she'd tried hard to hide and avoid. The pain consumed her, welling up from all those excruciating memories, from the devastation of losing someone so utterly adored and admired. Someone who had understood her with just a look. Who had been her best friend for the first ten years of her life and the best man she'd ever known. Her heart felt as though it was breaking all over again. The sound of her mother's lovely voice, hushed and reassuring, finally broke through Sophie's pain.

"Sophie, my baby. It's okay. It will be okay."

Sophie choked in a breath. "But Sheridan can't get away with this. It isn't right."

Her mother shushed her. "I know, darling, but it's been twenty years. We've been burdened with this for too long. We know the truth now. That's enough." Angelica's voice cracked, pain seeping through. She quickly cleared her throat. "It's time for us to let it all go and look to our future. You have such a bright future, darling."

"B-but, Mum," Sophie stammered. She wanted to argue but knew her mother was probably right.

"It's time, darling. Let it go."

"But could we not try to clear Dad's name?"

"Yes, we could." Angelica agreed. "We could report it to the police, tell the local council, the media, but what good would it do? We have no evidence and any remaining from the accident has surely been tampered with. The Garlands would also fight us the whole way, using their money, their influence, their lies, to discredit us again. We're outsiders now, while the Garlands are still very much respected in Moorhenvale and the surrounding towns." There was a pause, and then her mother sighed heavily. "No, Sophie. These uncovered truths do one thing and one thing only. They give us closure. Put the past to rest my darling. You finally have the chance to move on with your life."

"Mum?" Sophie pleaded.

"Sophie, listen to me. Let it go. Let your father and his memory, and all the sins of the past, rest in peace. Move forward. It's time."

Sophie inhaled shakily as tears cascaded down her cheeks. Her mother was right. They didn't need any more pain. They weren't like the Garlands, weren't anything like Sheridan. Revenge wasn't something they would destroy lives for, especially their own.

"I. . ." she began, but the words crumbled in her mouth. She swallowed, her raw throat aching, and tried again. "I love you, Mum."

Sophie could sense her mother's warm, loving smile before she even uttered a word. "I love you too, Sophie."

CHAPTER 36

After the recent rain, the rise leading to Bitterbark Creek's ranch house had sprouted long tendrils of pear-green grass, which whipped wildly in the gusty breeze. Though the vivid blue sky had been clear that morning, the warmth and humidity of the day had conceived an afternoon storm, building a mass of gloomy clouds in the west. As thunder gurgled menacingly in the distance, the birdlife in the surrounding trees stirred. A loudmouthed gang of noisy miner birds took off, squawking, into the sky.

Sophie followed the property's gravel road, careful to keep her footing on the crunchy surface. Before she'd even laid eyes on the farm dogs on the veranda, she heard their low howl of greeting. They raced down the stairs like furry little missiles and were at her feet before she'd gained five paces. They circled around her, weaving figure eights, before rubbing alongside her terracotta skirt. Laughing, Sophie paused to dote on them, patting their soft heads and accepting loving licks before continuing towards the main house. While Banjo lingered by her side, Boris ran ahead a few paces. Then he glanced back, tongue lolling proudly, before running ahead again. When Sophie finally reached the timber steps, both canines bounded in front of her, beating her to the veranda and greeting her all over again as they tried to usher her towards their trampoline beds and the mess of toys strewn nearby.

"Later, boys," she promised, skirting around them to the front entrance. "I've got to see your sister first." She snuck inside and clipped the barrier door closed. The pups pressed their damp snouts to the screen. "I'll be back," she cooed sweetly.

"Hello?" Aunt Robin yodelled from the depths of the spacious rustic-style dwelling. "Is that you, Sophie? I'm in the kitchen."

"Yes, it's just me, Aunt Robin." Sophie slipped off her brown boots, leaving them in the entryway with the other pairs of outdoor shoes, and then padded in sock-covered feet over the polished wooden floors. Cutting through the expansive living room with its impressive cathedral ceiling of bare beams, Sophie ducked into the large country-style catering kitchen.

Her aunt glanced up at her and smiled sunnily. She was in the middle of carefully adding slivers of pastry lattice to an apple pie. "Hello, beautiful." Robin beamed. "Have you come to help me prepare the pies for tomorrow's picnic at the lookout? I know we only have a few new guests since the wedding festivities, but it's always the more the merrier when it comes to baked goods." She winked and carefully placed another strip of pastry.

"Actually," Sophie began apologetically, "I've come to see your daughter, but I'm happy to stay and help if you need me."

"No, no." Her aunt chuckled. "I'm in my element here. The kitchen has always been my favourite spot in the house. No, you go and find Laura. She should be in her room."

"Okay. Thank you." Sophie breathed a sigh of relief, grateful she wouldn't be ruining any picnics with her lack of baking skills. "I'll still be around to help you feed the menagerie later."

"Sounds good, love." Robin grinned and focused back

on her task.

When Sophie stepped out into the corridor connecting the kitchen to the rooms beyond, she heard her aunt call after her.

"Oh, Soph?"

She glanced around the corner, back into the kitchen. "Yes, Aunt Robin?"

The older woman wiped her flour-sprinkled hands on a dishcloth and rounded the sizeable kitchen island. "Laura told us you've been having a bit of a difficult time since yesterday."

Sophie gulped in shock at the thought of what Laura might have exposed, but her aunt quickly raised a hand to calm her.

"Don't worry. My daughter didn't go into any details about what happened this time around. She just wanted us to know why you may be out of sorts today."

"Okay?" Sophie narrowed her gaze warily.

"Laura did tell us that you were planning to call your mum last night though." Placing a clean hand over the thick strap of Sophie's white singlet, she squeezed her niece's shoulder reassuringly. "I'm sure talking with her helped you work through the issue, but just know, sweetheart, if you ever need to talk about anything, your uncle and I are always here for you too."

Sophie's throat tightened, and she choked back heartfelt appreciation. Swallowing deeply, she blinked away the dampness that had begun to warm her eyes and forced a genuine smile. "I know, Aunt Robin." She let her aunt pull her into a brief but snug embrace and was secretly pleased when it ended, knowing she'd narrowly escaped another meltdown.

"Well, off with you then." Robin dismissed her with a wave and wiped at her own eyes as she headed back to her baking. "I know Laura would love the company," she called over her shoulder. "She's been locked in her room all day."

Jumping at the opportunity to escape, Sophie dashed

down the hallway. She halted at her cousin's closed bedroom door, sniffed a couple times, and wiped again at the traitorous tears. She coughed to clear her throat and hoped she looked more composed than she felt. After a deep breath in and out, Sophie braved a knock on the door. "Laura? It's Soph. Can I come in?"

There was a scuttling, a scrambling, and then something crashed to the floor.

"Oh. Ah, Soph. One minute." Laura sounded startled and strangely anxious for someone who was usually so chirpy and confident.

"Laur? Are you okay?" Sophie twisted the doorknob, ready to assist, but found that it actually was locked, just as her aunt had said.

"Yeah, I'm fine," Laura hollered back. "Just a moment." She muttered something under her breath, but Sophie didn't catch it.

"Laur?" Feeling a little unsettled by her cousin's odd behaviour, Sophie rested her ear against the door. "If this is a bad time, I can come back."

"No. No, it's okay. I'm coming." Again, her cousin mumbled, as though she wasn't talking to Sophie but someone else in the room. Suddenly, a latch clicked, and the door swung inward, revealing her frazzled cousin. "Hi." Laura offered her a wide, nervous smile and waggled her fingers.

"You said you were okay," Sophie said sceptically. "But you don't look okay."

"I'm fine, really," Laura panted, but her pink cheeks and rumpled outfit suggested otherwise.

Sophie leaned against the timber doorframe and peered over her cousin's shoulder, noticing the normally tidy room mirrored her dishevelled cousin. "So, can I come in or do you want to talk elsewhere?"

Laura glanced behind her and then back at Sophie. "Elsewhere?" There was a high-pitched uncertainty in her voice. Sophie's curiosity grew.

"What's going on, Laura?" Sophie pressed her hand against the door, testing her cousin's hold.

"Nothing."

"Laur, you look every bit the naughty child. What kind of mischief are you getting up to?"

"Only the good kind, I swear."

"Hey!" The displeased outburst came from somewhere inside the room. "I am *not* a kind of mischief." The bedroom door was yanked back to reveal the rest of the room and Laura's secret visitor.

"Ella?" Sophie gaped at the pair, her mortified cousin and a proudly indignant Ella Larsen, sporting matching messy clothing and tousled hair.

"And," her childhood friend continued, "hiding was in no way my idea."

"I never would have thought otherwise," Sophie promised. She tried to stifle the excitement swelling inside her before she burst into a grin. She didn't want to embarrass Laura or make a big deal out of something so new, but she was overjoyed for her cousin. "Laur doesn't often keep secrets, but when she does, she's usually bad at it."

Ella laughed and wrapped an arm around Laura's waist, pulling her close and forcing the shorter woman to look up at her. "The joey's out of the pouch, babe. Looks like it's official. We're dating."

Laura gazed adoringly up at Ella. When her curvy partner shot her a wink, she smirked, cute and bashful. "I'm sorry, cuz." She shrugged. "I wanted to tell you, but you've got enough to process as it is. We've only met up a couple of times. After that night at the cave, there was just a connection, you know?"

"If you say we just clicked, I'll pinch you," Ella teased.

Laura chuckled and bumped her hip against Ella's. She blushed when she noticed her cousin's beaming grin. "Oh dear, Soph. Say something. That look is beginning to scare me."

"What?" Sophie giggled. "Don't be silly, Laur. I'm thrilled for you both." She placed a hand over her heart and repeated Laura's earlier words. "*I swear.* I'm just a little speechless. You thought you had to go to the big city to find love, but it turns out it was here all along."

That statement had Sophie thinking of Jack, and how her love for him had returned and grown ever stronger since coming back to Bitterbark Creek. After yesterday's horrible conversation with Sheridan and her difficult conversation with her mother, Sophie had been hoping to find comfort in Jack's arms again today. Whether they had a chance to talk their own issues through or whether they had to wait until dinner the following evening, it wouldn't have mattered. Sophie just missed him and longed to be with him. She felt her truest self with him, so peaceful, so happy. Yet when she'd knocked on his door that afternoon, during his usual break from farm chores, no one had answered. It had left Sophie feeling a little lonely and blue, so she had hoped to find solace with Laura. Never in a million years had she expected her cousin to be in the middle of her own romantic interlude with Ella.

"Whoa, don't jump on board the love train just yet." There was a cheeky twinkle in Ella's eyes. "We've got to get to the like-like you stage first."

Laura snorted. "Please ignore my fiancée here. She forgets the wedding has been planned for next month," she joked.

Ella tickled Laura's ribs until she squealed. After catching her breath, Laura turned to Sophie. "So, cuz, what brings you by this afternoon? Secret Santoro business? A lesson in love?"

Sophie pouted. "Actually, nothing quite so grand. I just wanted some company. I went looking for Jack, but he wasn't in his cabin."

"Nope." Laura shook her head. "He was moping around, so Dale dragged him into Warwick for a beer and a game of pool. If I had to guess he was moping over you."

She eyed Sophie carefully. "Looks like you're both on the sulky side today. What's happened?"

Sophie shrugged. "Nothing, Laur. I just wanted a little space to get through yesterday, and now I'm missing his company."

"Sounds like he feels the same way." Ella clicked her tongue.

Laura frowned. "Why don't you just text him then?"

"I don't want him to think I'm needy."

"Has he messaged you?" Ella asked.

"A few times yesterday. But I never answered."

"Oh my gosh, you two," Laura scolded. "Just talk to each other!"

"And don't get distracted in the bedroom like us," Ella joked.

"I can't promise that." Sophie giggled softly.

"So, not that I'm complaining about playing second fiddle"—Laura wiggled her eyebrows—"but what were you going for when you knocked on my door?"

"Oh, nothing." Sophie backed up. "It doesn't matter. Like I said, I was feeling lonely. I just thought maybe we could watch a movie tonight or something, but now I see you probably have other plans."

"Hey!" Ella feigned surprise. "What a coincidence! I also like movies."

"How about that?" Laura fed off her girlfriend's good humour. "We *all* like movies."

"Well, what do you think?" Ella gazed at the ceiling and then raised her index finger as though struck with an epiphany. "Do you think we could *all* watch movies *together*?"

"Why yes, I think we could," Laura agreed.

They grinned cheesily at Sophie, and she chuckled at their silliness. "Clearly, you're made for each other."

When they giggled and ushered her inside to continue the conversation, Sophie felt all her tensions ease. Although she would have made it through a lonely night alone, the strenuous events of the past few days had left her wanting some affection and camaraderie. She needed support and understanding to restore her strength, especially considering what lay ahead of her tomorrow. But that was a worry for *tomorrow*. Tonight, she would take a moment to relax and hide from all the drama. If anyone could keep her spirits up, it was bound to be Laura and Ella.

CHAPTER 37

As shadows smothered the violet of the day's final light, the dimly lit veranda of Bitterbark Creek's main house became a beacon in the darkness. Adding to the already ominous mood, a lonely storm bird bellowed out a droning whoop, reaching a shrill crescendo before repeating the performance. It was only the chirpy indistinguishable chatter and the melodic tune of an Elvis love song drifting out the open windows that provided any contrast to the gloom.

From where he sat propped against the timber balustrade—Banjo's furry head on his lap—Jack watched another line of drool slip free of Boris's jowl as the canine peeked through the screened entrance. Delicious smells from the house spilled outside, wafting through the air like an invisible mist, igniting hunger in all creatures, human and canine alike. While he caressed the velvet of Banjo's forehead with one hand, Jack pressed his smartphone firmly to his ear with the other, his attention waning with each passing second.

"Are you listening to me, Jackson?" his sister screeched. "Do you want to ruin our lives? Because that's what will happen if you tell the Santoros the truth."

"We don't know that for certain, April-Rose, and even if it does, maybe that's what we deserve."

She growled her frustration. "You're just as difficult to get through to as Sophie."

"Don't you mean *manipulate*?" He smirked half-heartedly as he glanced down at Banjo.

His sister roared her displeasure, and Jack heard a loud *whack*, as though she'd hit something. "You can't be this naive, Jackson. Sophie finding out was one thing. It's a problem we still need to address. But the Santoros? They'll tell the whole town. Our family and the company will never overcome that kind of scandal."

Jack shrugged. He didn't care what his sister said or how she tried to convince him otherwise. He knew what he needed to do. "It's time, April-Rose. I can't live like this anymore."

She huffed. "Stop being selfish, and think this through. Do you really plan on destroying all of our lives just to win over a sad, lanky daddy's girl who probably doesn't love you anyway?"

Jack felt anger boil in his veins. It rocked him with adrenaline, but he held it contained, tensing all of his muscles to lock it there. "You were once a daddy's girl too," he reminded her. "But this is bigger than that, more than just about Sophie or the relationship we have together. This is about doing the right thing, April-Rose. It's about freeing myself from a secret that's been weighing me down for far too long. It's about telling the truth and opening up to the people who care for me, letting them in so they have the opportunity to really know me, to truly love and accept me without any falsities. Up until this point, all I've been living is a lie, little sister, and I'm tired of it."

"That lie allows us to rule this town, Jackson." Her snarl cut through the receiver. "Without it, we would have nothing. We would have to start over in another place, another city. Is that what you want? Could you inflict that on your family? On Mother?"

Jack closed his eyes. She thought she couldn't get through to him, but he was having an equally difficult time reaching her. They might have been siblings by blood and birth, but it had been twenty years since they'd had anything in common, since they'd formed a single thought on the same wavelength. He'd often wondered if she'd ever grown a conscience, its formation had been stunted by their mother's meddling. Or whether—like Sheridan—April-Rose had just been born evil.

"Could you really do that to us, Jackson? Could you really be that self-centred? Think hard before you make a mistake you can't repair."

Jack brushed his hand over Banjo's side. He heard the sound of footsteps approaching and glanced through an illuminated window. "Look, April-Rose," he told her forcefully, his patience fading. "You know I've already made my decision. No amount of whining or cajoling will alter that. I've prepared myself for the repercussions. I suggest you do the same."

When a shadow approached the screen door, Jack lowered the phone from his ear, hearing a last muffled shriek before he tapped the screen and ended the call. With luck, his sister might never speak to him again.

"Back up, buddy," Laura told the eager farm dog through the black mesh of the front entrance. "On your bed."

Jack watched as Boris hurried obediently over to his bed, well-trained in the ritual of feeding time. Banjo, on the other hand—struggling between his love of pats and his veneration of food—reluctantly followed his brother only once Jack had removed his fingers from the dog's soft fur. When both pups were seated on their separate trampoline beds, Boris's tail noisily thwacking the firm fabric, Laura used her hip to prop open the door and slip outside. In each hand, she carried a large silver dog bowl, the foodstuffs within smelling almost as interesting as the scents drifting out of the house.

"Wait," she drawled, ordering the pooches to stay as they wiggled with excitement. She skipped past them to where their water bowls lay on a brightly patterned plastic mat and then lowered the silver dishes. When everything was safely in position and she'd stepped away from the firing line, Laura gave the dogs a nod. "Go ahead," she told them. They dashed over to the chow. It was only as she turned back to the house, a pleasant smile on her lips, that she noticed Jack for the first time. She froze for an instant and then her grin widened. "Hiding outside in the dark, are we?" Laura teased. She propped her hands on her hips. "I don't think that will save you from your duty tonight."

"No, not hiding." Jack climbed to his feet. "Just thinking."

"Nervous?"

"Hell yeah." He sucked in a breath through his teeth.

"Take heart in knowing you're choosing to be the good guy this time," she reassured him. "I know my parents. They'll understand."

"And Sophie?" Just thinking about it made him nauseated.

"She loves you, Jack." Laura laughed. "I'm not sure there's much more you can tell her that she doesn't already know. She just needs to hear it in your words. Be brave, be honest, and I'm sure you'll get through this together."

"But I haven't heard from her in a couple of days. I haven't even seen her around the cabins." He sighed. They'd been like ships passing in the night. Every time he checked for her, she wasn't at her cabin, and she hadn't answered any of his texts. That old fear of his, that she'd leave without a word, had reared its head until the Santoros had reassured him otherwise. Sophie was still at Bitterbark Creek. They just hadn't crossed paths. But his heart was still in his throat. What if she had changed her mind about staying in town? What if her feelings for him had altered?

"I heard how slack she's been in replying." Laura laughed again. "I wouldn't take that to heart, Jack. She's just nervous is all. Tonight will be good for you both. We'll talk everything through, and it will all be fine. You'll see."

Jack eyed her carefully. "Do your parents know you've been playing matchmaker?"

"Who do you think has been encouraging me this whole time? Come on." She shoved him playfully. "It's time to go inside and confront the family." She chuckled again as she led him to the front door and then glanced back at him before opening it. "Just think, in an hour's time all of your sins will have been laid bare and you can start living your life guilt-free."

Jack groaned. "That's still an hour of agony, Laur."

"Yeah, and it will all be worth it." She grinned and ducked inside.

Jack followed her and shut the screen door behind him. He knew his beloved new sister was right. Grief and guilt had been eating at his soul like acid. He needed to do this. He could be brave and vulnerable. Not even the devil herself could stop him.

Jack heard a jovial blend of feminine and masculine voices intermingle with the jaunty chorus of Frank Sinatra's "Fly Me to the Moon" as he followed Laura down the corridor to the kitchen. He was positive that one of the voices was Sophie's.

"What did you do, cuz, sneak in the back way?" Laura asked as she entered the room and continued across the tiles to the adjacent dining area. She smiled at the three people already seated there as Jack shuffled along behind her.

Though the table before them was laid with all the appropriate cutlery and tableware, only water, wine and buttered bread rolls had been served. The enormous feast was being kept warm in a low-temperature oven to Jack's right.

"Look who I found lurking out front." Laura poked a thumb in Jack's direction and then turned to her cousin. "Were you trying to avoid this handsome face?"

Jack forced a friendly smile and squared his shoulders.

For an instant, he locked eyes with Sophie, and the sight of her gorgeous face all but stopped his heart. She looked angelic there in the gilded glow of the overhead lamp, so elegant and perfect in her white cotton dress, with her golden hair twirled atop her head, soft curls framing her face. She was seated at the head of the table opposite her uncle and aunt. The dark, reflective glass of the picture window stretched out behind them like a frame.

"I thought it best not to interrupt what seemed to be an important conversation," Sophie explained, quirking an eyebrow.

Jack mentally berated himself for answering April-Rose's call. Perhaps if he hadn't, Sophie would have made her way past him, and they could have talked alone for a moment. It was a wasted opportunity.

"Important conversation?" Laura scoffed as she took a seat beside her cousin. "Jack and I weren't talking about anything special. You should've interrupted us."

"It doesn't matter what entrance you used, Chooky," Nick told his niece. "We're just happy you decided to join us."

"Yes." Robin looked over her shoulder past Laura to Jackson. "You too, Jack." She motioned to the empty chairs across from her. "Are you going to come take a seat?"

It was only then that Jack realised he'd been frozen in place beside the kitchen island as though he were merely an onlooker peering in on the event. Rubbing his hands together nervously, he nodded and joined the rest of the party. He caught the scent of Sophie's hair and perfume—jasmine and vanilla—as he slipped past her, and savoured it while he hesitated. He desperately wanted to sit next to her, but there were only two chairs left at the dining table. Did he take the one closest to Sophie or the one next to Nick? When Jack finally sat beside Sophie, he realised he didn't care. Being close to her was all that mattered.

He knew he'd made the right choice when she gave him a sweet, sincere smile. He wanted to take her hand, to reforge that link between them, but fought the urge. He knew she may want her space again after listening to what he had to say.

"We hear you have something to tell us, Jack." Interest shone in Robin's kind eyes.

Jack cut a glance at Laura, and she reassured him with a nod. "Yes," he said, swallowing deeply as he intertwined his fingers atop the table, "I do have something important I'd like to discuss." He looked between Nick and Robin, saw them brighten with warmth and affection. He wondered how much of the story they already knew, how much Laura might have told them.

"Go on then, Jack," Robin encouraged. "We're all keen to hear what you want to share."

At that, his throat became arid and scratchy. He snatched up the water glass in front of him and took a long sip. He had to find the right words. He needed to make sure they understood the reality of what he went through all those years ago and what led him to make those terrible decisions.

As he lowered the glass to the tabletop and inhaled a calming breath, he felt a soft hand wrap around his own, fingers entwining with his. He looked from Sophie's hand in his to her beautiful face, soaking up the support and love radiating from her eyes. It brought tears to his own, and he quickly blinked them away.

"You've got this, Jack," Sophie told him.

He nodded and took a deep breath. "At the Garland dam twenty years ago ... it was *my* fault that Sophie nearly drowned."

"What do you mean, Jack?" Robin asked. "How could it be your fault?"

He sighed and looked at the couple who had become like parents to him, who had welcomed him into their family and given him a place to belong when he'd desperately needed one. "I'm saying that I'm the one who forced Sophie out onto the jetty that day. It was me. I'm responsible. She never would have gone out there had I not given her no other choice." Jack glanced over at Sophie, concerned this was it, the moment she would decide she could no longer love him. Yet although her expression was serious, intent on his words, her gorgeous dark brown eyes were warm, and her hand was still wrapped supportively around his own.

Jack squeezed it lightly, assuring himself that her touch was real, and then he continued. "The plan had been to take her out there and make her swim back to shore. It was supposed to be a punishment, a way of earning back our friendship and trust. But I knew how much Sophie hated that murky water and how scared she was of something waiting beneath the surface. I knew that it terrified her, but I knew the thought of losing her friends, of being an outcast, would scare her even more. So those were her only options. Swim back to shore or lose our friendship forever." He choked on the words. They hurt even now, as though he could hear his young voice echoing him as he spoke. Jack looked at his adoptive parents, searching their faces. Nick wrinkled his weathered brow, while Robin steepled her hands together in front of her. When Jack sneaked another look at Laura, she offered him a gentle smile.

"While I don't want it to act as an excuse, I feel I need to explain more about how the events of that day transpired." Jack licked his lips nervously. "After almost losing my father, my mother was obsessed with the idea that some kind of punishment should befall Sophie and her mother. Every day she would infect my sister and me with her hatred, convincing us that the Wendalls' grief was nothing compared to our own. Sophie losing her father wasn't enough. My mother wanted Sophie and Angelica to suffer more pain, more heartbreak. When the opportunity presented itself, we were tasked with carrying out her plan. Although I was initially reluctant, my mother forced me to choose between Sophie's family and my own. I still regret choosing the Garlands, but I was only a child, and I loved my family. My mother knew I had no other choice, just as she knew that Sophie would be forced to make the same difficult decision when choosing between her friends and abandonment."

Jack hung his head in remorse. "I know there is nothing I can say that will ever be able to justify what I did to your niece. Just please understand how truly sorry I am for all of it and how deeply I regret the pain and devastation I've caused." Jack released a shaky sigh and looked at Sophie. Her eyes were misty with tears, her cheeks flushed, but she held fast to his hand. "I'm so sorry, Sophie," he told her, allowing the sorrow he felt inside to leak into his voice. "All I can say is that I'm so infinitely, devastatingly sorry for hurting you and for all the agony I've caused your entire family. If you give me the chance, I'll spend the rest of my life making it up to you."

Jack's heartbeat pounded away in his ears as he waited in deafening silence for someone to say something. He could handle them yelling or telling him to get out and never come back. He deserved that—he probably deserved much more than that—but the silence was killing him.

Sophie lifted their clasped hands to her lips and pressed a kiss to the back of his palm. "I forgive you, Jack," she whispered. A tear trickled down her cheek.

Jack felt his lower lip tremble with emotion. Relief flooded every part of him. He fought back the wave of tears and cleared his throat before he braved a look at Robin and Nick. They were also holding hands, and their kind, compassionate expressions were more than he could have wished for.

"Over one year ago, Jack," Nick began, his booming voice shocking some life into the heavy quiet, "we welcomed you into our home, into our family. We gave you a place to stay, a job—a purpose when you needed grounding, when you sought stability and peace. Robbie and I like to think of you as our adopted son, and I know Pat and Laura see you as a brother. We've loved you, cared for you, and you've reciprocated that at every turn.

"But we've known you much longer than that. Your whole life in fact. We have known you through the good and the bad. We have known you as Jackson Garland and now as an adopted Santoro." Nick looked at his wife, who smiled tenderly and squeezed his hand. "While we might not know every good or bad deed you've ever done—we know your past, Jack. We know who you are and how you came to be. We know what sort of person you are and what truly lies in your heart, and our love and acceptance of that person will never ever change."

Jack rubbed at his eyes as his vision blurred again. He rolled Nick's words over and over in his head, testing them for some hidden insincerity, but there was none he could find. He choked back a sob. Laura had been right. His family, his *real* family, wouldn't give up on him. They believed in him. They knew he was a good person.

Jack felt Sophie wrap an arm around his shoulders and lightly kiss his forehead. Her support and affection lifted his heart. As he choked back another sob, those persistent tears finally broke free and rolled down his heated cheeks.

At Laura's unexpected hoot of approval, Jack jumped and glanced back up at the wonderful people seated before him. He brushed a hand over his face, embarrassed he'd let his emotions overcome him so.

"Well said, Dad. Okay, who's ready for dinner?" Laura grinned at everyone in an obvious attempt to refresh the mood.

"Actually, love," Robin interrupted, patting her daughter's hand "there's something Jack forgot to mention."

Jack and Sophie both looked at the petite older woman. "There is?" Jack asked cautiously, feeling his jittery heart skip a beat.

"Yes." She checked with her husband, who nodded for her to continue. "It's something you've kept to yourself for a long time, Jack, but we've always known the truth. I don't think you've even told Laura or Pat."

Laura gasped.

"Laura. Sophie." Robin cast a look from one to the other. "You now know that Jack is partly responsible for what happened to Sophie all those years ago, but did you know he's also the reason Sophie's alive and with us today?"

"What?" Laura squeaked.

Jack hadn't meant to keep this part of the story a secret, but it was so intrinsically linked to his misdeed that he could never bring himself to speak of it. The fear of what might have happened had he not been successful still haunted him. He thanked the Universe every day for ensuring he had made it in time.

Nick nodded. "It's true, Sophie. It was Jack who saved your life that day. When Ella ran to get help, and the others left you for dead, Jack dove into the dam to rescue you. He pulled you out and had you back up on the jetty by the time I arrived. If he hadn't been there, I know you wouldn't have made it."

"Oh my gosh." Laura covered her gaping mouth and stared at Jack. "Why didn't you say anything before?"

"Why, Laur? It wouldn't have changed anything, and it didn't absolve me of what I had done." Jack winced at the pain the memory triggered. He'd been so close to losing her, his sweet Sophie. He risked a glance at her then. "I couldn't lose you," he told her, the words catching in his throat. "Then, I lost you anyway. You left town. You left me. I never want to lose you like that again, Soph." Jack felt a hot tear trail down his cheek again and he wiped it away.

Sophie's lips quivered as she studied him, her face a mix of emotions. Then she launched herself onto his lap and into his arms, cuddling him against her. "You won't," she assured him, kissing his neck. "You won't lose me again." She pulled away to look at him, gazing into his eyes as she brushed a hand through his hair. "I love you, Jack, and I'm not going anywhere." Then she kissed him, her soft mouth moulding to his in the tenderest of touches.

"We're so pleased to hear that, sweetheart," Robin

announced, her gentle interruption drawing everyone's attention back to the older Santoros. After seeking silent approval from her husband once more, she continued. "Because *we* have something to tell all of you."

"Oh gosh," Laura said weakly. "More surprises."

Nick laughed at his daughter. "No, only the one, Laur."

"It's about Bitterbark Creek," Robin explained.

"You're not selling?" Sophie lurched forward in shock.

"No." Nick shook his head. "Not at all. But we have made some changes to our will."

Robin smiled. "As Pat and Marilyn have other plans, and Laura will eventually move on to bigger and better things in the city, we have decided to leave the farmstay to someone who loves and appreciates it as much as we do."

"We wanted to give it to someone who respects the bushland," Nick clarified. "Someone who loves our animals and thrives in the country. A person who understands the lifestyle we're inviting people to enjoy here."

"That's why," Robin interjected, "we have decided to leave Bitterbark Creek to . . . Jack."

"*What?*"

It was a feminine whisper, barely a whimper of sound. Jack had only a second to take in the shock and distress on Sophie's beautiful face before she freed herself from his arms and hurried out of the room.

CHAPTER 38

A gentle wind rustled through the leafy shrubbery edging the dark veranda, while far off in the distance, the night sky grumbled moodily as a flash of jagged lightning scarred the swollen clouds. The air felt crisp and smelled fresh, like the invigorating scent before rain, enticing a lone green frog to bellow out his croaky song from the rotund water tank nearby. As though it wished to join in, the wide outdoor hammock on which Sophie lounged began to creak. With her feet dangling over the edge, she let her bare toes tickle Banjo's exposed belly below as she swayed softly back and forth. When Boris—from his guard dog position by the wooden railing—raised his head and twitched his ears, Sophie knew she had company. As the interloper neared, the canine let his tongue loll freely and wagged his tail in merriment.

"Is there room on there for me?" Jack didn't wait for an answer. He steadied the hammock and slid in beside Sophie.

"Oh Jack, I'm so sorry," Sophie whimpered as Jack spread an arm around her shoulders. She let him cuddle her closer on the coarse but cosy fabric. "I didn't mean to run out like that." She felt her throat tighten around the words. She'd shed so many tears lately that she was sure she'd cried out every bit of shock and pain and fear, but still more seemed to come.

"It's okay, Soph." Jack caressed her bare shoulder comfortingly. "There was a lot to process tonight. For all of us."

"But I—" Her voice broke into a sob, but she swallowed it back, gathering her breath before trying again. "I shouldn't have left the way I did. I wasn't trying to be rude or ungrateful. I'm so happy for you, Jack. Truly I am. I'm so glad my aunt and uncle can entrust their beloved Bitterbark Creek to someone they love so much. It's just. . ." She had to tell him.

"It's okay, Soph. Really." Jack hugged her tighter. "Nick and Robin know how much you've been through. They weren't upset. Robin and Laura even offered to go after you, but I told them I could handle it." He sighed. "I really appreciate your kind words, Soph. But geez, that last part was a shock, wasn't it? I didn't see it coming. I always thought Pat would want to take over, but me? In charge of Bitterbark Creek one day? Wow." He looked as if he still couldn't believe it. "It's incredible, but do they really want someone like me running the place?"

"A Garland?" Sophie asked quietly.

"Yeah. Who would ever have thought a Garland would eventually own Bitterbark Creek?"

"It could change everything," Sophie mused.

"Or nothing." Jack rested his head against hers. "I may be a Garland in name, but I'm a Santoro at heart. This place is my home, and I would never do anything to jeopardise that."

Sophie released a shaky breath, encouraging the tightness in her chest to loosen just a little. For a moment, she saw Jack as the happy, cheeky little boy she used to adore. The Garland boy with a caring, good-natured soul, who used to hand-draw her birthday cards and help her climb down from Pat and Laura's tree house. The little boy who had so bravely risked kissing her all those years ago, on that special day by the creek, beneath the weeping willow.

Of all the many things Sophie loved about Jack now, the fact that he was still a good man, that he'd always tried to be, was something that had never truly changed throughout the years. Whether she could accept it as a child or not, Sophie had always known deep in her subconscious that Jack's family had truly been to blame.

That's why she had agreed to help Ella in her pursuit of vengeance, even though she'd told her mother she would let things be. Sophie had been so grateful for Ella's willingness to speak to her that night at the troll's cave when no one else would tell her the truth. Now Sophie wanted to do all she could to return the favour and help Ella finally free herself from the Garlands' web of secrets and lies. Ella deserved the opportunity to move forward, hopefully with Laura.

Jack shifted in the hammock, and the movement drew Sophie's thoughts back to the present. When he smiled at her and pecked her lightly on the lips, Sophie realised she still hadn't told him that she'd met with his mother, and that she'd unearthed worse crimes than the incident at the Garland dam. But there would be time for that later. They had the rest of their lives to talk through it all, to work through all the shock and pain and sadness together. Their love for one another would help to put all that darkness behind them. She hoped to help Ella and Laura do the same.

But right now, there was something more important Sophie had to tell him. Something that would change everything.

"I wanted to tell you. . ." Sophie searched for the words to properly explain. "Sorry, I tried to say it before. . ."

Jack frowned and pulled back to study her face. "What is it, Soph?"

"I wanted to tell you that I remember, Jack," Sophie confessed happily. "I remember."

"You remember?" Then it hit him. "You *remember*? Your memories have come back?"

Sophie nodded, and tears once again clouded her vision. "I remember everything, Jack. *Everything*. I finally feel whole again, like my mind is once more my own." Her body buzzed with a flood of emotion—relief, exhaustion, anger and excitement.

"Oh my god, Soph. I am so happy for you," Jack gushed, holding her closer and kissing her again.

The joy and relief in Jack's grin mirrored Sophie's own. Tears rolled down her cheeks. Her lost memories had started unravelling ever so slowly as her Uncle Nick told them all about how it had been Jack who had rescued her from the dam twenty years ago. Her surprise at her aunt and uncle's final announcement had acted as the last trigger, flooding Sophie's mind with every memory of that horrible day. Shock and the sheer force of it all had sent Sophie running outside for fresh air and quiet. She had needed a moment to get her head in order, to process that tidal wave of imagery and emotion.

Everything in her life was settling into place, and the possibility of their future together felt more real than ever. Sophie just had one final thing to do. Ella deserved to experience the same freedom Sophie now felt. She would do whatever was in her power to help her old friend achieve that. And having Jack onboard with their plan would increase their chances.

Sophie gave Jack a secretive smile and prepared to take him into her confidence once more.

CHAPTER 39

In the grand alfresco setting behind Garland Manor, a live orchestra and a sea of elegantly laid tables spread out beneath a colossal jacaranda tree, which was wrapped trunk to twig in links upon links of twinkle lights. As though that display weren't enough to enliven the already dazzling Saturday afternoon sunshine, a web of fairy lights crisscrossed above the crowd, creating a pattern between five glorious chandeliers.

April-Rose had desired a most extravagant, unforgettable engagement party and upon being faced with the gaudy atrocity before him—a giant stage topped with thronelike chairs—Jack believed his sister had achieved just that. It had been a long time since he'd visited his childhood home, but self-aggrandisement and prejudice still clotted the air like a suffocatingly pungent perfume. Although a mix of pleasant, sociable guests mingled about the space, alleviating some of that spirit-sucking ambience, frenemies, lackies and aspirants abounded, adding their noxious auras to the suffocating gloom.

Jack was more disgusted with his family than ever, since Sophie had told him about her conversation with his mother. If he hadn't been so determined to support Sophie in her endeavour to assist Ella and Laura with their plan of revenge, he would have refused to attend. As it was, he was glad to be nearby in case things didn't go quite as expected and the love of his life needed assistance. Especially since she hadn't made the guest list.

"So, things seem to have heated up between you and Sophie while Marilyn and I were away," Pat said quietly, dodging a waitress balancing a gold tray of champagne. He moved closer to his friend.

"You could say that." Jack fiddled with his cufflinks and glanced around, searching for the beautiful woman in question. "There was a lot to talk through, but we're finally in step with each other again."

"That's not exactly what I meant." Pat eyed Jack inquisitively. "I saw you leaving her cabin early this morning when I passed by the creek on the four-wheeler."

"Mate, you have missed a right debacle," Dale quipped as he stepped beside them, "and this one right here all sulky-like for much of it." He poked a thumb at Jack before tugging at his own tuxedo. He glowered when the collar wouldn't budge. "Gah, why do we have to wear these penguin suits? It's only an engagement bash."

"Because you wouldn't have been allowed in otherwise." Jack snatched a bottle of beer from a weaving waiter and took a sip. April-Rose's dress code was non-negotiable.

"Is that why there's security at the door?" Pat glanced over his shoulder. A couple of burly men, also outfitted in dress suits, clutched their clipboards tightly as they checked the attendees against a list before allowing them to enter the event.

"Yes." Jack took another swig from his drink.

"So, tell me," Pat turned to Dale. "I'm curious—what exactly have I missed?"

"Well, Jack and Sophie are. . ." Dale cringed, his voice trailing off as Camille sidled next to him and slid her arm through his.

"Well, they're an item, aren't they?" She shared a proud

grin with the group.

"Camille," Dale scolded. He pulled his elbow free of her. "I know you love gossip, but you can't just go around spreading rumours like that."

"Hey, it's not a rumour." She shrugged off the chiding. "They pretty much said so at the Santoros' dinner that Tuesday after the wedding."

"Yeah, but things could have changed," Dale snapped.

"Have they?" It was a question in chorus from both Pat and Camille.

Flustered, Dale waved for Jack to take over.

Jack ignored him. His attention was focused solely on the women he'd just helped sneak into his sister's precious engagement party.

When Sophie and the other two women had come to him to ask if there might be a way for the uninvited to still attend, Jack had informed them of the old, overgrown gate in the rose garden. It looked to him as though their mission had been successful.

Laura had colour-matched her stylish feminine suit to Ella's funky teal evening gown, and Sophie had let her golden waves curl over the thin straps of a classy taupe cocktail dress. Doing their best to remain inconspicuous, they huddled at the edge of the gathering, keeping out of sight. Though Jack wondered how someone as naturally stunning as Sophie could ever go unnoticed.

"So, are you going to spill, Jack?" Camille probed, inching closer. "Has something happened between you and Sophie?"

"More than can be shared in an afternoon of gossiping," Jack teased.

"But we have all evening as well." She winked.

"I think he means it's a chat for another time, Camille," Dale interpreted.

"Another time then," Pat vowed with a smirk.

As Jack returned his good friend and new brother's cheeky look, there was a flutter of commotion beside them.

Marilyn—shimmering in her glittery gold dress and matching accessories—dashed to her husband's side with her sister Addison in tow. The women were hand-in-hand and completely flustered.

"Has anyone seen Tiffany?" Marilyn wailed.

"No one can find her," Addison clarified.

"April-Rose is beside herself without her maid of honour," Marilyn continued, releasing her sister's hand to gesture madly. "Apparently, Tiff sent a message this morning saying she might be a little late, as she needed last-minute alterations to her dress. Everything seemed okay at the time, but now no one knows where she is."

"Hang on," Dale held up a finger to pause the procession of words. "Isn't a maid of honour just for weddings? How would it affect the engagement party?"

Camille gaped at him and raised both hands skyward. "Oh my god, Dale. I can't believe you just said that."

"Tiffany was involved in everything, Dale," Addison explained. "I don't think you realise how important it is that she be here."

"We have to find her," Marilyn told Camille. "I need you to start calling around—find out if anyone has seen her in the last few hours."

Pat shared a look with Jack and then winced at his wife. "Can't you just call her mobile?"

"We've tried, babe, but it just keeps going to this message saying the number is not in service." Worry crinkled Marilyn's pretty features. "It's like it's been disconnected."

"That's weird." Camille crossed her arms. "Did Tiffany and April-Rose have a fight?"

Marilyn whipped her head from side to side. "No. They say they never fight."

"Everyone fights," Dale said in disbelief.

"But that's no reason to disconnect your phone." Pat cuddled his wife, calming her.

"Has anyone seen Bradley?" Camille jutted her chin in

accusation. "My money is on them running away together."

"Cami," Addison reprimanded, slapping her friend lightly on the shoulder. "Just because you saw them having dinner together—once—doesn't mean they're going to betray April-Rose and elope."

"No, but it does look suspicious." Dale nodded approvingly at Camille.

Pleased with his support, she grinned. "Maybe we should start looking for both of them?"

"Hold it." Jack stepped forward and sliced his hand through the air in an effort to halt the growing panic. Once all attention was on him, he pointed up at the stage to where his sister stood before a microphone. A crowd had gathered below, waiting intently. "It looks like my sister has something to say."

"There's Bradley," Camille clucked, aiming her index finger towards the perfectly preened hulk of a man climbing the steps to the stage.

"And your mother, Jack," Pat said.

Bradley had paused to assist Sheridan. She was gussied up in yet another dramatic silvery-white evening gown as though she were the true centre of attention.

April-Rose waited for Bradley to escort Sheridan up the stairs and over to the line of special wedding party seating in the middle of the stage. From this distance, Jack couldn't tell if his sister was upset about Tiffany's disappearance. She stood tall in her sleek forest-green dress and looked as she always did—haughty and contemptuous.

Once Sheridan and Bradley had taken their seats beside one another, April-Rose flashed a smile at her audience and gripped the microphone stand. "Good afternoon, everyone, and what an extraordinary afternoon it is for us to celebrate such an immensely special occasion." His sister's voice cut sharply through the speakers at the foot of the platform, her saccharine tone more painful in its heightened volume. "Unfortunately, our mistress of ceremonies—Tiffany McDowall—is running late, but she should be with us shortly."

"I thought you said you couldn't get a hold of her," Pat whispered to Marilyn.

His wife shrugged her shoulders in obvious confusion. "We can't."

"While we wait," April-Rose continued, lifting a hand to encompass the orchestra below, "I thought we could begin the music. The first song on our setlist is—"

There was an incomprehensible shout from the right side of the podium, and April-Rose swivelled her head to stare at the three intruders storming her stage.

"Is that . . . Sophie?" Addison asked. "Marilyn said she and Laura had been uninvited."

"Well, it looks like Laura didn't get that memo either." Camille laughed, and the rest of the group silently watched the youngest Santoro follow Sophie to the top.

"And that's Ella." Marilyn paled in surprise. "What is she doing here? She hates the Garlands."

Murmurs multiplied through the audience in front of the stage like ripples through silken water, their voices growing louder and then hushing as the trespassing trio approached April-Rose. In the seats behind the disturbance, Bradley perched on his throne like an obedient king, while Sheridan straightened abruptly and gripped her soon-to-be son-in-law's hand.

"What do you think you're doing here?" Although April-Rose wasn't speaking directly into the microphone, it caught her growl and shouted it at the spectators below.

"Your queendom has come to an end, April-Rose," Ella roared. She clutched Laura's hand like a grounding anchor and confidence booster. "We're here for justice."

CHAPTER 40

The smartly attired guests crowded closer like a rowdy mosh pit at a rock concert, vying to see and hear more of the furore on stage. Every time words were hurled across the platform at one person or another, the speakers below released a resounding echo, parroting it across the Garlands' decadently dressed estate. Fury ripped through the air and melded with the warm afternoon breeze as the serene twinkle lights continued to sway innocently, a reminder of the happy occasion they had come to celebrate.

As Sophie looked on, Laura pulled her weeping girlfriend away from the venom-spitting harpy that was April-Rose. Although Ella had fought bravely, throwing herself on the front line to cast the first dagger into the heart of the Garlands' reputation, April-Rose had been just as quick in her retaliation. She'd regaled the audience with familiar falsities about Ella—stories of drug use, mental health disorders and a girl all but broken by the terrible loss of her mother. Ella screamed with rage, losing the thread of her argument and deteriorating into heart-wrenching sobs. Sophie couldn't bear to witness any further destruction of her friend's character. Although she had only come as moral support, it was time for her to step up and fight April-Rose with something bigger than a slash to her reputation. She had something even scarier up her sleeve, something so lacerating that she doubted the devilish Sheridan had shared it with her daughter.

Sophie reached the microphone in a few smooth strides. She felt an eerie calm claim her, pushing back her violent anger and the desire to shout or cry. She was consumed only by a fierce determination to see her mission through.

"Is it your turn now, little Suicidal Sophie?" April-Rose jeered.

But her taunting bounced right off. Sophie stared out at the captivated crowd and found the serious, supportive faces of her aunt and uncle. She was relieved she'd been brave enough to tell them what she'd learned from Sheridan, all the truths hidden under years of rumours and lies. Sophie had even had several more meaningful conversations with her own mother. Although Angelica didn't agree with seeking retribution, she was proud of her daughter for wanting to help Ella move on with her life.

As Sophie searched the crowd, she finally locked eyes with the person whose encouragement and support she wanted the most. The look Jack gave her told her everything she needed to know. She was doing the right thing. It was time everyone knew the extent of the Garlands' secrets and lies. She and Jack had talked for hours and hours on end—they'd even stayed in bed a whole afternoon just talking everything through. They had finally burned through the remnants of the past that plagued them. There were so many more beautiful memories they shared. Sophie hoped what they achieved here today would become one of them.

"What is this?" April-Rose scoffed. "The silent treatment?" She shoved at Sophie's shoulder. "Get off the stage and go back to the big city, Suicidal Sophie. None of us want you here."

Some brave souls in the crowd belted out their protests, declaring that Sophie was very much welcome in the tiny town of Moorhenvale. Taking that as her cue, Sophie reluctantly tore her gaze from Jack's and turned to the infuriated socialite beside her. She leaned closer to the microphone. "After hogging the spotlight your entire life, April-Rose, I thought it was time you learned to share." Sophie's heartbeat raced at the sound of her voice reverberating loudly through the speakers.

A warble of light laughter spread throughout the throng of guests but was silenced quickly under their hostess's brutal glare.

"Who do you think you are? This is my engagement party, and your invitation was rescinded. I should have you thrown out."

"Why don't you try?" Sophie dared, narrowing her eyes. "You know nothing short of killing me will stop me, and we all know you failed at that last time."

There were gasps among the guests milling around the stage, their shock evident in furtive glances and suspicious chatter.

Sophie's palms were sweating, but still she pressed on. She wouldn't give up this fight. She was doing this for Ella, for her mother, her beloved father, for all the years of heartbreak she herself endured because of the Garlands' lies.

April-Rose gawped at the audience and then ducked closer to the microphone for an instant. "She's lying," she yelled indignantly.

There were doubtful mutters from within the assembly.

"Don't worry, April-Rose, my *old friend*," Sophie told her. "I'm not here to tell everyone about that time twenty years ago when you physically assaulted me until I fell into your family's dam. Nor am I here to mention that you planned to leave me there to *drown*." She put her lips to the microphone and emphasised the word so loudly that it reverberated off the champagne glasses.

Again, there were sharp breaths and astonished whispers from the onlookers at the foot of the podium. Their eyes were glued to Sophie's performance.

April-Rose spluttered, seeking a suitable defence but finding none. Sophie ignored her. Although her heart still pounded in her chest and adrenaline still vibrated through her veins, Sophie's task seemed to become easier with each breath, with each word. Everyone deserved to know the truth about April-Rose and Sheridan Garland. They all deserved to be set free from their control.

"No. I'm not here for that." Sophie smiled, feeling somewhat more confident. "I'm also not here to reveal the pathetic mind games and manipulation you employ to keep the whole town under your control, or how you learned all of those scheming techniques from your calculating mother." Sophie looked over her shoulder and caught Sheridan's smouldering glare. She threw the Garland matriarch a patronising nod before readdressing the gathering. "I'm not even here to support the accusations spoken by our lovely Ella over there." She gestured to where the young woman and Laura were embracing at the side of the stage. "Although everything Ella told you about what the Garlands' did to her family, how Sheridan destroyed her mother, is *true*.

"No." Sophie shook her head and grasped the microphone stand with both hands. "I'm here today to tell you all about my wonderful father." She warmed at the thought of her dad—of his kind, loving nature and the fond memories of the time they spent together at Bitterbark Creek. "You see, that accident all those years ago—you remember—the one in which my father lost his life and Barton Garland suffered only minor injuries? Well, you were all sold a lie. You were told that it was my father, Jim Wendall, who was driving the car. But Sheridan Garland and Chief Ambrose concocted that story to protect Barry Garland from being punished for the crime *he* committed."

There was another rumble of gasps and chatter from the crowd below. Infuriated guests were edging even closer to the stage, while others were casting foul looks at the Garlands. Yet as Sophie watched on, never once did those looks of disappointment or anger target Jack. She met his gaze again, saw his concern for her beneath the firm support, and smiled when she noticed Pat place a hand reassuringly on Jack's shoulder. The men acknowledged each other with a look and then Jack nodded for her to continue.

Sophie took a shaky breath. "The reality is that it was Barry Garland who was driving that night, and it was *Barry Garland* who *killed* my father in the crash *he* caused."

"That's enough!" April-Rose screeched from somewhere behind her. "I will not be subjected to this drivel any longer."

Sophie spun just in time to see the redhead reach for her. April-Rose grabbed Sophie's upper arm and yanked her sideways away from the microphone. Sophie stumbled but caught her balance and settled beside Laura and Ella.

"I hope you all don't believe this utter rubbish," April-Rose sneered, waving her hand grandly across the assembled guests before firing a scowl of contempt at the trio of intruders. "You have known our family, worked with us and been a part of our lives for decades. You know what the Garland family name represents, so why would you believe the nonsense spouted from these lunatics?"

"Because they're probably right," grumbled a gruff masculine voice from among the horde.

"We all know what the Garland name really represent*s*," scoffed a woman from somewhere to the left.

"Money and exploitation," yelled yet another guest.

The gathering erupted into a roaring ruckus of opinions, complaints and endless accusations.

"Friends," April-Rose began, but the din drowned her out. "People, please, calm down." When the commotion only grew louder, and the townspeople surged with anger, she tried again. "Please, you know us. You know my family. We are the *Garlands*. You can't believe this. You can't treat us like this."

Visibly overwhelmed by the chaos as it crashed down

around her, April-Rose lowered her trembling hands and slowly backed away from the edge of the stage. She glanced at Sophie, and for an instant, a look of absolute terror chilled her violently blue eyes. All the blood had drained from her cheeks, and her mouth hung open in horror. Shaking, she turned and reached for Bradley. Her bony knees buckled and she teetered unsteadily on her heels. Bradley jumped up from his throne and surprised everyone when he lunged away from her. He launched himself in front of Sheridan like a member of the Secret Service protecting the president. April-Rose yelped in pain as she crashed to her knees and reached for him again.

"Bradley—why?" Her voice broke into a sob, and she stared at him with wide, disbelieving eyes.

Bradley took Sheridan's hand and helped her up from her chair. He wrapped a brawny arm around her shoulders, and she clung to him, gripping his finely pressed tuxedo. She stared down her nose at April-Rose.

"It's time you finally learn the truth, my darling daughter," Sheridan said, her sharp voice dripping with scorn. "Just know—you did all of this to yourself."

Bradley shot a similar look of contempt at his fiancée. "I'm sorry, April-Rose, but the wedding is off." He held his chin high in defiance before whirling back to address the audience. The microphone was a few feet away, but it picked up his booming voice without issue. "Months ago, my fiancée convinced me to get close to her mother, to seduce her and eventually trick her into signing over the controlling share of the company. But in that time, I got to truly know the magnificent woman next to me—the real Sherry Garland—and she stole my heart." He gazed lovingly at Sheridan and held her closer. "I love you," he told her.

"I love you too, Bradley dear." She kissed him.

So, this is the we *Sheridan had been talking about when she'd said she would be leaving town with someone,* Sophie thought to herself. The absurdity of it had her holding back a chuckle.

"What the—?" Laura exclaimed. Noises of shock, awe

and disbelief once again exploded among the guests viewing the farce-like display.

"You idiot, Bradley!" April-Rose shrieked when the lovers broke apart. The redhead clenched her fists and sat back on her heels. "You were only supposed to flirt with her, not lose your mind to the old woman. This is *our* engagement party. Have you forgotten? We're planning *our* wedding!"

"Not anymore," Bradley proclaimed. "Sherry and I are eloping. We want to start a new life together in Bali. And we've made the executive decision to sell the company to the Harts. Finalised the paperwork this morning." He chuckled sourly. "Not that there was much left to sell after Tiffany had finished with us."

"Wait—what?" April-Rose gasped. "Tiffany?" She climbed awkwardly to her feet. "What does she have to do with any of this?"

Bradley squinted at his ex-fiancée as though surprised by her ignorance. "She's been blackmailing us for weeks, April-Rose. I'm surprised you didn't notice the money disappearing. Tiffany found out about my affair with Sherry and threatened to tell everyone unless we paid her to keep quiet. She was also the one who stole your phone and all of your passwords. She's taken hundreds of thousands from our personal accounts and millions from the company. We were lucky to sell the business to the Harts for half its original value. After the creditors take their chunk, there won't be much left."

"What?" April-Rose panted, on the verge of hyperventilating. "What—my phone? It was Tiffany? *She* took it?"

"She's probably fled the country by now." Bradley nodded. "She never had any intention of showing up today."

April-Rose rested her hand over her heart as she fought for air. "Are you telling me," she wheezed, "that I'm . . . *poor*?"

"Well, we're not rich anymore." Bradley's answer echoed across the decorated alfresco area and left his ex-fiancée frozen stiff.

"Like I said," Sheridan told her. "You brought all of this on yourself, daughter dear."

April-Rose clenched her hands into claws and bared her teeth at her mother, but when she opened her mouth, she seemed lost for words. She looked around helplessly.

"Look—I'm sorry, April-Rose," Bradley said, not appearing apologetic in the slightest. "But Sherry and I have tickets for a late-night flight up to Cairns. I know I should have told you earlier. I probably should have called off the wedding sooner, but, well ..." Bradley shrugged, indifferent. "You never would have listened or understood—you never would have let us be together. Face it, April-Rose, you're just a heartless bitch in a nice dress, and you'll never be able to outshine your extraordinary mother."

"Thank you, dear," Sheridan purred as she cuddled him closer.

Bradley winked at her before aiming a final comment into the microphone. "Sorry, Mum and Dad," he called out, waving a hand in the air. "I'll write to you once we're settled." With that, he ushered Sheridan towards the stairs on the opposite side of the stage before anyone could intervene.

After watching one-half of the engaged couple make their mad escape, Sophie focused her attention on April-Rose, who was still struggling to catch her breath. The young woman slapped a hand to her forehead, and her eyes darted crazily from side to side as though desperately trying to comprehend what had just happened. She looked completely bewildered—a total mess without the crutch of her beloved money and status.

Deciding to do what any *good old friend* would do, Sophie approached the microphone once more and waited for the rambunctious crowd below to settle a final time. "Well, now that the niceties are out of the way," she told them, smiling reassuringly, "let's get on with the party, shall we? We might no longer have an engagement to celebrate, but surely the Harts' purchase of Garland Grain is as special a reason as any to resume the afternoon's festivities."

When a cheer burbled up from the group, the spattering of applause became contagious. April-Rose let out a pitiful wail and crumbled to her knees again in a sobbing heap.

CHAPTER 41

The slowly sinking sun was trailed by coral-kissed clouds, while the sky above had become a wintry lilac. It was no longer the blaze of warm afternoon and not quite the chill of dusk, but the atmosphere held a unique sort of magic, a crispness or spark of excitement, as though a new chapter in life was just beginning. Dragonflies flit through the air, skimming the murky waters of the Garlands' dam and dipping their feet to create circular ripples that spread ring upon ring to the outlying shore. On the wooden jetty in the very centre of the dark, peaceful waters, stood a lone silhouette bathed in the golden glow of dying sunlight. Her feminine curves were accentuated as she hugged herself tightly and stared, still as a statue, down into the muddy depths below.

As though approaching a wild animal, Jack made his way warily along the timber planks. When one creaked underfoot and alerted her to his approach, Sophie turned and surprised him with a tranquil smile instead of the tear-streaked cheeks he'd expected.

"How are you doing?" he asked cautiously. "Hopefully not considering a swim back to shore in that dress?"

She glared at him and then twitched her lips in a smirk.

"Sorry." He bowed his head. "I say stupid things when I'm nervous." He raked a hand through his hair and braved a step closer. "Just know that if you felt the urge to jump in, I'd save you like the last time. You're the stars in my sky, Sophie Wendall. You're my best friend, and I don't plan on ever losing you again."

She smiled warmly, and Jack found the courage to take another stride. "That was some kind of chaos you ladies released back there." He pointed his thumb back towards the house. "The Garlands will never be the same."

Sophie chuckled and shook her head. "Jack, *you're* a Garland," she reminded him.

He took a final step forward, now within arm's reach. "Sophie, I thought you understood it all by now. Just like your aunt and uncle said, I'm part of the Santoro family. That means I'm a part of your family. I'm nothing more than a Garland in name."

"So, you're not upset?" Sophie tilted her head to study him, and her eyebrows drew together in concern. "I know I already told you about what happened with your father, but that blow-up back there—that was rough. Rougher than any of us could have expected."

"Sophie." He touched her arm soothingly and then held her hand in his. "I don't know about you, but I am tired of allowing the past to affect our present. I don't want it to ruin our chance at a happy future. It's only brought us pain and heartache. I'm ready to move forward and focus on what's important to me now. That's you, Sophie. I want to be with you. I want us to make this work." As he spoke, Sophie smiled and swiped at the tears welling in her eyes. "I know we've both experienced trauma—whether it be twenty years ago or last week—but I know we can get through anything together. We've been blessed with something special, Sophie. We've known that all of our lives. Let's finally give ourselves the chance to let that connection grow."

Hope glowed brightly in Sophie's face as she squeezed his hand affectionately. "I love you, Jack," she told him, her voice thick with emotion.

"I love you too, Sophie. I always have and always will."

With a giggle, she started to say something but appeared to think better of it. Before Jack could ask her about it, she threw her arms around his neck, dragged him closer and pressed her mouth to his. As he enveloped her in his arms, hugging her tightly, she moulded perfectly against him, and he lost himself in the thrilling sensation. He revelled in her warmth, the feel of her heartbeat racing in time with his and the sweet scent of her that made him feel at home.

Jack's heart swelled so much he thought it might pop or lift his feet off the ground and carry him away. He never tired of hearing those three little words, and yet he was still so unprepared for the wave of emotion that crashed over him. He felt euphoric, finally free of all secrets and games. Now, it was just him and Sophie. They could finally start their lives together, build a future together beyond their painful past.

When Sophie finally broke their kiss, she smirked at him, mischief shining in her gaze. "I should tell you, Jack. I have one final secret to reveal."

"Oh gosh," Jack joked, copying Laura's cheeky tone. "More surprises."

Sophie laughed at his terrible impression. "No, only the one," she reassured him.

Jack stared lovingly into her deep brown eyes. He had an inkling as to what it might be, had heard a little something from Laura, but he had hoped Sophie would confirm it herself. "Well then, put me out of my misery."

"I'm staying, Jack," she told him excitedly. "At Bitterbark Creek."

"You're staying?" he gushed. It was just as he'd hoped.

She grinned and nodded. "Uncle Nick and Aunt Robin have invited me to stay indefinitely, but I have to work out a few things in Brisbane in the meantime. They want me to move into the main house while they rent out the cabin."

"Or you could move into my cabin with me?" Jack asked

hopefully, remembering that he'd made the suggestion once before. He bit his lower lip.

Sophie laughed and gave in to him with ease. "I couldn't think of anything more perfect," she agreed, echoing her response all those nights ago when they first made love under the stars.

Jack whooped in excitement. He cuddled her close and kissed her before hoisting her up into his arms, spinning her around and around. As Sophie giggled gleefully, Jack felt the fireworks of euphoria burst through him, buzzing through every nerve ending. He knew this precious moment was just the first of many they would share in their happy future together.

EPILOGUE

As the sun had risen in the clear blue sky, so had the midsummer heat. Insects hummed and danced, enjoying the fiery Queensland temperature as they hopped from plant to plant or marched along the rocky path. In the lower branches of the surrounding eucalypt trees, pink and grey galahs cawed, their astute little eyes watching every move of the couple wandering along the dirt track below.

Pointing towards Gap Creek, Jack quietly gestured for Sophie to follow him. Holding her hand outstretched—smartphone aglow in her palm—she did as instructed.

"What are you two doing right now?" Laura's voice burbled out of the device.

"Just walking," Sophie answered her, smirking at Jack.

"I can hear water. Are you near the creek?"

"Just hold your horses, Laur," Sophie ordered jovially. "We're almost there."

"I'm just sick of looking up your nose," her cousin teased. "Whose idea was it to video chat anyway?"

"Yours, you loser." Ella's voice, all cheeky sarcasm, piped out through the speaker.

"Hey! You're my girlfriend, you're supposed to be on my side."

"I'm for truth and justice," Ella proclaimed, doing her best superhero impersonation before becoming serious. "Just give them a second, babe. They'll settle soon."

"Thanks, Ella," Jack called over his shoulder, aiming the comment towards the gadget.

"No probs."

"Okay, we're here," Sophie told them.

Jack perched on a boulder beside the placidly flowing water. He'd led Sophie to a picturesque spot, where the nearby bushes still blossomed, and the riverbed on the other side reached into the lush emerald of a grassy lawn. Bitterbarks, she-oaks and gums stretched out overhead, their leafy branches covering the creek and surrounding land with cooling shade. Sophie sat down on the boulder beside Jack and then faced the phone towards the creek, knowing the familiar beloved view was sure to stir a reaction.

"Oh, wow," Laura fussed. "You're making me homesick."

"That's so charming," Ella agreed. "Very romantic." Sophie and Jack watched as Ella slid an arm around Laura's shoulder and kissed the younger woman's cheek.

"You'll have to come back to visit one day soon," Sophie encouraged. "Mum and my stepdad are driving out for a long weekend in February. Maybe you could join them? There's just so much you've missed."

"Gossip?" Laura whooped with anticipation and rubbed her hands together. "Like what?"

"Well . . ." Sophie glanced at Jack, unsure of where to begin.

"Well, Sophie's boss has decided to commission some of her artwork," he offered proudly. "She loved Soph's designs so much, she's hoping to use them as the main print for her next fashion line."

"Oh my god, Sophie," Ella praised. "That's amazing."

"Incredible, cuz," Laura agreed whole-heartedly. "I'm so happy for you."

"Hold that thought," Sophie warned her, "because you might not be so happy when you see what I've done with your room."

"Your mum and dad let her turn it into an office." Jack grinned and rubbed Sophie's knee. "She needed a base of operations for her work here, and it was the best available space."

"Why would I care?" Laura threw up her hands. "You gave Ella and me the lease to your apartment here in West End. As far as I'm concerned, it's a fair swap. This is our home now, and that's yours. Do whatever you need to."

Sophie laughed and rested her head against Jack's shoulder. "Okay, Laur. Thank you."

"So, what else is new?" Her cousin's face crowded the screen. "Any news on Tiffany?"

"Yes." Jack nodded. "Apparently she's shacked up somewhere in South America. I don't think she's planning on returning to Australia anytime soon."

"Probably not," Laura said. "If she does, she'll have to give all the money back."

"If there's any left." Ella shared a knowing look with her girlfriend.

"And what about Bradley and your mum?" Laura directed her question at Jack and grimaced as if just the thought was nauseating. "Are they still in Bali together?"

"Yes." Sophie chose to answer the difficult question for Jack. "They're still together." She handed Jack the phone as she fought to keep her humour in check. "Much to Jack's dismay, he now has a new *stepdad*." She struggled not to smirk. Jack shot her a playful glare and kissed her cheek affectionately.

"What? Really?" Laura looked genuinely repulsed. "I didn't think it would last that long."

"Yep, it's been confirmed," Sophie squeezed Jack closer. "Bradley sends his parents postcards updating them on all of his and Sheridan's adventures together. It's been big news around town ever since."

"Well, at least they're out of your hair," Ella said. "It would have been much worse if they had stuck around town." She looked at her girlfriend. "Ugh, imagine if they have children."

Laura stuck out her tongue and gagged.

"You two think that's bad," Jack grumbled, "but you're not a blood relative."

"Too true, Jack. Sorry, mate," Ella apologised.

"Yeah. Sorry, Jack," Laura echoed. "Didn't mean to spit in your meat pie. Let's focus on happier things, like the downfall of the she-devil herself." Laura leaned closer to the screen until her whole face filled it. "What new calamity has befallen our dear April-Rose?" She grinned excitedly, a glint of mischief in her eyes, and backed away from her phone's camera.

"You'll be happy to hear she's finally sold Garland Manor," Jack said. "It was the Hart family who bought it, actually. It was the one Garland asset not included in the company's holdings, and once the Harts had acquired all of the shares in Garland Grain, they were determined to have the house as well. They wanted a complete takeover. To start fresh and build the whole business up to the success it once was. They wanted a fair price for the manor, but April-Rose fought them all the way. Eventually, she had to relent and take their offer. If she didn't realise it after her engagement party, she sure knows it now—she's no longer welcome in town. The people of Moorhenvale have made it quite clear." He glanced at Sophie, tilting the phone in her direction, offering to let her jump in.

"She doesn't have her beloved wealth or reputation to prop her up," Sophie continued. "So, I think she's finally realised there's nothing here for her anymore. The gossip around town is that she's heading south. Melbourne, maybe? Or Adelaide? She wants to go somewhere where no one knows who she or the Garlands are."

"Understandable," said Ella. "Hey, pass on our congratulations to the Harts next time you see them?"

"Will do." Jack saluted her.

Laura glanced at Ella and then back at Jack and Sophie. "So, any other news besides the fact that my parents have lumped you with the farmstay while they travel through Europe?"

Jack laughed. "You know how much we love Bitterbark Creek, Laur. You might see it as a burden, but to us, it's home." He gazed adoringly at Sophie and kept the phone steady while he pulled her in for a kiss.

As they embraced, Sophie placed her left hand on Jack's cheek and let it linger there.

"Wait a minute," Ella burst out, shocked. "Is that a ring?"

"What is that?" Laura screeched. "Oh my gosh! Oh my gosh! You two!" She let out a squeal. "You're engaged!"

Screams of excitement rocked the phone's speaker as Sophie broke the kiss. She and Jack were laughing as they looked at the screen of her mobile only to find that her cousin and Ella had disappeared.

"Ladies, I think you've dropped your phone," Jack yelled out to them, trying to be heard over the racket. "Laura? Ella?"

Shadows could be seen bouncing around what looked to be cream-coloured carpet. The animated screams waned, and something bumped the phone. There was a curse, then a scratching, scrambling noise before the screen went dark and the video call lost connection.

Jack chuckled. "What was that?"

"Overexcitement?" Sophie offered with a grin.

"And what could there possibly be to get excited about?" he teased, pulling her closer to peck her lightly on the mouth.

She shrugged and then looked at the simple but perfect diamond ring on her finger. "I don't know," she pondered, slipping her arms around his neck. "Maybe it has something to do with the fact that I'm marrying the love of my life— the most cheeky, kind-hearted, handsome man in all the world." When she moved to kiss him, he pulled back slightly, stopping her.

"But he's a Garland," he warned.

"Only in name," she replied lovingly, and then caught his lips with hers.

THE END

Check Out Another Amazing Book by Tammy Mannersly

You can't hide from destiny....

Callum Hawthorne is one of those lucky guys who seem to have it all. He's a wealthy property tycoon, the CEO of his family's company. He's handsome, intelligent and charming and has a gorgeous new woman on his arm every week. But there's one thing still missing – the love of his life, Lucy Spencer.

Fourteen long years ago, Lucy left for college and cut off all contact with Cal, leaving their mutual friend Madison as his only connection. That was until in his effort to save his deceased father's beloved Gold Coast property, The Calypso, Cal contacts Insight Marketing, the best advertising firm in Melbourne, and discovers his Lucy among the team.

Successful marketing executive, Lucy Spencer had managed to avoid her ex-best friend for nearly half their lives. Fearful of trusting him, loving him and having her heart broken all over again, Lucy tries to keep her distance from him, but discovers that there is a fine line between love and hate, and maybe – just maybe – Cal could be her inescapable destiny.

~PERSUADING LUCY, a 1st Place WINNER for the prestigious 2018 CHATELAINE BOOK AWARDS FOR ROMANTIC FICTION, will quickly become your new favorite read!~

EXCERPT

Cal was flabbergasted. What had happened? What had he missed?

Then, distracted by her outburst, he made another mistake and his grip on Lucy's wrist loosened slightly. As if sensing his lapse in control, she used the whole weight of her small frame to jerk herself free of his hold and with a triumphant sigh she began to back away.

"So, you orchestrated this together, did you? What, did you seduce Maddy too? Why can't you just leave me alone?"

Cal's gaze narrowed with concern. "What are you talking about, Luce?"

Worried that she'd run before he had a chance to explain, Cal reached out and took a step toward her. But, Lucy immediately backed farther away, taking two steps for his single stride.

"What did you give her to make her finally tell you where I was?"

Her fiery glare was enough to make his fingers ache to touch her, to soothe her. He hated seeing her in so much distress.

"Nothing." His voice was calm, pacifying. "She didn't tell me."

Lucy frowned and her gaze dropped from his, confusion clearly clouding her expression.

"But I—" She shook her head with irritation and

glanced back up at him. "But how did you know that I'd be here?"

Cal smiled as he remembered the moment of pure serendipity, the second he'd seen her gorgeous face on the team's profile page on the Insight Marketing website. *Executive Manager Lucy S.*, it had read. Cal had tried searching the internet for her before, but to no avail. There had always been too many Lucy Spencers and he'd been convinced that she must have altered her name. Yet, this time he'd found her, so simply found her, as though the universe had finally pointed her out to him.

"Fate," he said confidently.

Available Now Where Books Are Sold

If You Love Your Romance with a Little Danger- Don't Miss

Drawn to him

TAMMY MANNERSLY

The new doctor in town is attracting some attention, especially of the female persuasion, but art teacher, Erica Townsend is blissfully unaware until she ends up injured and in his office. Too bad she'd vowed to resist love—that traitorous emotion, the destroyer of lives—after numerous failed relationships. Something about Matt, about their electrifying connection has her wondering if he might just be...*the one*.

Dr. Matthew Garrick is tired of playing wing-man for his best friend. It isn't that he wishes to look for love, rather the opposite. But the eagerness of some of the single women in their small country town unnerves him. That is, until a certain stunning brunette appears in the waiting room of his medical practice. Her touch sparks something deep inside him, jolting his heart into a new rhythm and Matt makes it his mission to win's Erica love. Can he convince her to take a risk on him and what they share together?

As the good doctor strives to show Erica that love doesn't have to come at a price, his dangerous secret admirer threatens to prove otherwise.

Whoever said love wasn't dangerous?

~DRAWN TO HIM was a FINALIST in the prestigious 2020 CHATELAINE BOOK AWARDS FOR ROMANTIC FICTION~

EXCERPT

Then it happened, that final breath, her lips snuck closer, brushing his, leaving a scalding spark, a blistering burn where they'd briefly, barely touched his skin—and then they were gone.

Matt wasn't exactly sure *when* he'd closed his eyes, but when he opened them again Erica had disappeared.

The *click* of the door handle had him turning around. She was halfway out of his office before she turned back to look at him, to give him that deadly sexy smile, making his insides smolder and ache with a want he'd never experienced before.

A torrent of thoughts whirled through his head, driven to swirl faster with the knowledge that in these final few seconds, his last words needed to leave an impression, a very good impression.

"Make sure to keep it clean."

Erica's gorgeous eyes glittered back at him, and then she was gone, heading back into the waiting room to see Melina and Jocelyn.

Make sure to keep it clean?

Matt could have died right then and there. He could have said anything, anything at all. He could have said he hoped she had a nice day. He could have mentioned he'd see her at the art class on Friday. Even the corniest *"That was nice"* would have been a better option. But, no, the doctor voice in his head had won out and his concern over wound care had been the final impression his suave self had been willing to make. No *"Thanks for the kiss, you beautiful babe,"* just *"Make sure you don't get dirt on your injured knee."*

He slapped his hand over his face and closed his eyes.

Available Now Where Books Are Sold

ABOUT THE AUTHOR

Tammy Mannersly is an award-winning Australian author frequently praised for her heart-warming stories full of romance, dedicated friendships, and stunning Australian locations. All her books ensure a great Happily Ever After and a love story that will sweep you off your feet. Tammy has a Bachelor Degree in Creative Industries majoring in Creative Writing from Queensland University of Technology. She lives on the coast near Brisbane, Queensland and loves to write about her favorite Australian destinations.

You can find more information about Tammy and her work on her website: www.tammymannersly.com or by visiting:

Facebook:
https://www.facebook.com/tammymannersly

Goodreads:
https://www.goodreads.com/author/show/16935790.Ta
mmy_Mannersly

Instagram:
https://www.instagram.com/tammymannersly/

Twitter: https://twitter.com/TammyMannersly

Bookbub:
https://www.bookbub.com/authors/tammy-mannersly

Inkspell   Publishing:
http://www.inkspellpublishing.com/tammy-
mannersly.html